FIRE
PRINCE

EMILY GEE

SOLARIS

First published 2014 by Solaris
an imprint of Rebellion Publishing Ltd,
Riverside House, Osney Mead,
Oxford, OX2 0ES, UK

www.solarisbooks.com

US ISBN: 978 1 78108 239 3

Maps by Pye Parr

10 9 8 7 6 5 4 3 2 1

A CIP catalogue record for this book is available from the
British Library.

Designed & typeset by Rebellion Publishing

Printed in Denmark

A thousand thanks to Moss,
without whom this book wouldn't be what it is!

The Seven Kingdoms

Esfaban
(territory of
Osgaard)

Osgaard

Lundegaard

100 leagues
300 miles

Lomaly
(territory of
Osgaard)

Horst
(territory of
Osgaard)

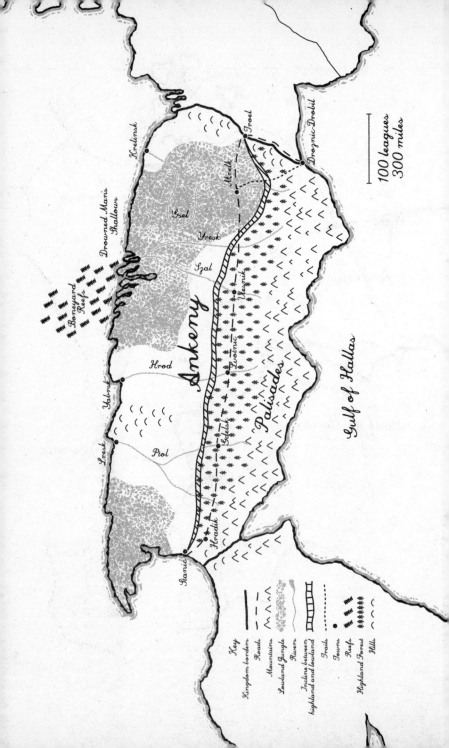

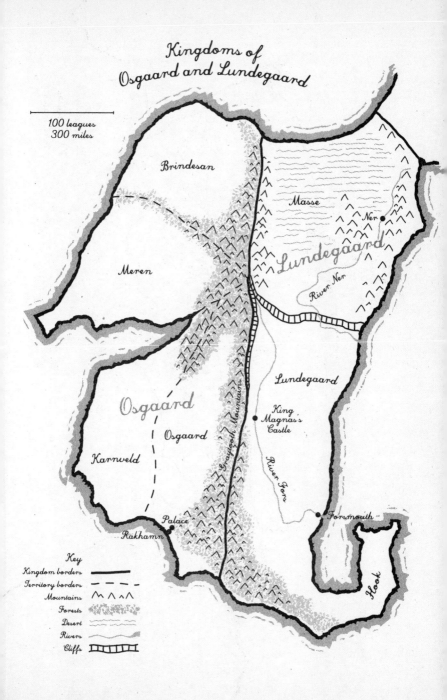

Kingdoms of
Osgaard and Lundegaard

100 leagues
300 miles

Brindesan

Masse

Ner

Lundegaard

Meren

River Ner

Osgaard

Lundegaard

Osgaard

King
Magnas's
Castle

Karnveld

Graylothi Mountains

River Fens

Palace

Forsmouth

Rakhamn

Hook

Key
Kingdom borders
Territory borders
Mountains
Forests
Desert
Rivers
Cliffs

CHAPTER ONE

JAUMÉ RODE A tough little pony with short legs and a bony spine.
He used his folded blanket as a saddle. The one thing he knew
he mustn't do was complain. These men watched him, even
Bennick watched, with a scant glance now and then, and they
had ears for everything, without seeming to listen.

Bennick gave a grin of approval when he saw the use Jaumé
put his blanket to.

The other men didn't grin, or wink at him the way Bennick
sometimes did. They were neither friendly nor hostile. Jaumé
knew they'd all been what he was—orphaned—but it was
Bennick who'd found him. Bennick whose charge he was.

Before dusk, Nolt led his band away from the road. They
followed a stream across the fields to a small copse.

Jaumé let his pony drink, then rubbed her down, copying the
actions of the men. He helped Bennick dig a firepit and ring it
with stones, watching the other men unload the packhorses,
seeing the way they worked together with the ease of long
familiarity, hardly needing to speak. This was his second night
on the road with them and he knew all their names now. Nolt.
Old Maati and young Kimbel. Odil. Black-skinned Gant.
Steadfast, called Stead by the others, and Ashandel, called Ash.

And Bennick.

The men were Brothers, and Bennick had said he could be one
too, if he was quick and tough and brave enough.

When the firepit was finished, Jaumé sat back on his heels and
looked at Bennick.

"Now what do we need?" Bennick asked.

"Firewood," Jaumé said promptly.

Bennick laughed and ruffled Jaumé's hair, the way Da used to do. "Good lad." He crossed to the pile of unloaded equipment and fished out an axe. "Come on. Help me find some wood."

Jaumé hurried after him.

Not far into the copse they found a fallen tree. The wood was as pale and dry as bone.

Jaumé gathered the firewood Bennick chopped, stacking it in piles. After several minutes, Bennick stripped off his shirt. His chest was tanned, furred with red-blond hair. On his right bicep was a small mark, blue-black.

"What's that?"

"A tattoo. You never seen one?"

Jaumé shook his head. "Is it a picture?"

"It's a picture of this." Bennick reached down to his waist, where a round pouch of dark leather was fastened. One moment his hand was empty, the next, he held a metal disk. No, not a disk, a knife with five blades.

"What is it?"

"We call it a Star." Bennick flicked it in the air with a flashing twirl of blades and caught it again. He held it out to Jaumé.

Jaumé took the Star reverently. The metal was polished to a gleaming brightness, the blades as sharp as razors.

"The tattoo marks me for a Brother," Bennick said. "We all have them. If you join us, you'll have one too."

"Will I have one of these?" Jaumé didn't dare throw the Star as Bennick had done. Those blades would slice off his fingers.

His imagination took flight, showing him his fingers spinning in the air, like thick pink worms, and scattering across the grass at their feet.

"You can have as many Stars as you want." Bennick's blue eyes smiled the way Da's had used to. "Do you want that, lad?"

"Yes."

Bennick held out his hand for the Star.

Jaumé gave it back reluctantly. "Will you teach me to spin it, the way you did?"

Bennick laughed as he slipped the Star into the pouch again, showing a flash of white teeth. "You need to learn how to throw a knife first, lad. Once you've done that you can think about Stars."

"Will you teach me how to throw a knife?"

"I have the one I made when I was your age. If I let you use it, you'll have to look after it. Sharpen it. Oil the blade. You can only throw a knife when you know it well enough. But now, let's shift this wood."

That night, after they'd eaten, Bennick went to his pack and took out a small bundle wrapped in soft leather. He sat down by Jaumé and folded the leather back. Inside was a plain cowhide sheath, with a white bone handle poking out the top.

Jaumé's fingers went out, almost as if the bone handle pulled them towards it. "Can I...?"

Bennick nodded.

Jaumé wrapped his hand round the handle. It was cold, but the shape seemed welcoming. He felt his fingers fit in the shallow grooves Bennick had cut for his own fingers long ago. He didn't ask if he could pull the blade out; already, the knife was shifting from Bennick to him. He felt it. The bone seemed to take warmth from his skin and return it. He drew out the blade. It shone in the firelight.

"You made this?" he said with awe.

"Made the handle, chose the blade, put the two together," Bennick said. "That'll be one of your first lessons when you reach Fith."

"How old were you?"

"Same as you. Eight."

Jaumé felt a thrill of excitement. He wanted to make a knife like this.

"How does it feel?" Bennick asked.

"Good. Is it...?" *Mine?* He glanced at Bennick, asked the question silently.

"You can use it. If it lets you."

"How?"

"Practice. Touch the blade. Careful, now."

Jaumé put his finger on the sharp edge. At once he felt a sting of pain. He drew his finger back and saw a drop of blood form.

"It cut me."

"No, you cut yourself. You went too fast. There's no easy way. There's only hard work. Can you do that?"

"Yes." Jaumé turned the knife over in his hand. "Can I give it a name?"

"No," Bennick said. "It's a knife." He patted the pouch at his waist. "And these are Stars. They're not for games. They're tools. You learn what they can do, then you make them do it."

Jaumé nodded. *A knife is a tool.*

Carefully, he wiped the faint mark of his blood from the blade and fitted it back in the sheath. *I'll work hard. I want to be a Brother.*

THEY CROSSED INTO Sault on the ninth day out of Cornas, moving through throngs of refugees. The soldiers manning the border post made no attempt to control the press of dusty, ragged people and carts piled high with household goods. Here was the same smell Jaumé had smelled in Cornas—sweat, with a sour undertone of fear. The curse seemed suddenly real again. He heard howling laughter, heard the crackle of flames. Rosa's scream echoed in his head. The smell of Mam's blood was in his nose.

Terror wrapped its fingers around his heart, squeezing.

And then he looked at Bennick, sitting easily on his horse, and the terror vanished. While he was with Bennick and the Brothers, he was safe.

CHAPTER TWO

MID-AFTERNOON THEY RODE over the pass into Ankeny. Harkeld halted and looked back. Dry, rocky hills hid the Masse desert. The red sand and the ruined city, the catacombs, were ten days behind them. "Do you see something?" his armsman, Justen, asked. "Someone following?"

Harkeld shook his head. The only people behind them were dead. Lundegaard's soldiers in their fresh graves. The Fithian assassins lying where they'd fallen. The ancient desert dwellers crumbling in their tombs.

The long string of packhorses passed them. Ebril rode last, whistling, his red hair glinting in the sun. "All right?" he called.

Harkeld nodded. He unstoppered his waterskin and swallowed a mouthful of lukewarm water.

Justen wiped dust from his face. "Prince Tomas should be at the escarpment by now."

Harkeld grunted. In another week, Tomas would be at King Magnas's castle. *Telling the king I'm a witch.*

Memory swept over him: fire igniting in his chest, flames bursting from his skin, an inferno roaring in his ears. With memory came a surge of panic. He'd not been able to control the fire, had been on the point of bursting into flames—

Harkeld shoved the memory aside. He rammed the stopper into the waterskin.

"We'd best not get too far behind," Justen said. "Those cursed assassins..."

The back of Harkeld's neck tightened at the words. He nudged his horse forward. It picked its way between the rocks. Far to the north the sea glittered. Somewhere in that glitter was a port town called Stanic, and more witches sent to strengthen their numbers. The most powerful of the shapeshifters, Innis, had gone in search of them two days ago.

To the southeast were mountains, the long range called the Palisades that cut Ankeny off from the sea. The mountains marched into the distance, snowcapped. Ahead were forested highlands, a tufted green carpet that stretched east as far as he could see. Tomorrow they'd be down there, in among the trees. How long since he'd last stood beneath a tree? Three weeks? Four?

He yearned for green leaves and damp earth and cool shade, but that dense forest also made him uneasy. How many assassins did it hide?

THEY CAMPED BESIDE a riverbed. No water flowed, but in a deep hollow was a stagnant pool. They unloaded the packhorses, let them drink, fed them the grain carried from Lundegaard. Harkeld helped Justen pitch the tents, then fashioned a rough firepit and piled the last of their wood into it.

Cora, the most senior of the witches, crouched alongside him and snapped her fingers. Harkeld flinched as the branches flared alight. The memory of flames stung his skin.

He shook his head sharply, angry with himself, and glanced around. Had anyone noticed him flinch?

No. Justen was laying out bedrolls and blankets in the tents and Ebril was rubbing down the horses. Of the other shapeshifters, there was no sign. They'd be somewhere in the gathering dusk, keeping watch for danger.

Harkeld looked back at Cora, with her plain, weary face and thick plait of graying sandy hair. "Cora?"

"Yes?" She didn't look up from unpacking the cooking pots.

"Dareus said that Sentinels can strip witches of their magic."

Cora stopped what she was doing. She looked at him. "If a mage misuses his magic, then yes, Sentinels will strip him of it."

"Can you strip me of my mine?" *Please.*

Cora surveyed him for several seconds. Had she heard the desperation in his voice? "Myself? No. Only healers can do it. Innis could do it."

Innis? He felt his face stiffen. Memory swooped back: the catacombs, a smoking torch, skeletal corpses jostling each other as they guarded the anchor stone. He heard Innis's voice clearly in his head: *I thought you were braver than this.*

"Not someone else?" Harkeld said. "Not Petrus?"

Cora shook her head and went back to unpacking the pots. "He's not a strong enough healer. Some of the Sentinels who're joining us should be. We asked for more healers."

Harkeld watched her sort through the bundles of dried food. Her hands were brisk, competent, short-fingered. *If no new healers come...*

He clenched his teeth together. If it had to be Innis, he'd do it. He'd get down on his knees and beg her. Anything to be rid of the fire inside him. "How is it done? Will I still be able to travel?"

Cora laid down the bundles and met his gaze squarely. "Prince Harkeld, you're an extremely strong fire mage. Stronger than I am, at a guess—"

"I don't want to be a witch."

"Whether you want to or not is irrelevant. You are one."

He shook his head.

She looked at him for a long moment, as if weighing options. He saw a decision firm her mouth. "Once the third anchor stone is destroyed, we'll strip you of your magic. But until then, you must use it."

"What?" He shook his head, pushed to his feet. "No!"

"Your magic saved your life in the canyon. And from what Innis tells me, it saved you both in the catacombs."

He didn't look at her, didn't acknowledge her words. He stared at the sun sinking behind the horizon.

"We need every advantage we can get, sire. Surely you see that? If you die..."

If I die, so could everyone on this continent.

"Fire magic is frightening," Cora said matter-of-factly. "And the more magic one has, the more frightening it is. Until one learns to control it."

He turned his head to look down at her.

"Only a fool wouldn't be afraid." Cora held out a large iron pot. "Can you fill this with water, please?"

Harkeld walked down to the stagnant pool, filled the pot, brought it back to the fire. Cora looked at the scum floating in it and wrinkled her nose. "We'll strain it." She took another pot and laid a strip of cloth over it. "You pour."

Harkeld hefted the heavy pot.

"I'll teach you to use your fire magic," Cora said, as the dirty water splashed onto the cloth. "So you can use it to protect yourself. And once the curse is broken, one of the healers will strip you of it. If that's what you wish."

Use it again?

He remembered the canyon, red cliffs towering over him, the assassin screaming as he burned. He remembered the catacombs, the ocean of fire, the deafening roar of flame.

"Innis told me what happened in the catacombs," Cora said as he lowered the empty pot. "She was right; fire was the only way through, but the risk... You're lucky the two of you are still alive."

"What do you mean?"

"If my guess is correct, you're strong enough to set stone on fire. You could have burned everything. Not just the corpses, but the entire catacombs. There would have been nothing left. You and Innis..." She made a sharp gesture with one hand. "Incinerated. And then what would have happened? We wouldn't even have had your body."

And the curse would never be broken. And everyone in the Seven Kingdoms would die.

Cora hung the pot on an iron tripod over the fire. Harkeld's eyes followed the movement of her hands, but his mind was back in Masse. He saw a gray dawn, a smoky battlefield, Dareus lying broken-necked. *If you'd used your magic, you sniveling coward, he'd still be alive!* The voice was Gerit's, hoarse with rage and exhaustion. *He's dead because of you!*

He'd felt the truth of the words then, and he felt them still. Dareus would be alive if he'd dared to use his magic.

"If... if I agree to learn..." The words were astonishingly difficult to utter; they clogged in his throat and stuck on his tongue. Harkeld swallowed. "If I agree—"

"If you agree, you have my word that one of our healers will strip your magic from you once the curse is destroyed."

The word of a witch. What was that worth?

He stared at Cora. She wasn't Dareus, whom he'd grudgingly trusted, but Dareus was dead, buried beneath the desert sand, and Cora led them now. She was... perhaps not completely human, but not the monster he'd once thought witches were.

Harkeld took a deep breath, ignored the panic churning in his stomach, and nodded. "I agree."

"Good. Can you fill that pot again, please? We need to boil some water to drink."

They strained a second pot of water and set it on the fire. Cora opened bundles of dried meat. "We'll start small. Can you fetch a candle?"

"What? Now?" Harkeld rocked back on his heels, alarmed.

"Why not?" She looked at him, her eyes reflecting the firelight. "You want to be able to control it, don't you?"

"Uh... I should really help with the packhorses." He gestured to where Ebril and Justen worked.

"Prince Harkeld."

Her voice wasn't scornful, as Innis's had been. She sounded sympathetic, motherly. *As if I'm a child, not a man of twenty-four.*

Harkeld flushed. He pushed to his feet and went to fetch a candle. Fear built in his chest as he brought it back to the fire. The first pot was simmering. He watched Cora put in handfuls of dried meat, dried vegetables, a scattering of dried herbs; nearly the last of the supplies they'd brought from Lundegaard. She dusted her palms one against the other. "Sit down beside me."

He did, his legs stiff with reluctance.

"We'll start with this." Cora snapped her fingers. A single flame flared on one fingertip, and then went out. "Fire magic is inside me, in my blood, and I choose to release it. I could have it come out my nose if I wanted to, but this..."—she snapped her fingers again—"is simple and safe. My magic is focused on one point that I can see. I'm not going to accidentally burn myself or anyone else."

She looked at him as if expecting a response. Harkeld nodded.

"When I was learning, I found it easiest to visualize a tinderbox. Flint strikes steel and you have a spark." Cora snapped her fingers, the flame flared again for an instant. "You try. Concentrate on your hand. Try to feel the magic in your blood. Imagine that it's warm and stings a little."

Harkeld took a deep breath. He looked at his right hand. His mind gave him images of what might happen: his hand engulfed in flames, becoming a blackened claw. "What if my hand catches fire?"

"I'll put it out."

His gaze jerked to her face. "It can happen?"

"It's extremely rare for fire mages to burn themselves. It's... how can I put it? The magic is in your blood, and your blood is in your body, and it's as if the magic knows it shouldn't burn itself. Does that make sense?"

He nodded.

"I saw someone make fire come out of his ears once," Cora said. "A student fooling around. His hair caught alight. That's the only time I've ever seen a mage hurt himself with his own fire."

His mind shied away from the image her words conjured.

"I doubt you'll burn yourself, Prince Harkeld, but if you do, I'll put it out."

Harkeld tried to swallow his fear, but it stuck in his throat, a choking lump. *Stop being such a baby*, he told himself. He gritted his teeth and stared at his right hand, trying to feel the magic in his blood. Warm and stinging, Cora had said.

The magic hadn't been warm and stinging in the catacombs. It had been hot, a searing pain that had roared through him.

In a rush, he felt it again: fire sizzling along his veins.

"Can you feel it?"

Harkeld nodded, his jaw clenched. His hand felt so hot the skin should be blistering, smoking.

"Now imagine your hand is a tinderbox and snap your fingers."

He was sweating, afraid. It was stupidly difficult to breathe. "You'll put it out if..."

"I'll put it out."

Harkeld gulped a breath, visualized a tinderbox—flint striking against steel—and snapped his fingers.

Flame roared high, white-hot, lighting up the campsite like a flash of lightning.

Panic burst in his chest. He rocked backwards, thrusting his hand away from himself. His mouth opened in a shout, but before it was uttered, Cora laid her hand over his, quenching the flame.

Harkeld stared at her, his mouth still open, his heart beating wildly. Behind Cora he saw Justen and Ebril turn their heads, startled. The horses moved uneasily, one half-rearing.

Cora's lips twitched in a smile. "I see I shall have to teach you how to dampen your magic."

He closed his mouth, found his voice. "Dampen?"

"You don't need that much magic to light a candle. Just a tiny amount." She released his hand. "Now, try again. Feel the magic in your blood."

I don't want to. Harkeld took a deep breath. He looked at his hand again and tried to sense magic there. This time it came quickly, a painful flood of heat.

"Is it hot?"

He nodded, gritting his teeth.

"Dampen it."

"How?" His voice was tight with pain.

"Tell it."

Harkeld snarled at the uselessness of this advice. *Not so hot,* he said in his head. *Not so hot.* But it didn't make any difference. His skin felt like it was sizzling, his blood boiling. Panic rose in him. Any moment now his hand would burst into flames and—

"Not working?" Cora reached out and took his wrist. "Come with me."

Harkeld stumbled to his feet and followed her, down into the riverbed. Her fingers pinched his wrist, pinched back his panic. Curse it, but his hand *burned*—

Cora crouched, pulling him to his knees, and plunged his hand into the stagnant pool.

Harkeld hissed. He half expected to see steam rise.

"Keep telling your magic that you don't need all of it," Cora said. "You only need enough to light a candle."

He did, over and over in his head. *Not so hot. I only need a little. Just enough for a candle.* The water helped. His hand began to cool. His panic trickled away, leaving him feeling foolish.

"Better?"

Harkeld nodded.

Cora released his wrist. He could barely see her in the dusk. "Now, try snapping your fingers again."

Harkeld lifted his hand from the water. He felt the magic in his blood, warm, pulsing in time to his heartbeat.

He shook off the drops and took a deep breath. *Just enough for a candle.* He imagined his hand was a tinderbox and snapped his fingers.

A flame appeared, steady and orange, dancing on the end of his forefinger. The light it cast showed him Cora's face. She smiled. "See? You control your magic, Prince Harkeld. It doesn't control you."

He nodded, too relieved to be able to speak.

"You have the candle?"

He fished in his pocket with his left hand.

"Light it."

He did. It became even easier to see Cora's face. "Well done," she said.

He felt no sense of accomplishment. The flame burning quietly at the end of his finger, the lit candle—they weren't things to be proud of; they were the first steps to becoming what he'd reviled all his life: a witch.

No. It was the first step to having the magic stripped from his blood. The first step to *not* being a witch.

Cora stood. "Let's get back to the fire. I think the stew's about to boil over."

The flame still burned on the end of Harkeld's forefinger. "How do I put this out? Douse it in water?"

"Pinch your thumb and finger together and imagine you're snuffing a candle."

He did. The flame vanished.

"You won't always need to use imagery like that," Cora said, as he followed her back to the fire. "But for now it's easiest. Like the tinderbox." She crouched and stirred the stew. "Put out that candle and try lighting it again."

"But the pool—"

"You shouldn't need water to dampen your magic, now that you know you can do it. That's a lot of what magic's about. Knowing what you can and can't do. If you doubt yourself, if you're afraid, it becomes a lot harder. Magic is in the blood, but our ability to use it comes from up here." Cora tapped her forehead.

A black owl glided low over the camp and landed beside the tents.

"Ah, Innis is back. She'll need her clothes." Cora gave him the wooden spoon. "Keep stirring. And once that drinking water's boiled for five minutes, take it off."

Harkeld had just removed the water pot from the fire when Cora returned with Innis. The girl's face was pale and tired beneath her tangled black curls.

"You must be starving, Innis." Cora rummaged among the bundles of food. "Here, have these nuts."

His own stomach gave a quiet rumble, but Innis would be hungrier than he was; witches were forbidden to eat when they were in another shape, and she'd flown more than a hundred miles today.

"The water's too hot to drink. Wait, I'll fetch my waterskin." Cora hurried off into the darkness.

Which left just him and Innis at the fire. Harkeld put all his concentration into stirring the stew, ignoring Innis sitting on the other side of the orange flames.

"Sire?"

He kept his eyes on the pot for a moment, then glanced at her. It was the first time they'd been alone together since the anchor stone, when she'd shoved his cowardice in his face. She'd been fierce then, her gray eyes blazing at him. Now she looked fragile and exhausted.

"I want to apologize for what I said to you in the catacombs."

He frowned. "What?"

"I apologize," Innis said. "I was trying to make you angry enough to use your magic."

Harkeld looked back at the stew. It was bubbling. Lumps of meat jostled one another, pieces of carrot, peas. "It worked," he said flatly.

He tried not to remember, but it was impossible not to. Her words had been like slaps across his face: *I thought you were braver than this, sire.*

Harkeld stabbed the stew with the wooden spoon. She'd been right to call him a coward.

"What I said wasn't true. I shouldn't have said it."

He lifted his head and glared at her. "It was true."

"What? No! How can you think that? I was there when your father said he'd cut out your tongue if you disobeyed him. Even when he said he'd take your hands and your head, you stood up to him! You did what was right."

Harkeld looked back at the pot.

"And in the Graytooth Mountains, at the pass, you came back to fight, even though Dareus told you not to."

Harkeld stirred the stew slowly.

"What I said in the catacombs—it was to make you angry, sire. And I apologize. It was badly done of me."

Innis meant what she said. He could hear it in her voice.

Harkeld looked up, met her eyes and nodded.

The apology shouldn't matter—she was only a witch after all; what did he care about her opinion of him? But somehow it did.

Innis held the nuts in her hand, uneaten. She seemed thinner, as if she'd lost weight in the three days she'd been gone. "Eat," Harkeld told her brusquely, and turned his attention to the pot again.

INNIS HAD TWO bowls of stew, trying to eat slowly and not shovel it into her mouth. She was still hungry when she'd finished, but a glance at the pot told her it had been scraped clean.

"Tell us about Stanic," Cora said. "Who was there?"

Innis put down her bowl. The food was a pleasant warmth in her stomach. Her eyes caught movement overhead. A russet-breasted owl glided over the campsite, its feathers shimmering with shapeshifter's magic. Ebril, keeping watch. He drifted out of sight into the darkness. "Five Sentinels."

"Only five?" Gerit scowled, his beard bristling. "We need more'n that."

"Who are they?" Cora asked.

"Susa and Katlen. Hew. Rand and Frane." A yawn caught her on the last name.

"Don't know most of 'em." Gerit's scowl deepened. "What are they?"

"Frane's a healer, Hew's a shapeshifter, and Susa's a fire mage. They've just finished their Journeys and taken their oaths. Rand's a healer. He says he knows you and Cora. And Katlen's a fire mage. She was an instructor at the Academy."

"Only one shapeshifter." Gerit spat into the fire. "Don't they know we need more'n that? What with that bounty and those thrice-cursed assassins." He scowled at Prince Harkeld, as if it was the prince's fault he had a bounty on his head.

Prince Harkeld ignored him. Cora did too. "Two healers, two fire mages, and a shapeshifter?" she asked Innis.

Innis nodded. "Rand said the Council's calling in all the Sentinels they can. More will join us after the second anchor stone."

"Where?"

"At the delta, if a ship can get close enough. He said something about shallows making it dangerous. Otherwise, Krelinsk."

"Dangerous?" Gerit snorted. "It's not rutting shallows that are dangerous, it's those Fithian bastards and their throwing stars." He pushed to his feet and stamped off towards the tents. Across the fire, Justen—Petrus—rolled his eyes at her.

"So once they join us, we'll be ten Sentinels," Cora said, seemingly unruffled by Gerit's bad temper. "Double what we are now. Good."

"I gave them the list of supplies we need." Innis tried to smother another yawn. "They'll meet us the day after tomorrow outside Hradik. I told them you'd like to avoid the town, because of the prince."

She glanced at Prince Harkeld. He didn't appear to be listening. His face was half turned away, shadowed. He looked like a peasant, unshaven, dark hair chopped roughly short, clothes travel-stained, but he didn't hold himself like a peasant, didn't move or ride like one, and his face—the square brow and jaw, the strong nose and cheekbones—was memorable. Someone might recognize him as Osgaard's missing prince.

"Rand said the Council think the curse will already be in Sault when we get there. They reckon we'll need a lot of Sentinels for that."

"We will." But Cora didn't sound worried.

"They're trying to find us a strong water mage."

"Good. We'll need one of those. Now get off to bed. You must be exhausted."

"Shall I take a shift tonight?" Innis flicked a glance in Justen's direction, trying to convey the silent question: *Or be Justen?*

"No." Cora stood. "I'll take the second watch. You can share my tent."

Innis rose to her feet. Her muscles had stiffened while she sat. She followed Cora across the stony ground.

"You told Rand and the others about you shapeshifters being Justen?" Cora asked in a low whisper.

"Yes."

"And?"

"They were shocked. Breaking a Primary Law..."

"But they understood why? The shapeshifter—Hew?—he'll do it?"

"Yes."

"Good." She heard relief in Cora's voice.

Innis glanced back at Justen and Prince Harkeld beside the fire. "Has Petrus been Justen all day? Do you need me to swap with him?"

"He's all right for now. Less tired than you, at any rate."

"And tomorrow?"

"You can go back to being Justen most of the time." Cora held open a tent flap. "The bedroll on the left is yours."

"Thanks."

"It's good to have you back, Innis. We've been stretched without you." Cora turned to go, then halted. "Oh... the prince and I have made a deal. If he learns to use his magic, we'll strip him of it once the curse is destroyed."

"What?" Her mouth fell open. "Learn to use his magic? He agreed?"

"He did."

Innis shook her head. *Impossible*. "But he's so afraid of it!"

"With good reason. I've never seen a fire mage with more raw power. Until he learns to control it, he's dangerous."

CHAPTER THREE

AT DAWN, INNIS slipped away from the camp and swapped with Petrus, taking Justen's shape and clothes. "He's started learning to use his magic." Petrus handed her Justen's amulet of walrus ivory. "Did Cora tell you?"

Innis nodded.

"She had him light a candle. You should have seen it, Innis. Flame right up into the sky. Just about set the horses stampeding." He snorted a laugh.

The round Grooten amulet lay against her breastbone, warm from Petrus's body. "Did he light the candle?"

"Eventually."

Innis settled Justen's baldric across her back. The muscles in her arms and shoulders ached from yesterday's flying.

Petrus pulled on his trews. "Susa's joining us? That's good news. Always up for a laugh, she is. Frane's a bit glum for my taste, though, and as for Hew..." He pulled a face. "No fun in him at all."

"No." Innis looked down at her body. Justen's body—brawny and male, clad in Justen's clothes. "He was shocked about Justen, said he wouldn't break a Primary Law."

"What? He's refused to do it?"

"Rand talked him round, but he was shocked too. They all were. Especially... about me being Justen."

"Don't pay them any attention." Petrus pulled on his shirt, then combed his tousled white-blond hair with his fingers. "Dareus was right: it's got to be done if we're going to keep the prince alive."

Innis scuffed her boot in the dust, remembering Hew's exclamation. *You? A girl be a man? That's doubly wrong!* Even laughing, carefree Susa had looked appalled.

Petrus punched her lightly on the shoulder. "You're a good Justen. Better than me or Gerit."

Because I like being Justen and you don't.

"I'm glad you're back. I missed you. Now get over there to the prince."

"My clothes—"

"I'll pack them for you. Go." He made a shooing gesture, hamming it up, acting the clown.

Innis grinned at him, closest friend and almost-brother, and headed for the horses.

She helped Prince Harkeld lift bundled tents onto a packhorse and strap the load into place. She wanted to whistle, the way Ebril always did. It felt so right, being Justen. The amulet at her throat, the weight of the armsman's sword, her place at Prince Harkeld's side.

THEY REACHED THE forest in the mid-afternoon, tall trees Harkeld didn't recognize, bark hanging off in long gray strips. The air was damp and mild. That evening they camped beside a river. The fire burned fiercely, the wood crackling and spitting, giving off a strong resinous odor. He lit a candle several times, under Cora's watchful gaze. "Good," she said. "Tomorrow night you can light the fire."

They struck camp at dawn, heading east on animal trails, following the brown hawk that was Gerit. After several hours they came to farmland. It had been hard-won from the forest; sheep grazed around burned tree stumps.

The hawk landed and became Gerit. Harkeld lifted his lip in a sneer—*filthy witch*—but the sneer was half-hearted. He was one of them now.

Gerit scratched his beard. "You want me to lead you round the settlements, not through 'em?"

"Please," Cora said.

They followed the hawk, skirting straggling fields, then down a rutted lane. Justen rode at his side, Cora just ahead, Ebril and Petrus behind with the packhorses, and yet Harkeld felt exposed. In Lundegaard they'd had an escort of soldiers. Here, there was only a handful of witches between himself and anyone who cared to claim the bounty on his head.

"Prince Harkeld?"

He looked at Cora.

"Now that we're in populated areas, we should call you by another name. One no one will recognize."

He nodded.

Cora looked relieved, as if she'd expected him to protest.

I haven't been a prince for weeks. Haven't you noticed? Not since the moment in the canyon when his fire magic had burst out of him. He'd lost the home in Lundegaard that King Magnas had offered him, lost any right to call himself a prince. He was a commoner now. No, lower than a commoner; a witch.

"Do you have a preference what name we use?"

What did it matter? The witches had lost him his birthright, his family, his home. What was a name, compared with those things? A name was nothing.

A name was something he had to live with, until he could be rid of these people. Another two months, at least.

Harkeld scowled at his horse's ears. On either side of the lane, warped split-rail fences enclosed ragged fields. He needed a name that was ordinary, but also one he'd recognize when people said it. His memory skipped back to the game he'd played with his half-sister when she was a child.

"Flin."

Saying the name brought back a rush of memory. He heard Britta's voice, *Can we play Flin, please?* Heard her breathless giggles as he chased her across the palace lawns while the nursemaids and the armsmen tried to keep straight faces. Heard her squeal when he caught her and her whoop of glee when he swung her in the air.

They'd only played Flin for a few months, before he'd been fostered to King Magnas's court. When he'd returned two years later, he'd thought himself too old for such games. And Britta, sweet Britta, had asked only once and never mentioned it again.

I should have played with her more often.

His throat tightened. Tears stung his eyes. For a dreadful moment he thought he might cry.

But wasn't it something worth crying for? The sister he'd never meet again. The little brothers he'd never see grow up.

Harkeld lifted his face to the sky. *All-Mother, please keep them safe,* he prayed.

THEY SKIRTED THE town of Hradik. Gerit now rode, and it was Petrus who glided overhead, creamy wings widespread. A second hawk joined Petrus for several minutes. It had a speckled breast and tail feathers. Not long afterwards they came to a crossroad. Four riders and a string of packhorses waited there. Above, the strange hawk circled.

"Rand!" Cora spurred forward.

Harkeld watched the witches greet each other, assessing them. These people would be his companions, his protectors.

There were two men—one young, one middle-aged—and two women. Harkeld ignored the older woman and let his gaze rest on the younger one for a moment. Curling blonde hair, good breasts, and a pretty, lightly-freckled face. It seemed she knew Ebril. The two of them were laughing.

"The men are both healers," Justen said from alongside him. "From what Innis said. Rand and Frane. And the women—"

"Both fire witches."

Justen glanced at him. "You listened the other night."

Harkeld shrugged.

"Flin. Justen." Cora beckoned.

He nudged his horse forward.

"This is Prince Harkeld," Cora said. "But we're calling him Flin now. And Justen, his armsman."

The older fire witch returned the introductions. She was a tall, lean, brisk woman, with salt-and-pepper hair cut as short as a man's. "I'm Katlen. Hew's up there." A jerk of her thumb indicated the speckled hawk. "And these are Rand, Frane, and Susa." Rand was the more senior healer, with weathered skin and hair the color of sun-bleached grass. His younger colleague, Frane, had a dark, lugubrious face. The young fire witch was Susa. She smiled cheerfully, her blonde curls bouncing around her face.

"We brought the supplies Innis said you needed," Katlen told Cora. "I understand you wish to avoid settlements?"

"If possible. The bounty on Flin's head..."

"Yes. Annoying."

Harkeld snorted under his breath. Annoying?

"Hew says there's a good campsite a few miles along this road," Katlen said. "A meadow beside a river."

AT THE MEADOW, Katlen dismounted and proceeded to take charge. "Pitch the tents there. Is that all right, Cora?" and "The packhorses over there, I think, don't you, Cora?" and "Frane will gather the firewood, if that's all right with you, Cora?"

Cora didn't seem to mind. She took the firewood from Frane and laid it inside the ring of stones she'd made. "Would you prefer to have Katlen instruct you?" she asked Harkeld. "She's been teaching fire magic at the Academy for twenty years."

He shook his head. *I don't like bossy women.*

"Very well." Cora dusted her hands together. "There are a couple of ways of lighting fires. Normally I do this..." She snapped her fingers, and a branch flared alight. "But you haven't learned to throw fire yet." The flame snuffed out. "You'll need to touch the wood to make it burn. You can do it with a single flame, but it's quicker if you do this." Another snap of her fingers, and Cora opened her palm, showing him a handful of flames dancing there. The sight made him shiver.

Cora took hold of a branch, and a moment later it was alight. "See?"

Harkeld nodded.

Cora released the branch and closed her fist, extinguishing the flames on her hand and the branch. "You try. Visualize the tinderbox, but this time, when you snap your fingers, imagine holding a handful of flames. Small flames."

Harkeld stared down at his right hand, trying to feel the fire magic in his blood. It came more easily this time, a rush of sensation, warm and tingling. He visualized the tinderbox. *A handful of small flames*, he told himself and snapped his fingers.

Heat prickled across his palm. He was suddenly holding a cluster of flames.

Harkeld's heart began to gallop. He held his hand away from himself. What if he set his clothes alight?

"Close your fist," Cora said.

He did. The flames snuffed out.

"You're afraid you'll burn yourself."

Harkeld flushed. Had his fear been that obvious? "My clothes. I could set them on fire."

Cora nodded. "Very well, let's deal with that. Suppose your clothes did catch alight, what would you do?"

He had a vision of himself frantically beating the flames, while the witches laughed. "Beat it out."

"You could," Cora said. "But it's much more efficient to use your magic—"

A pale hawk swooped down and landed, became Petrus. "Three men on horseback approaching from the west."

Katlen came across to the fireplace. "Three men?"

The speckled hawk landed and changed shape. "They've been behind us from Stanic." The new shapeshifter was a stocky young man with mouse-brown hair and pale skin covered with freckles. "They're just travelers."

Katlen nodded. "I've seen them."

"Even so, we'll take no chances." Cora stood and raised her voice. "Justen! Over here."

Harkeld pushed to his feet. He loosened his sword in its scabbard. Justen came to stand beside him.

"Ebril, Gerit, Susa," Cora called.

Harkeld was conscious of the witches ranging themselves around him. He heard the sound of swords sliding from scabbards; he wasn't the only person checking his weapon. He looked around. The healers were with the packhorses, removing the last of the loads, and Petrus and the new shapeshifter were overhead again. The only witch he couldn't see was Innis. He cast a quick glance at the darkening sky, but couldn't spot her.

He heard the sound of hooves. Justen stepped forward, placing himself squarely in front of Harkeld. It was what Justen had been hired to do—protect him with his life—but, even so, Harkeld felt a flicker of irritation. *Curse it, I want to see.*

The clop of hooves became louder. Harkeld stepped sideways to see past Justen. Three riders and half a dozen packhorses emerged from the dusk.

The riders halted. "Evening."

"Good evening," Cora said.

The men were about his own age, wearing dusty jerkins and trews much like his own. They sat relaxed in their saddles.

Harkeld eyed them. A single Fithian assassin could take down two or more soldiers. If these men were Fithians, what did they see? Three women, a handful of men.

Easy pickings.

"Mind if we share your campsite? Safety in numbers, y'know."

Harkeld glanced at their packhorses, saw bows strapped to one of them.

"I'm sorry," Cora said, "but we wish to be alone."

"There's only three of us. We won't take up much room." The man grinned, a friendly expression. "You'll scarcely notice us." He held the reins in one hand, the other resting casually on his hip.

"I'm sorry," Cora said again. "I don't wish to be discourteous, but we prefer not to share our campsite."

Harkeld watched the man's gaze slide over their faces and return to rest on him. He glanced at the other two riders. They were both looking at him too.

The hair rose on his scalp.

The men erupted into movement, spurring their horses forward. Gleaming metal sliced through the air towards him: a throwing star. Harkeld ducked, a shout stuck in his throat. He drew his sword. Another throwing star whizzed past his head. Someone shoved him to his knees. Justen. "Stay down!"

A lion roared. He heard shouts, the *whoosh* of flames, a scream, the shrill whinny of a horse.

Harkeld pushed to his feet, sword drawn. Justen's blade swept a throwing star out of the air with a loud *clang*. "Down, sire!"

The melee was chaotic. One assassin was burning, still astride his horse. The horse squealed as it tried to dislodge him. A second horse galloped free, scattering the packhorses, its saddle empty. Harkeld looked for its rider; there, on the ground, with a silver-maned lion standing over the body. Two more lions dragged the third Fithian from his saddle while his horse screamed in terror. The assassin didn't scream; he fought, a snarl on his face and a blade gleaming in his hand. He hit the ground and tried to scramble to his feet. The lions pounced, tearing at him.

Justen glanced back. "You all right?"

Harkeld nodded.

The body of the burned assassin tumbled to the ground and lay smoking. His horse fled, still squealing.

Justen lowered his sword. The last Fithian was dead, his throat ripped out. One lion shook its head, spraying blood, and changed shape. Gerit. "What were you doing?" Gerit yelled at Katlen. "Why didn't you use your magic? Just stood there and let us do all the fighting!"

"There wasn't time—"

"There was plenty of time!" he bellowed. "Cora burned one. Why didn't you? And you!" He turned to the speckled hawk as it landed. "You should have been down here, fighting, not flapping around up there!"

The hawk changed shape. Hew's face was pale beneath the freckles, as if he'd never seen death so close before. "It's forbidden to kill with magic."

"Not if you're a Sentinel," Gerit snarled. "Not if you're fighting Fithians."

Harkeld sheathed his sword. He inhaled, smelling burned flesh, smelling blood. How long had the battle taken? A minute? Less?

The silver-maned lion changed into Petrus. His face was as blood-stained as Gerit's. He spat, wiped his mouth with his hand, spat again.

Gerit swung to face Katlen. "You should go back to Rosny, the lot of you, if that's the best you can do! Useless, cowardly—"

"Gerit." Cora's voice was sharp. "That's enough."

He turned to her, teeth bared in his bloodied face.

"If you're unharmed, get after those horses. Bring them back. You too, Hew." Cora flicked Harkeld a glance. "You all right?"

"Yes."

Justen took a step forward. "Ebril's hurt—"

"Rand and Frane can heal him." Cora beckoned to the healers and hurried over to Ebril. The witch was clasping his upper arm. Blood leaked between his fingers.

Justen looked down at his sword. He made a sound of dismay.

"Nicked?" Harkeld said. "I'm not surprised. You caught one of those things out of the air."

"Ach, that was luck, not skill." Justen looked back, pulled a face. His gaze fastened on something behind Harkeld. "Susa!"

The blonde fire witch lay on the ground, arms outspread, a throwing star buried in her throat.

"Cora!" Harkeld yelled. "We need the healers! Now!"

Justen dropped to his knees, touched the witch's face.

"She'll be all right." Harkeld crouched alongside the armsman, hearing footsteps running towards them. "The healers—"

Justen shook his head. Tears shone in his eyes. "She's dead."

CHAPTER FOUR

THEY DUG A grave for Susa and a pit for the assassins. "Why bother?" Gerit said, throwing down his shovel. "Let 'em rot where they lie."

Petrus opened his mouth, but Cora spoke first: "Because we must leave no trace of this."

"But—"

"Use your sense, Gerit!" Cora brushed strands of hair impatiently away from her face. "One of these men was obviously killed by magic. Do you want to let all of Ankeny know where we are?"

Gerit flushed.

"Even if there was no bounty on Flin's head, we'd need to hide this. You know what people here think of mages."

Petrus drove his shovel into the stony soil with a sharp crunching sound. "'The only good mage is a dead one.'"

Gerit picked up his shovel again, scowling.

Night fell while they dug. Petrus worked alongside Justen and Prince Harkeld, hacking at the ground, his chest tight with grief. He levered a rock from the soil, hefted it aside, and leaned on his shovel, sweating, panting.

On the other side of the meadow, Gerit and Frane were digging Susa's grave.

I didn't even get to say hello to her.

Petrus looked away. Ebril, his arm healed, held one of the assassins' mounts while Rand dealt with the slashes on its haunches. Petrus recognized the beast. His own claws had made those wounds.

The taste of the assassin's blood abruptly filled his mouth. Petrus clenched his jaw against the urge to vomit. He concentrated on his breathing and let his gaze drift around the campsite. Katlen was picketing the packhorses, Cora pitching tents, Hew flying overhead, his owl's body shimmering faintly. A pot of stew cooked on the fire.

It looked so ordinary. He could almost imagine Susa wasn't dead.

But if Susa was alive, they'd be talking as they worked, laughing. Definitely laughing. Susa always made people laugh.

Rage and grief boiled up in him. Petrus attacked the stony soil again.

When the bodies were buried, they stood at Susa's grave. Rand spoke the words, "All-Mother, we give this woman to your care, that she may rest peacefully."

Ebril crouched and placed his hand on the mounded dirt. What silent farewell was he saying?

Petrus crouched too and laid his hand on the grave. *Goodbye, Susa.* The unfairness of it boiled up in him again. He pushed to his feet and walked down to the river, stumbling on half-seen stones.

"Does anyone have the green touch?" he heard Cora ask.

"I do," someone said. Frane or Rand.

"See what you can do to hide these."

"Green touch?" The voice was Prince Harkeld's.

Petrus cupped water in his hands, rinsed his mouth, and spat. The taste of the assassin's blood lingered on his tongue.

Ebril came to stand beside him. "You all right?"

"Why Susa?" Petrus said in a low, savage voice. "Why couldn't it have been Gerit? All he does is spew bad temper! Why couldn't it have been him and not her?" He squeezed his eyes shut. "Rut it. I'm sorry, Ebril. I shouldn't have said that. I don't mean I want Gerit dead. It's just... Susa..."

"I know," Ebril said, crouching alongside him. "Everyone liked Susa. She made people happy."

Petrus rubbed his face and sighed. "Rut it."

"Cora wants you to swap with Innis for a while. Let her be herself."

Petrus stood and headed back to the camp. Frane knelt at Susa's grave, his hands resting on the soil, a look of concentration on his face.

Petrus blew out a breath, trying to find calmness within himself. *It could have been worse. It could have been Innis who died.*

DINNER WAS A silent meal. Fresh meat, for the first time in weeks. Petrus forced himself to eat; he could still taste the assassin's blood. Each time he swallowed, nausea churned in his stomach. Ebril ate quickly, shucked his clothes, changed into an owl, and flew up into the sky. A few minutes later, Hew came and took Ebril's place at the fire.

"These curse shadows are off-putting," Rand said. "I've never seen ones so strong."

Petrus glanced at the healer, seeing the dark stain of Ivek's curse lying over him, promise of the death awaiting Rand now that he'd set foot in the Seven Kingdoms.

"You get used to it," Cora said. "I hardly notice them now."

Rand looked doubtful.

Petrus could tell him it was true—he only saw the curse shadows if someone pointed them out—but he didn't feel like speaking. He stirred his stew without enthusiasm.

Katlen put down her bowl. "I don't understand how they knew to follow us. We did nothing to draw attention to ourselves!"

"You must have done," Gerit said.

"You look different," Prince Harkeld said. "If I'd been them, I'd have followed you too."

Katlen frowned. "What do you mean?"

"Look at you." He gestured with his spoon. "You're a woman, yet you're wearing trews and carrying a sword. It's not natural."

Katlen bristled. "Where I come from—"

"And you speak with an accent, all of you."

Katlen closed her mouth.

"You're obviously fighters—and you're obviously not from the Seven Kingdoms. So what does that make you? Mercenaries? Or witches?" The prince put the spoon in his bowl, and put both on the ground. "I've never heard of Sarkosians accepting women into their companies, so I'd pick witches." His gaze was direct, challenging Katlen to deny this. "And why would witches be in Ankeny, a kingdom where witches are beheaded and burned? Why would you take such a risk?"

They all knew the answer to that question, but the prince said it anyway: "Because of the curse. Because of me."

"You think they were waiting in Stanic for us?" Frane asked.

Prince Harkeld shrugged. "Maybe they were just there to try their luck. If we succeeded in Lundegaard, we had to cross into Ankeny somehow, somewhere. When they saw you, they must have thought the All-Mother was blessing them."

Silence followed those words.

Petrus glanced at Innis. Her face was bleak. He wished he could reach out and take her hand, but he couldn't, not while he was Justen.

"Do you think there'll be more?" Frane asked.

Gerit snorted. "In Ankeny? Without a doubt. There's a bounty on his head. They'll be wanting a piece of it."

Katlen turned to Cora. "But we need our swords! We need to be able to fight!"

"You've got fire magic," Gerit said flatly. "That's a better weapon than any sword."

Katlen ignored him. "And as for skirts! They're impractical! They're—"

Petrus stopped listening. He stared down at his empty bowl. *If only...*

If only, what? There were so many *if onlies*. Dozens of them, hundreds. If only King Esger hadn't placed the bounty on his son's head. If only Dareus had survived the battle in the desert. If only Susa had ducked a second sooner.

Petrus grunted in disgust at himself. What was the point of *if onlies*? They made things neither better nor worse. A waste of time. A waste of emotion.

"Let's see if we can mend that sword of yours," Prince Harkeld said over the sound of Gerit and Katlen arguing.

Petrus looked at him. "Huh?"

"Your sword. I'll get the whetstones." The prince stood.

Petrus unsheathed his sword. The blade was notched. He glanced at Innis. She was staring down at her bowl.

"Innis..."

She looked at him. Tears shone in her eyes.

His heart seemed to turn over in his chest. He wanted to hug her, to comfort her. Instead, he held out the sword. "How did this happen?"

Innis blinked back the tears. "Throwing star."

Prince Harkeld returned with two whetstones. "Here."

Petrus set himself to trying to remove the nick. Alongside him, Prince Harkeld sharpened his own sword. Petrus sent him a sideways glance. The prince had to be afraid. He'd been the Fithians' quarry, not Susa. But Prince Harkeld didn't look afraid. His expression was the same one he'd worn for weeks: grim, remote, distancing himself from the mages around him.

Gerit and Katlen were still arguing. *Shut up!* Petrus wanted to yell at them.

"For pity's sake," Cora said. "You're behaving like children."

"But—"

"Enough." Cora's voice was sharper than he'd ever heard it. "We won't discuss this any more tonight."

Gerit growled, pushed to his feet, and left the campfire.

"How that man ever became a Sentinel—"

"Enough, Katlen."

Prince Harkeld tested his blade with his thumb and sheathed it. He stood and walked to where their supplies lay piled.

Petrus worked on his sword, keeping an eye on the prince. He was going through one of the packsaddles. He was safe enough; Rand was near him, and Ebril flying overhead.

The prince came back carrying two swords in their scabbards. "You're not going to get rid of that notch. Here. Take a look at these."

Petrus laid Justen's sword aside.

The first sword the prince held out had Lundegaard's crest worked into the hilt. Petrus swiped it in the air a couple of times. The weight and balance were good. It must have belonged to one of the soldiers who'd died defending them in the desert.

The second sword... The weight and balance weren't just good, they were perfect. He hefted the sword in his hand, cut the air.

"Like it?" Prince Harkeld asked.

Petrus nodded. He examined the hilt. No crest was worked into the metal. "Whose..." And then he understood. "It's Fithian." The taste of the assassin's blood filled his mouth. He almost brought his dinner up.

"Crafted by a master, from its balance."

Petrus turned the sword over in his hands. An assassin's sword. How many men had it killed? He tested the blade with his thumb. It was razor sharp. "Well looked after."

"Naturally."

Petrus looked at the two swords. The Lundegaardan sword was perfectly serviceable, but the one he held...

"I'll take this one."

"Thought you might." The prince grinned. "Why not kill the bastards with their own swords, eh?"

Petrus bared his teeth in an answering grin. "Why not?"

The prince took the Lundegaardan sword back to the pile of supplies. Petrus watched, his grin fading. For a moment there, he'd actually liked the prince. He slid the new sword into its scabbard, disconcerted. When he wasn't being a surly mage-hating whoreson, Prince Harkeld was surprisingly pleasant.

But only to Justen, who he thought wasn't a mage. *He treats the rest of us like vermin.*

He scowled briefly and looked around. A dark figure knelt at the assassins' grave. Frane, using his magic to make the grass grow. Hew was no longer at the fire. He was at Susa's grave.

Petrus walked across to him. Meadow grasses now thickly covered the mound of stony soil. Hew knelt with his hand on the grave. Did he think he was to blame for Susa's death? Was he apologizing to her? Begging her forgiveness?

"It wasn't your fault," Petrus said.

Hew glanced at him. His lips pinched together in denial.

Petrus crouched alongside him, lowering his voice. "The first time Gerit and I fought Fithians, they were too smart for us, too fast." He grimaced at the memory. Compared with the assassins, they'd been blundering fools. "By rights, they should have killed us. They very nearly did. It's only by the All-Mother's grace we survived."

Hew's expression eased slightly, became less bitter.

"Next time you'll be faster."

Hew's lips pressed together again. He nodded.

Petrus stood and walked back to the fire. He sat down beside the prince, unsheathed his new sword, and began to hone the razor-sharp edge with a whetstone.

HARKELD DREAMED THAT he sat in darkness. A breeze whispered over his face. Stars glittered in the sky. He wasn't sure where he was sitting, or why, but he knew who sat alongside him without having to look. The witch, Innis.

They were close enough that her shoulder touched his upper arm, and through that point of contact he *felt* her. Not just the warmth of her body, but an awareness of her emotions. Tonight, grief was dominant.

In his dreams, he and the witch were friends. He'd given up trying to fight it. It simply *was*. Harkeld put his arm around her and pulled her closer. Innis leaned her head against his shoulder.

They sat without speaking. Hours drifted past, while the stars wheeled slowly overhead. There was something deeply comforting about being with Innis. He wasn't certain exactly what it was—empathy, friendship.

"You would have liked Susa," Innis said quietly, as the sky grayed towards dawn. "She would have made you laugh. She made everyone laugh."

"I'm sorry she's dead."

How many people had died trying to protect him now?

He didn't have to count. He knew the tally. Eighteen of Lundegaard's soldiers. And two witches.

Twenty dead, for me.

It was too many. *I am worth only my own life.* And yet, because of his blood— Rutersvard blood, tainted with witch blood—he was also worth tens of thousands of lives.

CHAPTER FIVE

SAULT SLOPED DOWN to the Gulf of Hallas, the great ocean that stretched a thousand leagues to Lundegaard. It was cropping country. Barley nodded in the sea breezes. The roads were crowded, the hamlets eerily silent; the people of Sault had joined the flight from the curse. Nolt led his men between the teeming roads and the coast. Now and then a harvester, sweeping with a scythe, shouted angrily as the horses trampled his crop, but it didn't matter. The barley still needed weeks to ripen. The farmers, the last to flee, were trying to fill carts with heads from which they might pick usable grains. Their shouts were the shouts of desperation.

Jaumé understood now the value of his pony. It could keep up its steady trot all day. The men's horses drooped by nightfall, but the pony—he didn't name it—drank at whatever stream Nolt chose to camp by, then fell to cropping grass. Another day done.

Sometimes Jaumé drooped like the horses, but a meal revived him, and then his excitement in learning took over—a hidden excitement. Although Bennick taught him cheerfully, and sometimes with laughter, nothing was a game. First Jaumé had to be useful. He gathered stones for the firepit and branches for Bennick to chop. He fetched water to be boiled for the pungent brew of dried leaves the men drank each night. It was bitter to Jaumé; he kept to plain water—water that would soon carry the curse. Only when the meal was over and his jobs were done could he practice with his knife.

It took him several nights to learn how to keep its edge sharp with a whetstone. Da had used a whetstone on the scythes he made and Jaumé knew the technique of drawing the coarse side down the blade and coming back lightly with the fine side. But this blade had to be sharper than a scythe, and each side equal to the other, and its point needle-like. Jaumé learned quickly. Bennick, taking the knife and testing it on his thumb—and not cutting himself—was satisfied.

"Can I throw it now?" Jaumé asked.

"An easy throw. You've earned that." Bennick chose a tree with its near side illumined by the fire. He showed Jaumé how to stand, how to hold the knife. "By the handle when you're this close to the target. When you're further back you hold the blade and the knife flips over, but you'll have to wait for that. I don't want you cutting your fingers off." He took the knife and flicked it at the tree. It happened so fast Jaumé scarcely saw it. The blade was buried so deep he struggled to pull it out.

Bennick taught him patiently after that, how to hold the heavy little knife, how to know the distance to his target without thinking and make the throw with no pause or calculation getting in the way. Jaumé was aware of Nolt watching, and knew he had to satisfy Nolt as well as Bennick. Again, as with the sharpening, he learned quickly. By the second night, the knife hit and stayed every time he threw.

"Can I make it flip now?"

"No. You're doing well, lad, but there are steps. I'll teach you when you're ready."

"So I can be a soldier like you?"

Bennick laughed. "A soldier, eh? I guess you could call me that."

"Can you show me how you throw your big knife?"

"This one?" Bennick patted the knife sheathed on his belt. Suddenly he turned and Jaumé heard a whirr like a quail leaping from the grass and a thud in the dark where a white shape stood.

"Bennick," Nolt said from his seat at the fire. It was a rebuke.

Bennick made a little bow of apology. "Nolt." He strode into the dark. Jaumé trotted anxiously at his side. The shape was a young tree with a white trunk no thicker than Bennick's arm. The knife had struck it at the height of Bennick's chest and sliced through. Half the blade showed on the other side.

"I didn't even know this tree was here."

"You've got to see everything, night as well as day." Bennick pulled out the knife with a single jerk. He wiped it as though wiping off blood. "All right, lad. To sleep with you. There's more riding tomorrow."

"Where are we going?"

"Where the road takes us."

Bennick's tone said it was a question he shouldn't have asked. But Jaumé already knew part of the answer. Bennick had told him in Cornas. They were going to Ankeny. To meet a prince. The rest, Jaumé could guess. Nolt and his men weren't running away like the farmers with their carts. They were heading north to fight.

Jaumé shivered in his blanket, in the cooling night. There was only one thing to fight and that was the curse. But how could you fight what you couldn't see?

CHAPTER SIX

KAREL STOOD AT parade rest scanning Princess Brigitta's
private garden—the tall hedges, the rose bushes, the paths of
crushed pink and white marble, the bower where the princess
sat with her maid, Yasma.

His gaze rested on the princess for a moment. She was
returning to herself slowly, returning to the person she'd
been before her brief, terrible marriage to Duke Rikard.

No, he corrected himself. *She can never fully go back to
who she was.*

The weeks when she'd lived in a daze of poppy syrup, when
the duke had raped her daily—those weeks could never be
erased. Princess Brigitta could move forward, though, and
Yasma was seeing that she did. The princess was eating
properly again. She was sleeping without the aid of the
poppy syrup. Her skin had regained its color, her golden hair
its luster, her eyes their alertness, but beneath those things
was damage, as it was with Yasma. The terror he glimpsed
in the maid's eyes when armsmen noticed her, the way she
shrank into herself—Princess Brigitta shared some of those
scars now.

He examined the garden again, and let his gaze return to
the two girls: Yasma dark and slender, with a bondservant's
iron band pinched about her upper arm, and the princess
pale and golden, a delicate crown woven into her hair.

If I could, I would free you both.

But he wasn't free himself. He was bound to this gold-roofed palace until the term of his service ended, the lives of his family his bond. Seventeen more years. An eternity.

He scanned the garden again, his gaze skimming over hedges and paths and the green oval of grass.

Here, three short weeks ago, Princess Brigitta had committed her act of treason, slipping Osgaard's plans for invasion to the Lundegaardan ambassador's wife. The risk she'd taken had been appalling, but the consequences were beyond anything he'd dared to imagine. Freedom for Lundegaard, and Duke Rikard's fall from grace. And his death.

Karel allowed himself to savor the memory of Rikard's death. The man's final words echoed in his ears. *Out of my way, you whoreson islander. She's mine.* He couldn't remember drawing his sword, but he could remember the jolt of the blade sinking into Rikard's neck, the smell of the man's blood.

A sharp, exultant satisfaction filled him. *This whoreson islander killed you,* he told the dead duke. *The princess belongs to herself again, not you.*

But that was untrue. Princess Brigitta belonged to her father, and he would bestow her on someone else now that she was widowed. Another man like Duke Rikard, most likely, who'd never see her for who she was. Her heart, her mind—those were what made Princess Brigitta special, not her face.

Footsteps crunched fast on the marble path. Karel swung around, gripping his sword hilt.

Prince Jaegar. The princess's half-brother and heir to the throne, his crown bound to his head by his long, ash-blond hair.

The prince's expression was usually cold, but today a fierce, gleeful grin lit his face. "Britta!" He strode onto the grass, half a dozen armsmen at his heels. "Father's dead."

For a moment everything seemed to stand still, and then sound and motion rushed back into the world. Birds sang, a rose petal drifted in the breeze, Princess Brigitta and Yasma scrambled to their feet.

"What happened?" the princess asked. Emotions crossed her face: astonishment, relief.

Yasma backed away as far as she could. She stood with her head bowed, trying to make herself invisible.

"Another of his rages. His face went purple and he dropped dead."

"Oh," the princess said. "How... how..." She was clearly groping for a word that wasn't a lie. "How shocking."

"Indeed." Prince Jaegar's teeth gleamed white. They looked as sharp as a wolf's, and then Karel blinked and the illusion was gone. "I thought you should be the first to know."

"Thank you."

Prince Jaegar didn't hug his half-sister, didn't take her hands, didn't offer any comfort. He turned on his heel, the grin still on his face. "You'll tell the boys? I have a lot to do."

"Of course."

Karel watched him leave. The prince wasn't as massive with fat as King Esger, his bulk was more muscular. Prince Jaegar controlled his appetites and his emotions in a way his father had never managed.

No, not Prince Jaegar. Heir-Ascendant Jaegar. Osgaard's rule was passing to a new king. One crueler than Esger and far more dangerous.

"Britta?" Yasma said, once the Heir-Ascendant was out of earshot. "Are you all right?"

Princess Brigitta nodded. She looked slightly dazed. And worried. *She's wondering how life will change for us now.*

"I'm fine," she said, and then more briskly, "We must hurry to the nursery. I must tell my brothers!"

AT MIDNIGHT, KAREL went off duty, leaving the princess's safety in her second armsman's care. The palace was more alive than it usually was at this hour. Courtiers bustled and bondservants scurried. There was a frisson of nervous energy in the marble corridors. He tasted it on his tongue, slightly metallic, as if the air itself knew that the world was dangerously different.

Karel joined the line of men queuing for food in the armsmen's mess hall.

He went over the afternoon as he waited. The cool late-autumn sunshine, the roses losing their petals, Prince Jaegar grinning. And then the nursery, smelling of cinnamon and hot milk, and the young princes bewildered by their half-sister's news.

Four-year-old Lukas had been inclined to tears. Not grief, but fear, if Karel read him aright. "You won't leave us?" he'd asked Princess Brigitta, almost frantically. "Promise?"

The boys were orphans now, and it wasn't just mother and father they lacked, but Prince Harkeld too. Small wonder Lukas was terrified of losing his half-sister.

"I promise," the princess had said, hugging him.

It had been a rash promise to make. Princess Brigitta was a pawn, with no more control over her future than Yasma had. And from the expression on her face, she had known it.

Karel reached the front of the line. A bondservant piled mashed turnips on a plate, and thick blood sausages bursting from their skins. The man was from the Esfaban Islands, his hair as black as Karel's, his skin as brown. There was a fresh bruise on his face, fresh welts on his arms; he'd taken a beating today. Their eyes met for a moment. Karel gave the man a brief nod, acknowledging the servitude he endured. If not for his own parents' bondservice, he'd be wearing an iron armband, not the golden breastplate of an armsman.

He took his plate and a tankard of ale to a table, picking one where men who guarded the king's audience chamber sat. If there were rumors about King Esger's death, he wanted to hear them.

More men arrived; the seats filled up. Karel cut his food slowly, chewed slowly, listening to the conversations around him.

"Shrieking one minute, then keeled over the next."

"His face was right awful to see."

"...dark purple. Like one of them plums."

"You reckon it was natural?" someone asked in a whisper.

Karel didn't raise his eyes from his plate.

"I dunno," someone else answered. "But did you see Jaegar's face when it happened? He just about pissed himself, he was so happy."

"Pissed himself? He looked like he was having the best rut of his life. I'll wager he was coming in his underbreeches."

An armsman gave a snort of laughter, choked on his food, and began to cough.

"Bet he's found himself a bondservant to tup tonight," someone said.

"More'n one, I'll wager," another armsman said. "He'll be rutting all night."

"Island girls," someone said slyly, to Karel's right. "He likes how they squeal."

That comment was aimed at him. Karel ignored it, chewing stolidly, his eyes on his plate.

"So do I," the man opposite him said. "I had a good one last night. Looked like this whoreson right here. His sister, I reckon."

Karel raised his eyes and gazed at the man, unresponsive, as if he hadn't understood the words. The armsman was baiting him, seeing if he'd rise. *You think I'd risk my family's freedom for one such as you?*

The armsman snorted in disgust. "Little better than an animal, you are. Nothing up here." He tapped his forehead.

Karel marked the man's face in his memory and looked back down at his plate, cut another piece of blood sausage. *I'll have you on the training ground.* During wrestling, he decided as he chewed. An accidental knee in the groin. The man wouldn't be able to rape bondservants for a week. Forever, if he kneed him hard enough.

And then he regretfully laid the fantasy aside. His position was too precarious, his family's freedom too precious. He dared not step outside the rules. He'd trounce the armsman, but there'd be no knee to the groin. It would be a clean win. Nothing anyone could cavil at.

"He'd've done it, if he could," someone said around a mouthful of food. "But I don't see how."

"Don't you?" The voice was low. "Don't you remember his visitor last week?"

Karel glanced to his left. The speakers were some of Jaegar's personal armsmen.

"Which visitor? He had several."

Karel looked back at his plate, listening intently.

"The peg leg."

"Him?" someone said scornfully. "What's he to do with anything?"

"Jaegar was real careful we couldn't hear anything, wasn't he?"

"So?"

"So what did they do?" the armsman said, his voice growing exasperated.

"I dunno. Talked."

"You're as thick as that idiot islander," the armsman said. "He gave Jaegar something in a flask and was paid for it. Don't you remember?"

"So?"

"I reckon peg leg's a Fithian poison master."

"What?" someone said loudly. "A Fith—"

"Keep your voice down," the armsman hissed.

Karel concentrated on keeping his expression bored, trying to look like a cow chewing its cud. *Listening? Me?*

"No way he was Fithian," someone disagreed, his voice prudently low. "Only got one leg."

"And even if he was, you need to keep your mouth shut. Jaegar'll have your head on a stake for a rumor like that. With your tongue cut out."

Karel silently agreed. He finished his meal while the mess hall emptied around him. Jaegar's armsmen departed, some to sleep, others to find bondservants to rut.

Karel sipped his ale, turning the conversation over in his head. A Fithian poison master with a peg leg? It sounded ludicrously far-fetched.

But from what he knew of Jaegar, he could believe the man had poisoned his father. *That* wasn't far-fetched at all. Three of Esger's four wives had been murdered. Why not Esger himself?

CHAPTER SEVEN

HARKELD SPENT THREE evenings practicing how to put out fire. On the fourth evening, when Cora held a flaming branch towards him, his hesitation lasted less than a second. He called up his magic and reached out to grasp the branch. There was a sensation of warmth, but no pain. *Snuff,* he told it. The flames instantly extinguished.

Harkeld put the branch back on the pile that was to be their campfire.

"Did you burn yourself?"

He shook his head.

Cora snapped her fingers. His right cuff caught fire.

Harkeld didn't jerk back in panic, as he had the first time she'd done that, two nights ago. He laid his left hand on the burning fabric. *Snuff.*

"Excellent." Cora flicked her plait over her shoulder and turned to the piled wood. "Fire-lighting. When you snap your fingers, tell your magic you want a handful of flames." She demonstrated, snapping her fingers, opening her hand to show him the flames burning on her palm.

Harkeld reached for his magic. It came easily, a warm tingle in his blood. He visualized a tinderbox—flint striking steel—and snapped his fingers.

His palm became even warmer, a tickling sensation. He opened his hand. Flames burned there.

Harkeld took hold of a branch, gripping it tightly. Within seconds it caught alight.

"Good. Light a few more."

Harkeld lit six branches, then clenched his fist. *Snuff*. The tingling warmth faded.

Cora smiled. "Well done."

Harkeld didn't return the smile. "Are we finished for tonight? I'll help Justen with the tents."

"Of course." Cora reached for an iron pot and hooked it on the tripod over the fire.

Harkeld walked to where Justen was pitching tents.

The armsman glanced up. "Going well?"

Harkeld grunted. He unrolled one of the goat-hair tents. Each time he used his magic it came more easily. Each time, he became more of a witch.

They worked without speaking. The armsman had been subdued the last few days, even though he hadn't known the dead fire witch.

Around them, tall trees crowded close, streamers of bark hanging from their trunks. Warm rain began to patter down.

"Wrestling?" Harkeld asked when the tents were up and blankets and bedrolls laid inside.

Justen hesitated, clearly unenthusiastic, and then shrugged. "Ach, why not?"

They stripped to their trews. Harkeld rolled his shoulders, loosening them, and crouched.

Justen took a deep breath and seemed to shake off his gloominess. "Ready?"

Harkeld nodded.

They circled, grappled, and broke off. Harkeld felt stiff in his muscles and sluggish in his blood.

They grappled again, swaying, each striving for dominance. Harkeld shifted his weight, flexed one hip, heaved.

Justen landed on his back. He showed his teeth, climbed to his feet and crouched again.

Harkeld won the first two bouts, but lost the next. Two of the witches, finished with unloading the packhorses, stripped to their trews and began to wrestle too. Harkeld ignored them, concentrating solely on Justen. The armsman's Grooten amulet caught the firelight, gleaming like a small moon.

Their bouts became more vigorous. Harkeld began to pant. His skin was slick with sweat, slick with rain. His ill humor was gone. He felt fully awake for the first time in days.

Justen circled and came in low, his shoulder taking Harkeld in the abdomen. He let the armsman's weight propel him back and twisted, tossing Justen aside. The armsman rolled and sprang to his feet and bulled forward again, even lower, catching Harkeld off balance. An iron-hard arm gripped behind his knees and heaved.

Harkeld hit the ground hard, rolling, ending up on his back.

Justen laughed. "Got you."

Harkeld sat up, grinning. He wiped rain and sweat from his face.

"Flin, Justen, dinner," Cora called.

Justen reached down a hand. Harkeld gripped it and let the armsman pull him to his feet.

They dressed in their damp clothes. "I need to piss," the armsman said, jerking his thumb at the trees.

Harkeld nodded. He walked across to the fire. Rand and Cora had hung a spare tent between two trees. He hunkered under it and accepted a bowl of stew. The stew was made with dried meat, but it was Ankenian meat, flavored with Ankenian spices, piquant and peppery. A couple of minutes later Justen ducked under the shelter, followed by Innis. Harkeld glanced at the witch. He'd not seen her all day. She must have been flying in wide sweeps, far ahead, far behind. Or was she taking some shape he'd not yet noticed?

The armsman filled a bowl and sat alongside him. No, Justen was more than his armsman; he was his friend. Harkeld wasn't sure when their friendship had happened, but he was glad it had. *I'd go mad without Justen.*

IT WAS STILL raining in the morning. Before they'd gone a league, they came across a woodcutters' camp. The forest had been felled on either side of the road for a hundred yards. Despite the rain, men were hard at work. Harkeld heard the *thock-thock* of axes, heard voices shouting, heard the sharp splintering sound of a tree trunk snapping. A tree fell with ponderous grace. The dull thud of its impact reached his ears a couple of seconds later.

Lukas would love this, he thought, and his half-brother's face filled his mind's eye—the gap-toothed grin, the bright blond hair, the blue eyes.

Grief ambushed him, choking his throat, stinging his eyes.

Harkeld cleared his throat, scrubbed his eyes with his sleeve, but the grief sat with him while the stretch of cleared land on either side of the road became broader. They passed more camps, passed oxcarts piled with tree trunks laboring eastward.

The rain became heavier, filling the ruts and potholes with water. Dirt churned into mud, making the road treacherous. Their pace slowed until they were little faster than the oxen. Each mile became a struggle.

At dusk they halted and set up camp among the tree stumps. Branches littered the muddy ground. Harkeld gathered several armfuls and piled them for a campfire.

"This is a good exercise for you," Cora said. "You'll find it harder than yesterday."

Harkeld snapped his fingers. Flames tingled across his palm. He grabbed a sodden branch. The flames hissed out.

Harkeld tried again—and again the saturated wood quenched his magic. He hissed annoyance.

"Make them hotter," Cora said.

It took intense concentration before he found the knack. The flames on his palm became fiercer, white-hot. He took hold of the branch again. This time his flames didn't snuff out. The wood caught fire.

Harkeld released the branch. The flames began to die. *Oh no, you don't*. He scowled at the branch. *Burn hotter, curse it. Spread*. The flames became white-hot, spread outwards. The branch started to burn in earnest, crackling and spitting.

"Did you touch the branch just then?"

"Uh... no."

"Well done," Cora said. "Now see if you can do that without losing your temper."

Harkeld felt himself flush. Cora had a way of making him feel like a child.

Perhaps because I behave like one?

Water dripped from his eyebrows, from his nose, from his chin. He wiped it away and tried to do as she'd asked. It took several minutes before he figured out how he'd done it. If he lit a branch, just so, and if he then directed his concentration, just so, thrusting his magic at the flames without touching them...

Fire spread across a second sodden branch.

"Excellent." Cora set up the cooking tripod. "Light the rest of the fire, please."

Harkeld went round the fire methodically. At last every branch was burning strongly, despite the heavy rain. He sat back on his heels, unsettled. *I am much more a witch than I was quarter of an hour ago.*

CHAPTER EIGHT

SAULT BECAME HILLY. Ragged slopes climbed away from roads as narrow as cattle tracks. Gray boulders topped with grass reared like corpses freed from their graves. The valleys twisting inland held thin streams watering meager pastures. It was poor country, and these were poor people. They hadn't yet run from the curse, and they cried out for news of it as Nolt and his men rode by.

Nolt never paused. At day's end he chose camping places hidden from farm cottages and hamlets. There, in the twilight and into the night, Jaumé continued his education. He told himself he was training to be a soldier, and the lessons were: keep busy, be useful, work hard.

He sharpened knives. He sharpened Stars—a tricky job that ended several times with his blood smeared on the blades. He rubbed oil into the bows to keep them supple, then watched closely as the men restrung them. He wasn't strong enough for that job yet. He asked if he could take his turn as watchman at night, but Bennick said no, boys needed their sleep, and watching was a man's job.

Nothing dangerous, or even interesting, came out of the dark. Now and then a horse snorted and stamped its foot. The night bird native to this part of Sault made its curious call: *What-now? What-now?* The watchmen moved in and out of the glow of the fire. There was never a footfall or a breaking twig. Except for the curse, creeping towards them, Jaumé felt safe. Waking, he looked to see who the guard was and felt, from nowhere,

Bennick's hand tap him lightly on the brow, a touch that meant, *Go back to sleep*.

In the gray dawn they rode again. Jaumé's pony, trotting hard, kept up with the horses.

Riding behind Ashandel, Jaumé noticed the man's horse begin to favor its left hind leg. He looked at Bennick, riding beside him, and pointed, but Bennick only said, "He knows."

They paused at midday, broke bread, drank from their waterskins. Ash led his horse apart and tied its reins to a tree.

Jaumé plucked Bennick's sleeve. "My Da was a blacksmith."

Bennick glanced at Nolt, received a nod. "Go help him then, lad."

Jaumé trotted over to Ash. Ash's hair was as silver as an old man's—the prickly whiskers on his cheeks, his eyebrows, even his eyelashes—but he wasn't much older than Bennick. His eyes were silver too, bright and shining. "Keep him easy, boy. Talk to him." So Jaumé stroked the horse's nose and whispered praise and comfort, while Ash raised its hoof and freed the pebble lodged in its shoe. The horseshoe was loose, and worn down on one side. Ash fetched tools from one of the packsaddles and levered it off. He handed Jaumé some nails and a new shoe and used his knife to pare the ragged edge of the horse's hoof. Then he took the shoe, fitted it, and hammered in the nails that Jaumé gave him one by one.

"So you know horses, boy?"

"I've helped Da shoe horses. We used a rasp, not a knife."

"Ha! What do I do next?"

"File the edges clean."

"So fetch me a file. Then hold his head."

When the horse was ready the band rode on. Jaumé, on his pony, simmered with pleasure. Now it wasn't only Bennick he was friends with. He wanted to be friends with them all, although it might never be possible with Nolt.

Nolt was fixed on his purpose. He gave orders, sometimes with a word, sometimes a gesture, and the Brothers obeyed. There was no warmth in him, but that was because he was leader and must always be alert. He was like a night watchman who watched in the day. Jaumé was uneasy whenever he came close—his leathery face, his close-clipped beard, his stone-hard eyes that saw everything—but his trust in Nolt was almost as great as his trust in Bennick.

Nolt would keep them safe. He wouldn't make mistakes.

CHAPTER NINE

KING ESGER'S BODY lay in state for only three days, massive and decaying. Princess Brigitta took the two little princes to say goodbye to their father on the first day. Karel examined the body with interest from his place behind the princess. The dead king's face wasn't purple; it was black.

The stink of putrefaction became so great that the armsmen guarding the body were rotated every hour lest they faint. The burial was moved forward. Five days after King Esger dropped dead, he was interred in the marble-and-gold Rutersvard vault. Princess Brigitta attended the ceremony with her young half-brothers.

The Heir-Ascendant wore robes that matched the long pitch-black pennants twisting and snapping above the palace's golden roof and at each guard tower. Tomorrow, those pennants would be replaced with new ones, black with threads of gold woven through, and every day for the next nine days new pennants would be raised, each woven with more gold than the last, until on the tenth day the pennants would be pure gold.

Jaegar's robes would change, too, marking his ascension from heir to king. Ten more days, and he would wear gold cloth and take the throne. *And Osgaard moves into a new era.*

Karel accompanied the princess back to the nursery, uneasy, and stood against the wall, his feet the regulation twelve inches apart. Princess Brigitta spent the rest of the afternoon with the boys, letting them know they weren't alone, that they were loved. Prince Lukas sat in her lap for most of that time, hugging the blunt little woodcutter's axe Prince Harkeld had given him.

"Will Harkeld come back now that Father's dead?" Prince Rutgar asked, as the tenth bell rang and daylight faded.

"No, sweetheart." Princess Brigitta reached out to stroke his hair. "He's never coming back."

Rutgar's lip quivered. "I miss him."

"So do I."

Karel saw the princess blink back tears, saw her smile at her little half-brothers. "Bath time," she said cheerfully.

But Princess Brigitta's expression, when he accompanied her back to her suite, wasn't cheerful. She looked preoccupied, worried. She disappeared into her bedchamber, with Yasma.

Karel stationed himself by the door.

Take me with you, the princess had begged Prince Harkeld when he'd fled the palace. Memory of that moment was vivid in Karel's mind. He could see Prince Harkeld, could see the witches flanking him—a man with gray hair, a middle-aged woman with a long plait—see the crushed marble path and the hedges and the tall wall and the guard tower.

Prince Harkeld had refused, but what would he have done if the prince had said yes? Stood back and let the princess go, and condemn his whole family to bondservice?

No. He'd have had to try to stop her, would have had to fight the witches. *And they would have killed me.* And by his own death, he would have won his family's full freedom. And Princess Brigitta's.

But not Yasma's.

Yasma would have gone back to the bondservants' dormitories. And spent the next thirteen years slaving in the palace and being raped.

Karel pushed away from the wall and paced the wide parlor, past the door to the bondservants' corridor, past the brocade and gilt settle, past the marquetry table. Twenty strides to the end, twenty strides back.

A map of Osgaard hung on one wall, tinted in delicate colors. He halted and stared at it, his eyes finding Esfaban.

The artist had shaded the islands green, with golden shores, and blue waters. Memories came to him: palm fronds waving in the warm breeze, the lap of waves, the night-song of insects. And with the memories came a rush of emotion, tightening his throat, stinging his eyes.

Karel blinked and forced his gaze away from the string of islands. He found the other kingdoms Osgaard had conquered—Horst and Lomaly, Karnveld, Meren, Brindesan. Lastly, he found the palace, marked with a speck of gold leaf. It should be marked with blood, to symbolize the misery generations of bondservants had endured within its walls. But perhaps the gold leaf was apt? Osgaard had conquered its neighbors out of greed, after all.

And would keep conquering.

If the Fithians caught Prince Harkeld, if his hands and blood were returned to Osgaard, Jaegar would possess the power to end Ivek's curse... or allow it to ravage unchecked through the Seven Kingdoms. Lundegaard, Ankeny, Roubos, Urel, Sault, would be given a simple choice: be overrun by the curse, like Vaere, or cede sovereignty to Osgaard.

Would Jaegar even care how many kingdoms fell to Ivek's curse? Empty kingdoms were easy to conquer.

Karel resumed pacing the room. Twenty strides to the end, twenty strides back. Prince Harkeld wouldn't be captured. The witches would protect him. Witches could throw bolts of fire. They could turn into lions. They were a match for assassins.

That depends on how many of them there are, doesn't it? a tiny voice whispered in his head. How many assassins were scrambling for a share of the bounty on Prince Harkeld's head? And how many witches were protecting him?

Karel halted by the shuttered window, stared blankly at it. Events were in motion that he was powerless to influence, a terrible future unfolding.

Don't think about it. The things he could do were simple: complete an exemplary twenty years' service as an armsman, secure his family's full freedom, and guard the princess with his life. Those three things were in his power. Everything else he had to ignore.

CHAPTER TEN

THE WOODCUTTERS HAD been busy. The forest was felled for half a mile on either side of the road, a wasteland of mud and stumps. The rain eased, but never stopped. Every item they possessed was sodden: tents, saddles, weapons. Harkeld's clothes smelled of mildew, his blanket smelled, his bedroll smelled.

They made slow progress. The days narrowed to rain and tree stumps and mud, woodcutters' camps and ox teams hauling logs, silent meals around the campfire. And dreams. The dreams were the only time the sun shone. The only time he was happy.

He became more adept at lighting the campfire. He could ignite wet branches by holding his hand an inch above them now. "Excellent," Cora said on the fifth evening of rain, when it had taken him less than a minute to turn a pile of saturated wood into a roaring blaze. "You didn't touch any branches, did you?"

He shook his head.

"I think you're ready to start throwing fire."

Harkeld remembered a boulder-choked gorge and a man screaming as he burned alive. He grimaced.

"What?" asked Cora.

"I won't burn people." He'd kill with his sword, pitting his skill against an assailant's, he'd kill with his bare hands if he had to, but he would never burn anyone alive again.

"No. None of us would ask that of you. It's forbidden to use magic to kill—unless you're a Sentinel and the circumstances are extreme. But you can burn arrows before they reach you. Burn a man's clothes."

Harkeld nodded, remembering the chaos in his father's throne room, the armsmen throwing down their swords, ripping off their breastplates, tearing off their burning tunics.

"But in order to do those things, you need to be able to throw your magic with focus and control, otherwise you *will* kill people." Cora looked across the campsite. Figures moved in the gathering dusk: Justen and Gerit pitching tents, the others tending the horses. She raised her voice, "Rand, can you take over the cooking, please?"

Rand raised a hand in response.

"Let's go over here."

Harkeld followed Cora, squelching through the mud.

"See if you can set this stump alight."

Harkeld obeyed, holding his hand a couple of inches from the dark, rain-soaked wood. *Burn.* The tree stump flared alight with a wet hiss.

"Put it out."

He closed his hand. *Snuff.*

"Now hold your hand a little further away, say half a foot."

From half a foot to a foot, then two feet, then a yard. Harkeld backed away, setting the stump alight, quenching it, setting it alight again.

Night fell. Cora lit a nearby stump to give him light to see. Two yards, then three. It took concentration to push the right amount of magic at the now-charred stump—too little and it failed to light, too much and it ignited with a *whoomp* that lit up the sky. The first time that happened, his heart gave a panicked kick in his chest. Harkeld hastily closed his hand. *Snuff!* The flames vanished.

"Try again," Cora said, as if nothing had happened.

Harkeld glanced up at the black sky. Petrus and Innis must be up there. "I could burn one of the shapeshifters."

"I hope they have more sense than to fly over a fire lesson," Cora said.

Harkeld tried again. *Burn.* This time the stump caught fire with a demure crackle.

"Good," Cora said. "Another half-step back."

And another half-step, and another. Throwing fire wasn't as alarming as he'd thought. Under Cora's tuition, it was methodical and almost boring. Nothing like the catacombs. There was no searing pressure building in his ribcage, no feeling that flesh and blood and bones were on the point of bursting alight.

"Do you feel in control of your magic?"

Harkeld lowered his hand. "Yes."

"Even at this distance?"

He measured the distance to the stump with his eyes. A good seven yards. "Yes."

"Good. That'll do for now."

THAT NIGHT HIS dreams took him to the desert. He stood outside the catacombs. His palm stung. Blood dripped to the sand. Around him were bodies. A soldier with a throwing star buried in his forehead. A charred assassin. A dead horse. People crouched at the gaping mouth of the catacombs, tending a wounded soldier. Cora, Prince Tomas, Innis. Emotions flooded through him. Rage, despair. He turned his back to the scene.

Innis stood in front of him, her face solemn. "This isn't a good memory."

Harkeld glanced over his shoulder. Innis was still healing the injured soldier. He turned to the other Innis standing in front of him. "No."

"Let's go somewhere else." She held out her hand.

He took it and let her lead him away. His boots squelched. He looked down and saw mud, looked up and saw tree stumps stretching in all directions.

"I don't like this either," she said, tugging his hand.

They walked further. There was soft grass beneath his boots, sunlight on his face, the scent of roses. They were in the palace gardens.

Innis turned his hand over and looked at his palm. Blood still trickled there. "You should have let me heal this."

"I was too angry."

Innis smoothed her thumb across his palm, wiping away the blood. The edges of the cut grew together and sealed. "There."

The rage and despair that had gripped him at the catacombs were gone. Vanished, as the cut on his hand had vanished. Innis's presence was having its usual effect. He felt calm, happy.

They sat in a rose bower. Harkeld put his arm around Innis's shoulders and pulled her close. Her hand rested on his thigh, a light, casual touch. He let himself relax into the quiet contentment of the moment.

The light pressure of Innis's hand on his thigh wasn't sexual... but gradually it became so. He felt the heat of her palm. It almost burned through his trews. His imagination told him what it would feel like if she stroked his leg. Her fingers would tickle their way from knee to groin...

His cock stiffened. He wanted, quite suddenly, to rut her on this lush, green lawn. No, rut was the wrong word. He didn't want something rushed. He wanted to linger over the pleasure of it. He wanted to make love to her.

Harkeld stared across the lawn, his eyes narrowed, considering this. Sex with a witch?

In Lundegaard, when his dreams had headed in this direction, he'd broken free in revulsion. Tonight, instead of revulsion was... curiosity.

Harkeld gave a mental shrug. Why not? He hadn't had sex in weeks. Not since Lenora. And it was only a dream, after all.

He glanced at Innis. She was slender rather than voluptuous, shy rather than boldly confident, but... why not?

Harkeld placed his free hand over hers, on his thigh.

Innis tensed slightly and looked at him, her gray eyes wide.

He drew her hand up his thigh and cupped it over his groin, letting her feel his heat, his arousal. "Shall we?"

Innis blushed vividly. Her gaze fell, looking at his chest, not his face. She nodded.

Harkeld led her onto the lawn and stripped off their clothes. The grass was velvety beneath his bare feet. He drew her to him, skin to skin, stroked his hands down her back, bent his head and kissed her.

The dream segued sharply. They'd been standing; now they lay on soft grass. Innis kissed him back. Her kiss was shy, hesitant, virginal.

It doesn't have to be that *realistic,* Harkeld told his imagination.

His imagination took no notice.

But his annoyance was momentary. There was pleasure to be had in coaxing a virgin into readiness to be bedded, in being the first man to caress her breasts and tease them with nipping kisses that made her gasp, the first to trail his fingers up the silkiness of her inner thighs, the first to slide his fingers inside her.

She was tighter than any woman he'd ever bedded, but she was also hot, slick, ready.

Harkeld settled himself between her legs. Arousal thrummed in his blood.

"Harkeld—" She clutched his arm. He felt her fear.

"Don't worry." He bent his head and kissed her. "This is only a dream. It won't hurt."

He slid deeply inside her, uttering an involuntary groan of pleasure. By the All-Mother, it felt *good* to be inside a woman. For several seconds he held himself still, eyes tightly closed, savoring the moment, then he began to move, setting a rhythm for them.

He lost his awareness of Innis. The dream narrowed until it was nothing but rhythm and heat and pleasure. His climax went on endlessly, so intense it was close to pain.

INNIS LAY AWAKE in the dark tent, listening as the prince's breathing slowed and became steady again. *Don't worry,* his voice whispered in her head. *This is only a dream. It won't hurt*. But it had hurt, hurt so much it had jolted her awake. She turned her head and looked at the prince, but it was too dark to see him.

Did he realize what they shared when they dreamed together? Thoughts. Memories. Emotions.

No. Of course he didn't.

She reached out and found him in the darkness, laid her hand lightly on his shoulder, felt his warmth through the damp blanket.

A strong bond. That's what Dareus said the dreams meant.

Friendship. Empathy.

Love?

CHAPTER ELEVEN

THE HILLS CLIMBED to a plateau between Sault and Roubos. Sweeping winds chilled Jaumé to the bone; he rode with his blanket knotted round his shoulders. Bennick found him a cap to pull over his ears and boots for his bare feet. At a hamlet of four dwellings—huts built of dried mud and wood—an old woman scuttled inside as they approached.

Bennick halted. He felt in his pouch and held up a copper coin.

The woman's door opened a crack. "There's no food here."

"It's not food I'm buying. A jacket for this boy."

"What good's a penny? What good's ten? It's twenty miles to market and I've no horse to get there. I buried my husband two moons ago. Give me a loaf and you can have his jacket."

Bennick put the coin away. "Get one, Jaumé."

Jaumé dismounted and went to the packhorses. "Shall I give her two?"

"One," Bennick said.

Jaumé found the largest loaf. He carried it to the hut, where the woman opened the door half way and held out a garment.

"Spread it out," Bennick said.

The woman drew the door wider and showed a sheepskin jacket. "My man shrank. It'll fit the boy."

"Jaumé?" Bennick said.

"It looks all right." The jacket had worn patches, but looked clean enough, and the stitching was sound. It was like the jacket Mam had made for Da.

Jaumé took it and gave the woman the loaf of rye bread. She grabbed it, held it like a baby in two hands. He wished it was fatter. He wished there were two. He was sorry for her, with her sunken cheeks and gap-toothed mouth and greedy eyes.

"Thank you," he said.

She didn't reply. The door slammed shut.

"Put it on," Bennick said.

Jaumé obeyed. At once he was warmer, with the hide holding off the wind and the wool inside next to his shirt.

He folded the blanket he'd worn and used it again as a saddle.

JAUMÉ SLEPT WELL that night, with the jacket spread on his blanket as wide as it would go. He half-woke and saw the moon low on the horizon and the watchman, Odil, moving like a shadow beyond the embers. Odil leaned and whispered to Nolt, risen on his elbow, and then melted away into the dark, and Jaumé slept again.

They breakfasted on rye bread. Jaumé saddled his pony with the folded blanket. Wrapped in the jacket, he smelled the old man, but that didn't bother him as long as he was warm. Today's ride would be more comfortable. Then, beyond the horses, by a scrubby tree, he saw a pile of old clothes. He looked harder. Not clothes—a body. A gray, gap-toothed mouth seemed to grin. Blood, drying black at the edges, spread from under a slackened jaw.

"Bennick."

Bennick paused in saddling his horse. He looked where Jaumé pointed.

"It's her. What happened?"

Bennick turned back to his horse. "She came in the night. She was after your pony."

"But—"

"Odil heard her. That's all."

"He killed her?"

"Thieves get killed. Don't snivel, Jaumé. There's nothing wrong with dying. We come, we go. She's with the All-Mother."

"But..." Jaumé whispered. He saw the others mounting, and Odil, stocky Odil, with his hair as brown and curly as Da's, leading the packhorses out to the road. Odil, who'd killed the old woman. "Shouldn't we bury her?"

"Let her lie. The wild dogs will find her, and the crows." Bennick mounted. "Stay with her if you like. Or come with us." He trotted his horse after the others.

Jaumé mounted the pony and followed. He took his place beside Bennick. *She wanted the pony so she could ride to the market. So she wouldn't starve.* But after a while he began to wonder if the woman had known she'd be caught. It might have been her way of—what? Going to the All-Mother? At least she wasn't starving now.

The blood from her throat reminded him of Mam.

Mam lying in the kitchen, the floorboards red with her blood, the stink of blood in his nose, his feet slipping in blood as he ran.

His mind took him back to the beginning. Da, with his mad face. Rosa's scream. Mam. And running. Running for the safety of Girond, only to find it wasn't safe any more. Howling laughter like dogs. Flames rising into the sky as the village burned. And always, the smell of Mam's blood.

Tears stung the inside of Jaumé's nose, pricked his eyes. He forced them back.

Whatever happened, these men must not see him cry.

CHAPTER TWELVE

KAREL WALKED FROM the training arena, wiping sweat from his face. He'd won each of his bouts. The last man he'd beaten jostled him as they went into the barracks, digging an elbow in his ribs, shoving him against the doorframe, but he was used to that now. He'd grown adept at collecting bruises without letting any emotion show on his face.

He washed at the long row of stone sinks and then dressed in the scarlet tunic and golden breastplate, the wrist guards, the greaves.

"Marten, Edvin, to the king's audience chamber, now!"

There was a moment of near-silence as the two armsmen slung on their swords and hurried out, and then a rising buzz of conversation.

Karel buckled his sword belt slowly. He knew the two men. They were sworn to Prince Rutgar and Prince Lukas.

What's happening?

In the mess hall, someone jostled him again as he turned away from the servers. He lost a slice of coarse bread from his plate.

"Sorry," the person said.

Startled, Karel glanced at him. It was one of the armsmen from Lomaly. Only two generations from bondservice himself.

Karel let his expression relax. He gave a nod.

The armsman grabbed another slice of bread and put it on Karel's plate. "A bit on edge today, you know?" he said as he followed Karel to a table and sat.

"What's happening?" Karel asked.

"Haven't you heard?"

Karel shook his head.

The armsman pulled a face. "The Heir-Ascendant is shuffling the cards in his favor."

BRITTA SAT IN front of the mirror. Her hair tugged at her scalp as Yasma wound strands around the crown and anchored them with a jeweled pin.

She kept her head still, but glanced sideways, catching a glimpse of blue sky through the window. It was another sunny autumn day. The frost on the lawns would have melted by now.

Restlessness boiled inside her. Britta clasped her hands in her lap. Another ten minutes and she could walk in the gardens. A long walk today, to the farthest guard tower and back. The guard tower Harkeld had escaped from.

Her restlessness changed to anxiety. Where was Harkeld now? Was he even alive?

The fifth bell rang. Noon.

Britta tore her thoughts from Harkeld. "You wish to come walking today?" she asked Yasma.

"Yes, please—"

A knock sounded on the bedchamber door.

Britta met Yasma's eyes in the mirror.

"I'm sure it's nothing to worry about," she said, but her chest had tightened and the fear that underlay every action, every day, rose to the surface. The answer to Osgaard's most pressing problem, Jaegar had called her a few short weeks ago. Was today the day she discovered what her use was to be?

Yasma opened the door.

Karel stood there. He looked past Yasma to her. Something in his eyes made Britta pushed hastily to her feet. "What?"

"Have you not heard?"

Britta's heart kicked in her chest. *I'm to be bait to catch Harkeld.* She hurried to the door, heedless of the half-secured crown on her head. "Tell me!"

Karel's lips tightened fractionally, the most emotion she'd ever seen on his face. "Jaegar has imprisoned your half-brothers on grounds of treason."

What? Britta gaped at him, speechless, her fears falling away and new ones scrambling to take their place.

"Their executions are planned for after his coronation."

Disbelief flooded her, followed by panic. "What? What treason? What executions? They're children!"

"Half-Lundegaardan children. Jaegar believes they played a role in leaking the invasion plans."

"What?" Britta stared at him, aghast. *But that was my doing!* She didn't dare utter the words; the armsman didn't know her complicity in that act of treason. "But they're only six and four!"

"Even so, he plans to execute them."

"This is absurd! I must speak to Jaegar!"

Karel moved, blocking her way.

"Out of my way, armsman!" She tried to shove past him.

Karel caught her wrist. "No."

Britta was abruptly aware of the hard, corded muscles beneath his brown skin, the sharp sword at his side, the eyes so dark they were almost black. Fear spiked beneath her breastbone. An image flashed into her mind: Duke Rikard lying beheaded on the floor, Karel's sword dripping blood.

She lifted her chin, trying not to show her fear. "Release me."

"No," Karel said. "If you anger Jaegar, he won't hesitate to get rid of you too."

Britta tugged futilely at his grip. "Your orders are to obey me, armsman!"

"My orders are to protect you. And if you go to Jaegar now, if you ally yourself with Rutgar and Lukas, then you're dead."

The last word echoed flatly, shockingly.

"Jaegar's signaling to all Osgaard that he's decisive and ruthless, and that nothing and no one will stand in his way. Not even his half-brothers. *Especially* not his half-brothers."

"But the boys had nothing to do with—"

"No. But their blood is too dangerous. They're heirs to the throne." His grip eased on her wrist. "Princess, if you anger him now, you seal your own death and lose any chance to save the boys."

"Save them? You think they can be saved?"

"Not if you go to him in the state you're in now."

Britta stared at him, trying to read his dark, hawk-like face. He'd guarded her for three years, but what did she know of him? Who exactly was he? An Esfaban Islander, one step away from bondservice, wearing the scarlet tunic and golden breastplate of a palace armsman. And not just any armsman, one with the silver torque that marked him as a royal bodyguard. The first islander to reach that pinnacle. An elite fighter. Ambitious.

Whose interests did he have at heart? His own.

And yet Yasma claims him as a friend.

"What do you suggest?" she said.

Karel's expression relaxed fractionally. He released her wrist. "That we consider your next move very carefully."

YASMA FINISHED BINDING the crown to her head. Britta rubbed her wrist. She could still feel Karel's hard grip.

Her gaze rose to the maid's face. Yasma's skin was as brown as Karel's, her hair as black, her features as hawk-like. But unlike Karel, she wasn't threatening. She was slender, fragile, beautiful.

"Yasma... do you trust him?"

"Karel? Yes. As much as I trust you." Yasma slid the last pin into place. "He would never harm me. Or you. He's kind."

Kind? Karel looked as dangerous as Jaegar.

"He paid for the poppy syrup, Britta. And the dung-root juice."

"What?" Britta turned to face Yasma. "He *what*?"

"The dung-root juice was Karel's idea. He thought the duke might annul the marriage if you didn't conceive."

Britta stared at her, astonished. "And the poppy syrup?"

"That was my idea, but Karel paid for it. He wanted me to make you drink less—he said it was killing you, and he was right! But then everything happened and... I didn't have to."

Britta rubbed her forehead. *It's thanks to Karel I survived my marriage?*

"Listen to him, Britta. Please."

Britta nodded and stood, panic and anxiety swamping her again. Rutgar and Lukas imprisoned? *I must get them out!*

She hurried to the door and opened it. Karel wasn't standing against the wall at parade rest. He was by the marquetry table.

He pulled out a chair, a silent invitation for her to sit.

Britta stared across the parlor at him, seeing the powerful muscles, the gleaming breastplate, the sword.

He'd killed Duke Rikard without a second's hesitation... and then he'd knelt beside her and held her until she stopped shaking.

Britta made a decision. *I shall trust him until I have reason to do otherwise.*

THEY SAT AT the table, she and Yasma and Karel. The armsman had moved the table, so none of the guards outside could see them. Sunlight shone through the window, making the marquetry glow. "I must get them out! They'll be terrified! Lukas is only four—"

"You can't get them out," Karel said. "Not today."

"But—"

"Far better that they endure a few days of fear, and then freedom, than to act rashly now and bring disaster down on you all."

Urgency bubbled in her chest—*Hurry! Get them out!*—but Karel was right. Britta stared down at the marquetry, wrestling for self-control. Birds glided on wings of walnut and cherry wood. Flowers unfurled petals of golden oak. "What do you suggest?"

"The choices are limited. Even if you confess to giving the invasion plans to the ambassador's wife, it won't save the boys."

"What?" Britta's head jerked up. She looked at him, aghast, and then turned to Yasma. "You *told* him?"

Yasma shook her head. "No!"

"Yasma didn't tell me," Karel said. "I figured it out for myself."

Britta stared at him, her mouth open. It took her several seconds to find the breath to speak. "How?"

"I watch you. It's my duty."

Britta digested this statement. "When? When did you find out?"

"Before the garden party."

He'd known before she'd given the invasion plans to the Lundegaardan ambassador's wife—and he'd not betrayed her. Britta stared at him. *Was it for my sake you held your tongue? Or Yasma's? Or Lundegaard's?*

"If you plan to save the boys by confessing, don't forget that it's not only your life that will be forfeit. Yasma will be executed, too, and every member of her family forced into bondservice. Twenty years of slavery." Karel's voice hadn't been harsh before, but it was now. "Just how much are those boys' lives worth to you?"

"Not that much." Britta closed her eyes, a feeling of sick despair growing in her belly.

"Good," Karel said. "Because a confession wouldn't work for long. He'll have those boys dead. If not by execution, then a natural-looking death, like their mother's. Smothering. Poison. An accident. It won't matter. He wants them *dead*."

"Why?" Yasma asked.

"They're blood-heirs. Someone could put them on the throne in Jaegar's place. That's the second option out of this. Raising a faction against Jaegar. Deposing him, proclaiming Rutgar Heir-Ascendant. But I don't see that working. Do you, princess?"

Britta shook her head. "Harkeld could have done it, but not me. I've stayed out of that kind of palace politics." If there were nobles willing to make Rutgar their king, she didn't know who they were.

"Is there another option?" Yasma asked anxiously.

"Escape."

Britta jerked slightly in her seat. "Escape?"

"Prince Harkeld escaped," the armsman said.

"But he had witches to help him!"

"We have a week until the coronation. There must be a way to get the boys out."

Escape? *Impossible*. But hope flickered in her chest.

"And you should go with them, princess. And you too, Yasma."

"I can't!" Yasma said. "My family will be punished—"

"Not if we stage your death."

"But..." Yasma said, and trailed off.

"Your family owes twenty years' bondservice to Osgaard. If you die loyal to Osgaard, that debt is wiped. No one else in your family will be called. They can move on to the next step. Send a son to bear weapons for Osgaard."

Britta exchanged a glance with Yasma. The maid's expression was shocked, afraid, hopeful.

"For you both to get out of Osgaard would be a good thing, highness." The armsman's face and voice were impassive... but not his eyes. She suddenly understood what Yasma meant. Karel had kind eyes. "But for the sake of Yasma's family and my own, it *must* look as if you acted alone."

Britta nodded.

"You need to see Jaegar today—he'll expect you—but we must have a plan first."

"He wants me for something. He told Father I was the answer to their most pressing problem."

Karel's black eyebrows winged together, making his face even more hawk-like. "What problem?"

"Harkeld. I heard them say his name, and then Jaegar said he knew how fond Harkeld was of me, and... I think I'm going to be bait to catch him." It was the fear that had haunted her for three weeks, the fear that she'd not dared to confront.

"You never said anything," Yasma said, her voice low and distressed.

Karel's eyes were still on her, but she didn't think he saw her. He was thinking. "If that's so, why hasn't he acted?" he asked, and then answered his own question, "He's waiting for something. Or someone." His eyes focused on her. "If he wants you for that, it gives you some power. We may be able to use it to your advantage."

Britta nodded again. Hope and fear mingled inside her.

"Now, how do we get the princes out from under guard? How do we get you all out of the palace? How do we get you out of Osgaard? And how do we make it look as if Yasma is dead?"

THREE HOURS LATER, Britta stepped into the palace gardens dressed in one of her finest tunics. The silk was snow-white, lavishly embroidered with gold thread. The crown on her head was golden, the girdle at her waist golden. Her cloak was carmine, the closest color she had to scarlet.

White, gold, red. A display of purity and patriotism.

Britta paused for a moment. The dread and panic and nausea churning in her stomach were familiar. She'd felt like this on the morning of her marriage to Rikard. *I can't do this.*

She took a shallow breath and pictured the boys' faces. If she didn't do it, they would die.

Britta set off for the king's private garden, following the curving pink-and-white path. Karel followed. His presence was reassuring. It was a wild plan, but with Karel to help, it could work. It *had* to work.

Two armsmen stood at the entrance to the king's garden, one on either side of the ornate golden gate. "I understand my brother is here," Britta said haughtily. "Is that correct?"

"Yes, highness."

She gave a regal nod and stepped past them.

The garden had clipped hedges and rose bushes and trickling fountains, but here the fountains were crafted from beaten gold, and jewels glittered on their rims. The delicate crunch of crushed marble beneath her shoes seemed to erode her courage. Britta stepped off the path, walking on soft grass. Past the rose bower, past the burbling cascade.

She rounded a curve in the lawn. There were Jaegar's personal armsmen; six of them, now that he was Heir-Ascendant. They stood at parade rest, their backs to a tall hedge, their golden breastplates and silver torques glinting in the sun. But where was Jaegar?

Britta halted uncertainly, scanning the garden.

He was by the goldfish pond, talking to a man. Not a nobleman or courtier or army officer. A stranger, dressed in plain clothes.

The dread and panic and nausea churned even more violently in her stomach. *I'm going to vomit.* Britta set off across the lawn towards Jaegar, past a tall hedge, losing sight of the armsmen.

The hedge curved sinuously towards the goldfish pond, giving her glimpses of Jaegar and the stranger. Their voices came faintly on the breeze. She passed through shade, sunshine, shade. Jaegar's robe looked black from this distance, but sunlight sparkled on gold thread woven into the fabric.

The end of the hedge drew near. Britta's steps slowed. *I'm going to vomit. I know I'm going to—*

Karel caught her elbow, halting her.

Britta glanced at him, opened her mouth to ask why he'd stopped her—and closed it at the expression on his face.

Karel pulled her into the shade of the tall hedge.

"What?" she whispered.

He shook his head and laid a finger to his lips.

Britta stood tensely, aware that something was wrong, but not understanding what. Jaegar's voice drifted to her. "...can't prove it wasn't natural."

"Which is what you asked for, highness." The stranger's voice had an accent her ear wasn't used to. Short vowels, clipped consonants.

"You take me for a fool? I'm not paying for an act of nature."

Britta glanced at Karel. He seemed to understand the cryptic words. His expression was grim. He hadn't released her elbow. If anything, his grip had tightened. What was he staring at so intently?

She followed his gaze. Two elongated shadows lay on the ground half a dozen yards ahead. Jaegar's was easy to identify from the crown on his head.

"You refuse to pay the Brotherhood the contracted sum?" the stranger asked. "That would be unwise, highness."

"Are you threatening me?" Jaegar's voice was at its most cool, its most dangerous. Their father had yelled when he gave orders to have bondservants flayed; Jaegar gave such commands coldly, emotionlessly. "Think twice before you do so. I rule this kingdom, and your brotherhood doesn't frighten *me*."

"No threat, highness. Merely an observation."

"Then the answer is yes. I refuse. I will not pay for the All-Mother's work."

"If that is your choice, so be it." The man's tone was impassive. "And the new contract? Do you wish to proceed? I've received word that the ship has left Lundegaard."

"About time! I could have arranged it faster myself." There was a crunch of marble chips. Jaegar's shadow moved slightly. Britta shrank back against the hedge.

"If you don't wish to continue, you may cancel the contract, highness."

"I'll continue," Jaegar said curtly. "But your competence to date hasn't impressed me. I expected better results, given your reputation."

"You will have no cause to question our competence again. You have my hand on it." There was a short pause. From the shadows lying on the ground, it looked as if Jaegar and the man were clasping hands. "The ship should berth in four days. As soon as I've briefed the men, it will be ready to take passengers."

One shadow bowed. Britta heard the sound of a person walking away. The crunch of footsteps was uneven, as if the walker trod more heavily on one foot than the other.

Karel's fingers flexed lightly on her elbow. Britta looked at his face, saw the finger held warningly to his lips. They walked soundlessly back the way they'd come, staying close to the hedge. When they'd nearly reached its end, Karel halted. Britta scanned the garden. Jaegar's armsmen were out of sight, but past the rose bower was the stranger, walking in the direction of the gate. His gait was awkward, limping.

Karel watched until the man was gone. Only then did he release her elbow.

"Who was that?" Britta whispered. And why was Karel's face so frighteningly stern?

"I'll tell you later. For now, you saw nothing, you heard nothing."

Britta nodded.

"Be very, *very* careful, princess. If your brother discovers we witnessed that, we're both dead." The sound of a bell ringing drifted across the garden; the day was one hour closer to dusk. "Are you ready?"

No. The panic and nausea returned.

For a moment Britta's feet refused to move. *I can't.* And then she saw Rutgar's face in her mind's eye. Lukas's face.

She turned and retraced her steps over the grass, back to the goldfish pond. The nausea churned in her belly and climbed her throat. Jaegar's shadow still lay across the ground. A dozen more steps and he'd be in sight. Half a dozen steps.

I'm going to vomit.

Britta halted.

The armsman halted alongside her. His hand reached out and gripped hers. Warm, strong fingers.

Britta glanced at him, mute with panic.

"You can do it," he said, his whisper fierce with the same certainty she saw in his dark eyes. "I *know* you can."

Britta took a shaky breath. She pictured the boys' faces.

She released the armsman's hand, gathered up her skirts, and ran across the grass towards her half-brother. "Jaegar! Is it true?"

* * *

KAREL WATCHED FROM the edge of the lawn. Princess Brigitta was bewildered, distraught, words tumbling from her mouth, begging for her brother's reassurance.

He watched as she allowed herself to be persuaded that her little half-brothers had betrayed Osgaard. He watched as she timidly proposed exile for them, and allowed herself to be convinced that the boys needed to be executed.

"Oh, dear!" she cried, wringing her hands. "First Harkeld, and then Father, and now this! There's only you and me left!"

Jaegar's performance was almost equal to the princess's. He was benevolent. He was patient. He soothed her fears.

Karel studied the man out of the corner of his eye. He wore an Heir-Ascendant's robes, black and gold, like the pennants flying at the guard towers. Long ash-blond hair was woven around the crown on his head. A prince's crown, not a king's. Not yet. Beneath the gleaming crown, Jaegar's face bore a smile that was simultaneously sympathetic and satisfied. He wasn't annoyed his half-sister had come to him. On the contrary, he was pleased.

The princess was correct; Jaegar wanted her for something. *What?*

Princess Brigitta touched on the subject of the coronation. Would it not be better, she tentatively suggested, to have the boys' executions out of the way before that event? Jaegar's ascension to the throne was the start of a new era in Osgaard's history. Surely it was best not to start his reign with bloodshed?

Karel held his breath and listened intently. This was the topic they'd spent longest discussing: how far she should go in her attempt to convince Jaegar she supported him. If Jaegar decided to ignore the constitution—

"Osgaard's constitution forbids it," Jaegar said. "I'm not able to execute our father's blood-heirs until after my coronation."

If he declared the boys illegitimate, he could execute them now, but Princess Brigitta didn't suggest that.

"If you don't mind, I won't be present at the executions." She dabbed her eyes with a silk handkerchief. "But if there's *any* other way I can show my support... We must stick together, you and I. We are the last—" Her voice broke.

"I had no idea your feelings for me were so deep, my dear." Jaegar's tone was smooth, amused. Disbelieving? "I had thought Harkeld your favorite, and the boys."

The back of Karel's neck prickled. *Be careful, princess.*

"Oh... well... yes..." Princess Brigitta stammered, twisting the handkerchief between her fingers. "But you are so much older than me! We never spent any time... And now with Harkeld a witch and the boys involved in that dreadful plot! You are the only family I have."

The tears in her eyes, the distress in her voice, were perfect. If Karel hadn't known better, he would have believed her.

Jaegar patted her shoulder, his smile growing more satisfied, more wolf-like. "There's one thing you can do that would greatly help matters."

"Yes?" the princess said, wiping her eyes and blowing her nose. "Anything."

"Help me catch Harkeld."

"What?" Her head jerked up.

"He was always fond of you. He'll pause his little quest long enough to save you... if you need saving."

"What?" Princess Brigitta said again, her expression bewildered.

"I need you to go to Roubos with some men, Brigitta. To catch Harkeld. The ship departs in five days."

Five days? Karel tensed.

"Harkeld?" Princess Brigitta shrank back. "But he's a witch! I don't want to catch him. His head needs to be cut off!"

"These men will do that. They're Fithian." Jaegar's teeth glinted in the sunlight. "You'll just be the bait."

"But... but that terrible curse—"

"Will be stopped. With Harkeld's blood and his hands, it's easily done."

Princess Brigitta twisted the handkerchief, fear plain to read on her face. "Must I go with them? Can't I stay here?"

"If Harkeld believes you're in danger, he'll try to save you." Jaegar smiled benevolently at the princess. "You won't actually be in danger, my dear. The men will take good care of you. And you may take your maid with you, and your armsmen."

The princess gazed beseechingly at him. "Must I?"

"You must. For the sake of Osgaard. Be brave, my dear."

Princess Brigitta twisted the handkerchief more tightly. "Five days?" she said tremulously. "But I will get to see your coronation, won't I, Jaegar? I must see it!" An edge of hysteria rose in her voice.

"Speed is of the utmost importance—"

"But your coronation!" the princess cried. "I must be there! I must show my support for you! I'm all the family you have left!"

"Harkeld's capture—"

"What difference can two days make to Harkeld? Whereas here—the coronation—the start of your reign... I must be here! We must show Osgaard the Rutersvards stand together! If you send me away, people will think I don't support you, and I *do*. I do!"

Karel held his breath while the Heir-Ascendant considered this. Princess Brigitta's face was pale. Her distress, this time, was unfeigned. "Please, Jaegar," she begged. "Let me stay for the coronation. I promise I'll go without fuss. I'll help catch Harkeld. I'll do everything you want. Please."

Was she praying? Karel was. *I implore you, All-Mother, let him give us those two days.*

Jaegar pursed his lips thoughtfully, gazing at his half-sister. Then he nodded. "Very well. But I expect your complete obedience in the matter of Harkeld."

"Yes, yes. I promise! I'll do everything you ask."

"And everything the Fithians tell you to do."

"Yes," Princess Brigitta said meekly.

Jaegar looked pleased. If Karel read that expression correctly, he'd not expected the princess to agree to travel across the Seven Kingdoms in the company of Fithian assassins. Or help catch Prince Harkeld.

"I think... I shall lie down now," the princess said, touching her temple. "Today has been most distressing." She took a step away from Jaegar and paused, turning back. "I'll have my maid start packing. How long do you think we'll be away?"

"Two months."

"And I may take my maid and armsmen?"

"Yes." Jaegar's gaze turned to Karel.

Karel stared stolidly across the goldfish pond.

"Armsman..."

Karel allowed himself to meet the man's eyes. Cold eyes, almost as pale as his ash-blond hair.

"Not a word of this, or I shall have your head."

"Yes, highness."

Princess Brigitta took another step away from her brother, halted again, turned back to him. "I think I should see the boys one last time... with your permission, Jaegar. It would be proper. But... not today." She touched her temple again.

Jaegar shrugged. "There's no need."

"It would seem ill-bred of me—don't you think?—if I didn't pay them a final visit."

Jaegar's eyes narrowed. "Don't let them deceive you with their lies. I know how fond you are of them."

"Oh, no! Not now. Not after what you've told me. Their own armsmen witnessing—" Her voice faltered. She pressed the handkerchief to her face. "A brief visit. Two minutes. Just to say a formal goodbye."

"If you must," the Heir-Ascendant said coldly.

Princess Brigitta lowered the handkerchief. She seemed to hesitate. *No more,* Karel cautioned her inwardly. *Leave it at that.*

The princess seemed to hear the silent words. "Thank you." She turned away from her brother. "I really must lie down..."

* * *

KAREL ESCORTED THE princess back to her rooms. Yasma met them, her eyes wide and anxious.

Princess Brigitta sank down on the brocade and gilt settle, pressed her hands to her cheeks. She looked pale enough to faint.

"Fetch her something to drink," Karel told Yasma. "Wine."

Yasma hurried to the cabinet in the far corner of the parlor, where the princess kept her goblets and her wine.

Karel crouched alongside Princess Brigitta and touched her shoulder lightly. She was trembling. "Are you all right?"

The princess exhaled a low, shaky breath and rubbed her face. "I can't believe we actually did it."

You *did it, princess.*

Yasma returned, holding a goblet of golden wine.

"Drink," Karel said.

The princess obediently drank.

"What happened?" Yasma asked, distress shining in her eyes. "Did something go wrong?"

"No." Karel stood. "Nothing went wrong. By the All-Mother's grace, it worked."

"Truly?"

"Truly. Jaegar believed every word."

"Oh." Yasma uttered a sound like a sob. Tears spilled from her eyes.

Karel put his arms around her. She was trembling as much as Princess Brigitta. Terror. And why should she not be afraid? If anything happened to the princess, her future was a terrible one. *I will keep you safe if I possibly can, little one.*

Princess Brigitta rose from the settle. "Yasma?"

"A drink for her, too, I think," Karel said, stroking Yasma's hair. "If you will allow, highness?"

"Of course." Princess Brigitta held out her goblet. "Here. Take mine."

"Oh, no." Yasma gave a shaky sob and pushed out of his embrace. "I'll fetch one."

"Is she all right?" the princess asked in a low voice.

"Scared," Karel said. "And rightly so."

Princess Brigitta grimaced. She took off her cloak and sat again, kicking off her silk slippers, curling her feet under her. She drank another mouthful of wine. Some color had returned to her face. "Who was that man? The one talking to Jaegar."

"I'm guessing... a Fithian poison master."

"You guess? How?"

"He had a peg leg."

"Who did?" Yasma returned and sat on the settle alongside the princess.

"A man who was with Jaegar," Karel said. "The armsmen had been sent out of earshot. It seemed too much of a coincidence, given the gossip I'd heard."

"Who was he?" Yasma asked.

"Karel thinks he's a Fithian poison master."

Yasma jerked, almost slopping her wine. "What?"

"It's all right." Princess Brigitta reached out to take Yasma's hand. "At least... I think it is." She frowned at Karel. "I understand the second part of the conversation. The new contract, the ship—that's for me. But the first part... What was that about?"

"That was Jaegar refusing to pay for your father's death."

"It was poison?"

"I think so." Karel briefly explained the mess hall gossip, then told Yasma about the conversation he and the princess had overheard, and Jaegar's plan for Prince Harkeld's capture.

"A Fithian ship? Us?" Yasma shrank back on the settle.

"Departing in five days' time. But the princess convinced Jaegar to let her stay for the coronation."

Princess Brigitta put down her goblet. "Let's hope his word was given truly. If not, our plans are for naught." She pressed a hand to her temple. "Yasma, can you take this crown off, please? It's giving me a headache."

Yasma stood, deftly removed the jeweled pins, unwound the hair.

The princess sighed and closed her eyes. "Thank you." With her golden hair tumbling down her back, she seemed suddenly much younger. He was reminded that she was barely a year older than Yasma. Eighteen. Scarcely into womanhood.

Princess Brigitta looked exhausted, delicate, easily broken. And yet she'd survived marriage to Duke Rikard. She'd ruined Osgaard's invasion of Lundegaard. And she'd masterfully deceived her brother today. She was shrewder, stronger, than she looked.

Yasma placed the crown on the floor and sat again, tucking her feet under her. "What did Jaegar say about your brothers?"

Princess Brigitta opened her eyes. "You tell her, Karel. And do sit, please."

Karel fetched a chair and sat. He explained rapidly. Yasma listened with wide eyes, clutching Princess Brigitta's hand. When he'd finished, she turned to the princess. "Britta..." Her voice was hushed, awed. "You're so brave. I could never have done it."

Princess Brigitta glanced at Karel. Her mouth twisted wryly. "But for Karel, I wouldn't have."

He shook his head. *You're braver than you think, princess.* "If Jaegar keeps his word about the coronation, we can pull this off." He didn't dare think about failure. The consequences were too dreadful. For his family. For Yasma's family.

"I didn't ask where the boys are being held," the princess said. "It seemed best to leave it."

"I can find that out."

Princess Brigitta's mouth twisted again, in anger this time. "How can those armsmen give false witness? Against children!"

"A fat pouch of gold and early retirement," Karel said. "Like Queen Sigren's armsmen after her death." Memory gave him a glimpse of Marten and Edvin's faces that morning. How hard had it been for Jaegar to bend them to his will? Had it taken threat of death? Or just promise of gold?

"The boys won't die," Princess Brigitta said fiercely. "I won't let it happen!"

"Britta... I've thought of where we can get blood from."

The princess's face lit with eagerness. "Tell us, Yasma!"

CHAPTER THIRTEEN

PETRUS SWAPPED WITH Innis behind one of the tents. He donned Justen's wet clothes, his clammy boots, his Grooten amulet, his sword. "Has he said anything I should know?"

"He hardly speaks at all, these days. None of us do."

Petrus tucked the amulet inside his shirt. He glanced around the camp. Rand and Katlen weren't talking as they prepared dinner, Ebril wasn't whistling as he gathered wet branches for the fire, Hew and Frane weren't chatting as they checked the horse's hooves. *We're all gritting our teeth and getting through each day.* "It's because of Susa," he said, putting an arm around Innis's shoulders and pulling her close. "And the rain. And the mud. And the Mother-forsaken ugliness of this place."

Innis rested her cheek against his chest. "Could you see how much further the woodcutting goes?"

"Forever."

Innis sighed and pushed away. She squeezed his hand briefly and headed for the campfire.

Petrus watched her for a moment. *I love you.*

He blew out a breath, adjusted his sodden cloak, and strolled across to watch Prince Harkeld's magic lesson.

As he approached, a tree stump a good ten yards from the prince flared alight.

"Excellent," Cora said.

Petrus stood to one side and watched while Prince Harkeld worked to increase his range.

He didn't like the prince, but to give him credit, the man was working hard. And he was clearly a strong fire mage. Petrus was reluctantly impressed. Once Prince Harkeld learned to use his magic to defend himself, they'd all be safer.

When the prince's range reached fifteen yards, Cora stopped him. "How does it feel?"

"It's not taking any more effort than lighting the campfire, just a bit more concentration."

"And your control?"

"It feels like the magic's only going to do what I tell it to. It doesn't feel like it could get away from me." His voice became doubtful. "But maybe it could?"

"Unlikely. Your magic is part of your body. It obeys you. You'd never tell your hand to scratch your nose and have it clout you on the head instead, would you?"

The prince's expression relaxed almost into a smile. "No."

"Your magic will obey you, just as the rest of your body obeys you." Cora let this statement sink in, and then went on, "Accidents can happen if you're exceedingly unclear about what you're asking it to do. Or if you're drunk, or panicked. But if you give your magic clear commands, if *you* know what you want it to do, you'll have no problems."

The prince nodded.

"Accidents can also happen if you exceed... not your ability, because you have exceptionally strong ability, but your training. Your experience. Right now, if I asked you to burn Justen's cloak, you'd probably burn *him*. Not because your magic got away from you, but because you don't know how to use it with sufficient precision. You don't have the experience."

The prince glanced at Petrus, his expression sober.

"So we'll expand your experience." Cora nodded at the burning stump. "Can you make that fire burn higher?"

Prince Harkeld raised his hand. The flames flared up into the sky.

A screech came from overhead. An owl tumbled down, the feathers on one wingtip alight.

The prince made an inarticulate sound. He clenched his upraised hand. The flames towering into the sky, the flames on the owl's wing, quenched instantly.

The owl landed hard beside the campfire, became Gerit. He staggered to his feet, his face red with fury. "You cursed fool!" he bellowed. "You *burned* me."

Cora muttered something under her breath—a swearword, Petrus thought—and hurried across to the campfire.

Petrus glanced at Prince Harkeld. The prince's face was starkly pale. His mouth was half open, but no sound came from it.

Petrus touched the prince's arm. "It wasn't your fault."

"It was me that burned him." The prince shook him off and headed for the campfire.

Petrus followed more slowly. *An arrogant mage is a dangerous mage.* He'd said that to Innis once, when they'd discussed the prince, and there was no doubt the prince could be an arrogant bastard when he chose to be. But he didn't appear to be an arrogant mage. Prince Harkeld's attitude to his magic was cautious. And frightened. He was frightened of it.

The healers clustered around Gerit, examining his arm. At a gesture from Cora, Hew stripped off his clothes, shifted shape, and flapped into the sky to keep watch.

Prince Harkeld observed the healers from a distance. His face was still unnaturally pale, his expression stiff.

He's upset. Not pretend upset, not polite upset, but truly upset.

Once the burns were healed and Gerit dressed, Prince Harkeld walked across to Gerit. Petrus followed.

"I apologize for harming you," the prince said.

"Magic's not to be played with," Gerit snapped.

"He wasn't playing," Petrus said, his sense of fairness bringing him to the prince's defense. "He was learning."

"Well, he shouldn't be. Shouldn't be using his magic at all, not if he can't do better 'n that."

Petrus snorted. *Hypocrite. You wanted him to use his magic back in Lundegaard without any instruction.* He couldn't say that aloud, though. Not as Justen.

"You're an incompetent fool."

Prince Harkeld inhaled sharply through his nose. "And you are a foul-tempered whoreson."

Gerit bared his teeth at him and swung away towards the tents.

"Well said," Petrus said.

The prince glanced at him, his mouth tight.

Cora hurried over to them. "What—?"

"Gerit was being Gerit," Petrus said. "Flin here apologized and Gerit slapped him down."

"Pay him no attention, Flin. He's cross because you made him look foolish. Dinner's ready. Go eat. I'll speak to Gerit."

For a moment, the prince didn't move. He looked as if he wanted to stalk away, as Gerit had done. Then he nodded stiffly at Cora and turned towards the fire.

Petrus followed. "It wasn't your fault."

The prince dismissed the words with a shrug.

Petrus lengthened his stride and grabbed the prince's arm, halting him. "I mean it."

Prince Harkeld's eyebrows pinched together. "Unhand me, armsman."

Petrus ignored the order. "The person who misjudged his magic tonight was Gerit, not you. Any shapeshifter who flies over a fire lesson deserves to lose a few feathers!"

Firelight and shadows flickered across Prince Harkeld's face. Was the prince even listening to him? His expression was haughty, remote.

The prince's mouth relaxed. He inclined his head in acknowledgement. "Thank you, Justen."

LATER THAT EVENING, after he'd swapped back with Innis, Petrus looked for Cora. She was with Rand at the picket line, checking one of the horses. Petrus crossed the mud to them.

"About Gerit..."

Rand glanced up, but didn't stop massaging the horse's hock. Cora straightened. "What about him?"

"He was cursed rude tonight. The prince—I mean Flin—apologized, and Gerit just—"

"I've spoken with him about it."

"He makes us all look bad."

"No, only himself."

Petrus conceded this with a shrug. But even so... "He shouldn't be a Sentinel." Sentinels weren't meant to incite trouble, they were meant to prevent it, or at the very least, minimize it. A good Sentinel was calm, diplomatic, even-tempered. Not argumentative and rude.

"His last mission was difficult," Cora said. "Both his companions were killed. He should have been given time to rest, not sent out with us."

"Oh." Petrus scuffed the muddy ground with his boot.

"I've suggested he leave us at Roubos. He has agreed."

"Oh," Petrus said again.

"I know it may be hard for you to believe, but Gerit has been an outstanding Sentinel. One of the best. He deserves our forbearance."

In the dim light, he saw Rand nod.

Petrus ducked his head. "I apologize," he said. "I didn't realize—"

"How could you? This is your first mission." Cora brushed strands of hair back from her face. "We've agreed—Gerit and I—that he shouldn't be Justen any more. This is the ideal time for Hew to start taking turns as Justen, but I'm not sure it would be wise. Hew doesn't know Flin as well as you three do. I fear him making a mistake."

And he doesn't know how to laugh, either. And Justen, whoever played him, had a sense of humor.

Cora sighed. "I realize that this places more strain on the two of you—"

"We'll be fine," Petrus said hastily. "Don't worry about us, Cora."

"Well... let me know if it becomes too much of a strain. Now, bed. Try to get some sleep before you go on watch." She turned back to Rand and crouched. "Does it need more healing?"

Petrus walked to the tent he shared with Ebril, feeling small.

CHAPTER FOURTEEN

BRITTA TALKED WITH Yasma and Karel late into the night. They sat at the marquetry table, the detritus of her and Yasma's dinner pushed to one end. The armsman had refused a share of the meal. "I get fed at midnight."

From blood, they moved to the sewer system and the river that flowed beneath the palace, and from that to kitchen trolleys and herbs and perfume vials and bondservants' corridors and Jaegar's coronation. Their plan came together.

Britta studied Karel's face in the candlelight. In a few short hours he'd tipped their relationship upside down. *I've looked at him for years, but never seen who he truly is.*

His stern, hawk-like face hadn't changed. And yet it had, profoundly.

The armsman pushed back his chair and stood. "You should go to bed now. Both of you."

Britta was abruptly aware of how tired she was. Her eyes burned. But how could she possibly sleep with her thoughts spinning so feverishly in her head?

"Tomorrow morning, the library. You know what to look for, highness?"

"Yes." Britta stood and took one of his hands in both of hers and held it at her heart in a formal gesture of gratitude. "Karel, thank you."

Karel dipped his head in acknowledgement. His face had become expressionless again.

Britta didn't release his hand. There were hundreds of

armsmen in the palace—and yet how many of them would have dared do what he was doing? Or cared enough to do it? What stroke of fortune had given her Karel? "I thank the All-Mother you were assigned to me."

"We haven't won through yet, highness."

"If we do, it will be because of you."

The risks the armsman was taking were appalling. He was the child of bondservants, his family's continued freedom conditional on his good service. For him, the consequences of failure would be worse than death.

Yasma rearranged the table to make it look as if only one person had dined, then came to stand beside her. "I wish you could come with us, Karel."

An emotion flickered on the armsman's face, gone too swiftly for Britta to identify. Did he love Yasma? Was that why he risked his own life and his family's freedom?

"Can't we make it look as if you're dead, too?" Yasma asked.

"Who would witness our deaths?" Karel shook his head. "We dare not involve anyone else." He removed his hand from Britta's clasp. "Princess, Yasma, it's nearly midnight. Torven will be here shortly. You must retire."

SHE SLEPT IN snatches. Plans churned in her head, and beneath that was worry for the boys. How terrified they must be! *I'm coming for you*, Britta promised.

She rose at dawn, feeling exhausted. Outside, the sky was gray. Rain spotted the windowpanes. Six days until the coronation. Six days until their escape.

Urgency swelled in her breast, pushing aside the exhaustion. Six days was a perilously short time.

She ate, bathed, dressed, barely noticing what she was doing, and then Yasma began the lengthy process of weaving the crown into her hair. The maid's fingers were less deft than usual, her dark eyes shadowed. "Tired?" Britta asked.

"I couldn't sleep. I can't stop thinking about Karel. I wish there was a way for him to come too."

"Yasma, do you and he...?" Britta paused, uncertain how to phrase the question.

"Oh, no," Yasma said, flushing. "We're just friends."

"Oh... I thought maybe you and he had an understanding."

"Karel did offer to marry me if I wanted. But only to make me safer. He promised he wouldn't touch me."

Britta looked down at her lap. She smoothed a wrinkle in her silk overtunic. *I think he loves you more than you know.*

When the crown was in place, Yasma vanished into the dressing room, emerging with the carmine cloak in her arms and a frown on her face. "Look, on the shoulder."

Britta glanced at the dark mark. "Jaegar touched me there. He must have had something on his hand."

"No, it looks singed. The fabric's eaten through..." Yasma bore the cloak away again, still frowning. She came back with a sable cloak and settled it over Britta's shoulders.

THE PALACE LIBRARY was cool, quiet, shadowy. Deep cubbyholes lined the walls, within which rested hundreds of scrolls.

"Do you have scrolls on herbs?" Britta asked. "Their properties? I'd like to plant a garden of medicinal herbs."

The librarian, a thin, fussy man, muttered to himself as he bustled around the library. "Herbs..." He climbed a stepladder, brought down several scrolls and laid them on a table. "Cultivation..." He shifted the stepladder, climbed again.

"Are there scrolls on how to make medicines from herbs?"

"*Pharmacopeia*..." the librarian muttered to himself as he climbed the stepladder.

"And are there scrolls on dangerous herbs?" Britta asked, aware of the armsman standing behind her. Torven was as impassive as Karel. Was he assessing every word she uttered? "I'd like to know what they are to avoid them."

"The *Great Herbal* has a section on that subject, highness."
The librarian indicated the scrolls piled on the table.

"Excellent. May I take these back to my rooms?"

The librarian hesitated. His gaze lifted to her crown. "...royal
princess," he muttered under his breath.

"I shall treat them with utmost care," Britta said. "You have
a bondservant to carry these for me?"

The librarian reluctantly produced two bondservants.
"Careful... careful..." he muttered as he tenderly piled the
scrolls into their arms.

Britta led the small procession back to her rooms. The
armsman halted inside the door at parade rest. "Be careful with
these, girl," Britta told Yasma. "No food or drink near them."

The bondservants were both islanders, men not much older
than Karel. The scars of old beatings, old lashings, knotted their
skin. Neither of them looked at her. They kept their gazes down
as they helped Yasma lay the scrolls on the table.

Where Karel stood tall and strong, these men were hunched,
cowed. One had hands like an old man's, his knuckles thick and
stiff with scar tissue.

How did Karel bear it? Living in the palace, seeing his people
treated like this? The women raped, as Yasma had been, the
men bearing the marks of terrible violence?

The bondservants finished laying out the scrolls. "Thank
you," Britta said.

One man flinched, as if frightened he'd been noticed. The other
glanced at her, a hasty, anxious flick of dark eyes. "Highness,"
he mumbled, ducking his head.

The two bondservants retreated across the parlor. Britta
watched Torven's face as he closed the door behind them. Was
that contempt beneath the blank façade?

Don't you dare sneer at them.

How many years' service did the two men have left? How
many more beatings would they endure before they could
return home? And they were just two of the hundreds of
bondservants within the palace. The number of miseries and

sufferings experienced daily within these marble walls was uncountable. Unbearable.

It was enough to make her go mad.

Britta pressed her hands to her temples. *Don't think about it.*

"Have you a headache, princess?" Yasma asked.

Britta looked at her, remembering the first time she'd ever seen Yasma—the wide marble corridor, the brush and bucket and damp, freshly-scrubbed floor, the off-duty armsman hauling Yasma to her feet. She remembered the despair on Yasma's face, the panic in her eyes.

Britta lowered her hands. *At least I saved you.* No one had raped Yasma for four years. "A little."

"Shall I fetch a tisane for you?"

"Yes. Lemon, please." Britta crossed to the table. She sat and turned her attention to the *Pharmacopeia*.

AT NOON, KAREL took Torven's place, and the atmosphere in the parlor changed. She could let her public face slip, be more herself. Britta knew the exact day it had first happened—nearly three years ago, when she'd noticed that Yasma didn't cringe from Karel, as she did from all other armsmen. Since then, she'd called Yasma by her name within Karel's hearing, not *girl* or *you*, had let him see that she allowed Yasma to sit in her presence, that she shared her food with her, that she treated Yasma as if she was free, not a bondservant. And Karel had observed their friendship and not shown by even a flicker of an eyelid what he thought of it.

But today the change was more significant than usual. With the closing of the door behind Torven, the air seemed to acquire a charged feeling. It wasn't just her public face that slipped, but Karel's too. He wasn't impassive today. His expression was alert, questioning. "You have the scrolls?"

Britta half-rose from her chair. "Yes."

"Karel." Yasma emerged from the bedchamber.

Britta sank back into the chair and watched the armsman turn to Yasma, watched his face relax into a smile, watched him hold out his hand to the maid and briefly clasp her fingers.

They love each other.

Britta looked down at the scroll she was reading, not seeing the words, the carefully tinted illustrations. *We have to find a way to bring Karel, too.* But how?

"Have you found anything?" the armsman asked.

Britta raised her head. "I've found a number of emetics. One has an antidote and looks promising."

Karel pulled out a chair for Yasma, and sat himself.

"My brothers? Have you heard anything about them?"

"They're being held near the dungeons, highness. They have a nursemaid attending them. I heard nothing to indicate they're being mistreated." Karel's voice was reassuring, kind.

Britta swallowed a sudden lump in her throat. She pushed scrolls across the table towards him and Yasma.

THEY SPENT THE afternoon reading scrolls. Sleet splattered against the windowpanes and wind rattled the frames, but the parlor was snug, a fire burning in the marble fireplace. Britta sat with her feet tucked under her and the sable cloak over her shoulders. Across from her, Yasma was curled up in an ermine cloak, reading intently.

"Here!" Yasma said suddenly. "Black Sugar Orchid. That's what you said, isn't it, Karel?"

"Yes." The armsman reached for the scroll. He read aloud, "'Black Sugar Orchid. An orchid producing long pods that shrivel and turn black upon maturity, the seeds of which, when crushed and distilled, produce a sweet-smelling tincture known as All-Mother's Breath, which induces temporary paralysis and loss of consciousness when inhaled or ingested. All-Mother's Breath has no known antidote, but Horned Lily root may be used as a preventative.'" He unrolled the scroll further. "'Horned Lily root. A tuber with pale pink skin and white flesh, from which the Horned Lily grows and which, upon ingestion in either its fresh or dried form, renders the eater immune to the effects of All-Mother's Breath for a period.'" He looked up, his teeth flashing white in a grin. "The quantities are all here. This is precisely what we need, Yasma!"

Yasma flushed. Her glance to Britta was shy, pleased.

A while later, Karel laid down his scroll. "'Pepperwort. A herb that, when infused overnight, produces a colorless, odorless liquid with a peppery flavor. Pepperwort infusion may be used to warm the blood of patients with sluggish circulation, in particular those whose extremities are cold to the touch. Its application upon an object or trail renders hounds unable to follow a scent.'" He looked up. "And the instructions for preparing the infusion are here."

"That's everything, then," Britta said. "Let's make a list of what we need to purchase." She glanced at the armsman. "What *you* need to purchase." The risk in this next step was his. "And I must write a formal request for your grace day. And one for Torven."

Yasma scrambled off her chair and fetched parchment, ink, and a quill.

Britta penned notes to the commander of armsmen first, requesting that Karel receive a grace day the day after tomorrow, and Torven the shift after that. She worded them as commands, signed her name in flourishing letters, and affixed royal seals of scarlet wax and gold leaf. Let him ignore *that*.

Then they spent an hour checking and rechecking quantities in the scrolls and compiling a list of everything Karel needed to purchase. "Let's see those perfume vials," he said, once it was done.

Britta fetched an inlaid wooden box. Inside were four delicate blue glass vials with silver lids. She lifted one out and removed the lid, showing the slender tube that descended from it. "You fill the vial, insert this and screw it tight, press the lid, and it sprays the perfume out through this little hole."

Karel examined the vial and its lid. He filled one with water, screwed the lid on, pressed. A puff of spray misted out. "Ingenious. I've never seen anything like this. There must be a spring inside the lid."

"They're not made in the Seven Kingdoms. They come from somewhere called Margolie." Britta touched a vial with a fingertip. How many gold pieces had it cost?

"None of these have been used?"

Britta shook her head. "Rikard gave them to me." His name seemed to choke in her throat. She hurried past it. "As a wedding gift. I haven't opened the box since he showed me them." How long ago that seemed. And yet her wedding had been less than two months ago. "They shouldn't smell of anything."

"I'll rinse them all," Yasma said. "Just to make sure."

Karel emptied the vial and replaced it in the box.

"What do you think?" Britta asked.

"I think they're perfect for the All-Mother's Breath. Better than a soaked cloth. And we can use them for the pepperwort, too. Two vials for each. We'd best check they all work, first."

Someone rapped loudly on the outer door.

Britta flinched, her heart lurching in her chest. Yasma's face drained of color.

Karel rose swiftly to his feet. He pushed his chair in and headed for the door, his hobnailed boots making no sound on the soft rugs.

Yasma scrambled from her chair, pushed it in, and ran on tiptoe to the bedchamber, the sable cloak bundled around her and the box of vials clutched to her chest.

The loud rapping came again. Karel glanced across the parlor at Britta. She nodded, hastily rearranging the scrolls on the table.

Karel opened the door. Britta heard the murmur of voices. After a moment the armsman turned and announced: "Duke Frankl and Lady Agata, highness."

* * *

KAREL LISTENED TO Princess Brigitta greet her guests. "...a private word," Lady Agata murmured. "Perhaps your armsman could step outside?"

Karel saw the princess hesitate, then nod. "Armsman, wait outside."

He opened the door, caught her gaze for a brief moment—*Be careful*—and stepped out into the marble corridor. Two other armsmen stood there: Duke Frankl's and Lady Agata's.

Karel closed the door and planted himself squarely in front of it, trying not to let his uneasiness show. What did the new commander of Osgaard's army and his sister have to discuss with the princess?

The corridor was wide, quiet, secluded, curving away to the right. The only other doors were the gilded one to Prince Harkeld's empty suite of rooms, and a smaller, discreet door to the storage room the prince had used as a wine cellar. No one passed by; this was no thoroughfare. Karel heard his own breathing and, once, the creak of boot leather as Lady Agata's armsman shifted his weight.

The door behind him opened while the tenth bell was ringing. Karel stepped aside. Duke Frankl and his sister emerged, and the princess.

"This is the room," Princess Brigitta said, crossing the corridor and opening the door to the storage room. All three of them entered. Karel heard the murmur of voices.

He scanned their faces surreptitiously as they came out, trying to guess what was going on. The duke was younger than Rikard had been, trimmer, with no gray in his close-cropped hair and beard. A tiny smile sat on his mouth.

"Thank you for your visit." Princess Brigitta sounded grateful, tremulous. Karel looked sharply at her. Her expression was almost child-like in its innocence.

Duke Frankl bowed and kissed her hand, his sister curtseyed.

Karel followed Princess Brigitta into her suite and closed the door. The princess went to stand before the fire. Her expression was suddenly a lot more adult. Thoughtful. Worried.

"What was that about?" Karel asked. Words he would never have dared utter two days ago.

"That—at least I *think* it was—was Frankl positioning himself to take Osgaard's throne."

"What?" Karel strode across to her. "How?" And how would this change their plans?

Yasma emerged from the bedchamber. Princess Brigitta glanced at her. "Did you hear any of what they said, Yasma?"

The maid shook her head.

"Sit, both of you. I'll try to explain."

Karel sat on the settle. Yasma perched alongside him.

Princess Brigitta touched her fingers lightly to her forehead, as if organizing her thoughts, and took a deep breath. "They started by telling me that the boys are innocent and someone's taking advantage of Father's death to destabilize Osgaard's throne. Not Jaegar. They said he'd been duped by armsmen's lies, but Frankl must know that's not true. He *must* know Jaegar's behind this!"

Karel nodded, his eyes on her face.

"He said the boys' arrest has caused alarm in court, and a number of nobles have petitioned Jaegar for a stay of execution and an investigation into the allegations." She shrugged. "That may be true. Frankl said he's trying to persuade Jaegar to agree. He seemed to think he would. And he seemed to think the boys would be cleared."

Karel nodded again.

"And then he said... and Agata said it too... that I would be safer if I were married to him. And the boys would be safer too. He could protect us all from further plots. And he said that if Jaegar were to die, he'd be a good regent until Rutgar is of age. And... and what I *think* is that he sees his way to the throne, because if he *is* regent and the boys die, it's a short step from regent to king. Especially if he's married to me. Unless... perhaps I misread him?"

"I think not," Karel said, remembering the tiny smile on the man's face. Frankl had won Rikard's dukedom and command.

Now he wants Rikard's widow. "He's risen high in Osgaard's hierarchy in a short time. No man does that without strong ambition and ruthlessness." The duke commanded Osgaard's army. Add to that, marriage to a royal princess and guardianship over two blood-heirs... Yes, Frankl could well be aiming for the top.

"What do we do?" Yasma asked anxiously. "Does this change our plans?"

The princess met Karel's eyes. "It doesn't, does it?"

"No. The coronation is the only time the bondservants' corridors will be empty. If we wait, we lose our opportunity."

Princess Brigitta's expression relaxed. "Yes, that's what I thought."

"Why did you show him the storeroom?"

"Oh! That's the last thing Frankl said... he's trying to get the boys moved to somewhere more fitting of their status."

Karel frowned. *That* could change their plans.

"I suggested the nursery, but he said it wasn't secure enough— doors to the bondservants' corridors and so on—and then I thought... why not here? In *this* wing? It would make it so much easier for us!"

Karel's frown deepened. "He wouldn't... would he?"

"To make me look more favorably on his suit? I think he'll try. I was *very* effusive about how much I'd like to have the boys close. And he did say the room was suitable. Only one door, and no windows."

If the boys were moved here... Karel quenched the hope in his breast. "Jaegar will never allow it."

"No. Probably not." The princess hesitated. "Should I tell him about Frankl's visit?"

"You have to. If he hears about it from someone else, it will look bad for you. He *has* to believe you still trust him."

The princess sat on the settle alongside Yasma and reached for the maid's hand, gripping it, as if needing reassurance. He saw fear in her eyes.

"You can do it," Karel told her. "I know you can."

Princess Brigitta smiled faintly. "That's what you said in the gardens." She took a deep breath. "When? Not tonight?"

"Tonight, or tomorrow morning. Tell him you've heard the boys may be innocent. Let him see you're confused and worried. Ask for his guidance. And make sure he knows you're still obedient to his wishes about the Fithians. He must have *no* reason to send you away early!"

"Tomorrow morning," the princess said. "I need to think what to say."

CHAPTER FIFTEEN

THE DAYS BLURRED together, rain-drenched, muddy, endless. Tonight's campsite was like last night's, and the night before's. Discarded branches, rotting bark, a muddy creek, tree stumps.

The lesson was much like yesterday's too. Cora had him practice throwing his magic, and then manipulating the fires he'd lit from a distance.

"Well done," she said, when Harkeld had built a pillar of fire into the sky and then managed to shrink it back to one, tiny, glimmering flame without putting it out.

Harkeld shrugged off the praise. At least tonight he hadn't burned anyone.

"Dinner!" Katlen called.

They walked back to the campfire, Justen trailing behind, and ate bowls of stew. The stew, with its Ankenian spices, was also becoming tediously repetitive.

We're doomed to ride through this landscape forever, Harkeld thought glumly, as the rain dripped steadily from his hood. Doomed to be perpetually rained on, to never be dry again, to eat peppery stew forever.

The dreams were good, though. Sunlight and sex. He was looking forward to crawling into his tent, rolling up in his damp blanket, and falling asleep.

After they'd eaten, Cora had Frane and Rand drape an unused tent between two tree stumps. She unrolled a map beneath its shelter.

Harkeld's interest sparked. This wasn't part of their evening routine. *Maybe we* are *getting somewhere.*

Everyone crowded close.

"Katlen, some light, please," Cora said.

Katlen snapped her fingers. The flickering flames on her fingertips illuminated the map.

The mountain range that cut Ankeny off from the sea to the south was marked with jagged saw-tooth shapes, but the plateau of forest and woodcutters' camps they rode across was blank apart from the black line of the road they followed and the blue lines of several rivers flowing north.

"This is where we are," Cora said, pointing.

Harkeld examined the distance they'd traveled into Ankeny. Were they even a third of the way to the next anchor stone? "Why didn't we go by ship from Stanic? Wouldn't it have been quicker?"

"Too dangerous," Rand said. "The coast east of Yabrsk has a fearsome reputation. There's hundreds of reefs, not to mention the shallows. Drowned Man's Shallows, they call them. Can't remember what the reefs are called."

"The Boneyard," Cora said. "A ship's going to try to get close to the delta, Flin. With luck, the shapeshifters will be able to fly ashore, but we'll probably have to ride to Krelinsk before we can rendezvous with the others."

Harkeld looked at the map again, finding Krelinsk. It was almost on the border with Roubos.

Cora pointed to a blue line running north-south. "We should reach the Ptol tomorrow. It's too wide to ford, but there's a boat that takes travelers across."

Petrus stirred. "The horses—"

"From what I understand, the boats take horses too. And wagons. Merchants use this route."

Harkeld frowned, trying to visualize a riverboat that large.

"We have to go through the town. Gdelsk. It's unavoidable." Cora paused to let the words sink in. "Rand, tomorrow I'd like you to ride ahead and purchase some clothes for me and Katlen and Innis. Skirts. Flin was right; we don't look like ordinary travelers."

Rand nodded.

"Buy provisions for us. And ask about the other side of the river. If it's like this, we'll need grain for the horses. They're losing condition. And take the assassins' horses with you. If we need grain, they'll do as packhorses. If we don't, sell them."

Rand nodded again.

Cora rolled up the map. "We need to be vigilant in Gdelsk. If people *are* watching for us, it's the sort of place they'll be."

People. Harkeld pulled a face. By that, she meant assassins.

That evening, he took extra care sharpening his sword.

CHAPTER SIXTEEN

AT MIDNIGHT, KAREL went off duty. He took the princess's note to the duty commander. The man scowled when he read it. "A grace day? With the coronation so close? Did you ask her for this?"

"No, sir."

The duty commander read the note again and swore under his breath. "When was your last grace day, armsman?"

"Eight months ago, sir."

"Eight months? Then you're due one, but this week of all weeks! If she'd asked for *next* week..."

Karel felt himself tense. Was the request going to be refused?

The duty commander glowered at the royal seal. "Very well." He tossed the note on his desk. "You can have the grace day— now get out of my office."

"Yes, sir."

Karel went to the mess hall. He took a plate of food and began eating, paying no attention to who he sat next to or what he was chewing. Duke Frankl's visit and its consequences spun in his mind. If Jaegar doubted the princess's sincerity, if he sent her with the Fithians before the coronation...

"D'you reckon he has the pox?"

"Then the blisters would be on his cock, not his face, wouldn't they?"

"How d'you know they're not on his cock? Had a close look at it, have you?"

Someone snorted with laughter. Karel glanced up. The men speaking were some of Jaegar's personal armsmen.

"He has a blister on his hand, too," one of them said, shoveling food into his mouth.

"He does?"

The armsman pointed at his right palm, his mouth full, chewing.

"I reckon it's the pox," someone said with relish.

Karel shut out the conversation. He looked down at his plate. If Jaegar doubted his sister's sincerity, if he sent her with the Fithians before the coronation...

Then Princess Brigitta and Yasma and Torven and I will join the hunt for Prince Harkeld.

Could they escape a boatful of Fithian assassins?

No.

Could they sabotage the hunt?

Perhaps.

Rutgar and Lukas would certainly die—unless Frankl intervened. Did Jaegar intend his half-sister to die too? Was she expendable?

AFTER HE'D EATEN, Karel headed for the barracks, deep in thought. Down a flight of stairs, along wide corridors where torches burned smokily in brackets. He turned a corner. Halfway along the corridor a handful of armsmen clustered. He heard laughter, a woman's cry.

Karel halted in mid-stride.

They'd found a bondservant to rape.

His heart seemed to stop beating for a moment. He couldn't breathe. Couldn't move.

"My turn," one of the men said.

Karel turned and strode blindly back down the corridor, shoved open the door to the training arena, burst out into darkness and sleet. His heart hammered in his chest, almost bursting with each beat. He was panting as if he'd been running. An inarticulate cry of anguish rose in his throat, choking to get out.

He stood in the darkness, in the freezing sleet, struggling for control, but with each breath he inhaled his anguish grew. How could he not go back and save her? And yet, how could he?

His mother had once been that bondservant—raped—and if he broke his armsman's oath, she would be again. And his sisters. And his aunts and cousins.

Shivering, sodden, Karel went back to the door. But he couldn't make himself go through it. He sat on one of the long benches against the wall. There was a shuddering in his chest, in his breath. *Don't cry. Don't cry.* But it was too late.

The tears drained the anguish, leaving him numb with despair. He'd seen bondservants raped before and not been able to act. It would happen again. Hundreds of times, before his service was over. *Seventeen more years of this.* And at the end of that, he would have won full freedom for his family, the threat of bondservice forever erased.

He'd lasted five years of training, three years of service. He could last another seventeen.

Karel wiped his face. It would be worse once the princess and Yasma were gone. He was one of the best fighters in the palace, trained as a royal bodyguard. He'd go to Jaegar. And Jaegar was nothing like the princess. In his service, he would see the worst of Osgaard. Every day. For seventeen more years.

Karel squeezed his eyes shut. *Help me endure, All-Mother. Please.*

CHAPTER SEVENTEEN

KAREL TURNED INTO the wing where the princess had her rooms. His footsteps echoed flatly as he passed gilded doors, plain doors. He came to a junction of corridors, three straight, one curving out of sight. He took the curving one.

His footsteps faltered as he rounded the bend. The corridor was lined with armsmen in scarlet and gold standing to attention.

Karel continued slowly, scanning the armsmen—Torven at the door to the princess's suite, and six others. All wearing silver torques. Royal bodyguards. Jaegar's men.

The Heir-Ascendant was visiting his sister.

This is not good.

He halted at the door. Torven glanced at him.

How long has he been here? Karel wanted to ask. Instead, he silently took Torven's place.

Torven's footsteps died away. The fifth bell rang. Noon.

Karel's ears caught the sound of movement behind the door. He stepped aside.

The Heir-Ascendant emerged.

Karel stood stiffly, staring directly ahead. He caught a glimpse of Jaegar's face as the man passed in front of him. Below his right eye were three red blisters.

Jaegar strode down the corridor, his armsmen following. The clatter of hobnailed boots was momentarily loud. The Heir-Ascendant's robes flared behind him, the fabric as much gold as black now. In five days' time, they would be pure gold.

Karel entered the parlor and shut the door. Princess Brigitta was on her settle, her face wan and tear-stained. Yasma knelt at her feet.

Alarm tightened Karel's chest. "What's wrong?"

Both girls turned their heads. A smile lit the princess's face. Yasma leapt to her feet. "Karel!"

"What happened?"

The princess stood and came towards him, her steps almost dancing. "Jaegar's moving the boys to this wing. They'll be right across the corridor!"

"What?" he said, blinking, trying to reorder his thoughts. "When?"

"Today."

The tension in his chest slowly subsided. "I thought something terrible had happened. Your faces—"

"We thought you were Torven."

Karel blew out a breath, blew out the last of his tension. "What happened? Tell me."

The princess sat again, curling her feet under her. "I was just setting out to see Jaegar when he arrived. Frankl had been to see him. I've never seen him so furious!" She shivered. "I thought it was all over."

"But it's not?"

"No. I did what you told me to do. I cried all over him and begged his advice. And it worked. By the All-Mother's grace."

"You're staying for the coronation?"

She nodded. "I showed him the packing Yasma has done. That pleased him."

"And the boys? Why is he moving them?"

"Frankl pushed for it, and he *is* commander of the army. I think..." She frowned. "I think Jaegar moved against the boys too soon. I think he overstepped himself. He didn't expect opposition, from Frankl or any of the nobles, and now he's trying to mollify everyone until the coronation. It looks much more reasonable to have the boys confined up here, less like murder about to be done. And it keeps me amenable, too." She pulled a face. "We're all manipulating each other. Me. Jaegar. Frankl."

Karel considered the implications of the boys' move. They wouldn't have to traverse half the palace to reach them, access to the bondservants' corridors was closer, and there'd likely be fewer guards.

"I don't think Frankl will last long. Jaegar's voice, when he spoke of him..." Princess Brigitta shivered. "He'll start his reign with bloodshed. Not just Rutgar and Lukas, but Frankl and anyone else who raised objections to the boys' imprisonment."

DUKE FRANKL AND his sister came to visit that afternoon. The princess greeted them warmly, shed a few tears, thanked the duke profusely. She sent Yasma to the palace kitchens for sweetmeats and Karel out into the corridor. He stood with his back to the door for an hour, with Frankl and Lady Agata's armsmen, watching bondservants carry furniture into the storage room. He recognized the small gilded beds, the little table and chairs. They came from the princes' nursery.

The officer in charge of the palace dungeons came to examine the room and departed again.

Duke Frankl and his sister emerged from the princess's suite. Karel watched the duke from the corner of his eye. Frankl was a more subtle man than Duke Rikard, wooing the princess like this, rather than snatching her as Rikard had done.

Karel entered the parlor and closed the door. The princess stood in the centre of the room.

"What did Frankl want? He looked pleased."

"Oh..." She pulled a face. "He thinks I've agreed to a betrothal."

CHAPTER EIGHTEEN

GDELSK CAME INTO sight. Harkeld saw a high log palisade and steeply pitched wood-shingle roofs. Rain drummed down, blurring everything.

Rand met them a quarter mile from the gate. "The river's too high for the smaller boats, so several crossings have been canceled. With the backlog, we won't get across today. I've booked for dawn tomorrow."

"Can't be helped." Cora glanced at the trampled mire of mud, ox dung, and refuse surrounding the town, and grimaced.

"I took the liberty of reserving rooms at one of the smaller inns."

Cora looked at Rand, eyebrows raised.

"Although we can certainly camp out here, if you wish."

"Wish?" Her nose wrinkled. "No, I don't wish." She sighed and looked over her shoulder. "Gerit, Katlen, your opinions, please."

Harkeld had a strong opinion, but he kept silent while the witches debated the merits of staying in the town or camping outside it. They were the ones risking their lives to protect him.

"Very well," Cora said, with a nod at Rand. "Show us to this inn."

"Do you and Katlen wish to change into skirts first?"

Cora grimaced again. "I suppose we'd better."

* * *

FIFTEEN MINUTES LATER, they rode through the gates. Harkeld looked out from under his hood. Gdelsk had to be the ugliest town he'd ever seen, a bedraggled collection of log buildings that appeared to grow haphazardly out of the mud. Justen rode beside him, hand on his sword hilt, watching the few people scurrying along the filthy streets, scanning the doorways, examining the windows overlooking them.

The inn was two-storied, with a central courtyard off which stables opened. The five bedchambers Rand had reserved were on the top floor. Justen looked up and down the narrow corridor, opened the door to a bedchamber, trod across to the window and peered out. "Better than I thought. I doubt if even a monkey'd climb up that." He turned to Harkeld. "Station one of the mages outside the door as a dog and we should be safe."

Harkeld nodded and looked around the room. Two narrow, sagging beds, a wooden bench, a fireplace, and some hooks hammered into the walls. Basic, and not particularly clean, but it was dry. Praise the All-Mother, it was *dry*. "I wonder if they do baths."

Justen's face brightened. "We can hope."

They did do baths. While water heated in the kitchen downstairs, Harkeld unpacked his spare clothes. They were damp. He lit the fire, pulled the bench close, and draped his spare clothes over it to dry. He sent the armsman downstairs for a basin of hot water and a shaving kit, if the inn possessed such a thing. Justen came back with his arms full. The towel was threadbare, the mirror small and spotted with age, but the water was hot, the razor sharp, and the sliver of soap worked up a good lather. Harkeld propped the mirror on the windowsill and shaved. He dried his face afterwards and ran a hand over his jaw.

"You want to shave?" he asked the armsman.

"Ach, in a bit."

The bath came a few minutes later, first the copper tub, and then bucket after bucket of steaming water. Justen watched the servants, his hand close to his sword, not relaxing until the door was locked behind them.

Harkeld stripped and stepped into the tub. It was small, nothing like the sybaritic bathtubs at the palace, but he could sit with his knees drawn up and water halfway up his chest. He gave a deep sigh of pleasure.

He lathered his hair and skin and scrubbed himself with the brush the servants had provided. When he'd finished, the bathwater didn't look clean any more.

Harkeld glanced over the side of the bathtub. The servants had left two more buckets of water.

"Justen, rinse me off, will you?"

The armsman turned away from the window.

"Oh, you've shaved. You did that fast." And quietly. He hadn't heard the rasp of the razor through stubble.

Justen touched his chin, almost self-consciously, and shrugged. "Rinse you?"

Harkeld nodded at the buckets of water. "Pour them over me."

Justen obediently picked up a bucket and hefted it over Harkeld's head. Harkeld rinsed his hair and face in the stream of warm water, then stood and let the armsman empty the rest of the bucket over his chest and arms and back.

Justen hoisted the second bucket, pouring the water over Harkeld's groin and buttocks, his thighs, not looking directly at him, as if embarrassed by his nudity. Harkeld suppressed his amusement. It was unkind of him to find the armsman's bashfulness comical. He took the nearly-empty bucket and rinsed his calves and feet himself, stepping out onto the floor. "Thanks."

Justen handed him a towel.

Harkeld went to stand in front of the fire. He was clean. Truly clean. "By the All-Mother, that feels good," he said, drying his hair. "You should have one."

"I will... if you don't mind one of the mages guarding you?"

Harkeld shrugged. "No."

His spare clothes, if not completely dry, were nearly so, and warm from the fire. He dressed and looked down at the sodden, filthy garments on the floor. How many weeks since he'd washed them? "I wonder if they can launder these?"

The inn couldn't, but at least he didn't have to wear them until tomorrow, by which time they'd be dry. And until then he was clean and shaved. Harkeld hung his wet clothes on the hooks and went downstairs with Ebril and Rand, while the armsman bathed in fresh, steaming water.

CHAPTER NINETEEN

RUTGAR AND LUKAS arrived in their new quarters at dusk. Princess Brigitta visited them immediately, taking Karel with her even though the storeroom was only a few steps across the corridor. He stood just inside the door and examined the room. It was windowless, lit by candles, warmed by a small brazier. The only openings were the door and a ventilation slit near the ceiling. The beds had been placed against the far wall. In one corner, a woven screen shielded a chamberpot.

Two armsmen stood inside, and another armsman outside in the corridor. Karel silently thanked Duke Frankl. He'd made this significantly easier for them.

The princess sat on one of the beds. The boys clung to her, bewildered, frightened, crying. She held them, rocked them, kissed away their tears. After an hour, Lukas fell asleep sucking his thumb. Rutgar stayed awake, clutching his half-sister, not crying any more, his distress silent.

A nursemaid watched from one corner.

When the twelfth bell rang, the princesss carefully covered Lukas with a blanket. "Shhh," she whispered to Rutgar. "Don't wake him."

She undressed Rutgar, helped him into a nightshift, and tucked him into bed. "Will you stay all night?" the little boy asked, an edge of panic in his voice. He was thinner than he'd been four days ago, paler. He looked fragile, terrified.

"I can't, sweetheart."

Tears welled in his eyes.

"I promise I'll come back tomorrow." Princess Brigitta smoothed the hair back from Rutgar's face, kissed him. "I *promise*."

She held his hand and sang lullabies until he slept, then stood, beckoning to the nursemaid. "How have they been?"

"Not eating well, highness, nor sleeping well. Calling for you."

"My brother has given me permission to visit daily. I'll be back tomorrow morning. They may eat better if I'm here." Princess Brigitta clasped the woman's hand. "Thank you for looking after them."

The nursemaid curtseyed. "Highness."

Karel followed the princess from the storeroom, took two strides across the corridor, opened the door to her suite, and stood aside for her to pass.

Princess Brigitta halted just inside the parlor. She pressed her hands to her face.

"Britta?" Yasma came from the bedchamber. "Are you all right?"

The princess lowered her hands. "How can he do that to them?" There were tears in her voice, tears on her face. "His own brothers!"

Yasma hurried across the room. "We'll save them, Britta." She hugged the princess. "Come, let me take off your crown. And I brought dinner from the kitchens."

Karel paced the parlor while the princess and Yasma were in the bedchamber, holding the boys' faces in his mind. Rutersvard princes. *Am I insane?* Rutersvards were conquerors, oppressors. And yet he was risking his family's freedom for them.

No, that was wrong. If he was honest with himself, he was doing it for Princess Brigitta, because she loved the boys. And because, if this wild plan succeeded, she and Yasma would be free. And for *that*, almost any risk was worth it.

When you love people, you save them.

He paced from the marquetry table by the shuttered windows, to the far wall, and back. A trolley sat beside the table, with ashets and tureens. The smell of food wafted from beneath the silver lids.

The princess emerged from the bedchamber, her hair caught loosely at the nape of her neck, a leather pouch in her hand. "Yasma has an idea, Karel."

He lifted his eyebrows. "What?"

Yasma came to stand beside the princess. "If you die serving the king's interests, there'll be no penalty to your family, will there?"

"No." His death in the line of duty would carry the same weight as twenty years' good service. The last portion of his family's debt of servitude to Osgaard would be erased; they would be fully free. "But I can't come with you. Someone needs to witness your death."

"Britta says there's an armsman in the corridor, guarding the boys' door. What if we get *him* to witness our deaths? Then you can come too!"

Karel frowned. "Witness how?"

"Suppose Britta calls to him for help and he sees us lying here..." Yasma gestured to the floor. "In the middle of *lots* of blood."

Karel shook his head. "His duty is to guard the princes. He shouldn't move one step from that door."

"Even if Britta is covered in blood and calling for help? Don't you think he'd at least look in? She *is* a princess. It would be his duty, don't you think?"

Karel chewed the inside of his cheek. *What would I do in those circumstances?*

"And once he's seen you both, I'll spray him with All-Mother's Breath," Princess Brigitta said.

"Don't you think it could work?" Yasma asked.

"It increases the risk," Karel said, ignoring the voice in his head that urged him to agree with them. *Caution,* he told himself. That's what would carry them through this: caution. And taking as few risks as possible.

But hope of leaving Osgaard blossomed inside him, bright and painful.

Karel forced himself to shake his head. "He might come to the doorway, but he might just as easily call for help."

"Everyone will be at the coronation," Princess Brigitta said. "No one will hear him."

"The two armsmen inside the storeroom will."

"Then we'd have *three* witnesses."

"Please, Karel." Yasma tucked her hand into his. "Come with us."

Karel hesitated. "No," he said, firming his voice. "It's too risky."

Yasma's brow creased in distress, but the princess merely gave him a sharp glance and said, "We'll discuss this later. Yasma, let's eat. Will you join us? No?"

CHAPTER TWENTY

THE WITCHES GATHERED around a table in the corner of the taproom. Hew was in dog shape, sitting on the floor, ears pricked, alert. All three women wore ankle-length skirts. In trews and carrying swords, the female witches were noteworthy. They looked capable, skilled, even a little dangerous. In skirts, they were ordinary. Harkeld glanced around, looking for Petrus. Perhaps he was an insect hiding in a cranny somewhere?

The taproom was empty but for themselves and a man seated in the opposite corner; a merchant, by his garb. His girth was far too large for him to be an assassin.

A plump, pretty serving maid brought platters of food to their table—roasted vegetables, a haunch of venison, gravy, fresh bread and cheese—and tankards of ale.

Harkeld ate, half-listening to the witches talk. Their conversation was sporadic but relaxed, not glum, not edgy. He wasn't the only person whose mood had lifted.

The maid flirted with them as she cleared their plates, giggling and sending pert glances to him and Justen, to Ebril, to Frane. He could have told her it was pointless trying to seduce Justen; the armsman had sworn fidelity to his betrothed back in Groot.

The maid brought more ale and lingered to flirt. Harkeld eyed her. She had generous breasts and hips. She'd make a warm armful. And she was clearly bold, experienced, willing—all things he liked in a woman.

He glanced at Ebril and Frane. Frane's mouth was prudishly tight, but Ebril looked... not precisely neutral. Harkeld interpreted it as *If I wasn't on duty, I'd bed you.*

Harkeld gave a mental shrug. If no one else was going to take advantage of what was on offer, he would.

PETRUS LISTENED, HIS face carefully expressionless, as the prince ascertained that the maid was more than happy to accompany him upstairs for some bedsport and that she wouldn't get in trouble if she deserted her duties for half an hour.

"Excuse us, Justen," the prince said. He departed the taproom, his hand on the maid's waist, Hew padding at their heels. Petrus glanced down the table and caught the expression on Ebril's face—rueful, envious, reluctantly impressed. He suspected his own expression was similar.

Innis's expression was *not* impressed. Petrus bit the tip of his tongue to stop himself laughing at the indignation on her face.

"Ebril," Cora said, her voice dry. "Keep an eye on him."

"Must I? I doubt she's planning on killing him."

"It's not the bounty on his head she's interested in," Petrus said. "It's the bounty in his trews."

Rand snorted with laughter. Ebril grinned.

"Even so," Cora said, with a wave of her hand at the stairs.

Ebril lost his grin. He pulled a face and obeyed.

Petrus looked down the table again. Rand looked amused and Gerit, alongside him, sour. But whatever Gerit's opinion of the prince's tomcatting, he kept it to himself. Katlen wasn't so circumspect. "I wonder you allow him to carry on like that," she said tartly to Cora.

"Allow? He's an adult."

Rand looked even more amused. He covered his mouth with a hand.

"He's an untrained fire mage. He shouldn't have sex until he can control his magic. The risk is too great."

"Do you wish to tell him that?"

Katlen thinned her lips.

Rand lowered his hand. "I'd say he's been having sex for years. If he hasn't burned anyone yet, he's not going to tonight."

"And that's another thing," Katlen said. "I really think it should be me who teaches him, Cora. I've had twenty years' experience at the Academy."

"I asked him if he'd like you to instruct him, and he said no." Cora's tone took the sting out of the words. "I'd consider yourself lucky, if I were you, Katlen. Our Flin is... prickly."

Petrus snorted at this understatement.

"But—"

"I will certainly involve you in the lessons when we reach more dangerous practices."

Petrus slid down the bench to sit beside Innis. The indignation was gone from her face; she looked wan, unhappy. "Tired?" he asked, touching his knuckles lightly to the back of her hand.

"Oh..." She glanced at him, shrugged. "Can you teach me how to shave? I faked it today, but he almost noticed."

"I will," Petrus said. "But not now. You look tired. Why don't you sleep as yourself tonight? I'll be Justen."

Innis shook her head. "Thanks, but it's not necessary."

Petrus caught Cora's eye. "Why don't I be Justen all night? Innis hasn't slept as herself for a long time."

Innis opened her mouth as if to protest.

"Good idea. Thank you, Petrus."

"And that's another thing." Katlen's eyebrows twitched into a frown. "Surely it should be the male shapeshifters who are Justen. Innis is a *girl*. Why break a Primary Law unnecessarily?"

"Innis is our strongest shapeshifter," Cora said, her voice mild. "Dareus felt she was the best choice for this task."

Katlen opened her mouth as if she'd like to argue further, and then shut it.

I'd not argue with Dareus's judgment either. Although, come to think of it, he had, when Dareus had first outlined his plan.

He examined Innis's face. She'd changed in the last two months, become more confident, more assertive. Had Dareus anticipated that? Was that another reason for his choice?

Petrus picked up his tankard but didn't drink. He stared down at the dark ale. An arrogant mage was a dangerous mage, and Innis had more reason to be arrogant than any mage he knew. She was the strongest shapeshifter in living memory. No one had found her physical limits yet; only her sanity and conscience kept her in check. *And* she was a powerful healer, *and* the youngest Sentinel ever to take the oath. She could easily have become cocky, reckless, dangerous.

Petrus swallowed a mouthful of warm ale and put down his tankard. But a timid Sentinel was also dangerous. And Innis had been... if not precisely timid, then diffident, lacking in confidence. Sentinels needed to be decisive, unafraid to act. And when Innis was Justen, she was.

He examined her face again, seeing the arch of her dark eyebrows, the scattering of freckles across her nose, the lines of cheekbone and jaw. His heart squeezed in his chest. He laced his fingers tightly together, repressing the urge to stroke back a strand of curling black hair and tuck it behind her ear.

Not now. Not while they were on this mission. But afterwards...

Afterwards, he'd tell her how he felt and ask if they could become bonded.

CHAPTER TWENTY-ONE

AFTER SHE AND Yasma had eaten, the princess emptied the leather pouch. Silver and gold coins spilled across the table. "How much will you need tomorrow?"

Karel counted the gold coins. "Do you have more?"

The princess shook her head. "I could ask Jaegar for some, but... I'd rather not."

He nodded agreement. "It'll cost more than this to hire a ship, but when you reach Lundegaard, I'm sure King Magnas will pay the rest."

They settled on a dozen gold coins for his grace day, and a score of silver ones. Yasma tore up a piece of linen and they wrapped the coins in scraps of cloth. Karel slid them between his breastplate and his tunic. It was a tight fit; the coins pressed against his chest as he breathed.

"Well?" the princess asked.

Karel strode across the parlor and back. Nothing clinked, nothing fell out. "It's fine."

The princess gave him the list of herbs. Karel folded the parchment and tucked it inside one of his wrist greaves. The sound of a bell pealing came distantly. He counted the strokes. Only an hour until midnight. "You'd best retire."

"About Yasma's idea, don't you think—?"

"No," Karel said firmly.

Princess Brigitta tilted her head and examined his face. "We'll discuss it after your grace day." She scooped the remaining coins back into the leather pouch and stood for a moment, looking at him. Candlelight gilded her hair, made her eyes dark. "Be careful tomorrow."

KAREL WALKED TO the barracks, alert to any shifting of the coins inside his breastplate. His bunkroom was empty, the armsmen on duty or in the mess hall. He crouched and pulled his trunk out from beneath the bunk, unfastened the lid. His few possessions lay inside: plain shirt and trews for his grace days, a cloak, a small pouch of copper coins. He hid the list under the clothes and quickly loosened his breastplate, fished out the coins, slid them into the pouch. He closed the trunk and pushed it back beneath the bunk.

Karel went to the mess hall and joined the line of men waiting for food.

CHAPTER TWENTY-TWO

THEY ROSE EARLY, loaded the packhorses, and were at the jetty as dawn lit the sky. A light drizzle fell. Innis stared at the Ptol. She'd never seen a river so wide before. It must be half a mile across. She had to squint to see the far shore.

The water was thick and brown, flowing past the jetty with a quiet hiss.

Prince Harkeld sat on his horse alongside her. He looked relaxed, well-rested, almost cheerful.

Innis gritted her teeth and looked away. It was irrational to be so furious with him. *I am Justen,* she reminded herself. And Justen wouldn't be upset that the prince had bedded a tavern wench.

Hew maneuvered his horse alongside them. "See the cable? That's how the ferry crosses."

"They pull it by hand?" Prince Harkeld asked.

"No. There's a rudder which angles the boat upstream, and then the current pushes the ferry across the river on the cable." Hew frowned. "At least, that's what the stablehand at the inn said. I don't quite understand it myself."

"Huh." The prince shrugged. "I guess we'll find out."

The packhorses were loaded onto the flat-bottomed ferry. Innis stayed close to the prince, scanning the riverside. She saw a couple of women with baskets, an elderly man pushing a handcart. A youth with hair even redder than Ebril's leaned against a wall, watching something downstream, chewing a hunk of bread.

She followed his gaze. Logs were being unloaded into the water. Tree trunks bobbed as far downstream as she could see. "Where are they going?" she asked, pointing.

Prince Harkeld shrugged again. "Ankeny's major cities lie on the north coast. At a guess, there."

They dismounted and led their horses on to the ferry, Gerit circling overhead, a faint shimmer of magic coating his feathers. The boat cast off. Innis examined the jetty. The red-haired youth was idly watching them, but even as she looked, he turned away in disinterest, still eating his breakfast. The nose of the ferry swung into the current. They began to drift towards the opposite shore.

The woodcutters had been busy on the eastern bank, too. A half-mile-wide strip of logged land stretched on either side of the road. "More tree stumps," the prince said glumly.

CHAPTER TWENTY-THREE

KAREL ROLLED OUT of his bunk, dressed in plain trews and shirt and cloak, tied his money pouch to his belt and tucked the list of purchases into his pocket. All around, men slept. He heard someone snore, heard someone mutter, heard someone fart. He collected a grace pass from the duty commander and the coins he was owed. Copper pennies, not silver groats like the other armsmen were paid, because he was earning freedom with his service.

He showed the pass at the gate, walked under the portcullis, and out onto the furlong of bare ground between the palace walls and the town of Rakhamn. The sleet had stopped, but the wind still came from the south, bitterly cold, cutting through his cloak.

Karel inhaled deeply. The air was different out here. He couldn't taste the bondservants' misery with each breath, couldn't smell their fear.

He crossed the bare ground, striding fast, hugging his cloak around him. Breath plumed white from his mouth, whipped away by the wind. The paved marble road the nobles and high courtiers used was a hundred yards to his right, linking the main gates of the palace and the town. This track, for armsmen and guardsmen, lesser courtiers and artisans, was of packed dirt, crunching frostily beneath his boots. He glanced to his left, narrowing his eyes against the biting wind. Half a furlong distant was the road the princess would escape on, where wagons lumbered between the palace and the town all day and long into the night. A wagon laden with barrels moved heavily along it now.

Rakhamn was stirring. Smoke rose from chimneys. The shutters being thrown open looked like eyes blinking awake.

Karel headed down the cobbled streets to the harbor. Twice a year he walked this route, twice a year was free for a day. The whitewashed stone houses were familiar, the market square with its covered well and the bell where the hours were rung out, the shops with wooden signs hanging above the doors— baker, shoemaker, weaponmonger, apothecary.

The street curved, widened, opened out onto wharves. Here was the ocean. Karel filled his lungs with sea air. He tasted salt on his tongue, smelled fish, seaweed, wet ropes, woodsmoke.

Beyond the sheltering arms of the breakwater, the sea stretched wide in the bay. It was the same sea that lapped Esfaban's shores, yet so different. Cold. Gray. Nothing like Esfaban's clear blue-green waters.

Within the harbor, fishing boats jostled alongside merchant ships and naval vessels. Nets hung, drying, and gulls swooped and screamed. The smell of the nets was familiar, the sound of the gulls, the slap of waves on wooden hulls. If he closed his eyes, he could almost imagine he was home. Except there would be warm sand beneath his feet, not slabs of cold stone.

Karel shook off the memories of Esfaban. He scanned the moorings, counting the merchant vessels—fourteen—and the naval ships—five. He inspected the merchant ships, his gaze halting on one smaller and narrower than the others. A two-masted schooner. To his eyes, it looked to be the swiftest ship in the harbor.

He turned into a waterfront tavern. A copper coin bought him a half-tankard of ale, a plate of stew, bread and cheese. He ate slowly, studying the other patrons. Sailors, most of them, looking as if they'd been up all night. He bought another half-tankard, fell into talk with a bleary-eyed sailor, and by the time he exited the tavern he knew a lot more about the ships in the harbor. His eyes skimmed the vessels, halted on the schooner. The sailor had implied the crew were little better than privateers.

Karel walked along the wharf and stopped to chat with a man mending nets. Talk about fishing led to talk about boats, and the fisherman willingly gave his opinion of the merchant ships. "Wallow like a sow in mud," he said, dismissing three of them. "And them's as slow as a turtle swimming upstream." Four of the ships, he allowed, were fairly smart, and two had some speed in them, but the schooner was the only one that could really fly.

"Faster than them?" Karel asked, pointing to the naval vessels.

"Do fish piss in the sea?"

Karel took that as a yes. "Has it been here long?"

"Three, four days."

Karel let the conversation drift back to fishing and left the man ten minutes later. A stroll up to the main square told him that the apothecary's shop was now open.

He retraced his steps until he came to a two-storied building squatting on the waterfront. *The Lucky Sailor*. Half-tavern, half-whorehouse. He'd been here once, on his first grace day as an armsman, and never since.

Karel pushed open the door. The taproom was dimly lit, warm, smelling of ale and food, sweat and woodsmoke. A fire burned in the wide grate. Despite the early hour, *The Lucky Sailor* was doing good business. A dozen men sat at tables or leaned against the tapster's counter.

He bought a half-tankard and stood at the scarred wooden counter, sipping slowly, eying the other patrons, keeping his hood up. A girl in a low-cut gown crossed to him. "Wan' come upstairs w' me, sailor?" she asked, her eyes half-focused. "Two pennies f' an hour."

"Later."

The girl pouted and drifted towards another customer.

Karel watched a sailor come down the stairs, buckling his belt. The man crossed to the tapster, opened his money pouch, emptied it. A thin copper half-penny fell out.

Karel waited until the tapster had poured the man an ale. "Leaving port soon?"

The sailor shook his head. "Not till next week."

Shame. The man would have been perfect. Drunk, but not too drunk. Short of money. And not Osgaardan.

Karel sipped his ale. Sailors entered the tavern, climbed the stairs to the wenching rooms, reappeared fastening their belts, ordered ale, wine, spirits, food. Some had too much money for his needs, some were too drunk, others too sharp-eyed and alert, or spoke with Osgaardan accents.

It took half an hour before he found what he was looking for. The sailor was less than half-drunk, genial, had spent his last pennies, and was leaving Osgaard tomorrow.

Karel bought the man an ale and invited him to sit at a table, choosing one in the darkest corner of the room. "Good bedsport upstairs?"

The sailor took a long swallow and wiped his mouth with the back of his hand. "Nice 'n plump," he said cheerfully. "Just how I like 'em."

"Shame you can't buy yourself another hour."

The sailor shrugged philosophically. "One rut's better than none."

"True," Karel said. He let his tone grow thoughtful, "You know, I could see my way to slipping you some coins... if you do me a favor."

"What kind of favor?"

"I need to buy some items from the apothecary." *And I need not to be seen doing it.* "He won't serve me because I look like an islander."

The sailor grimaced. "Osgaard. My least favorite kingdom. You're lucky you're not one of them slaves they have here, whatever they call 'em."

"Bondservants."

The sailor took a slurping mouthful of ale. "Sure, I can do that for you."

Karel took the list from his pocket. "Here."

The sailor unfolded it, read it squinting, and raised his eyebrows. "All-Mother's Breath? Need to knock someone out?"

"I'm a tooth-puller."

"Tooth-puller?" The sailor screwed up his face. "Rather you 'n me."

Karel shrugged. "Someone's got to do it." He unfastened his money pouch and took out four silver groats. Three, he slid across the table. The fourth, he held between thumb and forefinger. "This one's for you, afterwards."

The sailor grinned, drained his tankard, and stood. "Where's the apothecary?"

Karel told him. "And remember, no mention of me."

"My word on it." The sailor hitched his belt higher up his hips and exited the tavern, whistling.

Karel sat, counting the minutes, sipping his ale. Had he been wrong in his judgment of the man? Would the sailor return? Or would he decide that three groats in his pocket now was better than one later?

He'd just decided that the sailor wasn't coming back, when the man returned, a grin on his face and a small bundle wrapped in hessian under his arm.

Karel bought him another tankard. He checked no one was watching and unwrapped the bundle. He put the emetic and its antidote to one side, unfamiliar with them; he'd have to trust the apothecary was honest. The packet of dried leaves was pepperwort. They had no odor, but tasted strongly of pepper, burning his tongue.

Karel rinsed his mouth out with ale, glanced around the taproom again, and unwrapped the dried Horned Lily root. Four tubers, like shriveled pink carrots. They *looked* genuine. He picked one up, sniffed it, took a bite from the end. He recognized the taste from his armsman's training, slightly sweet. Karel chewed and swallowed, glancing idly around the taproom while he counted to one hundred. Then he uncorked the vial of All-Mother's Breath. He sniffed cautiously. The scent filled his nose, pungent, vanilla-like. That was familiar, too.

Karel recorked the vial. "Did he ask about this?"

"He did." The sailor winked. "I said I was the tooth-puller on our ship."

Karel laughed, relaxing. He rewrapped the bundle. "Here." He gave the man a groat. "Thank you."

The sailor fished in his pocket and pulled out four copper pennies and a silver half-groat. "Your change. I forgot."

Karel took the half-groat. "Keep the rest. As payment for your honesty."

The sailor grinned. "I'll spend it now. Good day to you."

Karel's smile faded as the man went upstairs. He'd climbed those stairs once himself, three years ago, holding the first coins he'd earned. He'd climbed those stairs and paid his pennies—and found himself unable to choose a whore. They weren't bondservants, terrified and trapped, they were paid for spreading their legs, but their eyes had seemed to stare right through him.

How could he bed a woman with eyes like that?

Karel stowed the bundle beneath his cloak, looping one of the strings around his belt, and headed out into the cold.

He walked the length of the wharf, examining the vessels. At the eastern end, coal was being unloaded. Bondservants labored, cringing from the overseer's whip. Beyond the breakwater, the river that ran beneath the palace flowed into the bay, carrying the palace's sewage. The wind carried the stink to him. Gulls wheeled and swooped, shrieking.

Karel turned and retraced his steps. He stopped to talk with sailors he met. *Which ship are you from? When are you leaving?* Casual, friendly questions. His eyes returned time and again to the two-masted schooner. It was almost noon. He had to make a decision, had to act. Which ship should he choose?

A rowboat pushed away from the schooner. Oars dipped, splashed.

Karel watched it intently.

The rowboat drew close. Three men were in it. They secured the boat and clambered out.

The sailors walked halfway down the wharf and entered a ship chandler's warehouse. Karel followed. The smell of the warehouse filled his nose. New rope, pitch and tar, tallow. He browsed the offerings—barrels of iron nails, of turpentine, of lard, of peppercorns—listening to the three men.

One sailor was giving orders. "Salt," he said. "And lamp oil." His vowels were round, his consonants guttural. He had a broad, ruddy face and a pointed sandy beard.

Karel fixed the man in his memory and strolled out of the chandler's. He waited on the wharf, listening to the gulls and the slap of waves against the piles. Yasma's voice whispered in his ear: *Please, Karel, come with us.* Hope stung in his breast, bright, painful. The All-Mother knew he *wanted* to leave Osgaard.

He went over her plan in his head. It could work. If it looked like he'd died trying to prevent the princess's escape, there'd be no penalty to his family.

But the risk...

And if he went with them, he could never return to Esfaban.

It was more than eight years since he'd left. Were his parents even alive? His mother, mute after her bondservice, his father with his scarred, broken hands.

If they weren't already dead, they would be before he returned. They'd all known that when he left.

Grief filled his eyes with tears. He blinked them back, scowled at the chandler's warehouse.

If their plan worked, Yasma would never return to Esfaban either. Her family would think her dead. They'd mourn her. But their debt of bondservice would be erased and they'd move to the next step, sending a son to train as armsman or guardsman or soldier. And after his service, they'd be free.

If it looks as if I've died for Osgaard, my family will be free.

Free, seventeen years early. Wasn't that worth never returning?

But the risk. The *risk*. He could plunge them all into bondservice if anything went wrong. Not just his parents again, but his sisters, his aunts and uncles, cousins.

It was a problem without a solution. Karel shoved it aside and focused on the chandler's warehouse. "Come out, come out," he muttered under his breath.

Quarter of an hour later, the sailors emerged and split up. Karel followed the man who'd given the orders. He lengthened his stride, caught up to him, then slowed, matching his steps to the sailor's. "You from the schooner?"

The man halted. "Who are you?"

"I'm looking to hire a ship. Departing in four days to Lundegaard. Could you do that?"

"What cargo?"

"A few people."

"A whole ship for a few people?" The sailor studied his face, and then glanced at his cloak and boots. "Doubt you could afford it."

"I'll pay in gold."

"How much gold?"

"You the captain?"

"First mate."

"I'll discuss payment with your captain."

The man stared at him, narrow-eyed, and then shrugged. "All right."

"Now?"

The sailor shrugged again. "If you wish."

THEY ROWED OUT to the schooner. Her name was *Sea Eagle*. Karel spoke with the captain and examined the ship.

"What do you think?"

The captain was darker-skinned than an Esfaban islander, but his eyes were light gray. He had a clipped, pointed beard like the first mate's, and a melodic accent.

"You're familiar with Lundegaard's ports?"

"Sailed into the Hook a few times, and Forsmouth once."

"How many days to get there?"

"Five to the Hook and another one to Forsmouth. Less, if the wind favors us."

Karel nodded and glanced around the deck, noting the stained planks, the messily coiled ropes, the bucket rolling on its side. "What cargoes do you usually carry?"

"All sorts."

"Such as?"

"Our last load was spices."

"What were you planning on carrying from here?"

"Hadn't found a cargo yet."

Karel turned to face the man fully. "I heard a rumor you're privateers."

"Us?" The man laughed. "Of course not!"

Something in his laugh struck Karel as false. If these sailors weren't privateers, they were close to it. Opportunists, ready to do dirty work if they could see a profit in it.

"I want to see the cabin again."

He inspected it carefully; a large room, with a closet off one end where a chamberpot could go. The bed was built into a wooden alcove, wide enough for the princess and the boys to sleep in together. Only one entry point, unless one counted the window looking out to sea, which was too small for a man to enter through.

The door was solidly built and had a crossbar. With the bar in place, it would be almost impossible to break down.

"Well?" the captain asked.

The ship was perfect. The cabin was perfect. But the crew...

Karel looked at the captain. *I don't trust you.*

He walked to the window and looked out. Choppy gray sea, stone wharf, whitewashed houses. The palace wasn't visible, but he could imagine it—creamy marble and golden roof tiles, armsmen in their scarlet tunics, bondservants. *Please, Karel, come with us.*

He'd have to, if he hired this ship. If he didn't, there was a chance Yasma and Princess Brigitta wouldn't reach Lundegaard. Two beautiful young women. What would these men do to them? Honor the contract? Sell them into a brothel?

One of the larger merchant ships would be safer. But he'd questioned men from most of them, and not found one that was leaving when he needed, in the direction he needed. The merchant ships had cargoes, schedules to keep. And they were slower. The naval vessels would easily outstrip them.

Karel stared at the sea and thought of his family. *The risk...*

But if it worked, they'd be free.

Wasn't that worth never seeing Esfaban again?

He turned to the captain. "I'll need two extra beds. Mattresses or pallets or truckles."

"Easily done."

"Oil lamps or candles. A brazier. A couple of chamberpots."

The captain nodded.

"I'll pay you ten gold pieces now, another twenty when we set sail, and twenty more once we reach Lundegaard."

BACK ON LAND, Karel headed to Rakhamn's market square. A mixture of hope and panic churned in his chest. He walked past the weaponmonger's shop, glancing at the swords hanging there. He'd need new weapons if he was to flee the palace.

He took a turn around the market square, weaving his way between stalls and wagons, past bleating sheep in pens, piled skeins of wool and bolts of fabric, cartloads of turnips and dried fish. A traveling metalsmith's wagon was drawn up on the northern side of the square. Pots hung on hooks, shovel blades and hammer heads and scythes. Karel paused. "You have any daggers?"

The metalsmith looked up from sharpening a long-tined fork. "A few." He hauled a wooden crate out from inside the wagon, pulled out a hessian-wrapped bundle and opened it, laying five daggers out.

Karel inspected them. They were plain, sturdy, sharp. "How long are you here for?"

"Leaving tomorrow," the man said. He was chewing a wad of tobacco. He shifted it from one cheek to the other as he spoke.

"What? Not staying for the coronation?"

The man shook his head, cleared his throat, and spat. The brown phlegm on the cobblestones seemed an indication of his feelings for the Rutersvards.

"When will you be back?"

"Couple of months."

"I'll take this one. I don't suppose you have any swords?"

The man glanced at him, trying to see his face beneath the hood. "Might have a couple."

"May I see them?"

The metalsmith brought out three swords. Two had decorated hilts, the third was plain. Karel inspected them carefully, examining the blades. "You made these?"

"Just that one." The metalsmith pointed to the plainest sword. "It's the best of them."

The man glanced at him again, his eyes narrowing as he tried to see Karel's face. "I know."

Karel hefted the weapon in his hand. The weight and balance were similar to his armsman's sword. "I'll take it."

The metalsmith stowed the other two away and put the daggers back in the wooden crate. A curving gleam of metal at the bottom of the crate caught Karel's eye. "Is that a throwing star? May I see?"

The man handed it to him silently.

"Ah..." Karel said, disappointed. "It's not real."

"Iron," the metalsmith said with a shrug. "Made it for fun."

Karel turned the throwing star over in his hand. It was no weapon. The balance was wrong, the blades not sharp enough, but it *looked* real...

Possibilities spun in his head, decisions clicked into place. "I'll take it. My son will love it."

He paid for his purchases with the last of the gold coins. The metalsmith wrapped the weapons in hessian and tied the bundle with twine.

"I wish you safe journey," Karel said.

The man nodded and went back to sharpening fork tines.

After that, the afternoon sped by so quickly that Karel almost felt dizzy. The large wooden trunk and padlock and bolt of red fabric he purchased himself, openly, with his hood pushed back, but everything else was bought by sailors leaving Rakhamn before the coronation. He spun tales, bought tankards of ale, gave out pennies and groats. In exchange they brought him clothes, food, a sword belt, a leather rucksack, a second smaller trunk and padlock. The edge of panic faded. In the late afternoon, he walked through the town, towing a hired handcart. On it were the trunks, one inside the other, and inside them, all the purchases except for the apothecary's parcel tied to his belt. The padlock he'd bought dangled from the hasp of the outermost trunk, rattling as the handcart lurched over the uneven cobblestones.

As dusk approached, he reached the gates used by wagons travelling to and from the palace. Here the cottages were poorer, the whitewash gray, the shutters hanging crooked. He glanced at the town wall. It was lower than the towering palace walls, the mortar crumbling around the blocks of stone. No guard patrolled its ragged top, no guards stood at the inward and outward gates stopping wagons. Such security measures were for the palace.

Karel stepped aside as a wagon piled with grain sacks passed. He watched it lumber through the right-hand gate, rumbling on the cobblestones. The sound of the wheels changed as it passed onto the paved road to the palace.

Another wagon labored up the street towards the gate. Coal, this time.

Karel listened as it passed beneath the gate. The rumble of wheels on stone became smoother. *Good to know*.

He turned his attention to the nearby dwellings. He wanted one with a shed and no dog.

There were a number that suited his needs, but one that he preferred. The yard was a small wedge of weedy ground between the back of the cottage and the town wall, not overlooked by any windows. The shed was in the farthest corner, lopsided, half tumble-down.

Karel knocked on the cottage door.

A woman answered, a crying baby on her hip and a toddler clutching her skirt. Her face was thin and tired. Wisps of hair straggled from her bun. "What?"

Karel pushed his hood back and smiled at her. "I'm an armsman at the palace. I wondered if I might pay you to store this trunk for me in your shed." He opened his hand, let the woman see the pennies he held.

Her eyes fastened on the coins, then lifted to his face. She squinted at him suspiciously. "You're an islander."

"Yes. My parents were bondservants; I'm an armsman."

The woman shifted the baby to her other hip. It didn't stop wailing.

"I want to send this trunk to my family once I've filled it." Karel gestured to the trunk on the handcart. "It'll take me a few years. Is there perhaps space in your shed for me to store it?"

The woman looked at the trunk, at the copper coins on his palm, and lastly at his face again. "Mebbe."

"Shall we have a look?"

The woman led him round to the yard, the baby wailing on her hip. The toddler came too, silent, dirty-faced, bare-footed, clutching at her skirt. Two wagons rumbled past from the palace, empty and rattling.

The shed held firewood, old tools, broken buckets.

"If you can fit it in, you can store it," the woman said, lifting the crying baby from one hip to the other.

"Your husband...?"

"He won't mind. Anything for a few pennies."

"You don't have a dog?"

"No. We got too many chil'en to want another mouth to feed."

"You have more?" Karel asked, feeling pity for her.

"Two more."

He cleared space immediately inside the door, piling the firewood higher. Was this all the fuel they had for winter?

They'll freeze. The toddler watched wide-eyed, its thumb in its mouth, as Karel slung the trunk down from the handcart, trying to make it look as if it was nearly empty.

He checked the padlock, then gave the woman the pennies. The baby on her hip still cried. "I don't know when my next grace day will be. Not for another six months or more, most likely. I only get two a year."

She nodded, gripping the coins tightly. Dusk was falling, darkness growing like fog around them.

"If you or your husband should change your minds, if you wish me to remove the trunk, you may send a message to me at the palace. My name is Karel. I'm personal armsman to Princess Brigitta."

"We won't change our minds."

He accompanied the woman back to her front door. "Thank you."

The woman nodded, hefting the crying baby to her other hip. She chivvied her toddler inside and closed the door.

Karel stood back to let another wagon carrying coal pass, then trundled the handcart down the street. It bounced along the cobblestones, rattling loudly. At the corner, he looked back. The sky, the wall, the buildings, had lost their color, become gray.

The tenth bell tolled. He heard it ringing from the palace and the town square. As the last notes faded, a wagon emerged from the left-hand gate. It wasn't empty. Something was heaped in its tray.

Karel watched it approach. *Is it...?*

The rich smell of horse dung filled his nose.

Yes.

Karel examined the wagon as it passed, carrying manure from the palace stables. He ran his gaze over the pile of dung, over the wagon's sides, its tailboard, turning and watching until the vehicle was gone from sight.

In four days' time, he'd be on that wagon, with the princess and Yasma and the boys.

*   *   *

KAREL RETURNED THE handcart to the market square and spent his last coins on a meal. He sat for a while, nursing a tankard of ale, going over everything in his head. Was there anything he'd forgotten?

When he'd finished, he walked back to the wagon gates, the hood pulled over his face. The streets weren't completely dark; torches burned in brackets.

The gates were lit with torches too. There was still no guard. Karel observed the torches thoughtfully, then glanced down the street. Fifty yards of darkness, and then another torch.

A wagon approached from the town. He heard its wheels on the cobblestones.

Karel stepped back into the shadows. He closed his eyes and listened intently. Yes, the change when the wheels went from cobblestones to paving stones was quite distinct; the choppy rumble became a smoother, lower sound.

He waited for a wagon from the palace and counted the seconds it took to travel from the illuminated gate, along the stretch of dark street, to the distant torch.

Twice more he listened, counting the seconds.

Nine seconds. Nine seconds to get five people out from under a pile of horse dung. *Can we do it?*

CHAPTER TWENTY-FOUR

THAT NIGHT IT took Harkeld a while to find Innis. She was in one of the gardens furthest from the palace, standing beside a water lily pond.

He walked across to her. "I've been looking everywhere for you."

Innis turned her head and looked at him, her gaze cool. "I don't want to be with you tonight."

"Why not?"

"Because I'm too angry with you." She turned and walked away.

"Why?" Harkeld called after her, baffled, irritated.

Innis swung round, fury on her face. "You had sex with that whore."

"What?"

Innis didn't repeat the words, just turned her back again and headed for a gap in the hedge and the path beyond.

Harkeld strode after her. "It was just a bit of *fun*, curse it!"

Innis didn't stop, didn't turn around.

"And she wasn't a whore," he yelled at her back. "She didn't ask for money. She *enjoyed* it."

CHAPTER TWENTY-FIVE

BRITTA SPENT THE morning with her brothers, drawing pictures on sheets of parchment for them to color in. Woodcutters with axes for Lukas. Horses for Rutgar.

The door to the storeroom opened. She lifted her head and watched two armsmen come in. The men they replaced left without uttering a word. The door closed again.

Britta laid down her quill. There were no windows, so she couldn't hear the noon bell, but she knew it was ringing. Which meant that Karel had replaced Torven in the corridor outside.

"Darlings..." She smoothed hair back from Lukas's brow. "I need to go for a while, but I promise I'll come back."

Rutgar's head jerked up. She saw panic in his eyes.

"We'll have supper together," Britta said, leaning over to kiss him. "I'll order it from the kitchens. What would you like? Fried blood sausage? Roast chicken?"

Choosing food distracted the boys from tears, but she was aware of their anxiety as she rose to her feet. "I expect to see these colored in when I return," she said cheerfully. "Frida will help you."

The nursemaid nodded and took her place at the table.

One of the armsmen opened the door. Britta waved to the boys and stepped into the corridor.

An armsman stood to her left, at parade rest. And across from him and two paces to the right, in front of her own door, stood Karel.

Britta crossed the corridor. Karel silently opened the door and followed her inside.

SHE SAT AT the marquetry table with Yasma, listening to Karel tell his tale. The armsman's face was sterner than usual, his black eyebrows slanting together.

"The *Sea Eagle*?" Yasma said. "It's a nice name."

"And a fast ship. The fastest in port. Faster than the naval vessels. But the crew..." Karel's eyebrows pinched even closer together. "I don't trust them. So... I'm coming with you."

Yasma gasped. "Karel!"

"There's no point risking everything to get you out of here," Karel said, "only to have you thrown overboard."

"You think they might do that?" Britta asked.

"That or worse."

"And if you come with us, they won't?" Britta frowned. Was he *that* good a fighter?

A smile touched the corners of Karel's mouth. "I bought a throwing star. Fake, but it looks real. I'll talk like that poison master. Use the same words, the same tone. If they think I'm Fithian, they won't dare touch you."

"You, a Fithian?" Britta lost her frown. "Excellent, Karel!"

He shrugged and continued with his tale. Britta listened closely. "You saw the dung wagon? It reached the town at dusk? But someone could see us getting out!"

"On coronation day, the palace gates are shut from noon till nightfall. The wagon won't leave until full dark."

"You're certain?"

"Yes. The orders were given last week. And all the guardsmen and armsmen are changing shift early. Everyone, on duty or off, will be at the ceremony. Yasma, what have the bondservants been told?"

"We're to kneel in the Great Courtyard from noon until nightfall. Every last one of us. Even if it snows."

"That includes the kitchen bondservants?"

"Until the eighth bell. Then they go back to work."

Karel nodded. "So, we get the pigs' blood first. Yasma, where exactly is the tub? Near the scullery?"

From the tub of pigs' blood, they moved to the sewer system. "The closest hole may be too small for Karel," Yasma said. "I'll check. How wide's your breastplate?"

"We can leave it behind," the armsman said. "In fact, that'll look better. Especially if there's blood on it."

"Will a dinner trolley carry both your bodies?"

They all looked at the silver trolley standing beside the door to the bondservants' corridor.

"Yes," Yasma said.

They went through everything in meticulous detail, planning the coronation day to the last quarter hour, making notes on a sheet of parchment. "I'll make the masks this afternoon," Yasma said. "Britta has some black silk sashes. I'll cut eyeholes."

"And we need to test these," Karel said, gesturing to the items he'd taken from his breastplate—pepperwort, Horned Lily roots, All-Mother's Breath, the emetic and its antidote.

"I'll set the pepperwort to steep today," Yasma said.

Karel picked up the vial of All-Mother's Breath. "We'll try this on me tomorrow. The dosage *has* to be strong enough to knock out an armsman for several hours." He glanced at her. "Did Duke Frankl come courting yesterday?"

Britta nodded. "With his sister, yes."

"What time?"

"Oh..." She glanced out the window. "About now." She pushed back her chair, suddenly anxious. "We should hide these!"

Britta concealed everything in her bedchamber, while Yasma went to fetch the boys' supper from the palace kitchens. When she went out to the parlor, Karel was looking at the map of Osgaard. Something in the set of his mouth, the tilt of his head, made her hesitate before crossing to him. "What is it?"

Karel was silent a moment. "I can never return to Esfaban."

"I'm sorry."

"It's not your fault. The choice is mine. And my family will have their freedom seventeen years early because of it."

Britta followed his gaze, seeing the string of islands arcing towards the equator, the blue-tinted seas, the golden shores. "Esfaban looks beautiful."

"It is," Karel said. "The most beautiful place in the world."

CHAPTER TWENTY-SIX

THERE WAS NO frontier post on the high plateau. Somewhere in the wilderness of saw-leafed grass and thorny scrub, Nolt took his band from Sault into Roubos. At times they saw small herds of black and gray goats that vanished into the scrub in the wink of an eye. One afternoon, Nolt nodded to Steadfast, a slender man with sleek black hair and slanting eyes. Stead strung his bow and rode away. He came back with two young goats, skinned and gutted, strung across his horse's neck. They ate fresh meat that night, tender and running with fat.

Jaumé got his share, and Bennick gave him a bone to gnaw. He washed his hands and face afterwards in the creek. He had seen how clean these men were—clean, tidy, quick—and he strove to be like them.

But mostly they ate food bought at the hamlets they passed. Bread, dried meat. There was no flight here from the curse. Some people refused to believe in it. Others thought it wouldn't cross the highlands into Roubos. They carried on with their lives, herding and harvesting and threshing barley. Some called out for news, but Nolt stayed silent.

The farmers calling questions made Jaumé think of Mam and Da, and his sister Rosa. He tried to keep them in his head the way they'd been before the curse, but never managed it for long; soon there was blood on Da's hands and blood around his mouth, and Mam lay in the kitchen, torn and dead, and the stink of blood was everywhere, and Rosa was screaming...

He pushed it out of his head the only way he knew, by looking at Bennick beside him, and the men ahead, and telling himself they were on their way to fight the curse. They were going to destroy it.

Smoke hazed the sky beyond a row of hump-backed hills. Nolt slowed their pace to a walk, and sent Stead and Odil scouting ahead.

"They're burning stubble," Jaumé said, trying to show his knowledge. There had been smoke from stubble-burning down on the plains, and Da had burned his fields that way.

Bennick shook his head. "Wrong smell."

Stead and Odil rode back and Odil spoke briefly with Nolt. Jaumé couldn't hear the words.

Nolt handed Odil an object that looked like a brass mug, and sent him up the hill. Jaumé watched, puzzled, as Odil turned the brass mug into a tube as long as his forearm and put the end to his eye. He glanced at Bennick.

"Spyglass," Bennick said.

Odil waved them on. They rounded the hill and found the back fields of a farm—unburned stubble. Beyond a red barn, smoking and blackened, stood the ruins of a farmhouse. Tongues of flame licked a half-fallen wall.

The men cantered into the yard, holding their horses steady against the smell of blood.

Five bodies lay in the yard. An old man and a younger, both disemboweled, two young boys, one headless, the other hacked almost in half, and a woman with blood running into her blonde hair and her skirts upflung to cover her face. Jaumé jerked his gaze away from the lower part of her body. He didn't want to see what had been done to her.

"Barn," Nolt said, and two of the men rode away.

Jaumé's ribcage seemed to squeeze tightly around his innards. Blood. Death. Fire. He turned to Bennick. "The curse! It's here. It's caught up with us!"

Bennick shook his head. "This is hillmen, lad. They raid the farms. And anything passing on the roads."

Jaumé looked at the bodies, jerked his eyes away. His arms and legs, his chest, were trembling. "Why?"

"For what they can get. Food. The killing's for fun. And the rape."

Fun? He wanted to cry, to vomit, and knew he must do neither of those things. "Will they come after us?"

Bennick shrugged, unconcerned, watching Ash and Kimbel trot back from the barn. Young Kimbel had a dead goose slung over his saddle.

"They've taken what they can carry. It's a poor place," Ash said.

They left the farm behind. Jaumé tried not to think about the bodies. He'd thought Nolt would bury them, but he'd left them lying where they died and not even said words to the All-Mother for them.

The road wasn't much more than a cart track, running between hills and a stream. Nolt sent Brothers out each side as scouts. Bennick was one, and Jaumé watched him anxiously; it was the most dangerous place to be. Copses of trees rose like islands in water, too small to hide a band of twenty or more men, which Nolt, reading hoof-prints on the track, reckoned was the strength of the raiders.

The prints turned off towards the hills, but Nolt left Odil out scouting, and soon Odil reined in his horse. He dismounted and eased forward and lay peering at something on the other side of the hill. He used the spyglass again, then made a series of arm movements.

"Twenty-six. Spears and bows. They're behind trees, down the other side," Bennick whispered to Jaumé.

Nolt waved in Odil.

"They know we're here," Odil said.

"So we'll make them come to us." Nolt led them across the stream to a low, dense copse. They broke into the center, leading the nervous horses. "Tie them, boy," Nolt said. "And stay with them."

The eight Brothers unstrapped their bows from the packhorses, stepped back into the trees and disappeared.

Jaumé tied the horses, and in a moment heard men talking and laughing from somewhere outside the copse. He smelled woodsmoke. Did that mean they were boiling water? Getting ready to cook the goose from the farm? The hillmen would see the smoke and come. Was that the plan? He needed to see.

Jaumé checked the knots securing the horses, then eased his way under sharp foliage to the edge of the copse. The fire was halfway between the trees and the stream. Two billies of water rested in the flames. The Brothers sat eating bread, joking and laughing in a way Jaumé hadn't heard them before. They had no weapons.

A bow and a sheaf of arrows leaned on the trunk of a tree, hidden from sight, and further along were other bows and swords and throwing knives. He understood: the raiders must show themselves as they rode down the track or down from the hill, whichever they chose, and Nolt and his men were only twenty yards from cover and their weapons.

But there were only eight of them, against twenty-six.

Jaumé wondered if he was going to die, then heard Bennick laugh. He wriggled half on hands and knees and half on his belly for a clearer look, and saw that it was no pretence; the men were relaxed and enjoying their bread. Young Kimbel walked away from the fire and pissed on the ground, then washed his hands in the stream.

The hillmen came with a thunder of hooves and a prolonged cry like the howling of wolves. They galloped along the track, spears held high. Nolt and his men pretended to act in fear. They ran like rabbits for the copse, Kimbel a dozen steps behind, and Jaumé barely had time to slide back into hiding. He drew his knife, but saw how useless it would be. He crept a little sideways, looking for a place where he could see what happened. The hillmen came charging, bareback, their wolf call rising until it filled the sky. Jaumé saw Bennick in the foliage. He was standing easily, an arrow nocked on his bow-string. Nolt was further along, and a shine of silver hair showed Ash on the other side.

The bunched hillmen clattered across the stream, yelling and joyous, thinking they had easy prey hiding in the copse. Each strained to get ahead of the others. Their skulls were shaved apart from a crest like a horse's mane. Their eyes glared, their teeth were bared as though to bite, and the dangling bones ornamenting their chests rattled like sticks on hollow logs. Their yellow ponies, as hairy as goats, were almost as fierce. Their nostrils flared.

Jaumé lay frozen in terror. These men were worse than anything he'd imagined. The rattling bones, the crested heads. He wanted to burrow into the ground and hide.

The hillmen reined in by the abandoned fire, and sprang from their ponies. With spears held high, they charged at the copse.

Jaumé didn't see Nolt's signal, but suddenly arrows sank into the chests or throats of the charging hillmen. Eight of the raiders fell—he didn't need to count, he knew none of the Brothers had missed—and then another eight as the hillmen turned and ran, their howls turning into cries of panic. The survivors used the ponies as cover and fled in a pack, crossing the stream and stopping out of bow-shot.

"Wait," Nolt said, and his men stayed hidden.

The hillmen captured some of their ponies and mounted. They milled and argued, some frightened, others still fierce. A thickset man, his mane of hair matted into long yellow tails, seemed to take charge.

"They want their dead," Nolt said. He looked at Bennick. "Too far?"

Bennick answered by taking another arrow and nocking it. Jaumé crawled under a branch to see better.

Bennick stepped into the open and ran his eye past the fire, past the stream, to the distant hillmen and their leader. Jaumé saw the way he didn't think or calculate again, but raised the bow, drew the bowstring back until his fingers touched his jaw, and released it. This time, Jaumé saw the arrow in its flight, rising quicker than a falcon and swooping downwards at the end. It buried itself in the throat of the man with the matted yellow hair. He tumbled from his pony.

There was a high shriek of fear, a clatter of hooves, and the hillmen fled back along the track. The riderless ponies galloped after them.

"Nine left," Nolt said. "They won't be back."

"They'll come in the night for their dead," said Ash.

Old Maati and young Kimbel moved among the fallen men. They slit the throats of three who were still alive. Jaumé looked away. Blood. Blood everywhere. The curse seemed to reach out towards him.

"Boy," Nolt said, not turning.

Jaumé crept from his cover, his heart thudding hard in his chest.

"I told you to stay with the horses."

Jaumé couldn't speak. He saw with terror that Nolt was going to leave him behind.

Black-skinned Gant came out of the copse. "He tied them," he told Nolt.

"He had his knife out," Ash said.

"Did you want to fight them, boy?"

"Yes," Jaumé managed to say.

Nolt looked at him, narrow-eyed. He grunted. "One mark. Another one and you're out. Now get the arrows and clean them."

Jaumé moved among the dead hillmen. Some of the arrows came out easily, others he had to work at with two hands. One, fixed in a man's head, wouldn't move. Bennick came and pulled it out. He said nothing, but pointed at the stream. Jaumé washed blood from the arrows. He checked them for damage and took them to the men, knowing who owned each pair from the color and set of the feathers. Gant and young Kimbel thanked him, Ash winked. The others made no sign. They had brought their horses from the copse while Jaumé worked.

Bennick came back from retrieving his arrow from the dead leader. "Better be quick," he said.

Jaumé ran through the prickly trees. He untied his pony and led it out.

He rode at the rear for the rest of the day. Nolt made up time, not stopping to eat. Jaumé didn't complain. He gnawed a crust of bread from his pouch. Dead farmers, dead hillmen. Blood everywhere. It made him feel sick, but the deadliness of the archers, Bennick's skill, returned and filled him with pride and awe. Could he be as good as that, one day?

He knew he would have died if Nolt had left him behind.

CHAPTER TWENTY-SEVEN

DUKE FRANKL VISITED in the afternoon. He patted Lukas on the head, praised the horse Rutgar had drawn, inquired after Britta's health. Frankl was using her, but her gratitude towards him was genuine. Rescuing the boys was a much easier task now.

At nightfall, Britta kissed the boys and left them in the care of the nursemaid.

Karel was at parade rest in the corridor. He opened her door and followed her inside.

Yasma emerged from the bedchamber, a blue glass vial in her hand. "I've made the All-Mother's Breath. Half concentration."

"Excellent. Where would you like to do it, Karel? In here?"

They gathered all the rugs in the suite and piled them on the floor, then spread cushions and blankets on top of them. The armsman took off his breastplate and laid it on the settle. "Make the fire smoke, afterwards. We need to get rid of the smell. Torven will recognize it." He unbuckled his sword belt. "I'll try move after you've sprayed me, and say something. If I can. Count how many seconds it takes for me to fall. And speak to me. I'd like to see how much I can remember."

Yasma brought the Horned Lily root. They both took a bite and chewed. It was sweeter than Britta had expected. She swallowed and counted to one hundred. Her palms were damp with nervousness as she picked up the perfume vial. "Yasma, you count the seconds."

Yasma nodded.

Britta took a deep breath. She raised the vial and sprayed All-Mother's Breath in the armsman's face. "The sun rose backwards in the sky today..." The scent of vanilla filled her nose. She saw Karel's nostrils flare as he inhaled, saw his pupils dilate, saw the tiny muscles in his face stiffen. "...and the sea was pink, not blue."

The armsman's hand rose from his side, he took a half-step forward. His lips parted.

"Birds flew upside down and—"

Karel fell, suddenly and solidly, not putting out his hands to catch himself.

Britta crouched hastily. "Karel?"

The armsman lay utterly still. He didn't move when she touched him, didn't move when she and Yasma rolled him over. His body was stiff, rather than limp. His eyes were half open.

"Karel, can you hear us? Can you see us?"

Breath came from his half-parted lips, his pulse beat at his throat, but he made no sign of awareness. His eyelids weren't blinking.

Britta carefully closed them.

"KAREL? KAREL!" It was an anxious voice, faint, at the edge of his hearing. A voice that he thought he should recognize. "Karel, wake up!" His eyes wouldn't open. His thoughts were turned in on themselves, coiled tightly in the deepest darkness of his skull, like a hibernating bear.

"Karel!" Someone took his jaw, opened his mouth, pushed something inside, closed it again.

Time passed slowly. Awareness came, creeping as unhurriedly as a glacier. There was something on his tongue. He tasted sweetness.

"Swallow it, Karel."

His mind sluggishly considered this request.

"Karel!" A slap on his cheek, but he felt no pain. "Swallow!" The edge of desperation in the voice stirred a vague knowledge. *I must protect her.*

The substance on his tongue was wet, pulpy.

The slap came again. "I order you to swallow, armsman!"

Obediently, he tried to follow the command. But the muscles in his throat didn't work. The pulp caught at the back of his throat.

"He's choking! Roll him over, Yasma. Quick!"

Hands grabbed him, rolled him.

The ability to breathe returned, and with it, a little more awareness. Karel tried to open his eyes.

"Is he breathing?"

"Yes."

"His eyelids moved. He's waking up." There was a relieved sob in the voice.

Karel managed to blink his eyes open for an instant. He glimpsed a blue silk cushion.

The pulp was still in his mouth. He tried to swallow it again. This time his throat muscles worked.

Someone rolled him back over.

Karel blinked and saw two anxious faces. His eyes shut again. He forced them open and stared up, trying to find names for the young women. One fair, one dark. Both with tears in their eyes.

The fair one pushed something gently against his lips. "Eat this, Karel."

He opened his mouth, chewed, swallowed. Gradually more awareness returned, a prickling tingle in his numb limbs, and then a flood of memory.

Princess Brigitta and Yasma. All-Mother's Breath. Horned Lily root.

Karel groaned, rolled onto his side, pushed up to sit as slowly as an old man. His head spun. He squeezed his eyes shut.

"Are you all right, Karel?"

"What time is it?" His voice was slurred, hoarse.

"Less than an hour until midnight."

He groaned again and rubbed his face with hands that didn't feel as if they belonged to him.

"Karel, here..." Yasma knelt beside him, holding a cloth. She wiped his face with it. Wet. Cold.

The headache eased, but his thoughts were still slow, sluggish.

"Would you like more Horned Lily root?" the princess asked.

Karel took the piece she gave him, chewed, swallowed. The pins-and-needles tingle in his limbs faded. "Did it say in the scroll to use it to wake people?" His thoughts were too fuddled to remember clearly.

"No, but we couldn't think of any other way to rouse you." Her gaze was bright, anxious. "Can you stand?"

With both girls' help, he managed to get to his feet. They sat him on the settle and hastily cleared everything away—rugs and blankets and cushions, blue glass vial and Horned Lily roots. The princess brought him a goblet of water. "How do you feel? Can you walk?"

"I have to," Karel said grimly. "Torven will be here shortly." *What a fool I was to suggest this.* But when he stood, the room didn't spin around him. He was drowsy, a little shaky, but he wasn't going to fall over.

Karel walked slowly across the parlor and back. "I'm fine. You'd best get to bed, both of you."

"Dress, first." The princess held out his breastplate.

The straps defeated his clumsy fingers. Yasma fastened them, then buckled his sword belt at his hip.

"How do I look?" He felt half-asleep.

"Not as neat as you normally are," the princess said. "And a bit dazed. Your pupils are dilated."

Yasma twitched his scarlet tunic, straightening it, and reached up to tidy his hair with her fingers. "Will you be all right, Karel?"

"All I have to do is eat and sleep," he said, trying to reassure himself as much as her. "I'll be fine. Now bed, both of you, before Torven gets here."

"Be careful," the princess said, gripping his hand for a moment.

The midnight bell rang less than ten minutes after the bedchamber door had shut. Torven arrived as the last note sounded. His expression was sour. "The duty commander wants to see you."

KAREL HALTED OUTSIDE the duty commander's door. His limbs shook and his eyelids were heavy. He wanted to lean his head against the wall and doze. He blinked hard, took a deep breath, knocked.

"Enter."

Karel's heart began to beat faster. Sweat sprang out on his skin. *Don't make a mistake.* He obeyed the command, saluted, stood at parade rest. "You wished to see me, sir?"

The duty commander leaned back in his chair and looked at him. Would the man notice that his pupils were dilated?

"Princess Brigitta is leaving Osgaard shortly. You're to go with her—but you already know that, don't you, armsman?"

Karel blinked, feeling a flicker of panic. *Was* he meant to know that? Yes. Jaegar had told the princess within his hearing. "Yes, sir."

"Then you know the details—a Fithian ship, hunting for Prince Harkeld?"

"Yes, sir."

"Your orders are to obey the Fithians in all matters. The retrieval of Prince Harkeld's hands and blood is of the *utmost* importance. More important than the princess's well-being. The Heir-Ascendant believes she may prove difficult as the hunt draws to its close. You have his permission to manacle her, if that's the case."

Karel's wits were too slow to hide his shock. He knew the duty commander saw it on his face.

"If such measures are necessary, you won't be punished, armsman."

Karel tried to speak stolidly. "Yes, sir."

"Be ready to leave at dawn, the day after the coronation. The quartermaster will issue you with a traveling kit. Here's a note for him. Dismissed."

Karel took the note, saluted, and exited the room. He stood in the corridor feeling groggy, sweaty, confused.

HE ALMOST DOZED off twice in the line waiting for food, almost dropped his plate when he sat at the table, almost spilled ale down his front when he tried to drink. Thank the All-Mother the meal was fish stew, not something he had to cut. Even so, he had to concentrate on getting the food to his mouth.

Undressing was even harder than eating. Unbuckling his breastplate and sword belt, untying his boot laces, were almost impossible tasks. Finally his uniform was off.

Karel crawled into his bunk and slept.

CHAPTER TWENTY-EIGHT

HARKELD APPROACHED INNIS cautiously. Was his imagination going to cooperate tonight?

Innis cast him an unsmiling, unfriendly look and went back to examining the water lilies. A dragonfly hovered like a bright jewel over one of them.

"All right," Harkeld said crossly. "I'm sorry." *Can we have sex now?*

Innis didn't respond to the apology. She stared across the pond.

"What?" Harkeld said finally, frustrated by the silence. "What do you want from me?"

"You could go away."

He glared at her. "This is *my* dream. I'm staying."

"Then I'll go."

He caught her elbow as she turned away. "Is this still because I tupped that girl in Gdelsk?"

She pulled her elbow free. He heard her *What do you think?* in his head as clearly as if she'd opened her mouth and spoken the words.

"What?" he half-yelled in exasperation. "What was wrong with that? She enjoyed it. I enjoyed it. How was that wrong?"

Innis folded her arms tightly. The emotion leaking from her was outrage.

"You think I've been unfaithful to you? Is that what this is all about?" Harkeld laughed, a loud, flat, disbelieving sound. This dream was even weirder than he'd thought. No, not weirder. *Stupider.*

Innis's lips tightened. "You think it's funny?"

"Not funny. *Ridiculous*." Harkeld waved at the pond, the high, clipped hedges, the blue, cloudless sky. "This is a dream! It's not real life. We're not betrothed. We're not married. You're something my imagination made up. Whether I'm faithful to you or not is irrelevant! So can we stop all this offended *I've-been-betrayed* horseshit and get back to what this is all about?"

"Sex?" She said the word like it left a bad taste in her mouth.

"Being happy. That's the point of these dreams, isn't it?"

Innis didn't answer. Her expression was unreadable.

Harkeld sighed. What more did his mind want from him? "Being with you makes me happy, whether or not we have sex. All right?"

Her lips pressed together. She conceded this with a tilt of her head.

Harkeld held out his hand. After a moment's hesitation, Innis took it. Her fingers were cool, slender. "But I'm not having sex with you tonight."

Harkeld decided not to argue. Right now he'd settle for the contentment of holding her hand.

HE WOKE AT dawn when Justen unfastened the tent flaps. "Still raining," the armsman said. He reached back for the naked sword he always laid between their bedrolls and slid it into its scabbard.

Harkeld grunted and sat up, rubbing his face. "I've been having the strangest dreams lately."

"Good or bad?"

Harkeld considered this while he combed his hair with his fingers. "Frustrating," he said finally. "Confusing. Bizarre." He rubbed his face again. Stubble rasped beneath his hands. "Maybe I'm going mad?"

Justen snorted a laugh. "Ach, I doubt it."

"Don't laugh," Harkeld said wryly. "It's possible." He shrugged aside his blanket and peered through the open tent flap. Tree stumps. Mud. Rain. "In fact, if we don't get out of this landscape soon, it's inevitable."

CHAPTER TWENTY-NINE

"How are you?" the princess asked. They sat at the marquetry table. Sleet slapped against the window panes.

"Fine," Karel said. "Normal." The effect of the All-Mother's Breath had worn off while he slept; he'd won his sword-fighting bouts this morning. "But if you hadn't used the Horned Lily root like that, I don't think I'd have woken for hours. Whoever's idea it was, it was a good one."

"Yasma's."

"You scared us, Karel," Yasma said.

Karel nodded. He'd scared himself. They'd come perilously close to ruin. "Thank the All-Mother we didn't use the full dose. I think we can safely say the tincture is a very strong concentration. It all happened much faster than I thought it would, and went on a lot longer."

"What can you remember?" the princess asked.

"You said that nonsense rhyme the boys love. I didn't hear any more than the pink sea. If you got to the barking cows—"

She shook her head. "I didn't."

"Tomorrow..." Karel frowned, thinking. "I think we should increase the dose by no more than one or two drops. And as for the boys... they need to be sedated, but not All-Mother's Breath. It's too dangerous."

The princess nodded. "I agree. I asked the nursemaid this morning about poppy syrup. She told me a dosage that will make them sleep all night. And we have almost a full bottle left from... before."

From her marriage, she meant.

"Good." Karel tapped a finger on the table, thinking. "Yasma... did you smell the All-Mother's Breath last night?"

She shook her head.

"You were what? Two yards away? So the boys shouldn't inhale any, but even so—get them to eat Horned Lily root as soon as you can, highness."

"I shall."

"The nursemaid, did you ask whether she'll be with the boys or—"

"She's going to the coronation."

"Good." That was one less person they needed to deal with.

Princess Brigitta took a folded piece of parchment from her pocket. "Last night you fell over so fast, Karel. There's no way I'll have time to tell the armsman what I'm doing with your bodies, or why. The bloodstains will be there for anyone to follow and they're sure to *guess*, but I thought—just in case—I should write Jaegar a note. So there's no doubt you both died loyal to Osgaard." She pushed the parchment across to him.

Karel unfolded it and read.

Jaegar, I won't let you kill the boys, nor use me in your plans to catch Harkeld. You are worse than Father ever was. I pray to the All-Mother for your death.

Then came a gap.

I thought they were mine to command, but they were loyal to Osgaard. For that, they die and their bodies shall rot in the sewers.

"I'll rewrite it tomorrow, the first sentences neat, and the last ones all messy and rushed and bloodstained. What do you think?"

"An excellent idea." He folded the note and handed it back to her.

"What else needs to be done?" Yasma asked.

"The princess's trunks?"

"Packed," Yasma said. "And the coronation clothes laid out. And I've put pepperwort infusion in two of the perfume bottles, and—"

Someone rapped on the door.

"Frankl," the princess said, shoving the note into her pocket and standing. "I'll take him next door to the boys. Tonight we'll go over everything, step by step. We can't make *any* mistakes tomorrow."

CHAPTER THIRTY

KAREL WOKE AT dawn and knew he wouldn't sleep again. Nervous tension clenched in his belly. The enormity of what they were about to do was horrifying.

Two hours until breakfast. He couldn't just lie here and worry.

Karel climbed out of his bunk and dressed quietly. All around him, armsmen slept.

He left the bunkroom and headed for the training arena. The sky was low and overcast.

Karel fetched his Esfaban bow. Handling it brought memory of home. Warm rain, tree frogs singing, palm fronds rustling in the breeze. He heard his father's voice: *Keep your arms relaxed, son. It comes from the back. From here.* He almost felt the tap of his father's fingers between his shoulder blades.

Karel practiced for an hour. The world narrowed to the straw-filled targets on the far side of the arena, to the smooth flex of the bow, the swift, sure flight of the arrows. It was relaxing, almost hypnotic. But when he laid down the bow, the day loomed over him again and he became tense once more.

He collected the arrows from the targets. A gust of wind blew across the arena, not icy, not blown up from the south pole, but raw and blustery, from the north. In its wake, rain started to fall. Karel glanced at the clouds. *Keep raining.* The bondservants would be miserable, kneeling all afternoon in the Great Courtyard, but the river flowing beneath the palace would run faster, flushing sewage into the sea, and no one would think it odd if his and Yasma's bodies couldn't be found.

He unstrung the bow and held it for a moment, remembering the day his father had given it to him. How could he leave it behind?

Karel laid a kiss on the smooth, dark wood. *Forgive me, Father.*

The third bell rang, and the morning seemed to speed up. Breakfast, surrounded by armsmen grumbling about starting their shifts an hour early, and then instead of training, they were set to polishing their gear. Karel went to the quartermaster for his traveling kit. The man hauled out a small trunk and filled it, not just with spare tunics, but a whetstone and buffing cloth, soap and razorblade, bootlaces, fur-lined hat and gloves, long-sleeved woolen vests and leggings, a warm traveling cloak.

Karel lugged the trunk to the barracks and heaved it up on his bunk. Then he went to the duty commander. "Sir, one of the cottagers by the wagon gate is storing a trunk for me. I'm filling it to send home to my family." He held out the spare key. "Will you see it's sent if... if something should happen to me?"

The man nodded. "Give it here."

For the rest of the morning, Karel sat with the other armsmen, polishing his breastplate and greaves and wrist guards, his gilded scabbard, the hilts of his sword and dagger. Lastly he buffed the silver torque that proclaimed him a royal bodyguard. Princess Brigitta's personal armsman.

But it wasn't the torque that bound him to the princess. Nor the words of his oath. His tie to her was much deeper than that.

There was a flurry of washing, of shaving, of donning crisp uniforms. Karel hung back in the bunkroom. He felt inside his money pouch, took out the second key to the trunk he'd stored in Rakhamn, tucked it under a wrist guard, then joined the armsmen straggling off to start their shift an hour early.

TORVEN WAS WAITING in the princess's parlor. "Lucky whoreson," he muttered sourly. "You won't be going to the ceremony. *She's* sick."

Karel watched him leave. Torven wouldn't get to his bunk until nightfall. He'd have a hurried meal, then stand at parade rest all afternoon while Jaegar ascended Osgaard's throne.

Yasma peeked through the ajar bedchamber door. "Karel!" She came towards him, half-running. "Jaegar came!"

"What?"

Yasma gripped his hands, words spilling from her lips: "We did it just as we planned—Britta falling ill—and she sent a message to the master of ceremonies, and *he* came. Jaegar himself!" Her fingers were trembling, her eyes bright with excitement. "He was so angry. He thought Britta was pretending—and she threw up *all over him*." She gave a choked laugh. "I wish you could have seen it!"

The bedchamber door opened fully. Princess Brigitta stood there in a loose night robe. Her face was shockingly pale, but her eyes were as bright as Yasma's.

"Are you all right?" Karel asked.

She nodded. "I took the antidote."

Karel crossed to her, holding Yasma's hand. "Jaegar came himself?"

"Yes."

"And she cried, too, because she's missing the coronation," Yasma said. "And he believed her!"

THEY WORKED THEIR way down the list of things to be done: preparing fresh All-Mother's Breath, filling two perfume vials with the mixture, blending poppy syrup and honey for the princes. Karel threaded the padlock key on a piece of cord and hung it around his neck. He sprayed pepperwort infusion on four empty wine bladders, and then on the princess and Yasma—their skin, their clothes, their hair. "Cover your eyes," he warned. "It'll burn if it gets in them."

The noon bell rang.

The corridors of the palace were now empty. The kitchens were empty. The armsmen's barracks, the stables, the palace laundry.

Bondservants would be kneeling in the Great Courtyard in the rain, and everyone else in the palace—armsmen and guardsmen, stablemen and gardeners, cooks, nursemaids, artisans, courtiers, nobles and ambassadors—would be packed into the throne room and the chambers and antechambers and courtyards radiating from it to witness Jaegar become Osgaard's king.

Everyone except us. And the guards on duty on the palace walls. And the guards in the dungeons. And the three armsmen keeping watch over the princes.

Princess Brigitta picked up the empty wine bladders. "Let's get the blood, Yasma."

KAREL WENT TO stand in the corridor, opposite the man guarding the princes' door, trying not to let his agitation show. Bored. He was bored, not worried. Bored, bored, bored.

Minutes crawled past. Where were Princess Brigitta and Yasma now? He tried to imagine how long it would take them to traverse the bondservants' corridors, how long to fill the bladders with pigs' blood, how long to return. What if a bondservant had been left on duty in the palace kitchens? What if there was no blood in the tub? What if they spilled it? Left footprints?

Stop it, he told himself. None of those things would happen.

Half an hour passed. Too long, surely? Something must have gone wrong—

The door behind him opened. "Armsman," Yasma said timidly. "The princess wishes to speak with you."

BRITTA TOOK ONE last look around the parlor. The smell of blood was strong in her nose and the taste of Horned Lily root sweet on her tongue. "All right. I'm doing it now."

Neither Karel nor Yasma moved. They lay on the floor, blood pooling around them.

Britta wiped her hands on her robe. Bloody hands, a bloody robe. She picked up the perfume vial, took a deep breath, laid a hand on the doorknob—*I'm distraught, half-hysterical*—and opened it. "Armsman!" she cried, her voice breathless, distressed. "There's been a terrible accident. Help me!"

She saw the man's shock as he took in her disheveled, blood-stained appearance. His eyes widened, his mouth opened. He pushed away from the wall, entered the parlor at a run, halted with an inarticulate cry when he saw the bodies—Yasma lying crumpled, Karel face-down, hand stretched towards his out-flung sword—and swung towards her.

Britta sprayed the All-Mother's Breath.

The armsman stood for a moment, swaying, horror frozen on his face. And then he fell with a clatter of breastplate and sword.

Britta shut the door. She knelt and rolled the armsman over, examined him. His eyes were open, unblinking, the pupils hugely dilated. He made no reaction when she pinched his cheek sharply.

Britta closed the man's eyes. "He's out."

Yasma lifted her head.

"Careful," Karel said. "We mustn't leave footprints."

BRITTA STRIPPED OFF her bloody robe and dressed in clean clothes. She put the flask of poppy syrup and two pieces of Horned Lily root in her pocket, picked up the perfume vial, and headed for the door. Karel caught her glance, gave her a nod. She didn't need to hear him speak to know what he was telling her: *I know you can do it.*

Britta went out into the empty corridor. Her heart pounded in her chest.

She opened the door to the storeroom, stepped inside, closed it. Armsmen stood at parade rest on either side of her.

Rutgar and Lukas were at the little table coloring pictures. Lukas's face lit with a smile. Rutgar scrambled to his feet. "Britta!"

"Stay there, darlings. Don't move." Britta raised the vial and sprayed to her left and right. Vanilla. She glanced at the men's faces, saw flared nostrils, wide eyes, rigid faces.

Britta crossed swiftly to the boys. Behind her, the armsmen toppled, one after the other, crashing loudly to the marble floor. "Don't worry," she said, crouching at the table, smiling at Rutgar and Lukas. "They're just asleep. Here, eat this. It will stop you falling asleep too."

"Why are they asleep?" Lukas asked in a tremulous voice, clutching the Horned Lily root.

"Because they won't let me take you to Lundegaard," Britta said. "Eat it, love. Quickly now!"

"Is Harkeld in Lundegaard?" Rutgar asked, brightening.

"No, sweetheart, but your grandfather's there, and your uncles. You'll like to meet them."

When the boys had eaten the root, Britta measured poppy syrup into their mugs. "Drink this and we can go."

Both boys obediently sipped.

Lukas lowered his mug with a whimper. "I don't like the taste."

"It's not very nice, is it?" She smoothed baby-soft hair back from his brow. "But you need to drink it before we can leave."

Rutgar drained his mug first, Lukas a few moments later.

She took their hands and led them past the fallen armsmen. Did the scent of vanilla linger in the doorway?

"I'm tired," Lukas mumbled.

Britta ushered the boys into her suite. Rutgar clutched her robe when he saw the armsman lying just inside her door. "Don't worry," she said, bending to kiss his cheek. "He's only sleeping."

Lukas's eyes were half-closed. He seemed not to see the armsman, or the blood-soaked rugs and Karel's sword lying abandoned, or the ashets and tureens from the dinner trolley tumbled on the floor.

Britta led the boys to the settle.

"Are we going now?" Rutgar asked drowsily.

"Soon," Britta said. "Have a nap first. I'll sing you a lullaby."

* * *

KAREL GRABBED THE iron ring, hauled the metal cover out of its hole, and reared back as the stink of the sewers filled his nose.

He leaned forward and looked in. Nothing but blackness. His ears caught the hiss of fast-flowing water far below.

"They say a bondservant fell in once," Yasma said. "Her body was never found."

Karel glanced at her. "Truth, or tale?"

She shrugged.

Karel took off his greaves and wrist guards and threw them into the sewer. The sword belt and scabbard followed, and his silver torque. Rather than unbuckle the breastplate, he slit the straps with his dagger. He laid the breastplate and dagger on the floor, as if they'd had been tossed aside. "There's some blood left? A little on the breastplate. Then throw the bladders in."

Yasma obeyed. She threw the emetic and its antidote into the sewer hole too, and the bag the pepperwort leaves had come in. Lastly, she pulled off her iron armband and dropped it down the dark, hissing, stinking hole. "Britta's slippers?"

Karel glanced at her feet, at the bloody slippers. "Wear them back to her rooms and leave them there."

He sat back on his heels and examined the scene. The dinner trolley smeared with blood, angled across the corridor, half tipped over. The breastplate and discarded dagger. The trail of bloody smears and drips leading back down the corridor. A woman's small footprints. The open sewer.

"Let's go."

He walked carefully back down the corridor. A single boot print would destroy the scene they'd crafted.

At the corner, he glanced back. The bloody breastplate looked like the carapace of some gigantic, dead insect.

YASMA AND KAREL emerged from the bondservants' corridor into the parlor. "Are they asleep?" Karel asked in a low voice.

Britta rose from kneeling beside the settle. "Yes."

They worked quickly, silently. Yasma packed the All-Mother's Breath, Horned Lily root, and poppy syrup into a pillowcase, and on top of those, Britta's jewels. Britta copied out her note to Jaegar, scrawling the last sentences in large, agitated writing, and smeared bloody fingerprints on it. She burned the original, making sure the parchment crumbled into ash.

The armsman went through the suite methodically, double-checking everything. "You have your masks?" he asked, coming out of the bedchamber, two blankets in his hand.

"Yes."

He touched his chest. "And I have the key to the padlock."

Britta handed him a leather pouch. "Twenty gold pieces."

He tied it to his belt. "And the rest?"

"In the pillowcase."

Britta looked around the parlor. No one could mistake that a struggle had occurred here. Or that people had died. The two drying pools of blood were appallingly large. No one could lose that much blood and survive.

They sprayed themselves and the boys with pepperwort infusion and refilled the vials with the last of the mixture. Yasma rinsed out the bowl it had steeped in. "That's everything, isn't it?"

Britta exchanged a glance with Karel.

He nodded, and rolled the two blankets and slung them over his shoulder. "Remember, we have less than ten seconds to get out of the wagon. Move fast. And get off the road fast. There'll likely be a lot of traffic since the gates were shut half the day."

He crossed to the settle, picked up Lukas, and handed him to her. The little boy was deeply asleep, his cheeks flushed. Britta cradled him in her arms and watched Karel pick up Rutgar. Apprehension was tight in her chest. Escape seemed so close, freedom almost a tangible thing.

CHAPTER THIRTY-ONE

THEY WALKED SWIFTLY through the empty bondservants'
corridors, the armsman first, with the blankets and Rutgar,
then Britta and Lukas, and Yasma last, carrying the
pillowcase, spraying the pepperwort to hide their trail. The
eighth bell tolled. The coronation ceremony was halfway
through. The kitchen bondservants would be returning to
their duties. Britta's chest grew tighter, her ribcage squeezing
her lungs.

When they reached the stables, the armsman held out his arm,
barring the passage. He crouched and laid Rutgar on the floor.
"Wait here."

Two minutes later he reappeared. "Spray low," he told Yasma.
"We don't want the horses to inhale it."

The stables were fragrant with hay and straw and horse
dung, dim, warm, full of life. Horses nickered and snorted, they
twitched their ears, flicked their tails, nosed each other over the
sides of their stalls.

The dung wagon was just inside the wide stable doors,
with the cobbled yard beyond. Britta halted in the shadows,
clutching Lukas, scanning the empty stableyard. Rain drizzled
down. She lifted her gaze to the golden roofs of the palace. The
guard towers were just beyond view.

Karel laid Rutgar down and shrugged the blankets from his
shoulder.

"Do you need help?" Britta whispered.

"No."

Karel lowered the wagon's tailgate and reached for a shovel. A few minutes' work and the manure was piled in the middle of the wagon. He took one blanket, spread it on the wagon tray, beckoned to her.

Britta trod across to him, holding Lukas. Karel took the boy while she scrambled up into the tray. She lay on the blanket with her back pressed to the side of the wagon, her head towards the tailgate, and reached for Lukas, tucking him into her body.

Karel spread the second blanket over them, then shoveled dung to cover them. "Too heavy?"

"No."

"Can you breathe all right?"

"Yes."

A pause, and then the blanket was lifted and Yasma crept in beside her. Another pause, she heard Karel whisper, "Here," felt Yasma reach to take Rutgar.

She heard Karel fasten the tailgate. He shoveled again, for longer this time. Finally the sounds stopped. Silence. Karel would be spraying pepperwort infusion around the wagon.

The blanket moved, pulling taut over her. Karel was joining them.

She could see nothing, but she heard movement and knew the armsman was drawing manure over the blanket.

Silence came. The smell of horse dung was strong, but fresh air crept through cracks in the tailgate and found its way under the blanket. Britta heard her own breathing, heard Lukas's breathing, heard the sound of her heart beating.

THE NINTH BELL rang, and time seemed to slow down. The final hour before nightfall lasted forever. Britta counted seconds, minutes, hours. Surely something was wrong? Was the silence because their escape had been discovered?

No, strident bells would be ringing alarm. As they had when Harkeld had escaped.

And then she heard the bells, not just tolling the hour, but announcing the ascent of Osgaard's new king, a loud pealing that went on and on and on.

The last note died. Jaegar would be feasting now. Would he send someone to check on her? Would Frankl?

Voices came into the stableyard. *Take the dung wagon now,* Britta begged them silently. *Before our escape is discovered.*

The voices passed them by.

Britta lay in the dark, tense, waiting for the bells to ring a warning. Manure pressed down on her. Lukas was warm in her arms, deeply asleep.

After an eternity came the soft *clop clop* of hooves. Someone spoke close by. "Easy there."

She heard a horse being harnessed between the shafts, felt the wagon sway as the driver climbed aboard, heard the crack of a whip.

The dung wagon lurched forward.

KAREL LISTENED INTENTLY. Cobblestones in the stableyard, rough and jerky, voices at the palace gate, and then the smooth rumble of wheels on paving stones. He gripped the edge of the topmost blanket, ready to fling it off. The town gate must be close now—

He felt as well as heard the moment when they entered Rakhamn. The wagon rattled, slowed slightly.

Karel counted the seconds under his breath. *Three, four, five.*

He thrust the blanket back—night, a torch flaring behind them—and reached for Yasma, tossing her out, handing Rutgar to her as she ran to catch up, reached for the princess, for Lukas. The rumble of wagon wheels drowned their footsteps, drowned the grunts of breath.

Karel grabbed the pillowcase, hauled the blankets out, leapt over the tailgate, and ran for the side of the road. He crouched low on the wet cobblestones, panting, his heart hammering in his chest.

Ahead, the dung wagon passed into a flickering ring of torchlight, then vanished into darkness again.

No shouts came, but another wagon was rattling towards them.

Karel moved back until he was pressed against a cottage. Where were the princess and Yasma? The boys?

Not on the street. The wagon passed without pause.

Karel straightened and walked quickly in the direction of the gate, blinking rain from his eyes. Four steps—and there was a dark shape huddled against a cottage. The princess, with Lukas in her arms. He took the prince from her and gave her the bulging pillowcase. Another five steps, and there were Yasma and Rutgar. He handed Yasma the blankets, slung Rutgar over his shoulder, and headed for the shed.

KAREL'S HANDS WERE covered in dung. He wiped them on his tunic as best he could and gave the key to Yasma. She unfastened the padlock and raised the lid of the trunk, things he heard rather than saw. It was like being blind, so dark was the night. "Don't lose that padlock and key," Karel whispered to her.

He moved forward, finding his way into the shed by touch, knocking the trunk with his boots. There was the top of the second trunk, nestled inside the first, and there were the rope handles...

Karel heaved the smaller trunk out and backed from the shed. Rain pattered down.

They unpacked the trunk swiftly, stripped off their palace clothes, dressed in the ones he'd purchased. Karel buckled on the new sword belt, unwrapped the sword and dagger and slid them into their sheaths. He tucked the fake throwing star inside his cloak.

"Give me your tunic," the princess whispered.

His and Yasma's bloody clothes went into the trunk first, then the folded blankets, and then both children, the princess's clothes tucked around them. He heard the rattle of wagon wheels on the nearby street, the patter of rain, the sound of their breathing, but other than those sounds, the night was silent.

Karel bundled the food into the leather rucksack—strings of dried sausages, cheese, hardbread, apples. They still needed cider, though. "Highness, can you get me out a groat? And a half-penny."

After a moment, she tucked the coins into his hand.

Karel piled the bulging pillowcase into the rucksack. "That should be everything. Feel on the ground."

"Just two padlocks," Yasma said. "And Britta's and my shoes."

"Shoes in the trunk," he said. "Tuck them down the end. Yasma, take the big padlock and fasten the trunk in the shed. The key on the cord fits it. Check inside the trunk first. You should feel a roll of fabric, nothing else. Then spray inside the shed, close the door, and spray outside too." He heard faint noises as Yasma obeyed.

He felt inside the boys' trunk one last time. The young princes were deeply asleep. Clothes wedged their bodies firmly. Their faces were clear of smothering fabric. *I should have drilled air holes in the trunk*. It was too late for that now. He checked their faces one more time. *Keep breathing*.

Yasma returned, pressed the key into his hand.

"The second padlock?" Karel asked.

The princess handed it to him.

Karel closed the trunk and locked it. He strung the key on the cord by touch, knotting it tightly. "Put this around your neck," he told the princess. The two keys clinked as he handed them to her. He stood and settled the rucksack over his shoulders. "You girls take one handle, I'll take the other. It'll be heavy, but it's only half a mile to the market square. We'll get a handcart there."

"Do we put our masks on now?" the princess asked.

"At the wharves. I'll tell you when. Until then, keep your hoods well forward."

*   *   *

THERE WAS AN element of nightmare to their journey—a sense of frantic haste, knowledge that something terrible was at their heels, a feeling of endlessness, that she'd be forever hurrying through darkness and rain, half-blind, never able to see more than the next torch flickering ahead. The rope handle bit into her hand, her fingers were painfully squeezed alongside Yasma's, her boots skidded on wet cobblestones, and always, always, she strained to hear past their panted breaths, past their footfalls, past the drizzling rain. When would the bells signaling their escape start ringing?

At the end of the street were firelight and voices.

"The market square," Karel said.

They halted. The square was large, filled with people singing, shouting. A bonfire burned in the middle. Light and shadows flickered over people's faces, making their eyes gleam blackly and their mouths gape like dark holes.

"Celebrating the coronation," Karel said, lowering the trunk to the ground. "Wait here, I'll get a handcart."

He vanished into the crush of people.

Britta flexed her fingers. Ridges were imprinted across her palm.

Yasma pressed close to her. Britta took the maid's hand, trying to project a confidence she didn't feel. She scanned the crowd. Which hooded head was Karel's?

He returned, striding around the outside of the square, towing a handcart. His rucksack and six full bladders lay in it.

"Hold the cart steady." He crouched and hefted the trunk up.

They circled the market square and headed down the cobbled streets to the harbor, trundling the cart.

"Masks on," Karel said.

Britta took the strip of black silk from her pocket, tied it over her face, pulled her hood up again.

"From now on, not a word. Unless it's life or death. I want them to think you're lads."

Britta glanced at Yasma. Cloaked and hooded, wearing trews and boots, she looked like a boy.

"When we get on board, bar the cabin door. It's the *first* thing you must do. And don't let anyone in but me. I'll call myself Eliam."

A FEW TORCHES lit the wharf. Britta was aware of openness to her right, and black water stretching out of sight. Pyres burned distantly, marking the gap in the breakwater. She saw the flickering lights of ships in the harbor. On board one were Fithian assassins.

She shivered and pulled the cloak more tightly around her.

They strode along the slick stones for a hundred yards, the handcart rattling, then Karel halted. "Hold this."

She and Yasma took the shafts.

Karel walked to the edge of the wharf, looked over. "Ho, *Sea Eagle*."

Voices rose in answer.

Sailors climbed up onto the wharf, two of them, and roped the trunk and lowered it into a rowboat. Britta scrambled down iron pegs set into the wharf, trying to move like a boy, confident, unafraid, swinging down into the boat. Yasma followed, then Karel.

The sailors pushed off.

Britta crouched alongside the trunk. Wild, painful hope swelled in her chest. *We're going to make it.*

The journey to the *Sea Eagle* took several minutes. The boat rocked through the water. Britta listened to the slap of waves and creak of rowlocks, watched the slowly shrinking lights of the town.

One sailor pulled in his oar. A ship loomed out of the darkness. The rowboat swung around, bumped lightly against its side.

Britta gazed up through the drizzle, her heart loud in her chest, her mouth dry with nervousness. The *Sea Eagle*.

Lamps glowed. A rope ladder dangled over the side. She saw people peering down at them. Sailors. The men Karel didn't trust.

A rope was lowered for the trunk. Karel double-checked the knots, settled the rucksack on his back again, and climbed the rope ladder. His voice floated down to them. She heard the words *careful* and *fragile*.

The trunk swung upward. Britta watched in paralyzing terror. *Don't drop it!* Her imagination gave her a picture of the padlocked trunk plunging into the sea. The boys would drown, locked in darkness.

Men grabbed the trunk, swung it out of sight.

Britta scrambled up the rope ladder.

CHAPTER THIRTY-TWO

KAREL FELT HIS hackles rise. The captain had greeted him affably, and the first mate too, but something in their smiles reminded him of Jaegar. He glanced around, counting the watching sailors. Six, and two more in the rowboat.

Yasma climbed onto the deck and came to stand beside the princess.

"Put the trunk and our belongings in the cabin, then I'll pay you," Karel told the captain. "You're ready to sail, I trust? Harbor fees paid?"

"Of course," the captain said, smiling.

Sailors hurried to pick up the trunk.

Karel crossed the deck, Yasma and Princess Brigitta at his heels. The door to the cabin stood open, lamplight shining inside. It looked safe, warm, inviting. He glanced inside, making sure no one lurked there, and slung the rucksack in. "In with you," he told the girls brusquely.

They filed silently past him.

He stood to one side of the door, his hood pushed back, scanning the deck, while the trunk and the bladders of cider were carried into the cabin.

A sailor hurried up with the last bladder. The princess took it and closed the door.

Karel turned to the captain. "Payment," he said. "And some instructions for our voyage. In your cabin."

The captain smiled, his eyes gleaming in the lamplight. "Of course." He glanced to the right, lifted his chin in a short jerk, turned towards his cabin.

The prickling on the back of Karel's neck grew as he followed the captain across the deck. He didn't like the *follow-me* head jerk the man had given to someone, and even more, he didn't like his swagger. That cocky, confident strut said the captain knew something he didn't. The first mate walked at Karel's side, swaggering too, smiling above his pointed beard.

The northerly blustered, throwing rain in his face. Karel didn't pull his hood up. He was aware of men walking behind him, several steps back. Two sailors.

The prickling at the back of his neck increased, climbing up onto his scalp. He knew—he *knew*—that he was about to be attacked.

The captain opened his cabin door and entered.

The first mate entered.

The two sailors closed in behind him, little more than an arm's reach away. Tension coiled in Karel's muscles. This was like a bout in the training arena, when everything narrowed to who moved fastest, struck hardest.

Except this time I kill.

Karel stepped through the door and moved sideways, keeping his back to the wall, unsheathing his dagger beneath his cloak, taking the cabin in with a glance—table, bed, the captain behind his desk.

The two sailors crowded into the cabin, slamming the door. Knives gleamed in their hands.

Karel found the same bright, fierce clarity that he did when he fought in the training arena. He grabbed the nearest sailor's wrist, yanked him closer and buried his blade high under the man's ribcage, angling for the heart. *One second.* He thrust the man away and lunged for the second sailor, avoiding his clumsy blow. *Two seconds.* Another upward stab and the man was dead. *Three seconds.*

Karel whirled to face the first mate.

The man was charging, mouth open in a roar, knife in hand.

Kill him? Or spare him?

Karel released his dagger. He met the man's charge, grabbed his upraised wrist with both hands, kicked his legs from under him, using the man's momentum to twist him as he fell.

The first mate screamed as his arm broke. The knife tumbled from his grip.

Karel dug a knee into the man's abdomen, winding him. He snatched up his bloodied dagger and spun to face the captain, crouching low.

The man had scrambled out from behind his desk and was coming at him, sword raised.

Karel took the fake throwing star out from under his cloak, displaying it.

The captain recoiled.

Karel straightened to his full height. "We had an agreement," he said softly.

The captain's mouth opened and closed. He looked as winded as his first mate. He backed away, his eyes fixed on the throwing star.

"You wish to renege?" Karel smiled a sharp, Jaegar-like smile. "That's the only way I can interpret this attack."

The captain shook his head. He dropped his sword with a clatter, held his hands palm out in a gesture of surrender. "No, no, no."

Karel took a step towards the desk. "I would advise against it. The Brotherhood knows which ship I'm on and when it's due in Lundegaard." Behind him, the first mate wheezed, groaned, struggled to sit up.

"A mistake," the captain said, raising his hands higher. "We didn't know—we won't—I give my word of honor you'll reach Lundegaard!"

"For your sake, I hope we do. You'll find the Brotherhood has a long memory." He emphasised the word *long*.

"Yes, yes, yes," the captain said, nodding, sweat standing out on his face.

"And your first mate? Does he give his word, too?" Karel turned to the man, let him see the throwing star he held between finger and thumb. "After I so generously spared his life?"

The first mate flinched back against the wall. His face was no longer ruddy, but bloodlessly pale. "My word of honor." Pain hissed between his teeth with each word.

"Very well." Karel stowed the throwing star beneath his cloak and untied the pouch of money. "Twenty gold pieces." His voice was bland, as if nothing untoward had happened. "You shall receive the rest when I'm paid for my contract in Lundegaard."

Britta tucked the sleeping boys into bed and went to stand at the window, staring out at the wharf and the town.

Why wasn't the ship moving?

Rain pattered against the tiny glass panes. She opened the window, straining to hear any sounds from shore. What time was it? Not even halfway to midnight, surely? Jaegar would still be feasting. She pictured him as he'd been that morning, dressed in gold cloth, a row of fading blisters beneath his right eye. He'd worn a prince's crown woven into his hair, but now he'd have their father's crown on his head.

Yasma joined her.

"Why isn't the ship moving?" Britta asked. "If the bells start ringing before we're out of the harbor, they might still catch us!"

"Do you think Karel's having trouble? He did say he didn't trust—"

A *clunk* echoed through the hull.

They looked at each other. "Is that the anchor?" Britta said.

Yasma ran across to the door and laid her ear to the panels. "I think they're raising the sails."

The ship stirred slightly.

Britta's heart seemed to be beating in her throat. "We're moving," she whispered. "We're moving!"

The *Sea Eagle* was sluggish at first, slowly picking up speed as it crossed the harbor. The lights of the town grew faint. The ship passed between the arms of the breakwater, between the burning pyres. Britta thought she heard the wild pealing of bells across the water. Had their escape been discovered?

The ship swung south and seemed to leap forward. Nothing could catch them now.

A knock sounded on the door. "Open up, it's Eliam."

Yasma slid the bar back.

Karel entered, carrying a bucket. "Sea water," he said. "To wash the dung off."

Yasma slid the crossbar back into place. "Is everything all right?"

"It is now. How are the boys?" He crossed to the bed, bent over the children. "They look well."

"They are." Britta closed the window and stepped over the two pallets on the floor. "What do you mean by, 'it is now'?"

Karel grimaced. "They tried to jump me. I had to kill two of them."

Britta halted, shocked by his words. "You *what?*"

His face became expressionless. Had he heard her question as an accusation? "Four against one. I had to kill some of them. A Fithian would have."

Four against one? And he'd survived?

"Karel..." Yasma crossed to him, took his hand. "Are you all right?"

"They didn't harm me."

That wasn't quite what she meant.

Britta looked at him. He'd just killed two men. How could he stand there so calmly?

But he wasn't completely calm. There was tightness around his eyes, around his mouth.

Her armsman. Who'd killed for her. "Thank you, Karel."

Something seemed to relax in Karel's face. He nodded and looked back at the boys. "When they wake, we must stop them crying. I'd like to disembark without the crew ever knowing there were children on board."

Britta crossed to the bed. "We'll keep the lamps burning. If they see me, hopefully they won't cry."

Karel glanced around the cabin, his gaze lighting on the rucksack and bladders. "I put the fear of death into the captain, but we should still take care, eat only our own food, drink only our own cider. I'll divide the food into six days' worth—although, with luck, we'll reach Lundegaard sooner. We've a good wind behind us."

"I'll do it now," Yasma said, releasing his hand.

"Highness, sleep in the bed with them," Karel told Britta. "They'll feel safer."

She nodded, bracing herself against the swaying of the ship.

Karel dragged a pallet over to the door. "I'll sleep here. Yasma, where would you like me to put yours? In the corner?"

Yasma, kneeling by the rucksack, didn't answer. Britta glanced at her.

"Yasma, are you all right?" Karel asked sharply.

Yasma pushed to her feet, ran to the open closet, and vomited into one of the chamberpots.

Britta hurried over to her. "Yasma?"

She heard Karel's boots cross the floor behind her, heard the sound of fabric ripping. "Here," he said.

She looked back. He held out the bucket of sea water and a strip torn off her palace robe.

Britta gave Yasma water to rinse her mouth with and cleaned her face with a wet cloth. "Into bed with you."

Karel had made up the pallet. He tucked Yasma in.

Yasma was shivering, her skin clammy. "I was ill all the way from Esfaban," she whispered. "I thought it was because I was upset at leaving home."

"I think not." Karel wiped strands of hair back from Yasma's brow.

"You were like this the whole way from Esfaban?" Britta said, worried.

"They gave me poppy syrup. I slept, mostly." Yasma closed her eyes.

Britta glanced at Karel, asking a silent question.

He nodded.

Britta measured some syrup out, mixed it with cider, and gave it to Yasma.

"How much is left?" Karel asked in a low voice.

"Less than half."

Britta threw the contents of the chamberpot out the window, rinsed it out, put it back in the closet, but the sour smell of vomit still lingered in the cabin. She crouched beside Yasma's pallet. "Is she asleep yet?"

Karel nodded. He pulled the blankets higher around Yasma and stood. "We need to save some syrup for when we reach Lundegaard. Pray to the All-Mother the boys aren't badly seasick too."

"Can we give Yasma All-Mother's Breath?"

"We may have to. You're all right? Not feeling ill?"

She shook her head.

"Let's eat. And then you should sleep. One or other of us should always be awake."

They ate sitting on the floor. The food was plainer and more delicious than any Britta had eaten in her life—dried sausages tasting of smoke, salty cheese, coarse hardbread, sweet cider. She hugged her knees after she'd finished. The cabin was cozy, the lamps glowing, Yasma and the boys sleeping peacefully. *Have I ever been this happy before?*

"I heard alarm bells ringing as we passed through the breakwater," Karel said.

"I heard them too. Jaegar knows I'm gone." But Britta was no longer afraid. "He can't catch us now."

CHAPTER THIRTY-THREE

HARKELD BURNED STICKS as Justen tossed them in the air. The precision and concentration required came easily. He eyed the final stick, smoldering in the mud where it had fallen. He couldn't—*wouldn't*—take pride in his magic, but surely he could take pride in his skill at controlling it?

"Tomorrow we'll reach Lvotnic," Cora said, rain dripping from her hood. "Once we're across the river, I'll start you burning arrows out of the air."

HE WENT LOOKING for Innis in the palace gardens and found her back at their campsite, sitting on a tree stump, observing his fire lesson. She looked up as he approached, boots squelching through the mud.

"What are you doing here?"

"Watching you."

Harkeld glanced at himself and away again. "Innis, can we please go to the gardens? I hate it here." He was surrounded by mud and rain and tree stumps all day. Why would he want to spend time here in his dreams?

"Watch yourself. You're good."

Harkeld shrugged this compliment aside. "Cora's a good teacher."

"Watch yourself," Innis said again.

"I don't want to."

Innis sighed. She stood. "All right. Where do you want to go?"

He took her back to the water lily pond, to sunshine and soft grass and the hum of dragonflies. There, he devoted his attention to making love to her. Afterwards, they lay on the grass, arms around each other. He sank towards sleep, relaxed, happy.

"Harkeld? Have you considered becoming a Sentinel?

His descent into slumber stopped abruptly. His eyelids snapped open. "What?"

Innis sat up. Her hand was on his chest. "Don't get angry. I know how you feel about magic, but *think* about it. Once the curse is broken, why not become a Sentinel? Your magic is more than strong enough."

The touch of her hand brought with it familiar warm contentment, but her words—

"Because I'd rather die." He pushed up to sit.

"Why? Being a Sentinel is a *good* thing."

"I don't want to be a witch."

Innis looked at him for a long moment, her eyebrows drawn slightly together. "What was it you liked about being a prince? The power? The status? The luxury?"

The words stung. "None of those things!"

"Then what?" Innis took his hand. "I'm not trying to make you angry, Harkeld. I'm trying to understand why being a prince was important to you."

His anger eased slightly. He tried to organize his thoughts. Where should he start?

How about at the beginning?

"I was twelve when I was fostered to Lundegaard, to King Magnas's court. At first all I saw was how plain it was. I wanted to go home, I wanted golden roof tiles and golden tapestries and golden bathtubs." He pulled a face. *What a spoiled, obnoxious brat I was.* "King Magnas was patient with me. Remarkably patient. And after a while I began to notice how Lundegaard *felt*, not how it looked. It was like someone had handed me a new pair of eyes. I saw... I saw how I want Osgaard to be. People weren't afraid." That had been the biggest difference:

the lack of fear. No bondservants cringing in the corridors, no nervous courtiers eager to flatter him. Fear was something he'd inhaled with each breath in the palace—invisible, odorless, pervasive—and he'd never noticed it until Lundegaard.

"King Magnas rules his kingdom for his people, not for himself. He's wise and just and fair. My father..." Harkeld grimaced. "Father rules by fear, and Jaegar will too, after him. When I went back to Osgaard—" His laugh was flat. The fear had no longer been invisible and odorless. He'd choked on it each time he'd drawn breath, had seen it in people's eyes, on their faces.

"I decided that if I got the chance to rule, I was going to change Osgaard." It sounded pompous, said aloud. He glanced at Innis. Was she laughing at him? No. "I'd stop bondservice. I'd give back the kingdoms we'd conquered. I'd stop taxing so heavily. Peasants in Osgaard starve to death, you know. They shouldn't. Our land is fertile. If my father stopped increasing the taxes, stopped putting golden tiles on the palace roof—" The familiar, futile rage was building in his chest. He blew out a breath, tried to expel his anger. "*That's* why being a prince was important to me. Because I wanted to rebuild Osgaard."

How arrogant it sounded. Who was he to think he could make Osgaard a better kingdom? But *somebody* had to.

"I could expect to outlive my father. Whether I outlived Jaegar or not—" He shrugged. "Chances are Jaegar will sire heirs before he dies. The probability of me ever becoming king was slight." But if he *had* inherited the throne, he would have tried to be like King Magnas. A king who ruled for his people, not for himself.

Of course, that would never happen now. Even if the traitor's bounty on his head was rescinded, he could never return to Osgaard. *I'd be lynched for my witch blood.*

Innis looked at him curiously. "Did you ever think of overthrowing them? The king and your brother?"

"It did cross my mind. But rebellions and coups, civil wars..." He shook his head. "I don't want to destroy Osgaard; I want to remake it." He glanced at Innis, and away. How much should he tell her? "It had occurred to me..." He plucked a few blades of grass from the lawn.

"What?"

"If my father and Jaegar died, there wouldn't have to be a coup. I could just... take power."

Innis was silent for a moment. He didn't dare look at her. "You planned to kill them?" Her voice was neutral.

"Plan? No." Harkeld pulled up more tufts of grass. "But maybe one day I'd have grown frustrated enough to... maybe... I don't know." To gain the throne by murdering his father and brother? "That's one good thing, I suppose, about all this. I don't ever have to make that decision. Be that person."

And Osgaard would continue on its path, a kingdom ruled by greed and cruelty.

"Did you ever talk to King Magnas about your plans for Osgaard?"

Harkeld shook his head. "Those sorts of conversations are too dangerous. But... I went back twice to Lundegaard, when I was older. Magnas and I talked obliquely. I posed hypothetical questions; he answered. How does one hand back an annexed territory without plunging it into lawless chaos? How does one set taxation at levels that don't cripple the peasants? I'm sure he guessed my reasons for asking." He threw away the blades of grass.

"I'm sorry you can't be the king who changes Osgaard."

Harkeld shrugged her sympathy aside. "I probably never could have been. It was all a dream." As this was. The water lily pond, the blue sky, the witch he was talking to.

"If you can't be a king... why not be a Sentinel?"

He cast her an exasperated glance. "Innis—"

"No, listen to me. Sentinels do good things! Not on the scale of kings, but we *do* protect people and we *do* change people's lives. We're sworn to stop abuses of power. Doesn't that sound like something you could do?"

When she put it like that...

"No," Harkeld said firmly.

"You could be a good Sentinel."

"No, Innis."

She frowned at him in vexation. "You're a very stubborn man."

"I know." He pulled her close enough to kiss. "It's one of my many faults."

CHAPTER THIRTY-FOUR

AT A CAMP in the woodlands of Roubos, Bennick told him which sapling to cut and how to harden the peeled wood at the fire. Jaumé shaped his bow—a flattened shaft, narrow ends, notches for the bowstring—and shaved his arrows with his knife, fletched them with goose feathers, and Bennick gave him three iron heads and showed him how to fit them.

"Why did you use arrows, not Stars, against the hillmen?" Jaumé asked, when Nolt couldn't hear.

"Stars aren't for scum like that."

Jaumé practiced with the bow each night after he finished his work about the camp. He could hit a tree at twenty paces. And he could make a blade-throw with his knife. But all the while he was watchful, he carried out his tasks with great care and as quickly as he could. He made sure not to show he was pleased with himself. The mark Nolt had scored against him was still there, he felt it like a smear of soot on his forehead—and knew he must never get another one.

"Did you ever have a mark against you?" he asked Bennick.

"No," Bennick said. And Jaumé wondered if his mark was somehow a mark against Bennick too.

CHAPTER THIRTY-FIVE

AT FIRST GLANCE, Lvotnic was indistinguishable from Gdelsk—the wooden palisade, the log buildings, the mud. At second glance, Harkeld discovered a difference; Lvotnic was dirtier.

Rand had ridden ahead to book them on a river ferry. He met them at the gate, his headshake telling them they'd not cross the river that day.

"How long?" Cora raised her voice to be heard above the rain.

"Noon tomorrow."

This time there was no debate about whether to take rooms in an inn. They followed Rand through streets that were ankle-deep in mud. A stench pushed its way into Harkeld's mouth and nose. The residents of Lvotnic threw their refuse out their doors and left it to rot. And their shit, too.

The inn was older, bigger, and dirtier than the one they'd stayed at in Gdelsk. "It's the best I could find. The only half-decent one is full, and the others are worse than this."

Cora shrugged. "It's only for one night."

The stables were slovenly, but there was plenty of feed for the horses. They followed Rand to a taproom unpleasantly thick with smells. Woodsmoke was dominant, and beneath that were stale cooking odors, a whiff of urine, sweat, mildew. The tables hadn't been wiped down; ale lay where it had been spilled. Rotting straw covered the floor.

Justen caught his eye and pulled a face.

Rand had reserved five bedchambers. He led them upstairs. "It's less easy to defend than the inn in Gdelsk," he said, once they were all crowded into the narrow corridor. "That door at the far end leads down to the stables."

"Flin, you and Justen take the room in the middle," Cora said.

The chamber looked as if it hadn't been cleaned for some time. There were cobwebs in the corners, dust on the floor, but the beds were a pleasant surprise. They were much larger than the ones in Gdelsk.

Harkeld crossed the room to look out the window. "Squalid little cesspit."

Justen grunted agreement.

Harkeld turned and surveyed the room, his gaze coming to rest on the beds. "Beds this big beg to be put to good use."

Justen's expression became disapproving.

Harkeld shrugged out of his sodden cloak. "You're a prude, Justen." He'd meant it as a joke, but irritation edged his voice.

Justen stripped off his own cloak and shook it, drops spattering the floor. He hung the cloak on a nail sticking out of the wall, his mouth tight.

Harkeld sighed inwardly. *I've offended him.* He drew breath to apologize.

Justen swung to face him. "What if she's pregnant? That serving maid you tupped in Gdelsk. *Your* child. Did you think of that?"

"What? Don't be ridiculous. She's not pregnant by me."

"Any time you tup a woman it can happen." Justen crossed to the packsaddle and wrenched the buckles open.

"No, it can't," Harkeld said to his armsman's back, growing angry. "Because any woman with a grain of sense uses a sea sponge."

"Did you ask her if she was?"

No. He hadn't asked. He'd been too busy undressing her. "It's none of your business."

Justen snorted. He went through the contents of the packsaddle, pulling out clothes.

Harkeld gritted his teeth. He hadn't done anything wrong. The maidservant had been an adult, and she'd been willing. He wasn't going to let Justen make him feel guilty.

"You were hired to protect my body, not my seed." He spoke coldly. His palace voice. "If I choose to bed a woman tonight, it's none of your business."

Justen straightened and turned to look at him.

"This isn't a conversation I expect to have with you again, armsman. Ever."

All expression was gone from Justen's face. He looked as if he'd been carved out of wax.

Rut it. Now he'd *really* offended him.

Harkeld felt a rush of guilt, and then a surge of annoyance. "Oh, for pity's sake, Justen!" he half-yelled. "I have a bounty on my head! People are trying to *kill* me. I'm going to cursed-well take enjoyment where I can, regardless of whether you *or* the witches approve!"

Justen lost his frigid blankness. He looked down at the floor. "I beg your pardon. You're right. It's none of my business."

Harkeld's irritation drained away. "Forget it," he said. "Don't let's argue." And then, after a beat, "I'm sorry I spoke to you like that." Not the yelling, but the cold, haughty tone, as if the armsman was nothing more than a servant.

Justen was his only friend here. *Without him on this journey, I'd go insane.*

THE INN DIDN'T have a bathtub, or a razor for guests. Two buckets of lukewarm water and a rusting basin were all they could provide. Harkeld stood in the basin and sponged himself clean. Then he borrowed Ebril's razor and scraped the stubble from his face. He left Justen in possession of the razor, the basin, and one of the buckets of water, and went down to the taproom with Frane and Petrus, Hew trotting at their heels as a dog. Rand, Gerit, and Katlen were already at a table in the far corner. Someone had wiped it clean.

Cora and Innis joined them, wearing ankle-length skirts. Harkeld's gaze slid to Innis. She looked feminine, attractive. He remembered the dreams, the sweetness of her kisses. But the dream-Innis was a figment of his imagination. She wasn't the real Innis.

A slatternly serving maid brought nine tankards of ale. Harkeld took a cautious sip, lifted his eyebrows in surprise, and drank more deeply.

Justen slid onto the bench opposite him with a cheerful grin. "That tankard for me?"

"You or Ebril," Harkeld said, hooking the last tankard and passing it to Justen, relieved the armsman wasn't bearing a grudge. "It's actually quite good."

"Mine, then. Ebril's guarding."

The food, when it came, wasn't as good as the ale. Harkeld chewed stoically, examining the serving maids. Unfortunately, they were as unappetizing as the food. Willing, certainly, to spread their legs for a few pennies—one of them had gone upstairs with a bearded woodcutter and returned fifteen minutes later refastening her gown—but none of them looked as if they understood the concept of bathing.

He pushed his plate away and drained his tankard. "Another ale," he said to a passing maid.

"Me, too," Justen said, his mouth full.

The maid returned, slopped ale on the table, departed.

Harkeld slouched back against the wall. He sipped his ale and scanned the taproom. Despite the squalor, the room was almost cheerful, a large fire burning in the hearth, the noise level rising as a group of men entered, shaking out wet cloaks and calling for ale. He scrutinized their faces. They looked like woodcutters—rough, bearded, none too clean. None of them so much as glanced at their table.

Justen beckoned over a serving maid and asked her a question. Two minutes later she returned with a board painted with black and red squares and a grubby cloth bag. "You know how to play Jumping Dames?" the armsman asked, opening the bag and shaking out several dozen wooden discs painted red or black.

"I know how to play King's Leap," Harkeld said. "If that's the same thing?"

Justen shrugged. "Ach, let's find out."

It was the same game. The only difference was the names the pieces were called once they reached the end of the board and were crowned. Justen emphatically won the first round. Harkeld put down his tankard and concentrated. He won the second round.

Across the taproom, the door to the street opened. A man and woman entered, pushing wet hoods back from their faces.

The woman drew Harkeld's attention. Tall, with coal-black hair and dark eyes. Definitely beddable. But already in the company of a man. Harkeld returned his attention to the board game. He'd just won the third round when a contralto voice said, "May I join you?"

He glanced up. The black-haired woman stood there. She was even more handsome in close proximity, eyes bold, lips red and sultry. "May I join you?" she asked again. "You look like you have the right idea for such an evening."

"Please do." Harkeld shifted along the bench.

The woman sat beside him. "My name is Broushka."

"Flin," he said. "And Justen."

Justen nodded and set the board up again.

"Would you like some ale?"

"No, thank you. My brother came here to get drunk. I came for the company." She glanced at him sideways. Was that an invitation in her smile?

They played another round. Harkeld was intensely aware of the warmth of Broushka's thigh against his. Several times her fingers brushed his when they both reached for the same piece. Her laugh each time was low and rich.

Justen jumped down the board, capturing two pieces.

"I think we should play that one." Broushka reached across him. Her breast pressed, soft and full, against Harkeld's arm. His throat went dry. He thought about the wide bed upstairs.

Justen won that round.

"You have a room here?" Broushka asked, while the armsman reset the board.

"Yes."

Her lips tilted in a smile. "Shall we?"

"Uh... your brother? Won't he mind...?"

"My brother is not my keeper," Broushka said, standing. "Shall we?"

"Excuse us, Justen."

The armsman didn't look disapproving. He did roll his eyes though, as Harkeld slid out from the bench.

He guided Broushka across the taproom, his hand lightly on her waist. They climbed the stairs to the bedchambers. Hew followed, his claws making small *clack clack* sounds on the wooden risers. Broushka looked back and frowned. "Is that your dog?"

"Yes."

"I don't like dogs."

"He's old," Harkeld said, opening the door to his bedchamber. "Toothless. He'll just lie out in the corridor and sleep."

He ushered Broushka into the room and shut the door.

"Petrus," Cora said.

Petrus sighed. *Rut it.* Just how he wanted to spend his evening. He stood. Across the table he met Justen's—Ebril's—eyes and got a rueful grimace in return.

He left the taproom, climbed the stairs, and stripped off his clothes in his bedchamber. He shifted into a lizard and scuttled under the door and back along the corridor. Hew, his ears at a disgruntled angle, lay in front of Prince Harkeld's room. He shifted his tail, letting Petrus squeeze beneath the door.

The prince and Broushka stood beside one of the beds. Broushka laughingly fended off Prince Harkeld's attempt to unlace her bodice. "No, no, you first."

Prince Harkeld yielded to her request. He shrugged out of his jerkin and pulled his shirt over his head.

Petrus heaved a lizard-sized sigh and climbed one of the walls while the prince stripped, Broushka helping, murmuring, laughing.

By the time he found a good vantage point, the prince was naked and Broushka's bodice was unlaced. Broushka ran her hands up the prince's chest, then slid them low, to his groin. She began to tease him with her fingers, stroking, caressing.

Petrus looked away. *Great. Just rutting great.* How long would this take? It clearly wasn't going to be a quick five minute tup. The woman wasn't even undressed yet.

Prince Harkeld uttered a choked scream.

Petrus jerked his head around. He saw Broushka take a half-step back, saw the prince collapse to the floor.

Broushka reached beneath her skirt. She knelt swiftly at the prince's side, thrusting a knife under his jaw, the blade piercing his skin. "Your money. Where is it?"

Petrus launched himself from the wall, grabbed his magic, shifted into himself. He landed hard on hands and knees behind Broushka.

Her head snapped round. She uttered a hoarse shriek.

Petrus hauled her away from the prince, one hand fisted in her hair, the other gripping her knife arm. The woman fought with the ferocity of a wild animal, kicking, biting, slashing with her knife. Petrus released her hair and hooked his arm around her throat. By the All-Mother, she was going to slice him with that knife if he couldn't choke her into submission—

The door burst open.

Petrus spun around, struggling to overpower Broushka.

Frane and Gerit barreled into the room, wrestling with a huge black-bearded man. Behind them, Rand seized the man's neck, concentration fierce on his face.

The man kicked, his teeth bared in rage, and collapsed.

"Murderer!" Broushka shrieked. Her struggles intensified.

Rand strode forward, his expression implacable, almost frightening, and reached for Broushka's neck. The woman fought with panicked strength to free herself. Petrus hung on grimly. Broushka gave a final desperate kick and went limp in his arms.

"Did you kill her?" Petrus asked, shocked.

Rand shook his head. He pushed past Petrus and knelt beside the prince.

Their whole party was crammed into the bedchamber. "Hew, stay outside," Cora ordered.

The dog backed out of the room. Innis, white-faced, closed the door. "What happened?"

"Did he attack her?" Katlen demanded.

"*She* attacked *him*." Petrus lowered Broushka to the ground.

"For the bounty?" Cora said sharply. "She knew who he was?"

Petrus shook his head. "Robbery. She was after money." He turned and crouched alongside Rand. The healer's hands were at the prince's throat, stemming the flow of blood.

"What did she do to him?" Rand asked. "He's in a lot of pain."

"I didn't see, but at a guess... grabbed his balls and twisted."

Rand grunted. He released Prince Harkeld's throat and began to examine his groin. "Innis, the throat's yours."

Innis knelt by the prince's head. Her fingers pressed the wound closed.

Petrus glanced back. The black-bearded man lay face-down on the floor. Gerit and Frane were belting his arms together behind his back while Katlen searched him. She pulled a skewer-sharp knife from one of his boots. Justen was holding Broushka's body to the floor. Cora bound the woman's hands together. "I'd check her for more weapons," Petrus said.

Cora nodded.

Petrus looked back at the prince. The pallor of his face was frightening. He seemed barely conscious. Each breath he took was wheezing, agonized. *He's hurt badly*.

"One of his testicles is ruptured," Rand said.

The muscles in Petrus's stomach clenched. No wonder the prince had screamed.

"Help me get him on the bed."

Prince Harkeld roused as they lifted him. He made an animal-like sound of agony. His body convulsed. "He's going to vomit!" Innis cried.

Vomit the prince did, emptying the contents of his stomach on the floor. Petrus grimaced and stood back.

The sound of the prince's retching was uncomfortably like sobbing. Petrus's revulsion became pity. *Poor bastard,* he thought, helping to pick the prince up and lay him on the bed. Prince Harkeld was shivering, sweating, bloodlessly pale. Now that he'd vomited, he'd slipped back into semi-consciousness.

"Can I help?" Petrus asked. "I'm not much of a healer, but I have a little skill."

Rand shook his head.

Petrus turned to Cora. "How did you know we needed help? Did you hear us?"

"Through that din downstairs? No." Cora fished a knife from Broushka's boot. "When that one left the taproom"—a jerk of her thumb indicated the black-bearded man—"Rand was worried something was wrong. It seemed prudent to check."

Petrus looked down at Broushka. "How long will they stay unconscious?"

"Not long," Rand said. "Frane, come here." He yielded his place at the bed to Frane and crouched alongside Broushka. His fingers probed the woman's throat, paused, pressed. An expression of concentration furrowed his brow.

"What did you do?" Petrus asked when Rand removed his fingers.

"Slowed the flow of blood to the brain."

"I didn't know healers could do that," Petrus said, disturbed.

"It's misuse of healing magic," Rand said flatly. "It's dangerous. You can kill someone this way." He raised his voice. "If I ever catch Frane or Innis trying this, I'll flay them."

At the bed, Frane's gaze flicked to Rand. His expression was sober. He nodded.

Rand crouched alongside the black-bearded man and took a grip on his neck. The man stirred, then subsided into unconsciousness again.

"There. They're both out for a few more minutes."

"What made you think something was wrong?" Petrus asked.

"A nod and a smirk." Rand nudged the man with the toe of his boot. "Between the tapster and this one, just before he headed up the stairs. I'd say our two friends are here on the tapster's say-so. He probably thought we looked like good targets for this ruse."

"He was correct," Katlen said dryly.

Rand shrugged. "A nasty trick, but as old as the oceans. I saw it done once in Piestany. Sweetmeats with a hook in 'em, they call it over there."

Petrus frowned down at Broushka. "Do you think the tapster will show up here? Will we have to deal with him too?"

"I doubt it," Rand said. "I imagine he'll think these two have taken the stairs down to the stableyard and slipped out that way. But I could be wrong."

"Should we go to the municipal guards?" Katlen asked. "Lay charges?"

Cora shook her head. "We can't afford the delay—or the attention." She turned to Petrus. "Did she see you change shape?"

"No. I was behind her."

"Then..." Her eyebrows drew together as she thought. "Then we take these two down to the stables and dump them in an empty stall."

"Let them wake up and walk away?" Petrus frowned. That hardly seemed fair, after what Broushka had done to the prince.

Gerit grunted. "Dump 'em outside in the mud, I say."

Rand shook his head. "Unconscious, no. They could suffocate." He went back to the bed and bent over Prince Harkeld.

"The stables," Cora said. "But I'd like a shapeshifter there all night, just in case. We don't want to lose a horse or any supplies."

Gerit and Justen hoisted the man between them and staggered down the corridor, Katlen leading the way and Hew trotting at their heels. Petrus glanced at Cora. "I'll be a dog up here?"

Cora nodded. "Please."

Petrus lay out in the corridor and watched Gerit and Justen return, panting, and then depart again carrying Broushka's limp body.

Katlen came back with them and they vanished into the bedchamber. Voices murmured and then the door opened again. Justen headed downstairs. He returned with a pail of water and some cloths. "You're lucky," he told Petrus.

Five minutes later Justen emerged with the pail, accompanied by the smell of vomit. He returned shortly, empty-handed.

Gerit, Frane, and Katlen went to bed. Petrus lay down with his chin on his paws, bored.

Justen came out of the bedchamber. "Flin's conscious. Cora told him what happened. He wants to speak to you." He leaned his shoulders against the wall and jerked a thumb at the open door. "I'll stand guard."

Petrus went into the bedchamber. He shifted into his own shape and closed the door. Did the prince want to thank him?

Prince Harkeld lay in bed, the covers pulled up to his chest. He was still extremely pale, but his eyes were open and alert. Rand stood beside the bed. Cora and Innis were at the fireplace.

Petrus crossed to the prince. "You wanted to talk with me?"

Prince Harkeld reached out and gripped his wrist. "You..." His voice was hoarse, edged with pain. "Spying on me."

"Not spying," Petrus said, stung. "Protecting you."

The prince's grip tightened, pinching skin against bone, making Petrus wince. "If I could stand upright, I'd kill you."

So much for being thanked. Petrus twisted his wrist free and rubbed it. "Then I guess I'm lucky you can't."

Rand's lips twitched.

Petrus went out to the corridor, massaging his wrist. Innis followed. "I thought he was going to thank you, not threaten you!" She sounded distressed.

Justen's eyebrows rose.

Petrus shrugged. "If I was him, I'd be angry too. I'd want to rip me limb from limb."

Justen nodded.

"But you saved him!"

"I was also in his bedchamber about to watch him tup someone."

Innis blinked, looking confused. "You're not angry he's angry?"

Petrus shook his head.

"I thought you didn't like him."

"I don't."

Innis frowned. "Is this a male thing?"

"Huh?"

"Male pride? Male solidarity?"

"Huh?" Petrus exchanged a glance with Justen. Justen shrugged, clearly not understanding the question either.

"Never mind." Innis shook her head. "Which is your room, Ebril? Cora wants us to swap."

Justen pushed away from the wall and headed down the corridor. "You're naked, you know," he said over his shoulder.

Petrus changed back into a dog.

PETRUS SWAPPED WITH Gerit halfway through the night. He let himself quietly into the room he was sharing with Frane and climbed into bed. The sheets smelled unwashed, but he was too tired to care. He woke at daybreak, scratching. Frane was dressed and doing the dawn exercises, moving across the bedchamber in a series of lunges and retreats.

"Morning," Frane said.

Petrus grunted. He sat up and rubbed his face and scratched the bites on his jaw. Three of them, curse it, and another couple on his throat.

"Don't scratch them," Frane said. "They'll just get itchier."

"I know that," Petrus snapped. And then after a pause, "I beg your pardon, Frane." He climbed out of the lumpy bed and pissed in the stained chamberpot. He was tired, he was hungry, and he cursed-well *itched*.

"I'll heal them for you," Frane offered.

"I can do it myself. Thanks."

Petrus used his healing magic on the bites, then dressed and did the dawn exercises. He went down to the taproom feeling more alert, less irritable. He wasn't the only one who'd been bitten overnight. Katlen had bites on her face and Ebril had them down both arms.

"Once we're back upstairs, I'll heal them," Frane promised. "Just *stop* scratching them."

Rand joined them.

"How is he?" Cora asked.

"No swelling, no pain. He's fit to ride. And sire children."

CHAPTER THIRTY-SIX

BRITTA WOKE TO the sound of Karel talking softly. She opened her eyes, saw lamplight and dark shadows. Rutgar lay alongside her, fast asleep, but Lukas—

She pushed up on one elbow.

Karel sat on his pallet, holding Lukas. The little boy was curled up against the armsman's chest, trusting and relaxed, his eyes open, his expression absorbed.

"The woodcutter ran all night," Karel said quietly. "With his axe strapped to his back, and at dawn he came to a huge cave in the side of the mountain." He glanced up and saw her. "He's fine. Go back to sleep."

Britta obeyed, lying down, snuggling close to Rutgar, feeling safe and warm.

When she next woke, it was daylight and she was in the bed alone. She could still hear Karel. "That's right," he said. "Hold it like that."

She sat up, rubbing her eyes.

Rutgar was drilling a hole in an old wooden plank, his tongue poking slightly between his teeth as he concentrated. Lukas crouched alongside, holding the plank steady, watching the drill bite into the wood.

Her eyes went from the hand drill, to the trunk standing against the wall. Karel had drilled holes in it yesterday, while the boys napped. "Now I don't have to worry about them suffocating," he'd said, sitting back on his heels to examine his handiwork.

"They could have?" So many things she'd been afraid of, but not that.

"I don't know," Karel had said. "But now they can't."

He hadn't returned the hand drill to the ship's carpenter; instead, he'd fetched a wooden plank. "All-Mother only knows what they think we're doing in here."

Not this, Britta thought. Not two children playing at being carpenters.

Stubble was dark on the armsman's face. His clothes were rumpled, his black hair tousled. He looked very different from the man who'd guarded her for three years.

He glanced up and saw her and smiled, his eyes creasing at the corners. "Good morning."

Neither boy looked up. They were too absorbed in the wonders of the drill.

"How's Yasma? Did she wake? Could she eat?"

Karel lost his smile. He shook his head. "She was ill again."

Britta scrambled out of bed and crossed to Yasma's pallet. The maid was thin and still beneath her blankets.

"I had to use All-Mother's Breath this time," Karel said, crouching beside her. "There's not enough poppy syrup. I gave her a third of the dose we used on me."

"She'll be all right," Britta said.

Karel smoothed hair back from Yasma's brow. "She deserves a better life than she's had."

"She'll have that from now on. You saved her, Karel."

Karel's mouth tightened. He shook his head. "Not soon enough. Or you, either."

Rape. That's what he meant. Her own rape by Duke Rikard. Yasma's many rapes when she was barely out of childhood.

Britta looked away.

"Osgaard destroys people," Karel said. "I pray to the All-Mother that Lundegaard is different."

CHAPTER THIRTY-SEVEN

JUSTEN AND THE prince entered the stables while Petrus was saddling his mount. The prince's gaze skimmed over him as if he didn't exist.

Arrogant bastard.

Petrus buckled the girth, then walked across to Prince Harkeld. He put his hands on his hips and lifted his chin. "I don't apologize for obeying my orders, but I do apologize for invading your privacy."

The prince looked at him, narrow-eyed, then gave a stiff nod. "Your apology is accepted."

Huh. Petrus lowered his chin. Maybe the prince wasn't such an arrogant bastard after all.

"Thank you for coming to my aid."

That must have hurt to say. Petrus almost grinned. "You're welcome." He turned back to his horse. A stiff-necked whoreson, Prince Harkeld, but not completely without merit.

THE RIVER HROD was wide and brown and turgid. Downstream of the jetty, oxen lowed and men wrestled tree trunks into the water. The rain clouds pulled back and weak sunlight shone down. Innis glanced at Ebril gliding overhead, and then at Prince Harkeld, seated on his horse.

The prince had been tersely civil to Rand when the healer had checked him, curtly polite to Petrus in the stableyard, but otherwise he'd not spoken a word to anyone. His simmering rage seemed to be directed at them all. *Except for Justen.* This was how he'd been when they'd fled Osgaard. Grim. Uncommunicative. Hating everyone except his armsman.

Innis sighed. She scanned the riverbank, looking for Broushka and the black-bearded man. She couldn't see either of them, but... That youth with the bright red hair leaning against a wall, chewing an apple, idly watching the packhorses being loaded onto the ferry... hadn't he been at Gdelsk?

She looked around for the nearest shapeshifter. "Hew?"

Hew lifted his eyebrows.

"Between Gdelsk and here, was anyone on the road behind us?"

"Other than the oxcarts? There was that merchant with all the pack mules, and... uh... a single rider was all I saw, quite a way behind us."

"How far behind?"

Cora turned her head to listen.

"He got closer, the last few days. Still about four leagues back when we reached here."

"So he could be in Lvotnic now?"

Hew shrugged. "Probably."

"That youth over there, the one with hair redder than Ebril's. Is that him?"

Both Cora and Hew looked briefly. The prince turned his head too, a quick frowning glance, before returning his gaze to the river.

"Can't say," Hew said. "I only ever saw him from a distance, and he had his hood up. It was raining."

"Do you recognize him?" Cora asked Innis.

"I saw him at Gdelsk. He was at the jetty, watching."

The prince's gaze was on the jostling logs, but he was listening. His frown deepened.

"You're certain?" Cora said.

Innis opened her mouth to say *Yes,* and changed it to, "I'm fairly certain." *Am I confusing one redheaded man for another?*

"You think he's following us?"

"I don't know." She began to feel foolish.

"Hew, point him out to Gerit and Petrus," Cora said. "See whether they noticed him between Gdelsk and here. In fact, point him out to everyone. It's as well we all know what he looks like. If he is following us."

THEY HALTED BEFORE dusk. Mud. Tree stumps. It was as if they hadn't progressed at all, but were just covering the same miles over and over. Harkeld pitched tents with Justen. Rage and humiliation fermented in his chest. The witches had been *watching* him have sex.

"Flin."

Harkeld stiffened. The voice was Cora's. He didn't bother to stand and look at her.

"Do you wish to have a lesson tonight?"

Wish? What he *wished* was that Cora was a man, so he could give her the beating she deserved. He hammered a stake into the muddy ground.

Cora crouched in front of him. "I'm not going to apologize for setting Petrus to watch you," she said, her voice matter-of-fact. "My task is to destroy the anchor stones and end Ivek's curse. If I have to, I can do it with your blood and your hands, but *my* preference—and I think yours—is to accomplish it with you alive."

Harkeld lowered the mallet. He met her eyes.

"Now, do you wish to have a lesson? I bought three hundred cheap arrows in Lvotnic. You can practice burning them out of the sky."

It was on the tip of his tongue to say *No more lessons*, but they had a deal. If he reneged, Cora would renege. And burning arrows from the sky was an exercise that suited his mood. Harkeld gritted his teeth and gave a curt nod.

Cora didn't stand. "Fire magic should never be used in anger. And you're angry."

Very angry.

"But I think it could be a good exercise for you."

Harkeld almost snorted. Exercise? It would be a good release of rage.

"Healers can't bring dead people back to life. If you think there's any risk of you losing control of your magic, we'll postpone tonight's lesson."

The words brought a flash of memory: the assassin's charred body in the canyon.

"Now, tell me truthfully... are you in control of your anger?"

Harkeld considered the question seriously. He unclenched his jaw. "Yes."

"Are you certain?"

"Yes." He might hate Cora, but to kill her with his own fire, to watch her burn, screaming... "I have control of it."

"Good." Cora stood. "Justen, can you get a bow, please? And a hundred of those arrows."

"IF YOU WERE a Fithian using a throwing star to knock an arrow out of the sky, you'd aim ahead of the arrow," Cora said. "Magic isn't like that. You're not trying to anticipate where the arrow will be. Take sight of it and throw your magic at it. As long as you keep your eyes on it, the magic will find it. Take your eyes *off* the arrow and you'll probably miss."

Harkeld nodded.

"Ready?"

He nodded again and flexed his hands, as if readying for a fight. Fire magic tingled in his blood. He eyed Justen, thirty yards distant.

"All right, Justen," Cora called.

Justen raised the bow and fired, sending an arrow upwards. At the peak of its arc Harkeld raised his right hand. *Burn.*

The arrow burst into flames.

Satisfaction flared in his chest. *Got the bastard.*

The arrow curved across the sky like a small comet, burying itself in the mud fifty yards away.

Harkeld lowered his hand. "Someone could see this. Woodcutters—"

"Petrus says there's no one within leagues of us."

He nodded and watched Justen draw back the bowstring again.

"Make your fire hotter," Cora said. "See if you can burn the arrow to ash."

Justen released the bowstring.

Harkeld watched the arrow climb. He threw the hottest fire he could. The arrow ignited in a white-hot burst of flame and then vanished, leaving nothing except a smudge of ash. Even the iron arrowhead seemed to have burned.

"Like that?" Harkeld said, conscious of smugness in his chest. He looked across at Justen. The armsman was gaping upwards, mouth open.

"Yes," Cora said. "Exactly like that." She gestured to Justen. The armsman obediently reached for another arrow.

Harkeld burned that arrow and the next and the next, leaving nothing but ash in the sky. Each white-hot flare of fire seemed to ease the pressure of his rage.

"Lower the angle," Cora called.

Justen obeyed. The arc became shallower, the arrows faster.

Harkeld had to concentrate harder. *Burn. Burn.*

By the time dusk fell, there was barely any arc in the arrows' flight. Justen was aiming a few yards to Harkeld's left, each arrow whizzing past almost too fast to see. *Burn.* And another arrow. *Burn.*

The light faded. Justen lowered the bow.

Harkeld glanced at Cora.

"Impressive," she said. "You didn't miss any."

Harkeld dismissed the words with a shrug. He didn't need Cora's praise, and certainly didn't *want* it.

"Tomorrow, if you feel confident, we'll have Justen aim at you."

His smugness faltered slightly. *At* me?

"Don't worry, Katlen and I will make sure none of them hit you."

Harkeld lifted his chin. "You won't need to."

INNIS COULDN'T FIND the prince in the palace gardens. She finally found him leaning against the topmost parapet of King Magnas's castle watching the sun set behind the Graytooth Mountains. "What are you doing here?"

He shrugged, not looking at her. Still angry, then.

Innis took his hand. Anger, yes, but even stronger was humiliation.

"They watched me. They rutting *watched* me. Why didn't they tell me they'd do that? If they'd told me I'd never have—" His humiliation rose. She could feel it, like an agitated, painful cramp.

Innis tried to heal his anger and humiliation, sending cool serenity flowing into him. "Let's go to the gardens." She stood on tiptoe and kissed his cheek, a silent invitation to sex. "It'll make you feel better."

Harkeld pulled his hand from hers and rubbed his face so hard she saw his fingertips whiten. "No."

"Why not?"

"I'm too angry. If I have sex with you, I'll hurt you. And I know you're only a dream, but I *can't.*"

Innis took his hand again. *Calm. Serenity.*

Harkeld sighed. "The first time I ever had sex was here. When I was fourteen. King Magnas arranged it." He turned his head and looked at her. "But you know that."

I'm not your dreaming mind. I'm me. But she kept the thought suppressed.

"I never asked why, but now I can't help thinking... why did he do that?"

"Perhaps he saw you were ready."

"Thinking about sex? Yes, all the time. But ready for it? I was only a boy, for all I thought I was grown up."

Innis thought back to King Magnas. He'd had the same astute wisdom as Dareus. "If he had a purpose, what do you think it was?"

Harkeld's frown deepened. "I think... he thought that if I went back to Osgaard, I'd start raping bondservants, the way everyone does there, and that's just cursed *insulting*. As if I would have! As if I *could* have, after two years living here!"

"I'm sure he didn't think that."

"Until I came here, I thought bondservants were lower than animals. I thought they were moving pieces of furniture. If I hadn't been fostered here, I'd have raped them just as... as *casually* as everyone else does."

"You were a child."

"I was a blind Osgaardan idiot!"

"*Were* a blind Osgaardan idiot. You're not now."

He turned away without a smile. "If I hadn't been fostered here, I'd be another Jaegar. King Magnas was right to do it. To arrange it, to give me that lecture."

"Lecture?"

"You remember."

No. I don't. "Tell me anyway."

For a moment she thought he'd refuse, and then he blew out a breath and stared out over the ramparts. "A month before I went home, King Magnas arranged for me to have a liaison with one of the maidservants. He sat me down and lectured me beforehand. I can still remember most of it word for word... 'Sex is about sharing, Harkeld. Make sure you give as much as you take.'"

The emotion coming from him now wasn't humiliation. She was aware of how deeply he respected King Magnas.

"'Never force a woman to have sex. Never punish a woman with sex. Never have sex in anger.'" He glanced at her. "And then he said to never hurt a woman during sex unless she asks you to. I didn't understand that then."

Innis wasn't sure she did. "What else did he say?"

"Oh... a man is responsible for his own seed." He grimaced. "I forgot that in Gdelsk. I didn't ask."

"I'm sure she used a sponge. She'd have been more cautious otherwise, wouldn't she?"

Harkeld shrugged. "And he said that personally he preferred women who were clean, and that out of respect, he always bathed before he went to a woman. Oh, and all that stuff about political marriages. But that was afterwards. Once I'd actually done it."

"What about political marriages?"

"That even if a marriage is loveless, one should visit one's wife's bed with respect and kindness and then seek one's own pleasure discreetly elsewhere."

"King Magnas's marriage was arranged?" There'd been no queen at the castle.

"His first was. A political match between Lundegaard and Urel. She died giving birth to Tomas. His second was a love match, but barren. Queen Berthe died several years ago. She was a very pleasant woman. Kind."

An image came into her mind—a woman with ash-blonde hair and humorous eyes. Was that Berthe? Was she seeing his memory of the queen?

"You liked her?"

Harkeld nodded.

"Your foster parents meant more to you than your own parents?"

He glanced at her. "That's a stupid question, isn't it?"

Innis felt herself flush. It was a stupid question. The prince's own mother had died when he was still in swaddling clothes, and as for his father...

Memory gave her an image of King Esger seated on his throne, obese and malevolent. *Be silent! Or I shall have your tongue cut out.* She repressed a shiver. "I'm glad you had King Magnas and Queen Berthe."

"So am I. I hate to think who I'd have been otherwise."

"You'd have been you. Just as you are now."

He shook his head. "I've have been like Jaegar."

"Or maybe like your sister."

"Britta?" Grief flowed from him, sharp, painful, before he broke their handclasp and turned away.

"I'm sorry," Innis said, dismayed. *He's trying not to cry*. She touched the prince's elbow, stepped closer, hugged him. She felt the turmoil of his emotions. Grief was dominant now.

"I hope she's all right." His voice was low, like a prayer. "And the boys. I hope they're all right."

CHAPTER THIRTY-EIGHT

THE NEXT TIME the armsman left the cabin, he returned with two pieces of rusted chain. He ripped up their palace clothes—his scarlet armsman's tunic, Yasma's coarse cotton shift, her own silk undergown and long, silver-embroidered overtunic—and tore the two dung-covered blankets into strips with his dagger. The boys spent several happy hours knotting the pieces of fabric to the chains. "They look like hairy caterpillars," Lukas said.

Britta tied her and Yasma's palace shoes to one of the chains.

"Now it has feet!" Rutgar said, giggling with delight.

Karel dropped the chains out the window that night. Faint splashes drifted back on the breeze.

Britta felt even safer. Her princess's clothes were gone, buried deep, where no one could ever find them. *Watch me vanish, Jaegar.*

CHAPTER THIRTY-NINE

The port towns that straddled the border between Roubos and Ankeny were Drobil on the Roubos side, and Droznic on the Ankeny. There was no difference in customs and dress that Jaumé could see. The border was marked by a placid river with muddy banks, crossed by a dozen bridges.

Jaumé saw how people made way for Nolt and his band. *They know we're soldiers,* he thought proudly. And he was one of them. He not only wore his knife, he carried his bow and the three arrows he'd made.

They rode through Drobil and crossed a bridge lined with market stalls. Nolt didn't stop, although there was food to buy. In Droznic, they turned down to the waterfront. Men worked unloading the barges that carried goods from ships anchored further out. Jaumé listened to their shouts back and forth, but nowhere heard the accents of his home, Vaere.

They turned into a street leading away from the wharves. Nolt stopped before a courtyard with wooden gates. He called out a word Jaumé didn't know.

"Is this an inn?" he asked Bennick.

"A house."

"Who lives here?"

"One of our Brothers." His voice told Jaumé he was asking too many questions.

A servant came and swung back the gates.

"See to the horses," Nolt ordered a man who hurried from the stables at the back of the yard. "You, boy, help him."

The men followed the servant into the house.

Jaumé watered the horses at a trough. He rubbed down three of them and his pony while the stableman tended the others. The man watched him critically and nodded now and then. When his jobs were done, Jaumé waited by the door Nolt and the Brothers had entered. He was hungry, but knew not to go in until he was called. After a while he found a patch of sun by the stable wall and sat there. Presently he dozed.

He was woken by footsteps. Nolt and an older man crossed the yard. They went into a shed on the far side. A few minutes later they came out. The man held a pigeon. It was gray, with darting eyes and a small head.

Nolt fastened something to the pigeon's leg. Jaumé understood: a messenger bird.

The man flung the pigeon into the air and it was gone in a flurry of wings, over the wall, over the roofs. Was it going to Fith? Wherever Fith was. North across the ocean was all Jaumé knew.

The man turned and saw Jaumé. He had hard green eyes. His mouth, lengthened on one side by a scar, turned down. "How old is he?" he asked Nolt.

"Eight."

"What are you going to do with him?"

"Take him with us."

"Leave him. The jungle's too hard for a boy."

"Bennick thinks he can make it. We'll see."

"One mark?"

"Yes."

"If he gets another?"

Nolt shrugged. "We'll do what we do."

They went into the house. Nolt jerked his head at the last moment, telling Jaumé to come.

The house was bigger than any Jaumé had ever been in. Bigger than the fishermen's houses in Girond, the farmhouses, even the alderman's house. It was made of wood and had two storeys and long corridors with rooms opening off one another.

The Brothers were at a table in a wide hall. Bennick pointed to a water bowl on a side table. Jaumé washed his hands. He sat beside Bennick and ate hungrily. Even here the food was simple— bread, cheese, meat, fruit. He tried not to look at the man with the hard green eyes. He tried to make it seem like the Brothers' talk held no interest for him, but he took in every word.

"So Esger's dead?" Nolt said.

"Kings come, kings go," the green-eyed man replied. His name was Kritsen. He had a wooden hand with a thumb he moved by flexing muscles in his arm. Jaumé guessed he'd been a soldier once, and a leader like Nolt.

"It was a kill?" Ash asked.

"By Meffren."

Several of the men knew the name. They grunted, nodded.

"This new king?" Nolt asked. "Jaegar? The contract stays the same?"

"Yes."

"And we're closest?"

"That I know of."

Across the table, Kimbel grinned.

"Jaegar's honest?" Maati asked.

"No. But he'll pay the All-Mother. Meffren's made sure of that."

Bennick snorted a laugh, but Nolt frowned. "How soon?"

"Five moons," Kritsen said. "You've time enough."

Nolt nodded.

"Who went to the first stone?" Odil asked.

"Moase. And ten."

"And ten? What happened?"

Kritsen shrugged. "Only the All-Mother knows that. You been in the jungle, any of you?"

The Brothers shook their heads, except for Gant. "Been on the edges," he said. He looked like a shadow, black hair, black skin, his teeth and the whites of his eyes gleaming.

Kritsen twisted his mouth sourly and looked at each of them, sliding his eyes past Jaumé with a grimace. "No failures this time, or our honor's gone."

Nolt nodded once.

Kritsen went to a cabinet at the back of the room and took out a roll of parchment. The servant cleared the dishes away and Kritsen spread the parchment out. From his seat Jaumé could make out colors—blue, yellow, green, jumbled together—and lines like twisting snakes.

Kritsen put his finger on a spot of black where one of the yellow parts met the blue. "You're here. Droznic-Drobil." He moved his finger across to the other side of the parchment. "And you go there. Where the rivers meet."

"The stone's there?" Nolt asked.

"And our prince. If he makes it through Ankeny."

Prince? Jaumé's ears pricked. Bennick had said they were going to meet a prince. Were they joining an army? Somewhere in the jungle? He had no idea what a jungle was.

"How do we travel?" Ash asked.

"Not easily." Kritsen put his wooden hand on the black spot that was Droznic-Drobil. "Now listen."

Jaumé remembered the name of the colored parchment: a *map*. He leaned forward to see better and Kritsen's eyes swung to him, harder and greener now, in the light of an extra lamp the servant had brought.

"What's the boy doing here?"

"Ach," Nolt said angrily. He'd been rebuked. "Bed, boy, quick."

Jaumé went. He almost ran. Outside the door, he didn't know which way to go. The servant approached with another lamp and led him down a corridor into a large room lined with bunks.

Jaumé saw his belongings on a lower bunk. Bennick must have put them there.

The servant left the lamp on a shelf.

Jaumé sat on his bunk. He was angry with himself for attracting Kritsen's attention. He might have seen where they were going. He might have found out more about the prince. But he was too tired to be angry for long. He found the latrines through a side door, came back to his bunk, burrowed under the blanket, and fell asleep. He didn't wake when Nolt and Bennick and the others came in late in the night.

CHAPTER FORTY

"Open up, it's Eliam."

Karel shivered as he waited. A knife-sharp wind stung his eyes, bit into his skin, whipped his cloak around him.

The crossbar slid back. Karel stepped inside. Princess Brigitta barred the door behind him.

The cabin was cozy, the brazier burning. Rutgar and Lukas were drilling holes again.

Karel placed the bucket of fresh sea water on the floor. "We've rounded the bottom of the Hook. We're heading north. And the wind is favoring us. A southerly." Fresh from the icy waters of the south pole. "We should reach port in a day and a half."

"Good. I'm worried about Yasma. She needs to eat."

Karel shed his cloak and crossed to Yasma's pallet and crouched. He smoothed strands of hair back from her face with cold fingers. So thin and fragile.

"When we're at King Magnas's castle, she can eat and eat and eat," Princess Brigitta said at his shoulder. "I'll see that she grows fat."

"Princess..." Karel glanced up at her. "Yasma and I can't come to the castle with you."

"What?" Shock was vivid on her face. "But—"

"If word gets out that you and the boys were accompanied by two islanders... You must see we can't come with you."

"But..." Tears filled the princess's eyes. "Won't I ever see you again?"

Karel looked away. "Perhaps, in a few years, you could visit us. Perhaps not."

Princess Brigitta was silent for a long moment. "You'll marry her." It was a statement, not a question.

Karel shook his head. "I doubt Yasma will ever want a husband."

"But... I thought you and Yasma loved each other."

"We do, but not in the way you think. We're brother and sister. Here." He touched his chest above his heart. *It's you I love.* But Princess Brigitta was as far out of reach as the sun. "We'll pretend to be refugees, find a place to live far from the castle. I'll keep her safe."

"You must take my jewels."

"We won't need that much. We'll live plainly, draw no attention to ourselves." A simple life, but free, away from the brutality of Osgaard.

"How can I ever repay you?" The tears shone even more brightly in the princess's eyes, trembled on her lashes.

"By being safe and happy."

Princess Brigitta uttered a short laugh, but the sound had a sob in it. She wiped her eyes with her shirtsleeve. "The day you were assigned my armsman was the most fortunate day of my life." She took one of his hands in both of hers, raised it to her mouth, kissed it. "May the All-Mother bless you, Karel. Forever."

CHAPTER FORTY-ONE

THEY WAITED FOR a pigeon all morning. The men exercised in the yard, wearing only breech-clouts. They were so lithe they could tie their bodies into knots, it seemed to Jaumé. They could jump higher than a horse and twist in the air and land facing the other way, even old Maati, short and wiry and with his whiskers growing gray. Steadfast, with his sleek black hair and slanted eyes, was the smallest and quickest. Ash had muscles like huge slabs of meat. He was tallest and strongest.

The men all had a five-bladed Star tattooed somewhere on their bodies. It meant they were Brothers. Jaumé counted the dagger tattoos they also wore, on shoulder blades, chests, arms. Those were something to do with battles. Nolt had more than twenty, and Maati too. Bennick six. Ash and Stead both nine. Stocky Odil had four. Gant's were hard to see on his black skin. Jaumé thought he had six, too, like Bennick. The youngest Brother, Kimbel, had none.

Kritsen stripped off his clothes and joined the men, even though he had a wooden hand. He had daggers tattooed along his ribs, more than thirty of them.

Jaumé sharpened knives and arrowheads all morning. After lunch, Bennick let him practice with his bow, shooting at a butt set up in the yard. Kritsen, crossing from the stables, stopped to watch. Jaumé ran through everything Bennick had taught him, then stopped thinking and let his body do what it had to do. All three of his arrows hit the center of the butt. Kritsen grunted and went on. Bennick winked at Jaumé.

In the afternoon, Kritsen sent Jaumé with a kitchen woman to buy vegetables at the market. Jaumé didn't let his face show he was insulted. Kritsen had seen him using his bow; he knew he was a soldier, not a servant. But maybe Kritsen was telling him he was a boy with a mark against him?

The kitchen woman was bossy. "Hurry up, boy, don't dawdle." Then, "Not so fast, it's not a race." They bought greens for boiling and sweet potatoes to roast with meat. On the way back the woman said, "Wait here," and went into a pastry shop.

Jaumé put down his woven sack of vegetables. His shoulders ached and he was sweating in the humid air. It was hotter here than Vaere, even though it was nearly winter. It didn't look like Vaere, either. The buildings were built of wood, not stone, with galleries on stilts leaning over the streets.

A barmaid came out of a tavern and served three men tankards of ale. Jaumé would have liked something to drink, but knew he'd have to wait until he was back at Kritsen's house.

One of the men at the table was a sailor. He was talking about the kingdom of Lundegaard, across the gulf, and a battle that had been fought there. Jaumé caught the word "prince" and moved closer to hear.

"He crossed this desert, see, and the witches was chasin' him. These witches"—the sailor spat, his companions spat too—"they's the ones that set the curse. So they was tryin' to stop him. He had to get to the stone and they wakes a whole army of dead men from out of their graves to stop him. All bones, see, with skin hangin' off like bits of rotten cloth. There was thousands comin' at him, and the witches was comin' too, spittin' fire the way they can, and turnin' theirselves into oliphants—"

"Nah," said one of the men.

"They does! But this Prince Harkeld—"

"Where's he from?"

"Osgaard. He had an army of men from Lundegaard too, and they gets to this stone—there's three curse stones and he's the only one who can chop 'em—and he takes his axe, he's got this big axe, no one else can lift it, and he hits the stone dead center, big stone, red as blood, with the curse on it in witch language what no one can say, and it breaks in half, clean as that..." The sailor chopped with his hand. "And then it kind of crumbles into dust, and this army of dead men, their bones all comes apart and their skulls fall off their shoulders—it's true, I talked to a soldier who was there—and the witches, they give this big howl"—he spat again and the gob landed near Jaumé's feet—"like pigs when you stick 'em, and they turn into crows and fly away. True as I'm sittin' here. The soldier, he were a sergeant, he seen it with his own eyes. He's got a scar on his chest where the witches spat fire at him."

"This Prince Harkeld? Where's he now?"

"Leadin' his army to find the next stone. He's got to chop 'em all and then the curse'll end. And the witches has come back and they's chasin' him."

"I never heard of curse stones, just poison water."

"There's three stones. The second one's here, in Ankeny. In the jungle—"

The kitchen woman came out of the pastry shop, eating a tart. She called, "Boy," round a sticky mouthful, and then, "Hurry," when Jaumé hesitated.

He picked up the sack of vegetables and followed her.

Harkeld. Prince Harkeld. Now he knew. He was on his way to join the prince's army and fight witches and end the curse. Jaumé sweated under his load, and shivered with fear and delight.

CHAPTER FORTY-TWO

"Cora wants me to shoot arrows again," Justen said, while they pitched tents in the rain. "She says I'm to aim at you."

Harkeld glanced at him. The armsman's face was hard to see beneath his dripping hood. "Does that bother you?"

"Yes. What if I hit you?"

Harkeld grinned at the armsman's tone.

"It's not funny! I could kill you."

"You won't. Cora and Katlen are going to burn any arrows I miss." *But I won't miss any.*

"What if *they* miss too?"

Harkeld shrugged. "Then the healers get to show off their magic."

"They can't resurrect corpses."

"Then aim for my legs."

Justen snorted. "Ach, you can laugh now, but you'll scream if I *do* hit you."

Cora strode through the mud towards them, accompanied by Katlen and Rand. "Well? Do you still wish to try this? You don't have to. We can practice some more with—"

"I want to do it," Harkeld said.

"Very well. Justen, grab another hundred of those arrows."

Justen hurried off.

Harkeld headed away from the campsite with the three witches. "Have Justen stand there," Cora said, pointing.

Katlen nodded and halted.

Cora led Harkeld another forty or so yards towards the ragged fringe of unfelled forest. "Justen will start by aiming off to your right," she said. "And gradually alter his direction of fire. Should be a dozen arrows at least before he's aiming directly at you."

Harkeld nodded.

"You want to burn the arrows as far away from you as you can. If you fail to burn them by here..." Cora walked a dozen yards back towards the camp. "Katlen and I will burn them."

Harkeld nodded again.

Justen had reached the point where Katlen waited. From the way the witch was gesturing, she was telling the armsman exactly what Cora had told him.

"If *we* fail to burn them, then my only advice is to duck." Her gaze flicked to Harkeld's left. "Rand is here, just in case."

Harkeld followed her glance. The healer had settled himself on a wet tree stump a prudent distance away.

"If at any time you want to stop, just say so. This isn't an exercise in courage." Cora paused, her eyes on him, until he nodded. "Any questions?"

"No."

"Very well. Let's get started."

Katlen joined Cora. Forty yards distant, Justen nocked an arrow and drew back the bowstring, sighting to Harkeld's right.

Harkeld wiped rain from his face, inhaled a deep breath and flexed his hands. Nervous anticipation coiled in his belly. He summoned his fire magic.

"Ready?" Cora asked.

"Yes."

Cora signaled to Justen. The armsman released the arrow. Harkeld followed the blur of its flight with his eyes. *Burn.*

A white-hot burst of flames and the arrow was gone.

Katlen waved a halt with her hand, frowning. "What happened to the arrowhead?"

"I burned it."

Her eyebrows rose. "To ash?"

He nodded.

"It's a waste of your energy," Katlen told him. "You should use just enough magic to destroy the shaft."

"I disagree," Cora said mildly. "The next weapon he's faced with may not be an arrow. It might be a throwing star. You or I couldn't burn one of those, Katlen, but Flin might be able to. It could save his life."

"Throwing stars are made of *steel*," Katlen said. "Not iron."

"Did we keep any throwing stars?" Rand asked.

Cora shook her head. "Buried them with the Fithians. A mistake."

"The assassin I killed in the canyon," Harkeld said. "His throwing star didn't burn."

"No," Cora said. "But you had no idea what you were doing. I think there's a good chance you can burn steel if you put your mind to it. Your grandfather could."

His grandfather. The witch who'd tainted his mother's bloodline. Harkeld felt a familiar surge of anger, and shoved it aside. He didn't want to be sidetracked into rage right now. "Shall we continue?"

Cora waved to Justen. The armsman released another arrow. *Burn.* The arrow burst into flames.

Each time Justen nocked a new arrow, he sighted closer to Harkeld. The arrows became foreshortened, harder to see. Harkeld concentrated on burning them as far back towards Justen as he could. The armsman was almost directly facing him now.

Cora waved a halt. Justen lowered the bow.

"When Justen aims at you, that means *you* will be aiming at *him*. How do you feel about that?"

"I..." He frowned and tried to organize his thoughts. "I'm not aiming at Justen, I'm aiming at the arrows."

"You don't think you might accidentally burn him?"

He shook his head with a certainty that was deep and instinctive. "My magic knows what it's aimed at. *I* know what it's aimed at."

"Are you certain?" Katlen asked. "Because that's extremely potent fire you're wielding."

"I'm throwing my magic at the *arrow*," Harkeld said, annoyed. "Not at anything else. If I wasn't, then tree stumps all over this cursed place would be on fire!"

Cora smiled. "Good. As long as you realize that."

Harkeld felt slightly mollified. She hadn't been doubting him; she'd been teaching him yet another lesson.

"Ready?"

He nodded.

Cora waved at Justen. The armsman raised the bow. His stance was nervous. *He's afraid he'll kill me.*

Harkeld took a deep breath. His heart began to beat faster.

Justen released an arrow.

Burn.

Two seconds' wait. Another arrow.

Burn.

Another two seconds. Another arrow.

Burn.

Harkeld realized he was holding his breath. He made himself exhale, inhale. His heart hammered beneath his breastbone. The arrows were coming at him faster now. *Burn. Burn.* There was barely time to aim his magic, barely time to blink rain from his eyes, barely time to think, let alone breathe. *Burn. Burn. Burn.* His heart was galloping. His lungs had no air. The arrows were coming even faster. *Burn. Burn.* How could he aim when they were this fast? They were too—

An arrow streaked at him. He felt a spurt of panic—

The arrow flared alight. Orange flame, not white-hot. The shaft disintegrated into ash. The iron arrowhead struck his jerkin, a brisk tap against his chest. Harkeld flinched back a step, splashing into a puddle. His mouth was open, a yell lodged in his throat. His heart felt as if it was beating its way out of his ribcage.

The arrowhead hissed in the puddle at his feet, steam rising.

Cora waved Justen to stop and burned the two arrows he'd released. Their heads tumbled to the ground.

Harkeld swallowed the yell and closed his mouth.

"Excellently done, wouldn't you say, Katlen?"

Harkeld tried to inhale. His lungs felt uncomfortably tight. His heart still trampled in his chest.

Cora smiled at him. "How did that feel? Would you like to try that again?"

Harkeld swallowed. He wiped rain from his face. *Do I have to?*

No, he didn't. Cora had said this wasn't a test of his courage. He could stop whenever he wanted.

Harkeld touched his chest where the arrowhead had struck and glanced at Justen.

The armsman stood with his bow lowered. *How does he feel, knowing he hit me?* Scared. The armsman would be as scared as him, right now.

"Flin?"

"In my opinion, he's had enough for one lesson," Katlen said.

Her tone annoyed him. "No." Harkeld moistened his lips. "I'd like to try again."

Cora looked at him appraisingly. After a moment, she nodded. "Katlen, please tell Justen we'll do that one more time. Tell him to start slowly, and gradually build up speed."

Katlen looked as if she wanted to argue. She thinned her lips and walked back to where Justen stood.

"Are you certain about this?" Cora asked. "Because if you want to stop—"

Harkeld shook his head. Cora had stood in front of an archer and learned to do this. *If she can do it, I can do it.*

"Watch Justen," Cora said. "See if you can anticipate when he's going to release each arrow. It may make it easier."

Harkeld nodded, his eyes on the armsman.

Katlen came back to stand with Cora. Justen nocked an arrow, sighted. Harkeld's heart picked up speed again. Fear was tight in his chest, in his throat. He forced himself to breathe.

He was too far away to see the armsman's fingers move as he released the arrow, but he saw Justen reach for the next arrow in his quiver. Harkeld aimed his magic at the arrow he couldn't yet see. *Burn*. Something ignited in the air between them.

Justen reached back again, another arrow must be speeding at him. Harkeld threw his magic. *Burn*. Another flare of fire.

Ah, yes, this was easier. Much easier.

The fear faded. Harkeld began to relax. If he watched the armsman he knew when an arrow was in the air. *Burn. Burn.*

Justen began firing more swiftly. Harkeld narrowed his eyes, noting each snatch from the quiver. *Burn. Burn.*

The arrows were coming as fast as the armsman could shoot, but he had Justen's rhythm, could anticipate each arrow's release and destroy it within half a dozen yards of the bow. *Burn. Burn.* There was no fear, no panic. His heart was beating normally, his breathing was steady. *Burn. Burn. Burn.* This was simple. He had the trick of it. *Burn.* If it wasn't Justen shooting at him—if it was an enemy—he could have burned the arrows as they leapt from the bow, could have burned them *in* the bow.

"Halt!" Katlen called, waving her arm.

Harkeld burned the arrow Justen had just released and lowered his hand. He felt like grinning, like whooping aloud.

Katlen crossed her arms and frowned at him. "Could you actually *see* those arrows?"

"Uh..." He gulped a breath that was a half-laugh. "Not really, no."

Katlen's frown deepened.

"What are you aiming at, then?" Cora asked.

"I'm..." He tried to find words through the buzzing exhilaration in his head. "I'm watching Justen. I know when each arrow's coming even if I can't see it, so I throw my magic at it."

"Without actually sighting the arrow." There was censure in Katlen's tone.

Harkeld began to grow annoyed. "I got them all, didn't I?"

"You threw your magic at things you couldn't see! Do you have any idea how dangerous that is?"

"He only burned the arrows, Katlen," Cora said, her voice mild. "Nothing else. How did you do it, Flin? Can you describe it?"

The exhilaration was trickling away, replaced by irritation. "I thought that's what you meant I should do, when you said to watch Justen."

"Not quite." Cora's smile was rueful. "Can you tell us what you did? How you're aiming your magic?"

Harkeld blew out a breath. He frowned past the witches at Justen. What had he been telling his magic? "I knew each arrow was there, between Justen and me, because I'd seen him reach for the next one, so I sent my magic to find it. I wasn't aiming at nothing. I was aiming at a very *specific* something. The arrow Justen had released."

"Even though you couldn't see it." There was no censure in Cora's voice; it was a statement, not a stricture.

"No, but I *knew* it was there."

"You could have burned Justen!" Katlen said. "It was incredibly dangerous!"

"No, I could *not* have burned Justen." He scowled at her. "I was very careful *not* to. I didn't let my magic ignite each arrow until it was far enough away not to hurt him."

Cora accepted this with a nod. Katlen looked at him narrow-eyed, as if she didn't believe him.

"If I'd wanted to, I could have burned each arrow in the bow," Harkeld told Katlen, growing more annoyed. "But I didn't. I could have burned the cursed *bow*, but I didn't!"

"It's a thought..." Cora tilted her head to one side. "Shall we try?"

"The bow? From this distance?" Katlen's expression became horrified. "He'll kill Justen."

Cora shook her head. "I don't think so. Look at what he just did with the arrows. That was extraordinarily precise use of magic."

"Very *dangerous* use of magic."

Cora shook her head again. "No. Flin was in control of his magic the entire time, weren't you?"

Harkeld nodded, feeling slightly confused. "Why was what I did wrong?"

Katlen opened her mouth, but Cora spoke first. "It's not wrong, if it works—as it did for you—but for most fire mages, to aim at something you can't see is—"

"Catastrophic!" Katlen snapped.

Cora ignored the interruption. "You aimed at something you knew was there, but couldn't see. A very small, fast-moving object. It was a phenomenal exhibition of control. *I* couldn't have done it. Nor could Katlen."

Harkeld shrugged, still confused. "It was much easier than waiting to see them."

Cora's lips twitched. "I'm sure it was." She glanced over her shoulder at Justen, waiting in the rain, his bow lowered. "How would you burn a bow without harming the archer?"

"Uh..." He blinked, focused on the question. "I'd... set fire to it at the top or the bottom."

"Could you do it at this range?"

Harkeld hesitated. When he'd been burning the arrows he'd *known* he could set them alight in the bow if he'd wanted to. This was almost the same thing, wasn't it? "Yes."

Cora turned to Katlen. "Let's try it."

"The danger—"

"Flin won't harm Justen, will you?"

He shook his head.

"You're rushing him, Cora! Instruction should be paced—"

"To the needs of the student. And this is a student with a bounty on his head."

Katlen closed her mouth.

"Flin?" Cora asked. "Do you wish to try?"

"Yes."

"Katlen, can you please tell Justen what we're doing?"

Katlen hesitated, her frown deepening.

"Tell Justen I won't burn him," Harkeld said. "He has my word."

Katlen's mouth tightened. She turned away and walked back to Justen, her boots splashing in the puddles.

Cora watched Katlen speak with Justen. "If, when the moment comes, you don't wish to do it..."

"I'm not going to risk Justen's life for the sake of my pride."

"No. I didn't think you would."

Katlen returned.

"Justen agreed?" Cora asked.

"*He* has faith in him." Katlen's tone made it clear that she didn't. "You'll have to make your fire less hot, young man, else you'll burn him, whether you think you will or not."

"I know." But he wasn't irritated by Katlen this time. He didn't want to hurt Justen either.

"After the sixth arrow, go for the bow," Cora said.

Harkeld nodded and took a deep breath and stared across at his armsman. Dusk was closer now, but the rain had eased to a light drizzle. It was no harder to see Justen than it had been before.

"Ready?" Cora asked.

He nodded again, reaching for his fire magic, raising his right hand.

Cora signaled to Justen.

Harkeld narrowed his eyes, focusing all his awareness on Justen's movements. *Burn.* An arrow flared alight. *Burn.* It was as easy as it had been last time, as effortless. His magic went where he wanted it to, did what he wanted it to do. *Burn. Burn. Burn.* One more and he'd aim for the bow. *Burn.*

He fixed in his mind what he wanted to do, threw his magic. *Burn.*

A small puff of orange flame blossomed at the top of Justen's bow. The armsman jerked back a step, tossing the bow from him.

No one said anything for several seconds. The light patter of drizzle was loud in the silence. Cora turned to look at him. "Well done."

Harkeld lowered his hand. He tried not to look smug. "Thank you."

Katlen crossed her arms tightly over her chest. "In twenty years of teaching fire magic at the Academy, I've never seen that kind of control." She said the words stiffly, as if it pained her to utter them.

"Well, now you have," said a voice to their left.

Harkeld started. He'd forgotten Rand was there.

"That was quite a display," the healer said, standing. He clapped Harkeld on the shoulder. "Well done."

"Thank you," he said again.

Justen jogged through the mud towards them. "That was incredible!"

Harkeld went to met him. "I didn't hurt you? The flame wasn't too hot?"

Justen shook his head, grinning widely. "A *poof...*" He mimed with his hands. "And the bowstring came off. I didn't get burnt at all."

"Good," Harkeld said, relieved. "Where's the bow? I'd like to have a look at it."

Justen trudged back beside him. Harkeld crouched and picked up the bow, turned it over in his hands. The top was singed, the bowstring melted through. Exactly what he'd told his magic to do.

"Katlen tried to talk me out of doing it," Justen said in a low voice. "But I figured that if you could let me shoot at you, I could let you throw magic at me."

Harkeld glanced at him.

"Mind you, I *was* scared you'd burn my hands off," Justen said frankly. "Most of the fire you throw is so cursed *hot.*"

"Thank you for trusting me," Harkeld said, standing.

Justen shrugged. "Ach."

Harkeld headed for the campfire, carrying the bow.

"Were you afraid I was going to hit you?" Justen asked, matching step with him. "Because *I* was."

"That first lot of arrows, yes. I was rutting *petrified.* Especially when I missed that last one. But I told myself that if they'd learned to do it"—he jerked his head back at Cora and Katlen—"I should be able to, too."

"I don't think they mastered it so fast," Justen said. He

turned on his heel and raised his voice. "How long does it usually take a mage to learn to burn arrows from the air?"

"Months," Katlen said. "Some never manage."

Justen turned to Harkeld and nudged him, grinning. "You're a prodigy."

"THERE'S A SINGLE traveler behind us again," Hew said.

Harkeld glanced up from his stew.

"The redheaded man?" Cora asked.

"Can't tell. His hood was up. It could be the person who was behind us from Gdelsk, the horse looks similar. But then all brown horses look the same."

"How far behind is he?" Justen asked.

"He stopped at that woodcutters' camp four leagues back, pitched a tent there."

Four leagues. Twelve miles. Harkeld started chewing again.

"This drizzle looks like it's clearing. He might have his hood back tomorrow," Rand said.

"He's probably nothing to worry about. Just headed in the same direction as us, is all. I mean, one man? What could he do?" Gerit shoveled a spoonful of stew into his mouth.

Harkeld agreed. But even so, he took extra care sharpening his sword that evening. Beside him, Justen whistled between his teeth as he worked. The drizzle stopped. The clouds thinned, showing them a full moon rising.

Harkeld laid down the whetstone and examined his sword. It was a beautiful weapon—the flames engraved on the blade, the flaring tang.

It had been a gift for a prince. But he was no longer a prince. It was now a witch's sword. A fire witch's sword.

He touched the engraved flames with his fingertips. Would King Magnas wish the gift unmade?

* * *

HARKELD LAY ON soft, sun-warmed grass, holding Innis. His body was relaxed, sated. *Life doesn't get much better than this.*

"You really should think about becoming a Sentinel," Innis said.

Harkeld's eyes opened. He frowned up at the blue, cloudless sky. "I've never seen anything like what you did today. Even Dareus couldn't throw fire like that."

"I don't want to be a Sentinel."

"But it's—"

"I know. It's an honor being a Sentinel. Protecting the weak. Saving the innocent." He rolled to face her. "*I don't want it,* Innis. And I don't want to discuss this again."

She sighed. "All right."

Harkeld tucked her in close to his body. "Sleep," he told her. He drifted towards slumber, holding her.

"Did you hear that?"

Harkeld slitted his eyes drowsily open. "What?" He turned his head, but Innis was gone. "Huh." He closed his eyes and fell asleep in the warm sunlight.

INNIS WOKE IN the dark tent. An owl's screech echoed in her ears. She pushed up on one elbow. Beside her, Prince Harkeld breathed quietly. He hadn't been wrenched from their dream. *Maybe I imagined it?*

Innis listened. The night was silent. No rain pattered on the tent. No wind blew.

I dreamed it.

She lay back down. There was nothing to worry about. A shapeshifter kept watch over the camp. No one could creep up on them.

But as she shut her eyes, she thought she heard a sound outside.

Innis sat up. She pushed aside her blanket, crawled down her bedroll, reached for the ties fastening the tent flap—and paused. If someone *was* outside...

It was probably a mage needing to pee.

Or it could be bandits. Or assassins.

Innis leaned close to the tent flap. A cool breeze seeped through the gaps. *If I shift into a dog, I could smell if anyone's there.*

But taking off Justen's clothes would take time, make noise. She'd likely wake the prince—

Her ears caught a sound. The back of her neck prickled. That had been a footstep, surely?

She needed dog's ears and a dog's nose, but partial shifting was forbidden.

The faint sound came again.

Innis gathered her magic. *A dog's head*, she told it, and shifted.

The disorientation made her lurch, even though she was kneeling. She had a man's body and a dog's head, and it was *wrong*. She pressed her hands to the ground to hold herself up, squeezed her eyes shut, breathed deeply to quell the dizziness—and froze, mid-breath. There *was* someone outside. She smelled him.

Her ears pricked. Yes, someone was treading quietly towards the tent. Halting. Crouching. Her nostrils widened, breathing in the scent. Male. And she smelled blood. Fresh blood.

Innis shifted fully into Justen and moved backwards on her bedroll. Where was the prince?

She found his ear, bent her head. "Harkeld," she whispered.

The prince jerked awake, inhaling sharply. Innis laid her hand over his mouth. "There's someone outside," she breathed in his ear.

He tensed.

"When he opens the flap, give us light. And make lots of noise. Wake everyone."

Innis removed her hand. She crouched on the bedroll, searching for her sword. Where was it? She always left it unsheathed at night...

There. She lifted it carefully, silently.

The prince sat up alongside her, a movement she felt rather than heard.

Innis breathed shallowly, gripping the sword, straining to hear, her attention focused on the tent flap. If the man was Fithian, he'd kill her before she could wield the sword. *Then I'll be a lion.*

The sort of lion Justen would be, large and male.

The tent flap rustled faintly. A sliver of moonlight shone into the tent.

Innis gripped the sword more tightly. She gathered her magic, feeling it sting over her skin.

The sliver of moonlight widened. A dark shape crouched in the entrance.

Flames burst into life on Prince Harkeld's hand, illuminating the tent and the stranger. Innis saw a startled face, wide eyes reflecting the firelight, red hair.

She opened her mouth to yell.

The man pushed his shoulders inside the tent. A throwing star gleamed in his hand.

Innis dropped the sword and launched herself forward, shifting shape so fast it hurt. The yell in her throat came out as a roar.

CHAPTER FORTY-THREE

JUSTEN IS A witch?

Shock held Harkeld frozen for an instant, a shout trapped in his throat.

Justen's charge knocked the man backwards. Assassin and lion disappeared into the darkness.

Justen's a witch?

Harkeld grabbed Justen's sword, scrambled over the remains of the armsman's clothes, and burst out of the tent, yelling at the top of his voice. He threw his magic at the campfire, making it tower high, casting light as bright as day over the camp.

Man and lion fought in the mud. He saw a booted leg kicking, saw the flash of a blade, saw dagger-sharp teeth sink into a pale throat.

The struggle ceased abruptly.

Around him, tent flaps burst open, witches scrambling out with swords in their hands. The lion lifted its huge head. The white teeth ran with blood. Blood stained the heavy mane.

Harkeld stopped yelling.

The silence was total. Shocked.

"Get down!" Cora snapped. "You're a target!" She turned and shouted orders. Witches changed shape, wolves bounded into the dark, an owl launched into the sky.

Harkeld crouched, gripping the sword, scanning the campsite. His gaze kept returning to the lion standing over the Fithian's body.

That lion was Justen. *Justen.*

Cora and Katlen and Rand surrounded him, facing outwards, swords bared. "What happened?" Cora asked.

Harkeld swallowed, found his voice. "Justen heard something. He woke me. It was the man we saw at Lvotnic." *And then Justen turned into a lion and killed him.* Justen. A witch.

His head still rang with the shock of it. He peered past Katlen's legs, looking for the lion. It no longer stood over the body. He watched the animal pad across to a tent and thrust its head inside.

The lion changed shape, becoming Justen. The armsman crawled into the tent. A moment later he backed out, his expression grim. "Frane's dead."

Justen's mouth and chin were bloody. A cut scored across his ribs, trickling blood. The armsman's eyes found him, crouching behind the witches like a coward. "You all right?"

Harkeld stood.

"Get down," Cora said. "There may be more of them."

"But—"

"Get *down*."

Harkeld crouched again, anger burning his cheeks.

"Justen, get up in the sky," Cora said. "See if you can find Gerit. He was on watch."

The armsman nodded, changed into an owl, flapped upwards. Harkeld followed the bird's ascent. A witch. Rage rushed into his chest, hot and acrid.

A silver wolf loped into the firelight and changed shape. "Definitely only one scent," Petrus said. "Leads up to the forest, then west. At a guess, he walked from the woodcutters' camp. You want us to follow it all the way back?"

Harkeld straightened from his crouch.

"Tell Ebril to follow it back a few miles, just to be sure. You look for Gerit. He must be somewhere."

Petrus nodded and shifted into wolf shape again. He vanished into the darkness.

Harkeld shouldered past Katlen and walked to his tent. He ducked inside. Justen's torn clothes were strewn across his bedroll.

He found the armsman's—no, the lying *witch's*—scabbard and sheathed the sword he'd been gripping. He grabbed his own sword and his boots and backed out of the tent.

"I've found Gerit!" someone yelled.

Harkeld jammed his feet into his boots and followed Rand and Cora and Katlen, jogging in the direction of the yell. Away from the campfire, it was difficult to see. He lit his palm, the flames pushing back the darkness.

It was Hew who'd shouted. The shapeshifter was pale-faced, close to tears.

"Let me see," Rand said, hurrying forward. "I might be able to... Ah...." He halted.

Cora halted too. "Is he...?"

"Yes. I'm afraid so."

The body lay behind a tree stump. Harkeld stepped past Cora. For a moment he saw nothing. Was this a joke? There was no pale, naked corpse in the mud—and then he saw the owl, an arrow piercing its breast: Gerit.

A wolf loped up and shifted into Petrus. The witch went down on one knee beside the dead bird.

"Why didn't he change shape when he died?" Harkeld asked, confused.

"You can't shift once you're dead." Petrus's voice was harsh.

Cora touched his elbow. "Come back to the fire."

Harkeld glanced at the dead owl one more time, and followed Cora back to the camp. The fire still roared into the sky, blisteringly hot. He sent his magic out to it, tempering the flames to a warm orange-red bonfire.

The Fithian lay where Justen had killed him, blood puddling on the ground. Cora walked across to the body. "What happened to Gerit is what shapeshifters fear most," she said, looking down at the assassin. The man's spine gleamed whitely at the back of his ripped-open throat. "And Frane..." Grief spasmed across her face. "His first mission."

Two more to add to the list of those who've died for me.

Harkeld looked away. "I'll get the shovels."

*   *   *

By dawn, they'd dug graves for Frane and Gerit. The assassin didn't get one. They loaded his body onto a packhorse and Rand took it into the dark forest to dump it.

Harkeld helped lay Frane in his grave. *He's no older than me.* He looked away, grimacing. Movement caught his eye: Rand, trudging back towards them, leading the packhorse.

Cora placed Gerit in the hole they'd dug for him.

Harkeld stared down, frowning. That limp, dead bird was Gerit? Gerit, with his bristling eyebrows and bristling beard and bristling temper?

He understood why the witches were so distressed. Gerit would go to the All-Mother as an owl, not a man.

Harkeld scooped mud into the hole. A couple of shovelfuls and it was done. The smallness of the grave was disturbing. He hadn't liked Gerit, but the man had deserved to die in his own body.

And Gerit didn't like me, but he died for me. Or because of me. Or both.

Harkeld grimaced again, looked away.

Cora spoke the words committing Gerit and Frane to the All-Mother's care. They ate a silent breakfast, while Ebril wheeled in the sky above them. Harkeld looked around for Innis, but couldn't see her. She must be flying further distant.

In his dream, she'd heard something and left him. Had his sleeping mind heard Gerit's dying screech? Or footsteps outside the tents? Whatever it had been, he hadn't woken.

But Justen had woken.

Justen. Who'd pretended to be his friend. Whom he'd trusted. Justen, who was a rutting *witch*.

Harkeld put down his bowl, rose to his feet, and walked across to his tent. He hauled out the bedrolls and blankets and the armsman's torn clothes and began wrenching the stakes out of the ground.

The Fithian must have been planning to kill everyone, tent by tent. *And then cut me up at his leisure.* Head and hands in a sack. Blood in a flask. And now, as the sun rose, the man would have been strolling back to the woodcutters' camp, whistling, counting the number of new tattoos his night's killing had won him and planning what to do with the bounty.

But for Justen, it might have worked.

Justen. Pretending not to be a witch.

Harkeld hissed between his teeth. He rolled up the tent, hefted it on his shoulder, and carried it to the picketed horses. He set to work loading the packhorses. Rand joined him, then Petrus and Katlen and Hew.

They'd known Justen was a witch.

Harkeld saddled his horse. The events of the morning jostled in his head. Everything had sharp edges. The shock of the assassin, the shock of Justen, the deaths. He shook his head and tried to focus on one thing. Not the gleam of the throwing star in firelight, not the assassin lying dead with his throat ripped out, not the bedraggled owl's corpse, but Justen's roar as he shifted into a lion.

Anger boiled up in his chest. Justen had lied to him. The friendship he'd valued wasn't real. Harkeld tightened the girth with a jerk. *He played me for a fool.*

"Flin?"

Harkeld stiffened. The voice was Justen's.

He turned to face the armsman.

"Can we talk, please?" Justen gestured towards the fire.

Harkeld didn't move, didn't acknowledge the request. Anger pressed against his ribcage. He knew he should thank Justen. The armsman had saved his life this morning. "You lied to me. You're a witch."

"Yes. I'm sorry."

"I *trusted* you, you whoreson." He took a step towards Justen, his fists clenched. "I thought you were my friend."

"I am."

The lie—on top of everything that had happened that morning—was too much. Harkeld's anger boiled over. He swung at Justen.

The armsman went down like a tree being felled.

"Whoreson!"

Harkeld spun round. Petrus came at him, face suffused with rage.

"Stop it! Both of you!" The voice was Cora's, cutting the air as sharply as a whip.

Rand caught Petrus's elbow, swinging him away. "Get back to the horses."

For a moment Harkeld thought Petrus would disobey—then the young witch shrugged Rand's hand off and turned back to the packhorses, glowering.

Rand strode past Harkeld and crouched at Justen's side. The armsman stirred, groaned, blinked dazedly.

Cora hurried up. She flicked a glance at Harkeld and crouched too. "Is he all right?"

"Broken jaw and concussion," Rand said. "It's a clean break, easy to fix, but the concussion will take a bit of work."

"How long?"

Rand shrugged. "Give us an hour?"

Cora nodded and stood. She turned to Harkeld, twitched her plait over her shoulder, and put her hands on her hips. Her plain, mild face was grimmer than Harkeld had ever seen it. "I know that this morning has been stressful." Her voice was curt. "But I will not tolerate fighting. Is that understood?"

Harkeld pressed his lips together and scowled at her. He *refused* to feel ashamed of himself.

Cora took his silence as an answer. She turned away.

Harkeld glowered at her back. He shook out his fist and turned back to the horses.

CHAPTER FORTY-FOUR

THEY FOLLOWED A wide road north, busy with mule trains and wagons, then turned off and climbed a dirt trail into the mountains. At least, Jaumé thought they were mountains, but Bennick told him they were only foothills. "The Palisades, now *they're* mountains, lad," and he'd waved his hand west, and when the clouds lifted, Jaumé saw sharp white peaks rising high into the sky.

The dirt track was narrow and steep, but Kritsen had said this way was quicker. It would cut more than a week off their journey.

A forest closed around them, tall trees with bark peeling in long, gray strips. "Is this jungle?" Jaumé asked.

"No," black-skinned Gant said. "This is highland. The jungle's lowland. You'll know when we get there."

"How?"

"It's wet and it's hot and it stinks. There's no mistaking the jungle, boy."

Encouraged by Gant's willingness to talk, Jaumé dared to ask why his skin was black.

"Because I was born in Issel," Gant said. "Everyone has black skin there. Just like everyone in the Dominion looks like Steadfast."

Stead glanced sideways out of his slanting dark eyes and nodded.

Jaumé had never heard of Issel, or the Dominion. The world was much bigger than he'd thought. Questions crowded on his tongue. What made people's skin black? Did everyone in the Dominion have names that meant something? But he encountered a look from Bennick and kept his mouth shut. Bennick didn't like it when he asked too many questions.

CHAPTER FORTY-FIVE

INNIS LOOKED AHEAD to where the prince rode, sitting stiffly in his saddle, radiating rage. *I trusted you!* She touched her jaw, remembering his expression as he'd spoken those words.

"Hurting?" Cora asked, riding alongside her.

"No." Innis lowered her hand. "He was upset."

Rand, riding on her other side, grunted a humorless laugh. "We're all upset, today."

They passed an ox team laboring westward, wagon piled high with tree trunks. The driver raised his hand in greeting.

The road curved and dipped. They picked their way through a muddy ford. "Cora..." Innis said, once they'd gained the far bank.

"Yes?"

"I broke another Primary Law this morning."

Both Cora and Rand glanced at her. "Which one?" Cora asked.

"Partial shifts."

"Don't look so worried," Cora said. "Tell me."

"I woke because I thought I heard an owl screech." And she had. Gerit's death cry. "But then I heard nothing, and I thought I should go outside and check, but I also thought that if something *was* wrong, it was best not to blunder around making noise. So... I gave myself a dog's head, so I could hear and smell better."

Cora's eyebrows rose.

"I knew it was wrong, but I did it anyway."

"Did you hear him?" Rand asked.

"Yes. And smell him. And smell blood. So I woke Flin."

"Innis..." Cora sighed. "I'm not going to tell you that what you did wasn't wrong. You know it was as well as I do. But you probably saved your own life by doing it. And his. And ours. I can't censure that. And I can't even tell you not to do it again. On this mission, *any* means are justified. Even breaking Primary Laws."

"I know." Innis twisted the reins around her fingers. She was breaking two Laws right now, being Justen. And two more every time she ate or slept in a shape not her own.

"You made the right decision. If you face a similar choice in the future, I'm sure you'll make the right decision again.

"I broke Justen's cover." And that was almost worse than breaking a Primary Law. She touched her jaw again, remembering the prince's face, the emotion in his voice.

"You did what Dareus would have expected. The whole purpose of Justen was to have a Sentinel with Flin at all times, someone who could use magic to protect him if necessary."

"I know." Innis looked down at her hands, Justen's hands. "Should I stop being Justen now? He's no use any more, is he? Flin hates him."

"By the All-Mother, no!" Cora said.

Startled, Innis glanced at her.

"He's going to be difficult to handle after this. If he knew you shapeshifters had been taking turns being Justen, he'd be unmanageable."

Rand uttered a short laugh. "Unmanageable? He'd be murderous."

"You'd be upset too, if you'd been deceived like that," Innis said.

"I don't disagree," Cora said. "And I'd like this mission to be no more difficult than it already is. Justen stays. In a way, it'll be easier; if Flin isn't talking to Justen, then Hew can take a turn being him too."

"Justen can patrol too," Innis said. "If he's no longer an armsman."

Rand frowned. "That's a difficult shift, isn't it? I noticed you did it this morning, but how long can you maintain it?"

"It was hard," Innis admitted. It had taken a surprising amount of effort to be a large, male lion and Justen-colored owl. Her magic had fought her, wanting her to be a lioness, wanting her owl feathers to be black, not light brown. "I could probably only do it for three or four hours. I don't think the others could do it for that long. Not that they're incompetent or anything, it's just... it requires a lot of magic and I'm... um, stronger than them." She felt herself flush.

"So you are," Cora said, with a smile. "Very well, Justen can patrol at night—which the four of you can do in your own owl shapes. And if he's ever required to shapeshift during the day, we'll keep it short. And delegate that task to you. Agreed?"

Innis nodded.

"And when we receive reinforcements for Sault, we'll send Justen home, and all these problems will go away. Thank the All-Mother." Cora glanced ahead to where the prince rode. "He'll have to have a shapeshifter share his tent until then. That will be a battle in itself."

"A shapeshifter?" Innis said dubiously. "I don't think he'll agree."

"He won't have a choice."

A ghost of a smile crossed Rand's face. "Good luck with that."

IT WAS A day like Harkeld had in his dreams. Warm sunshine, blue sky. Birdsong. A gentle breeze.

He scowled at a patch of daisies growing alongside the road. Anger gnawed in his chest, burrowing deep, twisting his innards into knots. And beneath the anger was humiliation. It was in his blood, just as the fire magic was in his blood. *How could I have been so gullible?*

And beneath the anger and humiliation, in the pit of his belly, was a cold eddy of shame. He hadn't behaved well. He'd hit Justen instead of thanking him for saving his life.

I behaved like a child.

But he *felt* like a child, curse it. A five-year-old who'd just lost his best friend. Betrayed and bewildered. And angry.

I liked him. I trusted him.

And the rage surged again and he was glad—*glad*—he'd punched Justen.

HARKELD UNSADDLED HIS horse, watered it, fed it, checked its hooves—not speaking to the witches—then took one of the damp, muddy tents and unrolled it between two tree stumps and set to work hammering the stakes into the ground.

"Flin."

He glanced up. Cora stood there.

Harkeld got to his feet, gripping the mallet. His eyes narrowed. *No lesson tonight.* His mouth opened to say the words.

Cora held up a throwing star. The sight of it arrested the words on his tongue.

"Shall we?"

Harkeld closed his mouth. He dropped the mallet and followed Cora away from the campsite.

They walked for nearly a hundred yards before Cora halted. She held the throwing star by one razor-sharp blade. "Do you know how to throw these?"

He shook his head. It took Fithians years to master that skill, or so he'd heard.

"None of us do either. I'll put it here." She jammed the tip of one blade into a crack on top of a tree stump.

"How many are there?"

"Five."

Good. He didn't have to master this the first time. He walked half a dozen yards back from the stump.

Cora came to stand beside him. "Whenever you're ready."

Harkeld summoned his magic. Fire crackled inside him. He stared at the star. Not iron like the arrowheads, but steel. Were the witches sniggering at him while they set up camp, thinking him even more of fool for believing himself able to burn steel?

Harkeld gritted his teeth. He'd prove them wrong. He willed his magic to become even hotter. Scorchingly hot, searingly hot, as hot as it had been in the catacombs. He raised his hand and concentrated on the throwing star. *Burn.*

There was a blinding flash of white light and a thunderous crack of sound. Scalding air buffeted him.

Harkeld stepped back a pace. He rubbed his eyebrows. They still seemed to be there. He blinked, trying to see past the bright imprint of flames on his vision. Gradually the tree stump came into focus. The top was charred, smoking slightly. The throwing star was gone.

Had the blast blown it off?

Harkeld walked around the stump, examining the ground. No blackened star, no blobs of molten metal steaming in the mud.

He glanced at the camp. *Laugh at me, will you?*

"Gone?" Cora asked.

Harkeld nodded.

"I thought you could do it."

Cora stuck a throwing star into another stump. Harkeld stared at it. There was little use being able to destroy a throwing star if he incinerated everyone nearby. If he'd used that much magic in the tent this morning, he and Justen would be dead, as well as the assassin.

So I need to keep my magic as hot, but focus it tightly. Not an explosive blast, but a tiny, controlled spurt.

Harkeld flexed his fingers and called up his magic again. He narrowed his eyes, staring at the throwing star, visualizing what he wanted his magic to do. Fire roared inside him, so hot his skin should be smoking.

Burn.

There was flash of bright white light, a crack of sound, but no roaring blast of heat coming back at him. Harkeld blinked, squinted. Was the throwing star gone?

The stump was black and smoking and bare.

"Excellent," Cora said.

By the fourth throwing star, he'd got his magic to an intense burst of fire that completely vaporized the weapon and left only a small scorch mark on the tree stump.

Cora took the last star from the leather pouch the assassin had kept them in. "I'll toss this in the air, if you like?"

Harkeld nodded.

Cora held one blade carefully between her thumb and forefinger. She extended her arm. "Ready?"

Don't lose a finger. He bit the words back and gathered his magic. "Yes."

Cora tossed the star into the air. It spun upwards, razor-sharp blades flashing in the last rays of sunlight.

Burn.

A flare of white flame, a small crack of sound, and the throwing star was gone. All that remained was a handful of ash drifting down.

"Well done," Cora said.

Harkeld accepted this with a nod. He turned towards the camp.

"Flin."

Something in Cora's voice stopped him. He glanced at her.

"You will have one of the shapeshifters in your tent tonight."

"What?" His anger came bursting back. "No!"

"You will have a shapeshifter in your tent, tonight and every night. For precisely the reason that Justen demonstrated this morning."

He drew breath to refuse.

"It is not negotiable."

Harkeld glowered at her. He trembled on the brink of an outburst of rage, a screaming, stamping, hair-pulling tantrum. *Like a child,* he told himself.

He took a deep breath, made himself unclench his hands, unclench his teeth.

"The choice of shapeshifter is yours. I suggest Justen. He has proven his ability to protect you."

Harkeld shook his head.

"Why not?"

Because I trusted him.

Cora waited for him to speak, then shrugged. "Let me know who you choose." She headed for the camp.

"Ebril," Harkeld said when she was half a dozen yards away.

Cora halted. She turned to face him, her hands on her hips. "Justen didn't volunteer to be your armsman. He was given no choice; he was the only one of us you hadn't seen. He wasn't happy about deceiving you."

Harkeld turned his back to her. After a moment, he heard Cora walk away.

He looked down at the ground, scuffing the mud with his boot. Ebril. He grimaced. It had been Ebril whom Dareus had chosen to share his tent that very first night. *And I said I'd kill him.* And Dareus's response had been to give him Justen.

"Rut it," Harkeld said aloud, gouging out a chunk of mud with his heel. Back then, he'd rather have murdered a witch than share his tent with one. But he'd been sharing a tent with a witch for two months. *And I am one myself.*

He looked at the camp, a hundred yards distant. He saw the picketed horses, saw the witches, saw the tents. The campfire was golden in the gathering dusk.

He didn't want to go back. He wanted to turn and walk towards the dark, distant fringe of unlogged forest.

Can't I leave the witches? Take my horse and set out alone? He didn't need them any more. He knew how to use his fire magic. A sword, a horse, his magic... what more did he need?

Harkeld kicked at the mud, gouging out another chunk. Without the witches, he'd have been dead many times over. He needed them, if he was to survive. If the Seven Kingdoms were to survive.

"Rut it," he said again, and then he headed back to the camp.

*   *   *

"BE JUSTEN UNTIL after dinner," Cora said, keeping an eye on the prince as he approached. "Then you're yourself for the rest of the night. Take the first watch. Petrus will take the second."

Innis nodded.

Cora smiled at her. "At least you can sleep as yourself again. That's one less Primary Law broken."

Innis tried to smile back. *I don't want to sleep as me. I want to sleep in the prince's tent and share his dreams.*

They ate a silent dinner. The campfire seemed very empty. Gerit had taken up so much space it felt as if they'd lost four people, not two. Innis looked at her bowl, stirred the stew with a spoon. She didn't feel hungry.

She put down the bowl, pressed her palm to the ground. *I killed him for you,* she told Frane and Gerit. *He's dead.*

Did they hear? Did they feel avenged?

Frane had had green magic, she remembered. He'd coaxed wild grasses to grow on Susa's grave. *And I gave her meadow flowers too,* he'd told her. *It will be beautiful for her in summer.*

No one had been able to do that for Frane.

Innis pushed to her feet and walked away from the fire. She'd taken a tent by herself. Justen's bedroll and blanket were in it. Innis crawled inside, stripped off Justen's clothes, and changed into herself. She wrapped the blanket around her. It was damp, smelling of mildew.

The Grooten amulet still hung around her throat, the walrus ivory warm and smooth. She pulled it off, clenched it in her fist. Today she'd lost what made Justen important. Riding at the prince's side, being his friend.

Footsteps stopped outside her tent. Someone crouched at the entrance. "Innis?" The voice was Petrus's. "Are you all right?"

"I'm fine. It's just... it's been such an awful day."

Petrus crawled into the tent. "You didn't eat."

"I know. I was thinking about Frane and the wildflowers he grew on Susa's grave."

Petrus put an arm around her, pulled her into a hug.

"I hardly noticed Frane, and now he's dead," Innis said. Regret and guilt and grief choked her. Tears spilled from her eyes.

"I know." Petrus held her close. "But you got the bastard who killed him, Innis. You gave him that much."

Innis wiped her eyes with the blanket and nodded.

"Innis... did Rand or Cora talk to you about that kill?"

"They asked if I was all right."

"Are you? Because killing someone that way is pretty awful."

At his words, the taste of blood filled her mouth. She was abruptly glad she hadn't eaten her dinner.

"If you want to talk about it, there's me and Ebril. We both know what it's like."

Innis nodded. "Thank you."

"How's your jaw?"

"Fine. Rand helped me. It didn't take long." She leaned against his shoulder, oldest friend and almost-brother. *Don't you dare die,* she told him. *You are all the family I have.*

"Bastard," Petrus said, his voice suddenly fierce. "Hitting you like that. I should have broken his rutting neck."

"He was upset. You'd have been too, if you were him."

"I'd never have hit you!"

"He'd never hit a woman, either. He didn't know it was me."

"He broke your jaw! He's as bad as those cursed Fithians, violent son of a—"

"No, he's not."

"Just because he's a prince, you think he's a hero. Well, he isn't. He's a bad-tempered whoreson who thinks he's better than us. If he didn't need us, he'd kill us all and not care."

"No, he wouldn't!"

They stared at each other in the dark tent. She couldn't see Petrus's face, couldn't read his expression, but she heard his breathing—short, harsh, angry.

Innis spoke quietly: "I've been Justen more than anyone. I've seen a different side to him." *I've shared his dreams.* "He's not a bad person, Petrus. He's just extremely angry right now." She found his hand. "Please, don't let's argue."

For a moment she thought Petrus wouldn't take her hand, but then he did. The handclasp wasn't as comforting as it usually was. It felt awkward, as if they were pretending to be friends.

INNIS PATROLLED FOR half the night, flying along the road, skimming low across the half-mile-wide strip of logged ground on either side of it, circling over the dark forest. The moon cast long, black shadows, and she understood how the assassin had crept up on Gerit. He'd have waited in the forest until he saw Gerit swoop off to patrol the road, then crept down through the stumps. And when Gerit returned, when the owl was silhouetted against the pale disc of the moon...

Innis swept into another circle. It was easy to imagine that arrows were aimed at her. Her skin prickled, as if her feathers stood on end.

BY THE TIME Innis swapped with Petrus, she was exhausted. Not from flying, but from the constant fear that she might miss something. "Be careful," she told Petrus.

"Don't worry about me."

Innis watched him flap upwards, his pale feathers gleaming in the moonlight. *If anything happens to Petrus, I think I should die.*

She walked to her tent, crouched, and pushed aside the flaps. The tent was dark and empty.

She didn't want to be herself tonight, didn't want to sleep in an empty tent. She wanted to sleep alongside the prince and share his dreams. She wanted lazy, sunlit hours in the palace garden. She wanted the side of him he never showed anyone else.

What was the harm? An extra shapeshifter in the prince's tent could only be a good thing. He'd be safer if anything went wrong.

A Primary Law broken, a tiny voice whispered in her head. But she'd broken *that* particular Law every night that she'd slept in Justen's shape. And really, what was the harm?

INNIS FOUND THE prince in a training arena, lit by the moon. A handful of men struggled in the centre of the arena. She heard gasps, grunts of pain. The prince's emotions flooded her—fear, panic. Innis ran towards the men, sawdust puffing beneath her boots. There was the prince, pinned to the ground, and there, his half-brother standing with a sword. "We'll cut off his hands, first."

Prince Harkeld fought, tried to break free, but his arm was wrenched outwards, his wrist laid bare in the moonlight. The sword swung up.

The prince's fear spiked. She felt his panic burst through her.

"No!" Innis cried. "It's only a nightmare—"

A loud crack swallowed her words. White fire lit the arena, so bright she couldn't look at it.

The light faded. Four charred bodies lay smoking on the sawdust.

Harkeld sat up, moving slowly, as if he ached.

"It was only a nightmare." Innis crouched beside him. He was trembling, panting, sweating. She felt how close to tears he was. "Harkeld, it was only a nightmare."

"I know." He scrubbed his face with both hands.

"I won't let anyone cut off your hands. I promise."

Harkeld raised his head, his eyes black in the moonlight. "You can't do anything. You don't exist outside my head." He pushed to his feet and walked away from her, striding across the arena.

Innis followed. They passed through a bustling stableyard, crossed a vast marble courtyard with statuary and fountains, and came to the palace gardens, where the sun shone brightly. The prince didn't stop. He walked through rose gardens and over smooth lawns, past sculpted hedges and groves of slender trees, finally halting at the water lily pond where the dragonflies hummed.

Innis stepped up alongside him. She reached for his hand. "Harkeld—"

"Don't." He snatched his hand away. "No more witches in my dreams. Do you understand me?"

Innis shook her head.

His expression grew fierce. "This is *my* dream and I won't have witches in it."

"You want me to go?"

"What I *want* is to tup a human, not a foul, lying witch. Anything would be better than that shape!" He gestured angrily at her. "Rut it, even *Broushka* would be better!"

Tears burned her eyes.

"And don't cry," he said, disgusted. "You don't even exist. You're nothing more than my imagination." He turned away from her. "Get out of my head."

Innis pressed her hands to her mouth, blinked back the tears.

The prince swung round to face her again. "I said, get out! Get out of my head. *Get out!*"

IN THE MORNING, while she was saddling Justen's horse, Petrus came over. "I saw you go to the prince's tent last night."

"What?" Her head jerked up. "I didn't."

"Yes, you did. As a fieldmouse. I saw you go in, and about half an hour later I saw you come out."

"I..." Blood rushed to her face. "I just wanted to check on him."

There was an expression on Petrus's face that she'd never seen before. Mistrust. "Ebril will keep him safe."

"I know, I know," Innis said hurriedly. "But after what happened, I wanted to check on him. I was just..." Her voice trailed off. "Checking."

"Petrus, can you give me a hand with these tents?" Rand called.

Petrus hesitated, then went to help Rand.

Innis watched him go. There was a bad taste in her mouth. She felt slightly sick. *I lied to Petrus*.

CHAPTER FORTY-SIX

IT WAS CLOSE to noon when they reached the northernmost end of the Hook. Karel went out on deck. The sea teemed with vessels. He saw merchant ships, fishing ships, naval ships.

A ship flying Lundegaard's blue and gold flag hailed them. Its crew were dressed in the forest green of Lundegaard's military.

"Say we're refugees from Vaere," Karel told the captain. "We went a little off course, too far south."

He listened to the shouted conversation.

"You heard that?" the captain said, signaling a sailor to furl the sails. "We're fourth in line to disembark."

"I heard. Follow their orders."

He went back to the cabin. "We're nearly there. There are three ships ahead of us. How's Yasma?"

"Close to waking," the princess said.

The afternoon slid past slowly. Yasma woke, pale and drowsy. She ate Horned Lily root, and later, some sausage and cheese. Some color returned to her thin face.

"You and I will carry the trunk," Karel told the princess. "Can you do that?"

"Yes."

Towards dusk, the *Sea Eagle* began to move again, sliding into the harbor. Karel went to the window. Hundreds of people milled on the wharves. At first glance it looked chaotic; at second glance, orderly. The refugees were moving in a single direction, directed by soldiers.

Karel watched the busyness, the orderliness, with satisfaction. There would be a high-ranking officer in charge of an operation this size, one he could trust with Princess Brigitta's safety. *And Yasma and I can blend in easily among so many people.*

"We need to have a drink before we can get off the ship," Princess Brigitta said cheerfully. "It won't taste very nice, boys, but we must all have some."

Karel drank a mug of cider and pulled a face that made Rutgar giggle. The princess drank too. "Gah," she said, shuddering and sticking out her tongue. She handed the boys cider mixed with poppy syrup.

They both drank, pulling faces and giggling.

Night had fallen by the time the *Sea Eagle* moored. Karel and the princess tucked the sleeping boys carefully into the trunk and padlocked it. "Ready? You know what to do? And you, Yasma?"

"No speaking," Yasma said. "Hoods up. And use the silk to hide our faces, like scarves this time, not masks."

"And stand at parade rest," Princess Brigitta said. "As if we're men."

Karel picked up the plank the boys had drilled holes in, playing at being carpenters. He dropped it out the window. Far below, water splashed.

Someone knocked on the door. "Master Eliam?" It was the captain. "Are you ready to disembark?"

THEY DESCENDED A gangplank. The captain came too, to collect his payment, and the first mate, his arm still in a sling. Neither man would meet the armsman's eyes directly. Their fear of him would have amused Britta if she hadn't been so full of jittering excitement. Lundegaard! Where they'd all be safe.

She stood beside the trunk at parade rest, as she'd seen Karel do a thousand times. Shoulders back. Feet twelve inches apart.

Karel spoke to the sergeant directing their disembarkation.

Her ears caught words. "...urgent... must speak with your highest-ranking officer."

"Everyone's business is urgent," the sergeant said sourly.

Yasma came to stand beside her.

"...a matter that closely concerns your king." Karel's voice was flat, authoritative. "Your highest-ranking officer. Now."

The sergeant hesitated, then turned away. He issued orders, sent a man running, directed them to stand to one side.

Britta helped Karel carry the trunk to the shelter of a stone wall. A brazier burned half a dozen yards to their right, a torch half a dozen yards to their left.

The captain and first mate came to stand with them, and six soldiers, ringing them. Yes, Lundegaard's military were right to be cautious after the nearly-successful invasion last month.

"Start the next disembarkation," the sergeant shouted.

Britta waited, struggling to remain patient. *We're in Lundegaard!* The paving stones beneath her feet, the soldiers guarding them, the black sea reflecting the torchlight... they were Lundegaardan stones, Lundegaardan soldiers and torches.

A dozen men in green uniforms strode down the wharf.

"Sire." The sergeant threw his chest out, saluted crisply.

Sire? One of those men was a prince? The boys' uncle?

Britta scanned their faces eagerly. Six soldiers, two armsmen wearing silver torques, the messenger, an older man whose epaulettes marked him as a general. The other two men were in their twenties. Neither had the long hair or crown of a royal prince. *But this isn't Osgaard.*

She studied their faces, looking for a resemblance to Queen Sigren.

"Your messenger said there was something that concerned my father?" one of the men said.

"This man claims to have knowledge that concerns the king, sire." The sergeant gestured at Karel.

Karel stepped forward and bowed. "Highness?"

"Prince Kristof," the man said. "And this is my brother Prince Tomas. You are?"

"No names here, highness. You have somewhere we can talk privately?"

Prince Kristof narrowed his eyes. He examined their party—the captain and the first mate, Yasma and herself. "Follow me."

Britta picked up one side of the trunk. Karel took the other. They followed the princes, striding fast, surrounded by soldiers.

PRINCE KRISTOF LED them to a wharfside tavern that had been requisitioned by Lundegaard's army. Karel scanned the taproom as they stepped inside. There was no tapster; instead, the room was filled with the murmur of voices, the rustle of paper. Men sat at tables with parchment spread before them, their fingers ink-stained.

The prince ushered them into a smaller room with a desk sitting solidly at its centre. The armsmen and the general followed, and six of the soldiers. The soldiers took places around the wall. The armsmen came to stand behind the princes.

"Your business?" Prince Kristof said, folding his arms. His brother, standing beside him, had recently been wounded. Half his right ear was missing and a newly-healed scar crossed his cheek. Both men's eyes were narrow, their expressions suspicious, and behind them, the armsmen's equally so.

Karel lowered his side of the trunk. The princess did the same.

He turned the trunk so that its hinges faced the soldiers, the armsmen, the captain and first mate. "I need to speak with you privately," he told the princes, and held up a hand to forestall the protest forming on their lips. "I'll show you why."

He reached beneath his cloak for the key to the padlock—the armsmen stiffened, their hands moving to their sword hilts—and unlocked the trunk. Karel half-raised the lid and beckoned to the princes. "Not one word," he cautioned.

Prince Tomas frowned and strode across the room. "What nonsense is this? There's nothing that—" He halted when he saw the young princes nestled asleep in the trunk. He glanced at Karel sharply, his mouth opening.

Karel laid a finger to his lips. "There are ears here, highness."

The prince turned. "Kristof! Get over here!"

Prince Kristof hurried over. His expression stiffened in shock. He turned to the armsmen, the soldiers, the general. "Out. Everyone, out!"

One of the armsmen hesitated. "Sire..."

"You may have my sword and dagger." Karel unbuckled them and gave them to the armsman. He glanced at the captain and first mate. "You two, wait outside."

Everyone filed from the room.

The door closed. "Who are you?" Prince Kristof demanded. "Are these—?"

"They are your nephews, highness," Karel said, fully opening the lid. "Rutgar and Lukas. And this is their sister, Princess Brigitta."

The princess pushed back her hood and pulled the black silk down from her chin.

Both men stared at her. Karel saw what they saw: youth, beauty, a quiet regality. Despite her attire, there was no doubting she was a princess.

Princess Brigitta nodded to the princes and knelt beside the trunk, checking the boys' pulses.

"By the All-Mother's grace!" Prince Kristof said, sounding dazed. "Can this be true?" He dropped to his knees beside Princess Brigitta. "Rutgar and Lukas?"

"Are they all right?" Prince Tomas asked, kneeling too.

"Sedated with poppy syrup," the princess said.

Prince Kristof touched Rutgar's hair lightly, wonderingly, then suddenly stood. "We must tell Father!" He hurried across to the desk.

Karel followed him. "This has to be kept secret, highness."

"Father must be told! He's in Forsmouth now, preparing to sail to Osgaard and plead for the boys' lives."

"Tell him, by all means. But he must tell no one else."

The prince shook his head. "Why?"

"Because the maid and I are from Esfaban." Karel gestured to Yasma, now standing bareheaded. "Jaegar believes us dead. If we're known to be here, our families will be sent into bondservice."

Prince Kristof stared at him for several seconds, looking deep into his eyes, as if seeing him fully for the first time. Then decision firmed his face. He nodded. "Absolute secrecy. You have my word. *Your* families will not be harmed because of what you've done for *my* family."

He scrawled a swift note, underlined several sentences, sealed it, and crossed to the door. "Take this to my father," he said to someone outside. "Use the fastest ship in the harbor. It's urgent!" Then he closed the door and turned back to Karel. "Now tell us all! How do you come to be here?"

THE ARMSMAN TOLD their tale. How simple it seemed when reduced to concise sentences. "You need gold to pay the ship's captain?" Kristof said, once he'd finished.

"Yes," Britta said. "We hadn't enough."

"How much did you promise him?"

"Another twenty pieces. We have seven." Karel opened the rucksack and pulled out the money pouch.

Kristof waved it away. "Twenty. And I think... a little more to persuade them to avoid these waters for a while." He exited the room.

Britta glanced at Tomas, still kneeling beside her. "Rutgar looks like Sigren," he said, reaching out to touch the boy's cheek.

"Yes, I think so too."

Tomas turned to look squarely at her. "To have Osgaard take our sister's life, and then to think it would take her children's too... We can never thank you enough, Brigitta." Emotion made his voice rough.

"They are my brothers," Britta said simply. "And it's Karel and Yasma you should thank. Without them, I couldn't have done anything."

"Yes." Tomas stood. He bowed to Yasma and took one of her hands and clasped it to his heart. "Our family owes you both a deep debt." He turned to Karel and bowed, took the armsman's hand.

Britta watched Tomas. He was Harkeld's closest friend. The man Harkeld had hoped she would marry.

Tomas wasn't quite as she'd envisaged. He looked more serious than Harkeld had described. But serious things were happening in the world.

Tomas released Karel's hand and stood talking to him. They were of a similar age, a similar height. Karel wasn't wearing his weapons, but his stillness, the stern hawk-like features, the dark, watchful eyes—those made him look dangerous. Tomas, with his sword and his scarred face, seemed boyish beside him.

Kristof returned holding a sheet of parchment. "The *Sea Eagle*'s paid off, and the captain and first mate have agreed not to enter our waters, or Osgaard's, for the next decade."

"What?" Britta said, standing.

Kristof waved the parchment. "They signed their names to it."

"In exchange for what?" Tomas said wryly.

"Gold."

"And what else?" Tomas reached for the document. "I wouldn't trust those men... ah, threat of death."

Kristof shrugged. "Match the incentive to the man."

Britta stepped closer to look at the parchment. "One of them signed with a handprint."

"The first mate," Kristof said. "Someone had broken his arm."

Tomas gave a snort of laughter.

Kristof's posture and expression shifted into something more serious. "Hoods up, ladies, and let's shut the trunk again. You may have my quarters upstairs. They're secure. I'll bunk in with Tomas."

CHAPTER FORTY-SEVEN

PRINCES RUTGAR AND Lukas met their uncles in the morning, in the large, sunny parlor adjoining what had been Prince Kristof's bedchamber. The boys were shy and a little overawed by the tall men who claimed kinship to them, but sweetmeats and a set of painted toy soldiers helped overcome their bashfulness. Prince Tomas proved to have a streak of the jester in him, and he soon had the children giggling.

Karel watched, trying to gain a measure of both men.

Prince Kristof, a few years older than his brother, was the quieter of the two. A man who watched, who thought. Prince Tomas was the one who acted, whether lying on the floor marshaling toy soldiers or doing whatever had earned him those wounds. Both liked to laugh—that was written on their faces—but they had the demeanor of soldiers. The uniforms they wore weren't just for show.

The resemblance between the boys and their uncles was strong. It was more than fair coloring; it was in the shape of their faces, the set of their eyes. Karel hoped the resemblance went deeper than that, to character. If Rutgar and Lukas grew up in their grandfather's court and were molded by Lundegaardan values, there was a good chance they'd become men worth serving.

"Is there any news of Harkeld?" Princess Brigitta asked.

Prince Kristof exchanged a glance with his brother. "I'll let Tomas tell you what we know."

Prince Tomas clambered to his feet and shifted the toy soldiers and sweetmeats to the sunshine by the window, where the boys would be out of earshot, and rejoined them.

Karel listened intently to his tale. When the princess heard her brother was a witch, she uttered a choked sound. "Oh, poor Harkeld," she said, pressing her hands to her mouth.

Prince Tomas described the final battle with the Fithians. "Harkeld and the witches went on into Ankeny. They must be near the second anchor stone by now."

"Poor Harkeld," the princess said again. "To be a witch. He must be so upset!"

Prince Tomas looked uncomfortable. He nodded.

"Are the witches nice people? Are they kind to him?"

The prince blinked, as if the question surprised him. "Nice enough." Karel heard the silent rider: *For witches.*

"I wish I could go to him."

"But... he's a witch."

"He's my brother! I'd like to help him."

"You have helped him," Prince Kristof said. "By not going with the Fithians."

The princess nodded, but her expression didn't change. Her anxiety for her half-brother was clear to see. Witch or not, she loved Prince Harkeld.

"And you too have a tale to tell, I believe," Prince Kristof said. "Father says we owe our knowledge of the invasion to you."

"Oh..." Princess Brigitta looked disconcerted. Beside her, on the settle, Yasma's expression became alarmed. "He told you?"

"No one but us knows," Prince Tomas assured her. "And Erik, of course. Our brother. Father swore us to secrecy."

"There's nothing much to tell," the princess said. "I found the plans and copied them. And Yasma thought of a way to give them to your ambassador without anyone seeing." She reached out and took Yasma's hand.

"Lundegaard owes you both a great debt," Prince Kristof said seriously. "We'd likely be under Osgaardan rule by now, if you hadn't warned us. As we may yet be, if the Fithians catch Harkeld."

"What news of the curse?" the princess asked.

"It's halfway across Vaere," Prince Kristof said. "And into eastern Sault. The situation in Vaere is... not good. The kingdom's in chaos. The king refused to believe Ivek's curse was real, claimed it was a plot by Sault to empty his kingdom, that as soon as everyone fled, Sault would invade. He started mobilizing for war—and then reports came in that it really *was* true. We had some observers in the Vaeran court. They say the king completely panicked. The royal family fled overnight. Left the kingdom to just... fall.

"Sault dismissed the reports too, at first. I mean, who *would* believe it?" Kristof shook his head. "But the king didn't run when he realized what was really happening. Sault's a mess, but it's an organized mess. They're evacuating as fast as they can. Ships are arriving here daily and there's a lot of movement north into Roubos.

"Roubos..." Kristof shrugged, pulled a face. "King Salavert always has been a little... eccentric."

"Nuts," his brother said frankly. "Makes his decisions based on signs from the All-Mother. You know, how many grains of seed his pet bird eats, whether the rain falls in the east or the west. That sort of nonsense."

"Salavert claims the All-Mother has told him Roubos will be spared," Prince Kristof said. "He issued a proclamation telling his people to ignore the eastern 'disturbance,' that it will blow over. Our observers say most of the court are preparing to evacuate, even if the king isn't."

Prince Tomas snorted. "Salavert'll probably be sitting in his garden counting raindrops on grass blades when the curse reaches Roubos."

"Last we heard from Urel, they thought they'd be safe," Kristof said. "Thought the curse wouldn't reach the archipelago. But Dareus was certain it would. They'll sail north if it does."

"Dareus?" the princess asked.

"The leader of the witches. He was killed in Masse."

"Gray hair?" Karel asked. "Short beard?"

"I never met him." Kristof glanced at his brother.

"That was him," Tomas said. "You saw him?"

Karel nodded. So did Princess Brigitta.

"We're not expecting many refugees from Roubos," Prince Kristof continued. "If I lived there, I'd sail north, across the equator. The Allied Kingdoms are safer than Lundegaard. Ivek never cursed *them*. And as for Ankeny... They're waiting to see whether the curse reaches Roubos or not. Most of their population is in the north-west. They'll have time to evacuate to the Allied Kingdoms if they have to."

There was a moment of silence. Karel imagined Roubos and Urel and Ankeny emptying, thousands of people sailing north across the equator, flooding the Allied Kingdoms.

"This plan of Jaegar's, to use Brigitta as bait to catch Harkeld..."

Karel glanced up, found Prince Kristof's eyes on him.

"He wants to hold the Seven Kingdoms to ransom, doesn't he? He won't end the curse until we cede to him."

"I believe so, highness."

"He's as bad as Esger!" Prince Tomas burst out.

Karel shook his head. "He's worse. He's smarter than Esger. More disciplined, crueler. If he gets Prince Harkeld's hands and his blood..."

"He won't," Prince Kristof said grimly.

There was another moment of silence. Were the princes praying to the All-Mother? *He* was.

"Do the other kingdoms know about Harkeld and the witches?" Princess Brigitta asked.

Kristof and Tomas exchanged a glance. "There are rumors," Kristof said.

"*Wild* rumors," Tomas amended.

"But they haven't been informed of the details of Harkeld's quest. Father decided it was safer to say nothing. The fact that there are witches with Harkeld..." Kristof grimaced, shrugged. "No one knows how the other kingdoms will react. They might help, or... they might not. It's even possible one of them might try to do what Osgaard is doing. A grab for power."

"They don't know about Harkeld at all?" The princess sounded shocked.

"They know he's attempting to end the curse, but they don't know precisely how," Kristof said. "Or where he is, or with whom. It's safer that way."

"They don't know he's a witch?"

"No. No one knows that but us."

The princess bit her lip, nodded. After a moment she asked, "How many refugees have reached here?"

"To date? Nearly four thousand."

"Four *thousand?*" Karel said. "But that's..."

"A logistical challenge? Yes."

"What have you done with them?"

"Set up camps." Prince Kristof rubbed his forehead, as if the thought of the refugees gave him a headache. "We'll send them home once the curse is destroyed. If it's destroyed. I pray every day that Harkeld will succeed. If he doesn't..."

"Is it as bad as the tales say?" Princess Brigitta asked tentatively. "The Ivek Curse? Murder and... and cannibalism?"

"There've only been a couple of refugees arrive who actually saw cursed people. If you get close enough for that, mostly you die. But from what they've said... Yes, it's as bad as the tales." Kristof glanced at the little princes by the window, lowered his voice. "Brothers killing sisters, then violating the bodies, eating the flesh. Parents drinking their children's blood and gnawing on their bones. It's... madness. Insanity."

"Harkeld has to stop it," Prince Tomas said fiercely. "He *has* to." The words seemed to echo in the air, an edge of desperation to them.

"How long before the curse reaches here?" Yasma asked in a frightened whisper. She was clutching the princess's hand tightly.

Prince Kristof shook his head. "We don't know."

"Dareus said it was advancing across Vaere at about a league a day," Tomas said. "He predicted it would move faster once it reached the first anchor stone. Which is in Sault."

"All we know for certain is that the curse will infect all seven of the kingdoms before the year's out. If Harkeld fails." Prince Kristof made an effort to smile reassuringly at Princess Brigitta, at Yasma. "But he won't fail."

Karel heard the words he didn't say: *He* mustn't *fail*.

Lukas crowed with laughter.

They all looked towards the window. Both boys leaned over the toy soldiers, intent on their game. Sunlight gilded their hair, making it bright as gold.

"Highness...?" Karel said.

"*Sire* will do," Prince Kristof said. "We're less formal than Osgaard."

Karel nodded. "Sire, when do you think the princess and her brothers can depart?"

"Father should arrive tomorrow. I imagine he'll want to take Brigitta and the boys back to the castle as soon as he can. As for you and Yasma... I have some ideas, but I'd like to discuss them with my father. Something that rewards you fittingly, but keeps your secret safe."

"We need no reward," Yasma said.

Prince Kristof's face relaxed into a genuine smile. "Lady, for your services to our family and to all Lundegaard, you *will* be rewarded. But I would like it to be something that matches your needs. A title would be of no use to you, though you deserve to be called Countess."

Yasma blushed, and looked down at her lap.

"And you wouldn't like a title either, I think," Prince Kristof said, his gaze shifting to Karel. "Or a prominent holding."

"Prominent, no." Karel shook his head. "But a small farmstead somewhere, where no one will notice us."

"A farmer? It can be done, if that's what you wish. We'll discuss it tomorrow." The prince's gaze shifted again, coming to rest on Karel's sword belt. "I should like to see you fight, armsman. Do you care to cross swords?"

Karel touched his sword hilt. "Now? Is it safe? The princess and the boys—"

"This corridor is guarded by my most trusted armsmen. No one will get past them alive. If you're worried about your face being seen, I can have the practice ground cleared."

"Yes, do!" Prince Tomas said, his eyes alight with enthusiasm. "I'd like to see you fight. Do you wrestle, Karel?"

CHAPTER FORTY-EIGHT

THE JUNGLE. THEY climbed down from the highlands and found it. Jaumé had asked Bennick what it was like and Bennick had joked, "It's full of things that want to eat you." Black-skinned Gant had said it stank.

Both were right. Nothing big had tried to eat Jaumé yet, but small buzzing things bit him all the time. They were called *gnats*, Gant said. The gnats came night and day, from scummy ponds and underneath damp leaves. They sucked your blood and left red lumps that itched. Kritsen had given them oil that stank like cats' piss to rub on their skins. It kept the gnats off, but the jungle was large, Nolt said, and he made them use it sparingly. As for the stink, the oil was the least part of it. It seemed to come from the wet ground and the fat leaves, from the brown fungus on the trunks of trees, from the yellow ponds with drifting bubbles breaking on their surface.

Jaumé hated the jungle. He hated the gnats and the stink and the wet heat and the howls of animals in the night. There were screaming things and things with shining eyes in the branches of the trees. He was afraid when Bennick was on watch, but told himself there was nothing out there that Bennick couldn't kill, with his bow, with his Stars, with his throwing knife, his sword.

He had one rule for himself: stay close to Bennick. Bennick let him stay. He rode beside Jaumé when the trail widened and held the pony's mane when her hooves bogged in the marshy ground. At night he laid his sleeping mat by Jaumé's. In Jaumé's dreams, Bennick's face sometimes changed into Da's.

"Where are we going?" Jaumé whispered to Bennick one evening, hoping to hear about the prince, but all Bennick said was, "A town called Mrelk, where one of our Brothers lives."

CHAPTER FORTY-NINE

Britta stood in the doorway to the bedchamber, watching the boys and Yasma. Rutgar and Lukas were chattering happily, telling Yasma about their grandfather. "He says he'll get me an axe," Lukas announced, bouncing on the bed. "A proper woodcutter's one!"

"And I can have my own horse!"

Yasma smiled as she listened. Britta didn't feel like smiling. *Soon I shall never see her again, or Karel.*

King Magnas had been everything Harkeld had said. Warm, welcoming, wise. And above all, kind. He'd hugged the boys, unashamedly shedding tears, and then hugged her too, as if she was his kin. *My home is your home, child. You shall be my daughter.*

"We're going on another ship," Lukas said, bouncing. "Tomorrow."

"And then we'll ride to the castle!"

"And we'll have rooms at the top of a tower!"

And I shall go back to being a princess. Why did that prospect bring her no joy?

"I can't wait, I can't wait, I can't wait!" Rutgar chanted.

Yasma glanced at her. Her smile faded. There was quiet grief on her face.

Yasma, what will I do without you? You have been my close friend for so long.

Britta turned away from the doorway and crossed to the parlor window, looking out at the busy harbor. She didn't want to leave Yasma. Didn't want to be a princess again. But to keep Yasma with her would be selfish; and worse, it could bring ruin down on Yasma's family.

Britta sighed and leaned her forehead against the glass. And as for being a princess, Lundegaard wasn't as formal as Osgaard. Neither Kristof nor Tomas wore crowns, and their uniforms were unembellished. Perhaps her royalness wouldn't be so constricting.

The street was two stories below. Karel was down there somewhere. He'd gone with King Magnas to discuss plans for his and Yasma's future. And then to visit the practice ground. *You must see him wrestle, Father,* Tomas had said, laughing. *He slaughtered me!*

A ship had just disembarked. The wharf swarmed with refugees and green-clad soldiers. A woman caught her eye, haggard, exhausted, with two young children and a baby. Britta watched them out of sight.

She touched the windowsill and sent a prayer through wood and stone to the All-Mother. *Be safe, Harkeld.* Only he could stop this exodus of people. Only he could save the Seven Kingdoms.

Someone knocked on the door.

Britta turned, hoping it was Karel, but the man stepping through the door wearing Lundegaard's forest green uniform and with a silver torque at his throat was fair, not dark. "Princess Brigitta?"

Britta frowned. Hadn't Kristof said his armsmen didn't know who they guarded?

The man came towards her. He moved like Karel, light-footed, with a sense of coiled muscles. A trained fighter. "Princess Brigitta?" he said again. "There's been a concerning development. The prince requests I bring you to him."

"What development?" Britta said, taking a step back, bumping against the windowsill. She didn't like the man's eyes. They were fixed on her as intently as a cat's upon a mouse. "Which prince?" She glanced at the bedchamber. Lukas was still bouncing on the bed, Rutgar was out of sight. She heard his voice, though, and the low murmur of Yasma replying.

"Prince Kristof," the armsman said, halting in front of her.

Britta stared at him. What was it about this man that she didn't trust? His face was clean-shaven, his tone polite, his uniform neat—

Was that a smear of blood on his torque?

Her eyes jerked back to his—cold, intent—and she knew with absolute certainty that he wasn't one of Kristof's armsmen. "Yasma! Lock the door!" She pushed past the man, tried to run for the armsmen in the corridor, but he grabbed her arm, swung her round. "Lock the door!"

She caught a glimpse of Yasma in the bedchamber, wide-eyed, saw her slam the door shut, heard the bolt shoot across, and then fabric pressed over her mouth. Damp. Smelling of vanilla.

All-Mother's Breath.

CHAPTER FIFTY

KAREL CLIMBED THE wooden stairs two at a time. He liked King Magnas. The man's reputation for fairness and wisdom was justified. The king listened shrewdly, hearing more than the words one spoke. *He holds his kingdom carefully in his palm, not crushed in his fist like the Rutersvards.* King Magnas would do a good job of raising Rutgar and Lukas, and in his care, Princess Brigitta would be safe, and happy.

No armsman stood on the landing at the top of the stairs. Karel frowned and stepped into the corridor beyond—and stopped. No armsmen stood on either side of the princess's door. Instead, three men in forest green uniforms were exiting through the door at the far end of the corridor, moving with awkward haste, carrying something between them. A person on a stretcher?

"Halt!" Karel shouted. He broke into a run.

One man turned and threw something.

Karel flung himself flat. Metal struck the stone wall, rebounding with a fierce *clang*. A throwing star.

Karel shoved up from the floor. "Halt!" he shouted again, but the men had vanished through the door.

He ran, his boots slapping on flagstones, and barreled through the door onto a staircase. He heard the echo of footsteps one flight down.

An armsman wearing a silver torque huddled dead against the wall.

Karel vaulted over the railing, dropping onto the landing directly below, reaching for his dagger as he rolled into a crouch. His thoughts moved with the same bright, fierce clarity as when he'd killed the *Sea Eagle*'s men. This was about speed, about striking hard.

The Fithian who'd thrown the star spun to face him, blocking the stairs, his lips drawn back from his teeth. Half a flight below, two men carried a stretcher. Karel caught a glimpse of a pale face, golden hair.

He launched himself at the assassin, catching the man around the waist, knocking him off his feet. He stabbed as they tumbled down the stairs, stabbed again. The Fithian snarled, kicked, tried to slam his head against the risers.

They hit the half-landing, rolling. Karel sank his dagger into the assassin's belly and sliced upwards until the hilt jarred against the man's sternum.

The Fithian uttered a choked scream.

Karel shoved the man away and pushed to his feet. He ran down the last flight of stairs and burst through the door onto the wharf.

People. People everywhere. Refugees streaming towards the camps. Green-garbed soldiers striding in all directions. He swung around, panting, his bloody dagger in his hand, a scream building in his throat. Where was the princess?

"GONE," PRINCE KRISTOF said grimly.

"Where?" his brother demanded.

"To be bait for Prince Harkeld no doubt." Karel turned to King Magnas. "I need a ship!"

"You'll have one," the king said. "But first we must find out what we can. Most importantly, how many of them are there?"

"There's no time for that!" Thoughts churned frantically in Karel's head, chasing one another. "I need a ship now!"

"The fastest ship is being provisioned," King Magnas said. His calm gaze seemed to see inside Karel's skull, to the chaos of whirling, panicked thoughts. "My best men are gathering.

Let us discover what we can before you sail." He turned to Yasma. "You said they didn't try the bedchamber door?"

Yasma shook her head, her face pale and distraught.

"This was nothing to do with the boys," Prince Kristof said. "Was it? This is about Brigitta. And Harkeld."

"Did they follow us from Osgaard?" Yasma asked.

The king shook his head. "Their ship arrived in port before yours—if we've identified the right vessel. The harbor master is checking his records."

"Then how did they know she was here?" Prince Tomas demanded.

"Fithians have ways of communicating," Karel said. He pressed his hands to his temples, trying to stop his thoughts from chasing one another, trying to remember back to the palace gardens. "The poison master said... he'd had word that a ship had left Lundegaard."

"But how...?"

"Pigeons?" Prince Kristof said.

"Perhaps." The king pursed his lips, frowned. "It's worth investigating."

"I'll see to it," Prince Kristof said.

"Do they know the boys are here?" King Magnas said, his eyes on Karel. "And you and Yasma? And if they do, will they tell Jaegar?"

Karel's heart seemed to stop beating for an instant.

"She called out my name," Yasma said, in a small, scared voice.

"They knew exactly where Brigitta was," the king said. "I think it likely they know the boys are here too. The question is, will they inform Jaegar? And will they mention you and Yasma?"

"By the All-Mother, I'll find out how they knew," Prince Kristof said grimly. "If any of our men—"

"Our families..." Yasma said, tears spilling from her eyes.

The king took both her hands in his. "You brought us our kin. We shall not abandon *your* kin."

"How?" Karel asked.

"If Jaegar can sail to Esfaban and take up your families, so can we. Just tell me their names and where to find them."

Karel opened his mouth, and closed it again. His tongue was frozen with horror—to uproot everyone, to tear them from their homes. *This wasn't what I wanted. I wanted them to have freedom in Esfaban, not flight and exile.*

"I think it unlikely the Fithians will mention you," the king told Yasma, his voice matter-of-fact and reassuring. "You're servants, and most people look at servants without seeing them—and even if they *did* identify you, their goal was Brigitta, not the boys, not you or Karel. But we'll take no chances. We have a ship in Osgaard's harbor, a fast fishing smack, and ears and eyes in the palace. I'll send word, tell the ship to stand ready. If Jaegar moves against your families, we'll act."

"Thank you," Yasma whispered.

The king released her hands. He pulled a handkerchief from his pocket and handed it to her.

Yasma wiped her face. She turned to Karel. He put an arm around her, hugged her. "Thank you," he told the king. "But I pray to the All-Mother it isn't necessary."

"I don't think it will be. You left convincing evidence of your deaths, and most men believe what's in front of their eyes. Now..." King Magnas's expression firmed. "What do we know of this plan to catch Harkeld? Will they intercept him as he passes through Roubos, or wait for him at the anchor stone in Sault?"

"Roubos," Karel said. "That's what Jaegar told the princess."

THE HARBOR MASTER came, bearing his records, and the sergeant on duty at the wharf. The Fithian ship was pinpointed as a sloop, low and fast, that had arrived five days previously. Half a dozen passengers had disembarked. Refugees from Vaere. All men.

"And today?"

"The captain paid the harbor fees this morning and sailed a couple of hours later." The harbor master shrugged. "I didn't pay much attention to it, sire. Didn't see any reason to."

"Did the captain say where they were going?"

The man shook his head.

"Did you see how many men embarked? Or you, sergeant?"

The harbor master shook his head again, but the sergeant said, "I saw a dinghy row out with maybe half a dozen men in it. Just a glimpse, mind. A ship was unloading; my attention was on that."

"You won't catch the sloop," King Magnas said, after both men had gone. He leaned over the map of the Seven Kingdoms unrolled on the table. "But you should be no more than a day behind when you reach Roubos." He tapped the map. "I'll give you the best fighters we have here, but it won't be more than a half-score. It's skill you need, not numbers. You need to be fast on the ground."

"Father, may I go?" Prince Tomas asked.

The king looked at his son for a long moment, then nodded. "Yes. But Karel leads this mission. He gives the orders."

"Me?" Karel said.

"You've demonstrated you can plan, and think fast on your feet."

"And fight," Prince Tomas said. "You killed a *Fithian*. Single-handed!"

Karel shook his head, rejecting the admiration in the prince's voice. "I'm a royal bodyguard. Your men could do it too."

"Demonstrably not," Prince Kristof said. "Four of mine are dead."

"The command is yours, Karel." The king stood. "Bring Brigitta back if you can. Help Harkeld if you can. I don't wish to place more value on one life than the other, but the curse *must* be stopped."

Karel nodded.

"If you do see Harkeld, tell him... tell him that I regret I can't offer him a home here, now that he's a witch." The king's mouth twisted. It seemed his regret was genuine. "But safe refuge for a brief time, a chance to see his half-brothers and say goodbye, that I can offer. And gold, if he needs it."

Karel nodded again.

"Tell him that in my eyes, he is Harkeld before he is a witch."

KAREL STOOD ON the wharf, dressed in Lundegaardan green. The king had outfitted him, given him clothes and weapons and gold. And armsmen. And a ship that was almost ready to sail. The crew and armsmen were aboard, the last provisions being loaded. As he watched, a barrel was hauled up over the side.

He shifted his gaze past the ship, staring at the horizon. *I'm coming, princess.* Fithians or no Fithians, he would rescue her.

When you loved people, you saved them.

He turned to King Magnas. "About Yasma—"

"She'll be safe."

"She was a bondservant, she's..." *Been raped, many times.* "She's not comfortable around men. She's—"

"I understand," King Magnas said, and something in his eyes told Karel he did. "Yasma has my full protection. No one will harm her. You have my word as king."

Karel nodded. He believed King Magnas—he *did*—but to leave Yasma here... He glanced back towards the buildings, remembering how she'd clung to him when he'd said farewell.

"We're ready to sail!"

It was Prince Tomas who'd shouted. He stood with Prince Kristof at the wharf edge, a fierce grin on his scarred face.

Karel bowed to the king. "Goodbye, sire. And thank you."

King Magnas held out his hand to Karel, as if they were equals. "Good luck."

CHAPTER FIFTY-ONE

THE DIRT TRAIL brought them to a river, and the river brought them to the town called Mrelk. Mrelk lay on the wide road from Roubos. It had houses of mud-brick and a marketplace and a ferry across the river on a cable. Downstream of the ferry, a wooden jetty thrust into the brown river. A large boat with crumpled sails and slack oars was being loaded with sacks of jungle moss, boxes of fruit, bales of dried leaves. Gant said that if you smoked the leaves, it made you dream you were floating to the All-Mother and feeding on honey, but if you used it too much your skin wrinkled and your brain wrinkled too and you grew old and died. They saw men with loose gray skin sleeping with the dogs on the riverbank—waiting to die, Jaumé thought.

The Brother had a house at the back of the town. He was an old man, stooped and bald—but not wrinkled, this one. A pigeon house on a pole stood in the yard.

"Loomath," the old man said. He made no sign of welcome. His left arm was bent and scarred, the muscles wasted.

"Nolt," Nolt replied.

"You're late."

"We're here."

Loomath gave a twist of his mouth. It might be taken for a smile. "Here and gone. Nolt, eh? I've heard of you. My house is small." He made a short gesture with his hand. Nolt went into the house, and Loomath followed.

"What did he mean, here and gone?" Jaumé whispered to Bennick.

"He's one of the old bastards. They get like that. Look after your pony, Jaumé. And keep your mouth shut here."

They watered the horses at a trough at the back of the yard, and found hay in a shed and fed them.

Nolt came out of the house. "The boat takes us four days downriver."

"The horses?" Gant asked.

"Our mounts, that's all. The packhorses stay. Loomath has saddlebags. Take only what you need. You, boy." He turned to Jaumé.

Jaumé's mouth went dry. *They're going to leave me behind.*

"The jungle gets worse. It kills people"—Nolt snapped his fingers—"like that."

Jaumé saw Loomath listening from the doorway.

"I'll come," he said.

"If you can't keep up, we'll leave you."

"I'll come." He saw a gleam of approval in Nolt's eyes. Bennick patted him on the shoulder. The old man in the doorway had a sour look, but maybe his eyes showed approval too.

"The boat goes mid-afternoon," Nolt told the men. "Be ready." He went back into the house with Loomath.

"What's downriver?" Jaumé asked Bennick.

"More jungle."

They ate and repacked, then led the horses to the jetty. The wide, brown river turned over slowly like a snake. The boat crew, half-naked and sweating, were nervous of Nolt and his men. They lifted the horses and the pony one by one in a sling and led them into stalls in the hold. The eight Brothers found places for themselves on the deck. A slow, warm breeze caught the sails and the oars dug into the water.

CHAPTER FIFTY-TWO

THEY HAD THREE days of fine weather, three days when they rode fast on drying roads, not stopping until after dusk. There was no time for lessons, no time for anything other than riding, eating, and sleeping. Harkeld's anger cooled, congealing into a cold, solid lump in his chest. He ignored Justen, spoke only when spoken to, and shared his tent with Ebril each night. The red-haired witch was subdued. Harkeld didn't hear him whistle once.

On the third night, after a meal eaten mostly in silence, Cora brought out the map. "We're only a few leagues from Vlesnik. Once we cross the river, we'll head north."

To the anchor stone. Harkeld's heart seemed to speed up.

"We need to restock in Vlesnik. My question is... do we stay the night there?"

There was silence. No one looked overjoyed by the prospect.

"For my preference, no," Rand said.

"I agree," Katlen said. "It's too risky."

Hew nodded.

"Tomorrow I'd like you to ride ahead with some packhorses, Rand. Leave before dawn. Take... not one of the shapeshifters... Katlen, you go with him. If anyone asks, we're headed for Roubos."

"What would you like us to buy?"

"Grain for the horses. Dried meat for us."

Harkeld reached for the map. There was Vlesnik, there the River Szal, and there, where the Szal joined the Yresk: the anchor stone.

His gaze drifted east, to the border with Roubos. Most of that kingdom was off the map. Sault wasn't on it, or Vaere. Where was the curse now? Had it taken all of Vaere in its inexorable advance westward? Was it into Sault, poisoning wells and streams? How many lives had it claimed?

There was no sense of impending doom here in Ankeny. The woodcutters felling trees, the ox teams hauling them away, the occasional merchant with mules or wagons, seemed to inhabit another reality, one where Ivek's curse and witches and assassins didn't exist.

That was the reality that he wanted to be in. He wanted to wake up and find the last two months had been nothing but a nightmare. That he was still in Osgaard. That he'd not been bred by witches to destroy a curse that everyone had believed was only a legend.

He glanced at the faces around the fire. Witches, weary and grim-faced and dirty. *I bet they wish this was a dream too.*

But it wasn't a dream. This was reality. And in the eastern kingdoms, there was yet another reality—one where the curse poisoned the water with blood lust, and towns and villages emptied in a wave of panic.

Harkeld tried to imagine it and failed. He rerolled the map. Cora and Katlen and Rand were discussing supplies, their voices a low murmur.

He pushed to his feet, rinsed his bowl and spoon in the creek beside the campsite, and stacked them ready for the morning. Then he lay down in his tent and waited for sleep, hoping that tonight the dream-Innis would visit. He wanted to hold her hand and feel the calmness, the contentment, she always brought with her.

But the dream-Innis didn't come. She hadn't come for many nights.

CHAPTER FIFTY-THREE

THE CABIN WAS smaller than the one on the *Sea Eagle*. It had been stripped of furnishings. A pallet to sleep on and blankets to keep her warm, a chamberpot, and a window to look out of; those were the things she had. And a candle at night while she ate.

I will not be bait to catch Harkeld. But escape was impossible.

Death was possible, though.

Britta sat on the pallet, hugging her knees, and went over the arguments for and against.

If she lived, Harkeld could be more easily caught. If he was caught, he'd be killed. His hands and blood would go to Jaegar. And Jaegar would use them to subjugate the other kingdoms. Only once they'd submitted would he end the curse.

If she died, she couldn't be used to catch Harkeld.

It was clear what her choice must be, however much she shrank from it.

She heard Karel's voice in her head, heard his fierce belief in her. *You can do it. I know you can.*

Britta stood and went to the window. It was small and narrow, nailed shut, with tiny panes in an iron lattice.

The options were three.

One. Break a pane and cut her wrists.

Two. Break a pane, cut off a strip of blanket, tie one end to the lattice and the other round her throat and let her body weight strangle her.

Three. Prise out the nails, open the window, and throw herself overboard.

The third option was the one Britta liked best. She didn't want to die in this bare little cabin, imprisoned by Fithian assassins. And there was always the chance that a passing ship would find her before she drowned.

CHAPTER FIFTY-FOUR

JUST AFTER NOON, Vlesnik came into sight. Rand and Katlen met them outside the gates, a string of laden packhorses behind them.

"The ferry crosses east once a day," Harkeld heard Rand say. "In the morning. We're booked on tomorrow's."

"Cora, it's not like Lvotnic at all," Katlen said. In her long skirt, she looked like a farmer's wife. "There's an inn that's as good as any at home. They'll launder our clothes for us!"

"How safe is it?"

"We're going to be noticed anyway," Rand said. "Can't sneak a party this large through the town and onto the ferry. If anyone's watching, they'll see us."

Cora frowned. "In your opinion—"

"It won't do us any harm to put up there for tonight."

THE INN WAS not only cleaner than the one in Lvotnic, it had bathtubs. Harkeld washed, shaved, dressed in his spare clothes and went down to the stableyard with Ebril and Hew.

He spent the rest of the afternoon sharpening and oiling weapons, seated on a bench in the sun, with a witch on either side. A dun-colored dog sat at their feet, ears pricked, alert: Justen.

Harkeld ignored the dog. It was either that or let the cold, congealed anger in his chest simmer into rage again.

Katlen and Petrus hung bedrolls to dry on the long lines strung across the sunny yard, and unrolled the tents and hung them out too. The tents flapped like great birds in the breeze. In the stables, Rand and Cora examined each horse, sending two to the farrier for new shoes. Katlen and Petrus inspected the saddles and bridles, checking the stitching, oiling the leather. Harkeld paused in his sharpening and watched as inn servants pegged their washed traveling clothes out to dry, and then their blankets. The blankets and clothes steamed.

At dusk, they packed everything away and moved inside. The tables in the taproom were clean, and fresh straw lay on the floor. Ebril sniffed. "Food smells good."

They sat at a long table in the corner farthest from the door. Innis joined them, dressed in a skirt, and Hew stretched out on the straw in dog form. A plump, cheerful maidservant brought them tankards of ale and served a meal that was simple and delicious: warm crusty bread, pats of golden butter, tangy cheese, a haunch of roasted meat with root vegetables. Harkeld ate heartily and pushed his plate away. He leaned back, sipping his ale, feeling more relaxed than he had in days.

Ebril heaved a sigh, shoving his plate to one side. "By the All-Mother, I needed that."

Harkeld nodded. He glanced around the taproom. Four gray-headed men sat at a table, engrossed in conversation. Locals, he thought. The innkeeper brought the men more ale and stayed to talk with them.

Rand stood. "I'll ask about the road conditions to Roubos," he said with a wink to Cora. He wandered across to the locals, tankard in hand.

The serving maid cleared their table. Harkeld saw Petrus glance at her, then at him. His good mood ebbed. *You needn't look at me like that. I'm not going to tomcat tonight.* Anger stirred in his chest. He gulped another mouthful of ale.

Ebril touched the girl's elbow, spoke to her, and followed her from the table. He returned a moment later bearing a board painted with familiar-looking squares and a small wooden box.

"Would you like to?" he said, his manner diffident, as if expecting a rebuff.

Harkeld shrugged. "Why not?"

Ebril's face lit with a smile. He opened the box and laid the pieces out on the board. "Red or black?"

"Red, please."

Ebril was as good a player as Justen had been. Harkeld lost the first game, and narrowly won the second. The serving girl brought them fresh tankards of ale. Ebril whistled between his teeth as he set up the board again. Harkeld glanced across at the locals. Rand sat with them. They were deep in conversation.

Harkeld won the third game, lost the next two, and won the next.

Rand returned to their table. "The road to Roubos is in good condition," he said loudly. "Not as rutted as what we've had lately; there's no logging on that side of the Szal." He leaned closer, and lowered his voice: "One of them's just returned from Droznic-Drobil. From the way he tells it, everyone's talking about the curse there. Wild rumors. This lot don't believe it yet. Or don't want to."

Ebril grimaced. He set up the board again.

"Do they know about us?" Cora asked, her voice as low as Rand's.

"No. They're so ignorant it's frightening. They truly seem to think Ivek's curse is a tale."

Harkeld looked down at his ale. His face frowned up at him from the surface of his drink. *Of course they think it's a tale. I did, until two months ago.*

"The other interesting information"—Rand's voice dropped to little more than a whisper—"is that Vlesnik has a one-armed inhabitant who breeds pigeons."

Ebril froze, one piece held above the board.

"He's not from Ankeny. Used to be a merchant in the Allied Kingdoms, before he lost his arm. From time to time, travelers visit him. Always men. Members of his old guild."

The silence at the table had an unusual quality. Harkeld glanced around at the grim faces. "What?" he asked Ebril in a baffled whisper.

"Tell you later," Ebril whispered back.

"Is anyone visiting him now?" Cora asked.

"No. His last visitor was several weeks ago. A young man with red hair, heading west."

Harkeld glanced at the witches again, still baffled. This was something to do with Fithian assassins, but he didn't understand what.

"So they'll know we've passed through," Cora said. "But there won't be anyone immediately on our trail?"

Rand nodded. "That's how I read it."

"WHAT WAS THAT about the one-armed man?" Harkeld asked Ebril when they were in their room. "He's Fithian?"

Ebril nodded.

"How do you know?"

"Well..." Ebril sat on his bed and yawned. "If a Fithian can't fight any more, the Patriarch finds other uses for him."

"Patriarch?"

"The head of the Brotherhood." Ebril eased off his boots. "Some of 'em become poison masters, others become... well, we call them 'agents.' Don't know what the Patriarch calls them." He shrugged. "They gather information and pass it on, and provide shelter and assistance to assassins passing through."

Harkeld shook his head, his bafflement growing. "How do you know this?"

"Because we study them, the way they study us."

"What?"

"Fithians study us," Ebril said patiently. "Because Sentinels are some of the few people who actually have a chance against them in a fight. Well, shapeshifters and fire mages do, healers don't. And we study them, because sometimes we come up against them, and we need to know what to do."

Harkeld sat on his bed. "So this man with one arm...?"

"It's classic. A foreigner living on a route between kingdoms, badly injured, visited by travelers who're always male. He even has pigeons."

"Pigeons... to send information?"

Ebril nodded.

"Where to?"

"Ah, now *that's* the question. Maybe somewhere in Roubos, or one of the cities on Ankeny's north coast. Or Stanic. There's an agent there." Ebril yawned again. "Someone, somewhere, is going to know we passed through. But we'll have a head start, so it shouldn't matter."

Harkeld frowned. "Do you think there were agents in Lvotnic and Gdelsk?" Did every Fithian in the Seven Kingdoms know where they were?

"Rand didn't reckon so."

"He asked?"

Ebril nodded. "Always has a chat with the locals, our Rand."

"Huh." Harkeld pulled off one of his boots. "I didn't notice."

"You wouldn't have, would you?" Ebril grinned. "You had other things on your mind."

Harkeld felt himself flush. He busied himself with pulling off the other boot. "So there'd be agents like this in Osgaard and Lundegaard?"

"They're everywhere. Isn't a kingdom in the world doesn't have 'em."

"And the red-haired man who was here a couple of weeks ago—"

"Is the one who killed Frane and Gerit." Ebril pulled off his shirt and tossed it aside.

Harkeld stripped out of his own shirt in silence. "Did you know Frane well?"

"We trained together, the last few years at the Academy. Me and Petrus and Innis. Justen. Hew. Frane and Susa."

"I'm sorry."

Ebril grimaced, shrugged. "We all knew this mission could be dangerous."

But not this dangerous. Not with Fithians after us. Harkeld shucked his trews and climbed into bed. Dareus had died because of the curse, but Frane and Gerit and Susa were dead because of the bounty on his head.

Ebril snuffed the candle.

Harkeld lay in the dark, staring at the ceiling he could no longer see, turning over everything he'd learned. He felt almost as ignorant as the villagers downstairs. *I need to pay more attention. I need to ask more questions.*

"Ebril... that assassin, the one with the red hair... isn't it odd that he was alone? Don't they usually travel in groups?"

"Not always. They start with a Journey, like us, but after that it depends on what contracts they take. Some of them like to work with companions, others don't."

"Journey?"

"It's the final part of our training." The bed creaked as Ebril rolled over. His voice became slightly louder. "We Journey for a year or so with experienced Sentinels, learning what it's *really* like. And then we go back to Rosny and take the oath. If we still want to. Some people don't, by that time. Journeys are meant to be challenging, y'see. Sometimes students even die." He yawned. "The Fithians do it a bit differently. They Journey after taking their oath. It's when they make their first kills, under supervision of an experienced assassin."

"How long did you train?"

"Me? All up, twelve years."

"Twelve!" He rolled until he was facing Ebril's bed. "Are you serious?"

Ebril laughed at his astonishment. "Twelve's standard. Fithians train for about that, too. Of course, they start younger."

"They do?"

"'Give me a boy before the age of ten'... Haven't you heard that?"

"No."

"The Patriarch will only take them before they're ten. The younger the better. And only orphans. By the time they're adults, they're masters of every weapon. And utterly loyal to the Brotherhood."

"The one Justen killed looked younger than us."

"He did, didn't he?" The laughter was completely gone from Ebril's voice. "Three kills, though. Rand found the tattoos on the back of his neck."

"Plus Gerit and Frane." *Five kills*. Harkeld rolled onto his back again. He stared upwards. "So what did you learn for twelve years?"

"The first few years was mostly how to control my magic. And ethics."

"Ethics?"

"What's appropriate use of magic and what isn't. They drum *that* in early. That's the biggest thing we deal with, y'see. Mages who abuse their power."

"It is?"

"Uh-huh. A while back in Noorn, there was a bandit family with fire magic. They killed scores of people. Took nearly a dozen Sentinels to catch them." Ebril yawned. "But usually it's smaller stuff. Burglars who can shift shape, or people who use threats of magic to line their pockets. Or curses. I saw a nasty one on my Journey. Boils." Bedclothes rustled as he shifted position. "Anyway, people who only have a little magic, they're at the Academy for a year or two. The more magic you have, the longer you stay. It's really only Sentinel candidates who stay past eighteen."

"What do you learn then?"

"More magic. And lots of fighting. How to defend ourselves with and without magic. Sentinels are expected to be able to fight as well as a soldier, y'know. And we learn laws and such, how to pass judgment, what kinds of sentences to give. And court etiquette, because Sentinels travel all over the Allied Kingdoms and are invited into royal palaces. And then there's the Journey. And then, when we turn twenty-four, we take the oath."

"Twenty-four?" Harkeld frowned. "Is Innis that old?"

"No. They made an exception for her. The Council debated for days over it. Could have gone either way." Ebril yawned again. "But this is a critical mission, and she's the strongest shapeshifter we've had in a century, so they decided ability was more important than age and experience."

"Huh."

"You thinking of becoming a Sentinel? You could do it. Your magic's strong enough, and you've already got the fighting skills. I reckon a year or two of training, and then a Journey, and you'd be ready to take the oath."

"No," Harkeld said. "One of the healers is going to get rid of my magic once the curse is destroyed."

"Your choice," Ebril said, his tone a verbal shrug.

Harkeld frowned up at the ceiling. "Ebril... how do healers remove a person's magic?"

"They kill the bit of your brain that makes magic."

"What?" He rolled to face Ebril again. "I thought magic was in the blood."

"It is, but it comes from the brain. There's a gland that puts magic in our blood."

Harkeld felt his eyebrows rise. *Oh.*

"You'd best ask Rand about it. Or Innis. They'd explain it better'n me."

Harkeld lay awake, considering this startling news. He didn't like the thought of someone tampering with his brain, killing part of it. *But the result's worth it.* He wrapped the bedclothes more closely around himself and shut his eyes. The bedding smelled clean, the pillow was soft, the mattress wasn't lumpy. *Sleep*, he ordered himself.

But sleep refused to come. Soon they'd be at the second anchor stone. What would it be like this time?

Harkeld opened his eyes.

This was when Dareus and most of the soldiers had died in Lundegaard—when they neared the anchor stone. *It gets more dangerous now, not less.*

Bedclothes rustled as Ebril rolled over. He was still awake too.

"Ebril..."

"Huh?"

"You know how the curse raised all those corpses... do you think something like that will happen again?"

There was silence. "You know," Ebril said, sounding much more alert, "you could have asked me that in the morning. Would have woken me up good and proper."

"Sorry."

There was more silence. "I don't know," Ebril said. "By the All-Mother, I hope not."

So do I.

"There's no ruined city," Ebril said, after another long pause. "It's just jungle and hot pools, so far as I know. Wouldn't be many corpses lying around to be woken up."

Harkeld nodded, relieved. "Good. Thanks."

"Flin... stop thinking and go to sleep."

Harkeld grunted a laugh. He closed his eyes again. This time, sleep came easily.

WHEN HARKELD WOKE, the sun had risen and Ebril was exercising barefooted in the middle of the bedchamber. He watched the witch complete a sequence of lunges and retreats. He'd seen something like that before, in Osgaard.

"Do all witches do that?" he asked, when Ebril had stopped.

Ebril shrugged. "We do it every day at the Academy. Becomes habit." He sat on his bed and reached for his socks. "We've been traveling so fast it's been a while since I've had time to do it."

"What's it for?"

"It wakes up your body and your mind. The instructors say it improves balance, too, and co-ordination and flexibility, and all sorts of things."

Harkeld pushed back the bedclothes and sat up.

"There are other sequences, but that's the one people do most often." Ebril hesitated. "I can teach you, if you want."

Harkeld considered this offer. He had a flash of memory: gray-haired Dareus jumping lightly down from the rope dangling over the palace walls. Dareus had been well into his fifties, as old as King Magnas, but he'd moved like a man twenty years younger. "All right."

THE EXERCISES WERE harder than they looked. Harkeld kept overbalancing. His movements were jerky compared with Ebril's smooth flow and he couldn't get as low in the lunges. He was short of breath by the time they'd gone through it six times.

"Wakes you up, doesn't it?" Ebril said. He sat down and pulled on his socks.

Harkeld nodded. He wiped his face. There was perspiration on his upper lip. "Most witches do that every morning?"

"Yes." Ebril hesitated, sock in hand. "Look, I don't know if you're doing it on purpose, but... you keep calling us witches. And to us that's like..." He screwed up his face. "It's like if I called you a whoreson all the time."

"Oh," Harkeld said.

"In Rosny, if someone called me a witch, I'd hit them."

"Oh," Harkeld said again. "I didn't realize." He'd known the witches preferred to be called *mages*—Dareus had corrected him several times—but he hadn't known *witch* was such an insult.

"I wasn't sure if you were doing it deliberately."

"It's the only word we have here for, um... mages." He shrugged awkwardly. "I'll try not to use it."

Ebril grinned. "Good enough for me."

Harkeld fished his boots out from under the bed. *Justen never told me this stuff!* he thought resentfully.

But Justen had been pretending to not be a witch.

Not a witch. A mage.

IT TOOK NEARLY four hours to cross the Szal. The river was several miles wide, braided into broad channels interspersed with shingle bars. The deeper channels had flat-bottomed ferries on cables, the shallower ones had fords. By Harkeld's count, they loaded and unloaded the horses onto five different boats, forded seven channels, and rode across a dozen bars.

A small, dark hawk circled above them—Innis—but there was no sign of Ebril or Petrus or Justen.

The forest on the far side of the Szal hadn't been logged. Instead of tree stumps and mud, tall trees cast cool shade. They followed the road east for half a mile, then turned north onto a narrow track. Innis was still the only shapeshifter Harkeld could see. In the late afternoon, he discovered why. A russet-breasted hawk arrowed down, a dead pigeon in its talons.

Cora took the pigeon.

The hawk changed shape. "I caught it heading north-west," Ebril said.

A tiny leather pouch was tied to one limp leg. Cora unrolled the scrap of parchment inside. "We can guess what it says, even if we can't read it." She held the message out to Rand.

Rand examined it and shrugged.

"May I?" Harkeld asked.

Rand passed the scrap to him. A dozen incomprehensible symbols were inscribed on it in black ink.

"Don't throw that pigeon away," Ebril told Cora, shoving his legs into trews, dragging on his shirt. "I'll have it for dinner."

Not long afterwards, Petrus brought another dead pigeon. "It was flying east."

The message this pigeon carried was longer; there were two lines of cryptic marks. Harkeld stared at them in frustration. What did they say?

He held it out to Ebril, riding alongside him. "Want to see?"

Ebril took it, looked at it, grimaced.

"Can you understand any of it?"

Ebril nudged his horse closer. "Well, this one, the one that looks like a lightning bolt, means *mages*. And that arrow is a compass point. And this symbol here..." He pointed at a triangle with a dot in the center. "Is their one for a target. And the circle with one side shaded tells when the message was sent. See? It's the moon a few days past full. And the one on the second line that looks like a throwing star is the symbol for an assassin, obviously. As for the rest..." He shrugged. "One of these marks will identify who sent the message, and one'll be a number, for how many of us he thinks there are." He handed the message back to Harkeld. "The first line says we've passed through Vlesnik heading east. The second... My guess is he's asking for assassins to be sent after us as fast as possible."

Harkeld's ribcage seemed to contract slightly. "But the message didn't get through."

"Not this one, but chances are he'll resend tomorrow. Very thorough, Fithians."

Harkeld folded the scrap of parchment and tucked it in his pocket. "That's not reassuring," he said dryly.

Ebril grinned at his tone. "Don't worry. We've got a good head start."

CHAPTER FIFTY-FIVE

THEY DISEMBARKED AND headed northwest, following Nolt's compass. Jaumé had heard of compasses, but never seen one. It looked like magic—the arrow always knowing where north was—but Bennick said it wasn't.

There was no trail through this jungle. The trees stood close together, vines creeping up them with splayed, sticky fingers. The vines were feeding, Jaumé thought. He could almost hear them suck. Heavy leaves stroked his legs as he rode by. They would curl around him if he stopped.

In the afternoon, the ground began to steam. The trees took crooked shapes; Jaumé thought they looked like creatures in the tales Mam used to tell—goblins with wide-stretched arms and sharp claws. Here and there were black rocks like clusters of tall stone trees. Pools, yellow at the edges, stood in their way, sending up steam. There was a murmuring deep down, like soft laughter.

Stead's mare stopped and refused to go on. He dismounted and led her, but soon she baulked again and wouldn't move.

"Leave her," Nolt said.

Stead threw his saddlebags on Maati's horse and rode behind young Kimbel until Kimbel's horse baulked too. They released it and both walked. The horse, whinnying with fear, followed for a while and fell behind and was lost.

"It's the stink," Gant said. "They can't drink the water, they can't eat the leaves."

"Sulfur," Nolt said. "Loomath said it gets worse."

They freed the horses and slapped them away, back to places where there were at least ferns to crop. Only Jaumé's pony was able to go on. They loaded her with their saddlebags and trudged northwest.

"Three days to where the rivers meet," Nolt said, when they halted for the night. They unloaded the pony. She nuzzled the leaves on the bent trees—refused them, then ate, snorting with distaste.

There was enough dried meat in the saddlebags, but Gant, afraid of nothing, followed a trail of bubbles in a pool where the black water didn't steam, and hauled out a fish with no eyes. The meat from its tail, charred in the fire, was eatable.

The wet heat and the walking had exhausted Jaumé. The Brothers talked around the fire, but he was too tired to listen. He lay down on his mat, steam curling thickly around him, and slept.

CHAPTER FIFTY-SIX

TONIGHT'S MEAL CAME with a spoon. No knife. They'd never given her a knife yet, but they didn't seem to think spoons dangerous.

Britta waited until the assassin had locked the door, then scrambled off the pallet. She crossed to the window and set to work prising out another nail. She needed to be gone before they reached Roubos. Here, in an empty cabin, she had a chance of foiling the assassins. On land, surrounded by them, she'd have no chance at all.

Outside the window, the ocean stretched forever, gray and restless. The Gulf of Hallas was a thousand leagues wide and they were somewhere in the middle. But the gulf wasn't empty. Each day she saw ships sailing towards Lundegaard.

One of them might see her in the water, might rescue her.

When she got the window open, when she jumped, she jumped not to certain death, but perhaps towards escape.

CHAPTER FIFTY-SEVEN

HARKELD PACED BESIDE the water lily pond, as he had every night for the past week. "I'm sorry," he said aloud. "Please come back." But the swathe of lawn remained stubbornly empty.

He paced some more, then sighed and sat on the marble edge of the pond. Dragonflies hovered over the water lilies, and it was all very restful and serene, but...

Harkeld jerked around.

The lawn behind him was empty, but it had *felt* for an instant as if she was here. He climbed to his feet. "Innis?"

Was that the crunch of footsteps on a crushed marble path?

He hurried across the lawn and plunged into cool shade between tall hedges. "Innis?"

The path curved out of sight, empty, but there was a sensation that someone had just walked past. Harkeld strode along it. "Innis?"

The path curved. He saw movement in the distance. Someone in a dark cloak hurrying out of sight.

Harkeld broke into a run. "Innis, wait!"

He chased the person halfway across the garden, finally cornering her where two hedges met. Harkeld halted, panting. The woman had her back turned and her hood up, but he knew—he *knew*—it was Innis.

He caught his breath. "Innis? I apologize for what I said last time." He stepped closer, touched her shoulder lightly. "Don't go. Please."

"I tried to change my shape, but it won't stick. I can only look like me." Innis sounded close to tears.

"It doesn't matter." Harkeld gathered her gently in his arms. By the All-Mother, it felt good to hold her again. "I like how you look."

She shook her head.

"I was angry, Innis. I took it out on you." Harkeld pushed back her hood and laid his cheek against her curling black hair. He felt the familiar rush of tenderness, the familiar sense of deep connection. "How can I care whether you're a witch or not when I'm one myself?"

This was what his dreams had been trying to teach him all week. *I am a witch. I accept it.* There was no satisfaction in the admission, just a sense of defeat.

"I'm a bad-tempered whoreson. It's past time that I mastered my temper." And that was the second lesson in all this. To be more like King Magnas and less like his father.

CHAPTER FIFTY-EIGHT

ASH SHOOK JAUMÉ roughly awake at dawn. "He's all right," he called out.

"What?" Jaumé said.

Bennick sat slumped alongside him, gasping hoarsely.

"Watch him," Ash said. He ran to Nolt, who knelt by Kimbel, thumping his chest. "Bennick, Odil, Stead, Gant, all sick. Maati's dead. The boy's all right."

Nolt turned back Kimbel's eyelids, put his ear to his mouth. "Dead." He showed no grief. "Two. We've lost two."

"What's doing it?" Ash said. Behind him, Odil was on his hands and knees, Gant upright but staggering, Stead on his mat, wheezing.

"That fish Gant caught. It's poisoned us."

"The boy ate it too."

"The steam, then. It's poisoned. Boy." Nolt jerked his thumb. "Give them water."

Jaumé scrambled for a waterskin.

THEY ATE BREAD and dried meat. The pony nibbled leaves, snorting with disgust, and the dead men lay on the ground. The food and water revived Bennick. He sat straighter, breathed more easily.

Ash circled the clearing, keeping watch. He seemed stronger than the others, more alert, and after him, Nolt, even though they'd been watchman for half the night each. *The jungle is the enemy,* Jaumé thought. He couldn't understand why it hadn't attacked him too.

They laid the bodies side by side on the ground with their heads pointing north, and Jaumé didn't need to ask: facing home. Fith was north. Nolt laid each man's bared dagger on his chest, under his hands, and took their Stars to send back to Fith.

Kimbel had been young, but his face was old with the life gone from it. Kimbel, who had no dagger tattoos yet. Maati— Jaumé couldn't remember how many tattoos he'd had. A lot.

Nolt went through the dead men's packs and saddlebags, taking what was useful. Then, without any farewell or looking back, he led his men into the jungle.

CHAPTER FIFTY-NINE

THE FORESTED HIGHLANDS they'd ridden across for the last month ended. It wasn't an abrupt boundary, like Lundegaard's mile-high escarpment. This was a gentle sagging, a falling away from plateau to marshland. They rode downhill for half a day, picking their way along animal trails, while the tall trees with their long streamers of bark yielded to scrub. The slope flattened. The scrub dwindled and became boggy marshland. The air was thick, warm, stinking. Insects swarmed and long-legged birds stalked among the grasses. Harkeld wiped sweat from his face, slapped at gnats.

Rand pulled a bundle from one of the packsaddles. "Rub this on your skin. It'll keep the gnats away."

The oil stank even worse than the marsh, but it worked. Gnats gathered in clouds around Harkeld's face while he rode, but few bit.

As dusk turned to darkness, Justen led them to the Szal. The river had descended from plateau to marshland in turbulent falls, the shapeshifters said, but here it had widened again, branching into channels and long shingle islands.

They set up camp on the riverbank, pitching the tents by firelight. Cora materialized out of the darkness at Harkeld's side. "Let's have a short lesson."

He straightened wearily, mallet in one hand, tent stakes in the other. *Now? Must we?*

He followed Cora down to the stony riverbed. She'd lit a small fire, and illuminated by its flames...

He took it for a man—and reached for his sword—and then blinked and saw it for what it was: a stout branch standing upright with a smaller branch lashed across it, armlike, wearing a shirt—a scarecrow.

"Can you burn the shirt without burning the wood?"

Harkeld released his sword. His weariness evaporated. "I can try." He stepped closer to the scarecrow and examined it. If he told his magic to burn just the fabric, kept the heat of the flames low...

He raised his hand, concentrated. *Burn*.

The shirt flared alight, burning merrily. But the wood was burning too—

Snuff.

The flames vanished.

Cora pursed her lips, contemplating the scarecrow. Scraps of burnt cloth clung to charred wood.

"I killed him."

Cora conceded this with a nod. "I have more."

Harkeld helped her wedge a second scarecrow upright. Whose shirts were these, travel-stained and smelling of sweat? But even as he asked himself the question, he recognized the scent: Gerit's.

Harkeld grimaced.

He stepped back, blew out a breath, and raised his hand. *Burn*.

Again, both cotton and wood ignited.

Harkeld hissed annoyance between his teeth.

Cora set up two more scarecrows, dressed in trews rather than shirts. Harkeld threw his magic with careful precision.

Both scarecrows caught fire.

Harkeld scowled at them. He could burn arrows better than Cora or Katlen. He could burn throwing stars. Why couldn't he do this?

"Dinner!" Katlen called from the riverbank.

*　　*　　*

AFTER THEY'D EATEN, Cora unrolled the map. Harkeld leaned close to look. "Do you think there'll be corpses?"

"There have never been cities here."

It was the same answer Ebril had given. Harkeld sat back, relieved.

"The curse shadows were darker too," Cora said. "If that happens again, we'll know to be on our guard."

"Curse shadows?" The witches had talked of them before, but he didn't completely understand what they were.

She cocked her head and looked at him. "You should be able to see them. You are a mage."

"Untrained," Katlen said.

"We could probably teach you to see them," Rand said. "If you want to learn?"

Harkeld nodded. "But what are they?"

"Shadows that lie on anyone who's cursed. The darker the shadow, the stronger the curse. Ivek's curse has the darkest shadow I've ever seen, and I understand it became even darker when you neared the first anchor stone." He glanced at Cora, who nodded.

Harkeld looked at his hand. No shadow lay on it that he could see. He flicked a gnat off his thumb.

"Some healers can lay curses. I can't." Rand turned to Innis. "Can you?"

"They said I was strong enough to."

"Innis hasn't completed her training yet," Petrus said, a protective edge to his voice.

"Then we're certainly not going to ask her to lay a curse," Rand said. "All-Mother forbid!"

A faint memory uncoiled in Harkeld's mind, something Dareus had once said. "Laying a curse is like un-healing?"

"Exactly."

"So Ivek must have been a healer?"

"Yes," Katlen said. "An exceptionally strong one. And he must have had water magic, too, since the curse is waterborne."

"And stone magic," Rand said. "Because how else could he craft the anchor stones and bind the curse to the kingdoms' soil?"

"Stone magic?"

"Stone magic and water magic are rare and minor branches of magic," Katlen said. "Stone mages can mold stone into shapes of their choosing. Likewise, water mages have an affinity with water and can manipulate it."

"Very handy, being a water mage," Ebril said. "You can stop rain falling on you and part streams so you can cross with dry feet."

"And water mages can't drown," Rand said. "As long as they're conscious."

"There's also metalbending," Ebril said. "You should see the things metalbenders can make! And there's green magic, like Frane had. That's more common."

Harkeld nodded, remembering the grass Frane had made grow on Susa's grave. He felt slightly overwhelmed. *So much I don't know.*

CHAPTER SIXTY

NOLT CHOSE A campsite beside a spiny outcrop of rock. It looked like the back of a giant creature that had died and half-sunk into the soft ground. There was a pool nearby, but the steam rose less thickly than from others they had passed. They'd collected dry wood as they walked. Hard to find, yet each man carried a few branches. Nolt started a fire. They ate dried meat and bread and drank water.

"Ash and I will watch tonight," Nolt said. "Double watch. The rest of you sleep. Tomorrow I want you well. No Brother dies until he hears the All-Mother call."

I'm not a Brother, Jaumé thought. *Or does he mean I am, now?*

Bennick was still groggy, but less than Steadfast and Odil. Jaumé whispered, "How can Nolt and Ash stay awake all night? And walk tomorrow?"

"A Brother is trained not to sleep. Two nights, three." Bennick's voice was slurred. "You too, Jaumé, you'll see..." He closed his eyes.

The night was still, aside from the drifting steam. Jaumé watched it for a while. Nolt and Ash circled the fire. Now and then one of them laid on a new branch and the flames rose. How could anything hurt them when Nolt and Ash kept watch? He made up his mind it was Gant's fish that had poisoned everyone. *But why not me?* He'd eaten it too.

After a while he slept.

In his dream someone made small sounds of satisfied greed, like a baby suckling. It was a dream without people or shapes of any kind. Only murmuring and sighing and satisfaction. Jaumé woke with a start, glanced around, saw Nolt watching the jungle while Ash put more wood on the fire.

Something pink and fat stirred on Bennick's chest. It had a plump belly and chubby fingers and a round bald head and testicles the size of a bull's. Its mouth was fastened on Bennick's.

Jaumé screamed.

The thing released its mouth and looked at him. Jaumé saw a wizened old man's face, with eyes as black as coal and wet lips.

He scrabbled for his knife, jerked it from its sheath. He was aware of Ash advancing round the fire, but didn't wait. He slashed at the thing. A cry so thin it hurt came from the creature's mouth.

Ash grabbed his shirt, jerking Jaumé off the ground. He saw the gleam of Ash's knife.

"No," he cried. "The thing. On Bennick!"

Ash dropped him and shouted. Nolt was there. They pulled the creature off Bennick's chest. It dangled like a dead baby in their grip.

Jaumé saw another one, crouched on Gant. And others on Stead and Odil.

He shouted and pointed, but Nolt and Ash couldn't see them.

Jaumé rushed at the one on Gant and plunged his knife in. When he pulled his blade free, there was a gush of foul air. Jaumé choked at the smell. He scrambled over Gant and stabbed the things on Stead and Odil. Again the thin cry, like a knife blade sliding on glass.

Bennick!

Jaumé ran back to Bennick and put his ear close to Bennick's mouth. Faint breath tickled his cheek.

"Bennick's alive!"

"Pump his chest, the way I'm doing," Nolt said, looking up from Gant.

"Odil's dead," Ash said. He knelt beside Steadfast, but wasn't pressing his chest. He shook his head in a way that seemed to say Stead wouldn't live. He grabbed his bow and strode around the fire, but there was nothing to see in the steam, so he lifted Jaumé aside from Bennick and started pumping his chest.

"Get your bow, Jaumé," Nolt said. "You can see them, we can't." It was the first time he'd called Jaumé by his name.

Jaumé circled the fire. He kept an arrow on his bowstring. He felt ill. He'd never dreamed of creatures so disgusting—their wet mouths and bloated stomachs and their balls and penises as big as a bull's.

Nolt got Gant breathing evenly and shifted to Stead. Gant struggled to sit up, wheezing. He looked at the dead creature beside him and scrubbed his hand across his mouth. The thing was shriveling, dissolving. Its eyes had almost disappeared in the jelly of its face. "What is it?" Gant said hoarsely.

"Breathstealer," Ash said. "I've heard of them. But they're meant to be a myth. They don't exist."

"Yet here they are," Nolt said sourly.

"They come at night. They breed in the steam."

"Why can't we see them?"

"We've all known women. Except Jaumé."

"Virgin," Gant said.

Ash nodded. "How many more days in this steam?"

"A couple," Nolt said. "We'll travel at night and sleep in the day. When we get to the river, you and me will cross."

"And me," Gant said. He managed to stand, staggered, but kept his feet.

"We'll see. But Bennick?" Nolt shook his head. "He stays with Jaumé."

"Where?" Jaumé asked.

"We'll find a place. Jaumé, if we have to sleep at night, you'll be our watchman. And one of us with you."

Jaumé nodded.

"Steadfast?" Ash said.

"He hears the All-Mother calling."

Ash and Nolt laid Odil's body beside Steadfast, facing north. Stead opened his dark, slanted eyes. He smiled with half his mouth and moved his hand feebly to the hilt of his dagger. He seemed to nod—Jaumé couldn't tell. Nolt drew the dagger from its sheath. He placed its point over Stead's heart, held Stead's hands around the hilt, and thrust. The dagger slid in easily; Stead died with only a jerk of his legs.

Jaumé watched. He knew he mustn't turn away.

Nolt left the dagger in the body, with Stead's hands clasped around it. He laid Odil's dagger on his chest and stood. "Eat," he said, "We travel till midday, then sleep. At night we'll make torches and walk again. Jaumé."

Jaumé thought, *I'm not 'boy' any more.*

"Bennick is weak." The words carried no judgement. "He rides. You lead the pony. We carry what we need in our packs."

They ate. Nolt and Ash went through the saddlebags, cramming everything they could into five packs, discarding the rest. Jaumé cleaned his knife and slid it carefully into its sheath.

CHAPTER SIXTY-ONE

When the sun was high, Rand set about trying to teach him to see curse shadows. "It looks like a shroud of cobwebs, clinging quite closely." He held out his hand to Harkeld, fingers outspread. "It's lying on my palm, see? And around each finger."

Harkeld stared at Rand's hand.

"It's black," Ebril said helpfully, riding alongside him.

Harkeld shook his head. "I can't see it."

"Try looking out of the corner of your eye."

Harkeld did. "It just looks normal."

"Well, to you, it would." Rand lowered his hand. "Look at Ebril against the sun. Do you see anything covering him?"

The sunlight was a bright halo around Ebril's head, making his red hair look as if it burned. Harkeld narrowed his eyes, examining the mage, looking for a dark shadow.

He shook his head. "No." His frustration found its way into his voice.

"You're not missing anything," Ebril said. "They're pretty unpleasant."

Harkeld gazed down at his right hand, at fingers and knuckles and—turning it over—palm. There was a curse shadow clinging to it. Rand could see it. Ebril could see it. *Why can't I?*

"The curse shadows darkened this year," Rand said. "When the curse came into its full power. Do you remember ever thinking that maybe a room needed more candles? Or that the sun had gone behind a cloud you couldn't see?"

Harkeld shook his head, his frustration building.

He'd thought he'd known everything there was to know about his world. Had thought himself observant, even clever, steering a course through the dangerous political currents of the palace, watchful and alert, never making a misstep, planning his future, Britta's future, all Osgaard's future.

Ignorant and blind, that's what he'd been, and the world he'd inhabited, so narrow. *So much going on around me that I was unaware of.*

"If we could show you someone who's not cursed, I think you'd see the difference," Rand said. "Your problem is that you've nothing to compare it with. Curse shadows are normal to you. This is how your eyes tell you people should look."

Their horses splashed through a marshy dip. The air was heavy, stinking. Insects rose in swarms.

"There are more mages coming to join us," Rand said, waving insects away from his face. "Depending on where we meet them, you may have a chance to see what people look like without curse shadows."

"Krelinsk," Harkeld said, remembering what Cora had said.

"Or the delta, if we're lucky."

"I hope we sail," Ebril said. "The Drowned Man's Shallows are meant to be quite a sight. Some fleet or other got wrecked there ages ago, and you can see the old hulls rotting and masts sticking up out of the water."

They rode silently for several minutes, then Ebril said, "Rand... can you tell Flin how healers strip people of magic? I couldn't remember what that gland is called."

"The Daubon gland. Named after the healer who discovered it. Every mage has one, but they're not all the same. Hence the variations in our magic."

"And you kill this gland?"

"We stop the blood flow to it. Within a few days, the gland dies."

It didn't sound too alarming, no knives digging around inside his head. "What does the gland do?"

"It produces a substance—lots of different substances actually—that enter the blood."

"What are the substances?"

"We don't have a name for them other than *magic*. Exceptionally powerful healers can sense magic in the blood, sometimes, or smell it on people's breath, but no one's ever been able to see it."

Smell magic? Harkeld felt his eyebrows rise.

"The gland is active from birth, but a person's magical ability usually doesn't develop until just prior to puberty," Rand said. "We test for it by breath and blood.

"Breath and blood?" Dareus had used that expression once.

"A drop of your blood mixed in Jussi's oil and poured into a bowl of water, and then your breath blown over it," Ebril said. "Makes different colors, kind of like a rainbow."

"Jussi's oil?"

"For the mage who developed it," Rand told him. "Everyone has the test when they're a child. It gives a good indication of what kind of magic they'll develop. If any."

"It'd be interesting to have you tested," Ebril said. "See if you have more than just the fire magic."

Rand nodded. "It would. But we don't have any Jussi's oil."

Harkeld wasn't sure whether to be relieved or not. Did he want to know if he had more magic?

"This gland... will I pass it to any children I sire?"

"There's a strong chance, yes."

"Even if you kill it?"

"Yes."

Familiar rage swelled in Harkeld's chest. The mages had done this to him—deliberately corrupted his bloodline—and the taint wouldn't end with him. It would infect his children. And perhaps their children too.

Harkeld clamped his jaw shut, refused to let the anger spill out of him. Rand and Ebril were mages, but they'd had nothing to do with that deceit. It had happened two generations ago. His grandfather, the lying whoreson of a Sentinel who'd given him this gland, was dead.

*   *   *

THAT EVENING, HARKELD went to the riverbed with Cora and practiced with more scarecrows. The shirts and trews weren't as travel-stained and sweaty. Frane's, he guessed. That knowledge was sobering. He concentrated hard, but did no better than the previous night.

He scowled at the last scorched scarecrow and turned away, heading back to the camp.

"Flin."

Harkeld halted. He took a deep breath and turned to face Cora.

"A month ago, you couldn't even light a candle," Cora said. "In a few weeks you've learned things that normally take students years to master. Don't be too hard on yourself."

He took another deep breath, blew it out, tried to let go of his frustration.

"You like to do things well, don't you?"

"Yes," he admitted.

"An excellent trait in a fire mage. Particularly one as strong as you." Cora smiled. "Don't worry, you'll master this too."

"CAN YOU SEE curse shadows?" Harkeld asked the dream-Innis that night, as they lay on the sunny grass.

"Yes."

He frowned up at the blue sky. If she could see them, why couldn't he? She *was* part of his mind. "Are you blocking it?" he demanded, rolling onto one elbow to look at her.

"What? No. Of course not."

Harkeld scowled at her. "Then why can't I see them!" He closed his eyes and sighed. "Sorry."

He lay back down and stared at the sky, disappointed with himself. "I want to be like King Magnas, but I keep behaving like my father." *Yelling at you. Punching Justen.* It was just as well he was never going to be a king. He'd be an awful one.

*   *   *

"Justen!"

Innis glanced up from the packsaddle she was fastening. Petrus strode towards her, his expression grim.

"What's wrong?"

"I need a word with you."

Innis secured the buckle and followed Petrus from the campsite. On the edge of the riverbank he swung to face her. "I saw you go into Flin's tent last night. As a mouse. You slept there, didn't you?"

She opened her mouth, but no words came out. Horror had frozen her tongue.

"In the All-Mother's name, what are you *doing*? Breaking Primary Laws because of an infatuation?"

She blushed. "It's not—"

"Dareus should never have let you be Justen! It's gone to your head."

The injustice of this stung. "You've been Justen, too! You've broken Primary Laws."

"Only with Dareus or Cora's approval. Never because I *felt* like it."

"He's safer with me there," she said, defensively.

"Fine! Go ask Cora whether you have permission to sleep in his tent as a mouse." Petrus gestured angrily back at the campsite. "Go on, ask her!"

Innis bit her lip. She looked down at her feet—Justen's feet—in their big leather boots.

"Innis..." Petrus's voice became quieter. "How can you not understand how important this is? A Primary Law! And you, a Sentinel."

The heat was gone from her face. She felt cold, and slightly light-headed. "Are you going to tell Cora?" What would her punishment be? *I'll be sent back to Rosny. They'll scratch my name from the Sentinels' register. Maybe take away my magic.*

"No. *You're* going to tell her."

Innis flinched inside herself. "Petrus, can't we just—"

"No. This isn't a minor transgression, Innis. She has to be told. Today. Tonight."

She gazed at him, her throat so tight she couldn't speak.

"Don't look at me like that." Petrus squeezed his eyes briefly shut and raked his hands through his hair. "One of us has to tell her, and it needs to be you, not me. It will weigh the judgment in your favor."

She nodded mutely.

Petrus looked at her for a long moment, as if debating saying something further. He shook his head and turned on his heel and headed back to the horses.

Innis didn't follow; her legs were locked in place. Confess to Cora!

THEY PRESSED NORTH, cutting across marshland, pushing through thickets of scrub. Ebril guided them, gliding ahead.

Outcrops of black rock pushed out of the scrubby marshland, some humpbacked like gigantic tortoises, some running in long, low ridges. The shapes were oddly regular. Harkeld squinted, trying to see them more clearly. "Is that a ruin?" he asked, as they came close to an outcrop. "Some kind of fortress?"

Cora shook her head. "It's natural. I've seen something like it in Margolie."

"So've I," Rand said.

"Natural? How can that be natural?" The black rock stood in tall pillars, as regular as if they'd been hewn by stonecutters.

Rand shrugged. "It's a type of basalt that cracks that way."

"Huh." Harkeld craned his neck to keep the outcrop in sight once they'd passed it.

The sun moved past its zenith. Ebril rode now, whistling under his breath, and Hew flew overhead.

Harkeld concentrated on trying to see the curse shadows. He studied the mages riding ahead—Justen and Katlen—but the only thing he saw was a faint shimmer surrounding Justen, as if he caught the light oddly. Harkeld blinked several times and looked at Justen again. The shimmer still seemed to be there, especially if he looked at Justen out of the corner of his eye.

I'm imagining things.

Harkeld gave up and looked ahead. A mile or so to the north, the marshland butted up against dark trees. The jungle, within which the second anchor stone lay. Movement in the sky caught his eye: Hew, climbing in ever-widening circles. The hawk's wings and speckled breast seemed to shimmer, like Justen. Harkeld rubbed his eyes and looked at Hew again.

The mage glided towards the jungle. He dwindled to a small dot and returned several minutes later, flying fast and low.

Ebril broke off whistling. "Something wrong?"

Hew arrowed down to land. "Men," he called out. "Just inside the trees. Preparing to ambush us."

Harkeld jerked his mount to a halt. "Fithians?"

Hew shook his head. "They're a pretty ragged bunch. Some have brands on their faces."

"Outlaws," Rand said.

"How many?" Cora asked, pushing her horse forward.

"Eight. And not well-armed."

Eight. *And we are nine.*

"Let's try to run them off," Cora said.

"Agreed," said Rand. "I don't feel like killing people today." His inflection was dry, ironic.

"We don't want them following us, either," Katlen pointed out.

"So let's scare the horseshit out of them," Ebril said. "Some lions, some fire. They'll run till they reach Roubos."

Rand's mouth twitched. "Agreed," he said again. "What kind of weapons do they have, Hew?"

"A couple of bows. Swords."

"They can't be certain how many of us there are," Cora said. "We're too far away. So, I think... Petrus, Justen, Ebril, fly there and wait for us, change into lions. When they attack, rough them up a bit, give them a good scare."

Harkeld glanced at the shapeshifters. Ebril was grinning, Petrus was grave, and Justen looked... miserable?

"Hew, stay in the air. Keep watch."

Hew nodded.

"Katlen, you and I will burn their clothes. Flin..." Cora waited until she had his gaze. "You deal with their bows and arrows."

Harkeld nodded. He glanced back at Justen. Why was he looking so unhappy?

"And Rand—"

"I'll sit back and watch."

CHAPTER SIXTY-TWO

THEY CAME TO a river. It was as wide as the one they'd sailed down and turned over on itself in the same way, but was a dark green-black, not brown.

Nolt had pushed them hard, and seemed exhausted. Ash showed no signs of tiredness, he moved with the strength and freedom he'd always had, and Gant had recovered his quickness, although now and then he panted as though climbing a hill. Jaumé saw how much older Nolt was than his men, and remembered the rows of daggers tattooed on his shoulder blade—a lifetime of battles. His face was grizzled, gaunt.

"Ash and Gant and I cross here," Nolt said. "Bennick, you and Jaumé stay on this side."

Bennick, slumped on the pony, didn't argue.

"Follow the river," Nolt told him. "We'll follow on our side. It joins with another one, and there's an island. We'll find the prince there."

And join his army, Jaumé thought. *But how do Bennick and I get across?*

"Wait for us. Out of sight. Loomath said there's rocks you can climb and hide in."

Bennick nodded.

"If we fail, make the kill. That much we'll salvage of our honor."

Kill witches? Jaumé hid a shudder.

"What does this prince look like?" Bennick asked.

"Your age. Dark-haired."

Nolt and Gant and Ash prepared themselves. They tied their bowstrings in pouches to keep them dry, strapped their Stars tightly at their waists.

Bennick dismounted, moving like an old man. "All-Mother bless your blades." He clasped hands with Gant and Ash.

Nolt gave Bennick the spyglass and compass. "Keep them dry."

Gant winked at Jaumé, and Ash patted him on the head.

The men walked into the dark water, floating their packs in front of them. Silver Ash, black-skinned Gant, Nolt. The current took them. They swam one-armed, holding the packs, kicking their legs. Ash and Gant were almost at the far side when a bend in the river carried them from sight. Nolt trailed behind, not even halfway across.

Jaumé watched the river sweep Nolt out of sight. Was he going to drown in the black water?

"Will Nolt be all right?" He looked at Bennick, but saw no anxiety in his face.

"If it's his time, it's his time."

CHAPTER SIXTY-THREE

THE OUTLAWS LAUNCHED their ambush once the last packhorse was under the trees. Harkeld instinctively drew his sword—and rammed it back into its scabbard. Arrows leapt through the air. *Burn. Burn.* He searched for the archers, peering through the dark-green gloom and tangled vines. There was one. *Burn.* The bow burst into flames.

The archer threw his bow aside with a scream. He wasn't the only person screaming. The jungle canopy echoed with shrieks, with shouts, with cries. Harkeld risked a glance sideways— there was Petrus rearing on his haunches, cuffing an outlaw to the ground, and there was Ebril chasing down a man with great leaping bounds—

An arrow speared out of the green-tinted gloom. A horse screamed in pain.

Burn. He caught the next arrow. *Burn.* Where was the archer? Behind that tree, out of sight.

Harkeld seized his magic, told it what he wanted it to do, sent it after the bow. A high-pitched shriek of terror came from behind the tree. A shadowy figure ran scrambling, heading deeper into the jungle.

Harkeld turned his attention back to the battle. *Rout* was a better word. Two of the outlaws tore off burning clothes, the others fled from the lions.

Ebril was having fun. The snarl on his face was definitely a grin. He pounced on an outlaw. The angle of his ears, the angle of his tail... he was like a cat playing with a mouse.

A lion bellowed, jerking Harkeld's attention to where a man with a murderer's brand across his forehead cowered from a silver-maned lion.

"Flin!" Rand was with the injured horse. "Give me a hand."

Harkeld dismounted and went to help him. Rand spoke soothingly to the animal, examining its pierced haunch. His hand closed around the arrow. "Hold its head, this'll hurt."

The horse squealed and reared as Rand ripped the arrow free. Harkeld hung on grimly, forcing the animal back to all four hooves. Rand staunched the blood with his hands.

The screaming had stopped. The outlaws were gone. Cora and Katlen sat astride their horses, knee to knee, heads inclined towards one another, conferring.

The lions padded back. Harkeld identified them by the color of their manes. Ebril, russet; Petrus, silver; Justen, dun.

"Where's Innis?" he asked Rand.

"Huh? Oh, further back." Rand gestured vaguely south with a bloody hand.

Cora and Katlen dismounted and came towards them. "Flin," Katlen said, frowning. "Could you actually *see* that second archer?"

Harkeld glanced at Cora. She wasn't frowning. "Uh... no. But I knew which tree he was behind." Although he'd tried not to, a defensive note had entered his voice.

Katlen's frown deepened. "So how did you burn his bow like that?"

"I, um..." He glanced at Cora again. She still wasn't frowning. If anything, she looked interested. "I told my magic what I wanted it to do."

Katlen crossed her arms. "You threw fire without seeing either the archer *or* the bow."

Harkeld stiffened. "It worked, didn't it? I didn't hurt the archer." There'd been no pain in the man's shriek, just terror.

"I sometimes wonder," Rand said mildly, his hands still pressed to the horse's wound, "if we stifle our magic with all the rules and restrictions we place on it."

Katlen's attention snapped to the healer. Her frown grew so deep it looked carved on her forehead.

"Wild, untrained mages, like our Flin, don't obey the rules because they don't know they're there," Rand said. "And sometimes they do things that shouldn't be possible. Perhaps if you hadn't been told a thousand times that you can't throw fire at something you can't see, you could do it too?"

Katlen scowled at the healer, but Cora looked thoughtful.

"At the Academy, we train mages to be safe and lawful," Rand said. "But we also take away their spontaneity and their risk-taking and their experimenting."

"Spontaneity and risk-taking and experimenting should have *nothing* to do with magic," Katlen snapped. "They're far too dangerous!"

Rand shrugged.

Katlen turned and stalked to her horse. Cora stayed where she was. "It's true," she said. "You're doing things that shouldn't be possible. But how much of that is because you're an exceptionally powerful mage, and how much because you don't know the rules? Maybe no one but you could do those things?"

Rand tilted his head, smiling. "Good questions."

By the time the shapeshifters had dressed, the horse was no longer bleeding. A raw-looking scar marked the arrow wound. "It'll need some more work," Rand said, stroking the horse's haunch. "But we can move on, if you wish?"

Cora nodded. "I'd like to put a few leagues between us and them."

"Somehow, I don't think they'll try to follow," Ebril said, swinging up into his saddle.

Rand snorted a laugh, but neither Justen nor Petrus did; they mounted silently, not looking at each other. Harkeld frowned, watching them. Had they fallen out?

THAT EVENING, THEY camped beside the Szal again, and Harkeld had another lesson on the stony riverbank. These clothes were cleaner and smaller than the others he'd burned: Susa's.

He tried to relax, to not concentrate so fiercely, to let instinct take over. The first shirt burned briskly, and the wood underneath was only faintly singed. "Well done," Cora said. "Did you watch us today?"

Harkeld shook his head. "I didn't have time."

Cora set up another shirt. Harkeld repeated what he'd done; let himself relax, trusted to instinct. Again, the shirt burned, but the wood didn't.

"Good," Cora said. "Try the trews."

He burned three pairs, one after the other, leaving the branches barely singed.

"Excellent," Cora said. "I don't think you're going to accidentally kill someone. Do you?"

"No."

They walked back towards the campsite, stones crunching beneath their boots. "Cora, do you use only one hand for your magic, or both?"

"Both, of course." She halted. "Ah... you've only been using your right hand."

Harkeld nodded. "Yes. And this afternoon..." He frowned, remembering reaching for his sword and having to jam it back into the scabbard. "I'd like to be able to hold my sword *and* throw magic."

"You should be able to." Cora picked up a piece of driftwood. "Burn this with your left hand." She threw it in the air.

Harkeld's right hand lifted automatically. He hurriedly raised his left, grabbing for his magic. *Burn*. He caught the stick just before it hit the ground, an uncontrolled burst of fire, too strong, too hot.

"Hmm," Cora said. "Let's try that again." She gathered more driftwood. "Ready?"

She threw the sticks one by one.

Burn. Burn. Rough blasts of fire. *Burn.* It shouldn't be so hard, curse it. He was struggling to keep up with Cora. *Burn.* The sticks were falling too fast. *Burn. Burn.* He was going to miss that last one—

His right hand reached out, sent a flick of magic, burned the stick with an economical spurt of flame before it hit the ground.

Harkeld grimaced. *Rut it.*

Cora looked at him thoughtfully. "Are you strongly right-handed?"

Harkeld nodded.

"What hand you use *shouldn't* matter." Cora's smile was rueful. "My mistake. At the Academy we're taught to use both hands from the start. I should have done the same with you."

Harkeld waved aside the apology.

"Practice. That's what you need. Lots of practice."

He helped Cora gather more driftwood, and then the practice began. After the first few minutes, Harkeld drew his sword and held it in his right hand. With that hand disengaged, it became easier to use his left for magic.

He focused fiercely on the sticks Cora threw. By the time Katlen called them to dinner, he was exhausted, but he was burning the driftwood almost as efficiently as if he'd been using his right hand.

Harkeld slid the sword into its scabbard and shook out his fingers. They ached from gripping the hilt so tightly. A headache sat behind his temples.

Cora cocked her head. "Well?"

"It's hard," he admitted.

"I can see that. You're slower with that hand, less precise. But you're already much better than you were half an hour ago."

Harkeld rubbed his forehead, trying to ease the headache.

"You're about where you were with your right hand at Gdelsk. Give it a fortnight and you'll be just as good with both."

INNIS BARELY MANAGED a mouthful of stew. Her throat was too tight, her stomach too tight. Even her lungs were tight. She left the fire, shifted into her own shape, dressed in her own clothes.

Petrus glanced up when she came back to the campfire, his

face half-shadowed, then looked away. "I'll relieve Hew." He pushed to his feet and left the firelight.

Innis crouched alongside Cora. She had to swallow twice to find her voice. "Cora... may I speak privately with you?"

"Of course."

Cora led her down to the river, lighting the way with her hand. She sat on a log, patted a place alongside her, and smiled at Innis. "What is it?"

Innis sat, gripping her hands tightly together. She wished Cora would put out her flames. It would be easier to confess in the dark. She inhaled a shaky breath and looked away from Cora. "I've been breaking a Primary Law. I've been shifting into a mouse and sleeping in Flin's tent."

Cora said nothing for several seconds. "Why?"

I could lie. I could say it was to protect him. Innis clenched her fingers more tightly together. "We share dreams. Dareus said healers sometimes do it." She risked a glance at Cora.

Cora's expression was grave.

Innis looked down at her clenched hands. "When I was his armsman, we shared dreams almost every night. I missed them, so... I broke the Law."

Justifications bubbled up on her tongue. *It's a Law I broke every night I was Justen! You and Dareus gave me permission to sleep in a shape not my own, remember?* But that permission had been for the sole purpose of protecting the prince.

Cora quenched her firelight.

The night was dark, but not silent. Water burbled. Frogs croaked. Insects sang. Voices murmured at the campfire.

"Explain to me what you mean by sharing dreams."

"It's like... there's him and me, and we talk and... and he tells me things, and I can feel what he's feeling—his emotions, I mean—and..." How to explain? "It's like we *share* who we are. Sometimes we argue, but mostly we just talk and... and stuff." *Sex.* But she couldn't quite bring herself to tell Cora that. "And we feel happy. Both of us. Happier than I've ever been before."

How lame that sounded: happy. As if happiness justified breaking a Primary Law.

Cora exhaled, a sound like a sigh. "It sounds very complicated."

Innis nodded miserably. "Dareus said it happens sometimes with healers who share a strong bond. So he must be a healer. Flin, I mean."

Cora was silent for a long time. Innis sat with her head bowed and her eyes closed, listening to the river and the frogs and the insects.

"Does Flin know the dreams are shared?" Cora asked.

"He thinks I'm something he imagines."

Cora sighed. She snapped her fingers and set a piece of driftwood alight.

Innis shrank back. She wanted to stay hidden in the dark. She forced herself to meet Cora's eyes.

"There are several issues here, Innis. First, you've been breaking a Primary Law without prior permission. Second, you've been sharing dreams with someone who has no idea it's happening."

"But—"

"For you to share dreams with Flin and for *you* to know what's happening, and *him* not to, is... it's a violation, Innis."

Innis closed her mouth.

"If you were to continue sharing dreams, he would need to know what's happening. And he would have to agree with it. And as for breaking that Law..." Cora sighed again. "We're partly to blame for that, Dareus and I. We've asked a lot from you, and it's not unnatural that boundaries between right and wrong should blur. If you're breaking several Laws a day, what's one more? At least you recognized your misjudgment and corrected it."

Innis looked down at her hands again. "Petrus caught me. He said I had to tell you."

"Ah..." Cora said.

"You have to send me home, don't you? I shouldn't be a Sentinel. I need to be punished."

Cora uttered a sound that was part-laugh, part-sigh. "I'm not going to send you home, Innis. We need you here. And I'm not going to punish you. The culpability for this must be shared. Your youth and inexperience and the demands we've placed on you..." She shifted her weight on the log. Her tone became matter-of-fact. "When this mission is over, I'll have to report this... this error. It will go before the Council, but I'm sure they'll not be too harsh, given the circumstances. A comment on your record would suffice, I'd think. That's what I'll recommend."

Innis stared down at her hands. For the first time in her life, she was glad her parents were dead.

"You made a mistake. Which you have now corrected." Cora's voice became more gentle. "We all make mistakes, Innis."

My parents never made mistakes. They'd be so disappointed if they knew, so ashamed of her. A tear trickled down her cheek. Innis wiped it away with her sleeve.

"Innis..." Cora reached out and took her hand.

"You never make mistakes," Innis said, her voice wobbling. "My parents never did."

Cora gave a half-laugh. "I most certainly make mistakes. Flin caught me out in one this evening. And your parents made mistakes too, for all they were good Sentinels. Everyone does. It's part of being human."

More tears spilled from her eyes. "They had such high hopes for me." Everything she'd worked for at the Academy had been in her parents' memory, been done *for* them. "And now I've ruined it."

"Hardly ruined," Cora said. "And I would hope you chose to be a Sentinel for yourself, not for your parents."

Innis blotted her eyes with her sleeve.

Cora released her hand. "Innis, look at me. This is serious."

Her tone pulled Innis's head around.

"If you're a Sentinel because you think it's what your parents would have wanted, that's the wrong reason to take the oath. Why did you become a Sentinel, Innis? Because they wanted it, or because you did?"

"Both."

"Innis... do you truly *want* to be a Sentinel?"

Innis hesitated, and turned the question over in her mind. "Yes," she said with certainty. "I do."

Cora looked at her for a long moment, and then nodded. "Good, because you're a good one, and this mistake you've made—whether you believe me or not—will make you even better. We learn a lot from our mistakes." Her lips twitched wryly. "If they don't kill us."

Some of the tight knots in Innis's stomach began to unravel. She dried her face.

"I'm glad you listened to Petrus."

Hearing his name made Innis's chest squeeze painfully. His expression this morning, the tone of his voice...

"Back in Osgaard, when Dareus asked me to be Justen, I was afraid. I asked Petrus to watch me and tell me if he thought anything was going wrong." She closed her eyes. Petrus had done as she'd asked, but his face—

To lose Petrus's friendship was worse punishment than being dismissed as a Sentinel. He was her brother, for all they shared no blood. Her closest friend.

"You had good reason to be afraid. Being someone else for so long... it was bound to have an effect."

"I feel more comfortable in Justen's body than my own," Innis confessed in a low voice, not looking at Cora. "I like it better."

"Ah." Cora sighed. "That's worrying."

Innis nodded.

"This is why we have the Primary Laws. Asking you to break them was dangerous. It's just as well we'll be getting reinforcements shortly. Justen needs to cease to exist."

Innis nodded again, miserably. She stared at the little fire Cora had lit.

"These dreams of yours. What did Dareus tell you about them?"

"He said it happens when healers share a strong bond. And that it's rare. He didn't know much else about them. It was just after the prince had burned that assassin and I realized the dreams I was having weren't... ordinary. So I asked Dareus."

"Did he say anything else?"

"He wanted to know how the prince was feeling." Innis looked down at her cuff, rubbed the dampness from the tears with her thumb. "If you could have seen inside his head then, Cora... He was terrified."

"I've no doubt. To grow up as he has, thinking mages are monsters, and then have this happen to him... Given his background, he's dealt with it remarkably well. I'm impressed with him."

Innis glanced at her, startled. "You are? But I thought everyone thinks he's prickly and bad-tempered and—"

"There's a lot more to our Flin than his temper," Cora said. "He has the makings of a good Sentinel."

"I've told him that. In the dreams, I mean. But he's so stubborn."

Cora uttered a laugh. "Yes, stubborn. But also determined. He doesn't do things by halves. And he has a lot of courage."

"And if he thinks he's made a mistake, he always apologizes."

"Yes. I've noticed that."

"He thinks you're a good teacher. I don't know if he's told you, but he said it once, in a dream."

"No." Cora studied her face. "You like him, don't you?"

Innis felt herself blush. "Yes."

But Cora didn't pursue this line of questioning. "Have you asked Rand about the dreams?"

"No. Do you think I should?"

"Dareus was primarily a fire mage. Rand's knowledge of the intricacies of healing magic will be much broader than his was." Cora tilted her head to one side. "Would you like to ask him?"

Innis nodded.

"Now?"

She hesitated, and then nodded again. Cora stood and cupped her hands to her mouth. "Rand! Can you come down here, please?"

A few moments later, Rand joined them. He sat on Innis's other side, his face lively with curiosity.

"Have you ever heard of healers sharing dreams?" Cora asked.

Rand's eyebrows rose. His gaze fastened on Innis. "You're sharing dreams? With...?"

Innis felt herself blush again. "Flin."

"What do you know about them?" Cora asked.

Rand answered her, but his gaze stayed on Innis. "They're rare. Incredibly rare."

"What else?"

"They're intense. Usually extremely intimate. Exhilarating. Euphoric."

Innis looked down at her hands. Her cheeks felt hot.

"Forgive me for asking, Innis... but are the dreams quite passionate?"

Innis's cheeks grew hotter. "Sometimes."

There was a moment of silence, and then Cora asked, "Is Flin a healer?"

"He'll have some healing ability, yes, but not necessarily great. Innis, you sense your patients' emotions and personalities when you heal them, don't you?"

"Yes." She risked a glance at him. "Is that why it's happening?"

"One of the pair must be that strong a healer, yes. The other one..." Rand shrugged. "Some have been that strong, but many aren't. The most important thing is the bond between the dreamers, the emotional connection. I might be a much stronger healer than Flin, but you'll never have those dreams with me, because we don't connect on that level." His eyes narrowed as if a thought occurred to him. "You haven't finished your training yet, have you, Innis? You're still a virgin?"

Innis nodded.

"Then I imagine you'll be told all this during your sexual training. I'd certainly tell you, if I was your instructor. You're one of the few mages who has a chance of finding this kind of connection with someone."

"Hmm..." Cora pursed her lips thoughtfully. "Is there anything else you know about sharing dreams, Rand?"

He shrugged. "It's meant to be a remarkable experience. The dreamers develop incredibly strong and long-standing attachments."

"You mean... they marry?"

"There was a pair of siblings who shared dreams, oh, last century, but other than that, yes. The bond between dreamers... this isn't something casual, Cora. They're inside each other's head. They know each other better than most people ever will. It's intense, powerful. If Innis is sharing dreams with our Flin, then they're both exceptionally lucky." Rand paused. "I take it Flin doesn't know what's happening?"

"He thinks Innis is something he's made up."

"Ah..." Rand said. "Do you plan to tell him?"

Innis glanced at Cora.

"A connection this deep between two people is rare," Rand said. "It's not something to be dismissed lightly. In my opinion, he needs to know."

Cora rubbed her forehead. "He'll have to be told at some stage. But not now. Definitely not now." She grimaced. "There's the problem of Justen, you see. Flin will be sure to wonder why he's sharing dreams with Innis when it's actually Justen who's been sleeping in his tent."

"Oh, of course." Rand grimaced too. "That's a complication."

"Just a small one," Cora said wryly. "I'd like to avoid him discovering *that* deception if at all possible. He'd be furious."

More than furious. But it wasn't the prince's outrage that Innis feared. It was how humiliated he'd feel. She laid her palm on the log they sat on and sent out a prayer: *Please, All-Mother, let him never find out.*

"And he should also be told he's a healer," Cora said. "It may influence his decisions about his magic. Thank you, Rand." She stood and took Innis's hand, pulling her to her feet. "Bedtime."

"Thank you," Innis said.

Cora smiled reassuringly. "Don't worry. We'll work this out."

CHAPTER SIXTY-FOUR

THEY TRAVELED PART of the night, and spent the rest huddled beside a tiny fire. Bennick sat upright, his head jerking forward whenever he dozed. Jaumé gripped his knife, listening to the cries of night creatures, watching the writhing steam. Eyes gleamed occasionally. Twice he saw breathstealers.

He hated the jungle, hated the bottomless steaming pools, hated the things watching.

They set off at dawn, following the river, forcing their way through the jungle. In the afternoon, they came to an outcrop of rock stretching downriver as far as they could see. It looked like a petrified forest with the tree trunks all clumped together. Some of the stone pillars stood upright, some leaned over, some twisted like seaweed.

"We'll have to leave the pony here," Jaumé said.

"The mages will find her." Bennick's face was gray. He looked an old man.

"Mages?"

"Witches, you call 'em. They can turn into birds. If they see the pony, they'll know we're here."

Jaumé swallowed. "I'll kill her. I'll... I'll use my knife."

"Can you do that, Jaumé?"

"If I have to."

Bennick looked at him, then shook his head. "No lad, you can't. Take her into the jungle as far as you can and let her go. She'll forage."

Jaumé took off his pack and led the pony away, past steaming pools and twisting vines, until he came to greener trees. He unbridled her and slapped her away and she trotted off and soon was lost in the shadowy foliage.

"Good luck," Jaumé said. He'd grown fond of the pony.

He made his way back to Bennick, who'd fallen into a doze with his back against a slanting rock.

Jaumé roused him. "We've got to get above the steam."

Bennick raised his head groggily. He groaned, grimaced, struggled to stand. "They've sucked out my life, Jaumé."

Jaumé shouldered his own pack and picked up Bennick's. He found a ledge sloping upwards, where the stone pillars had fallen over, and helped Bennick to climb. Bennick moved like a sleepwalker. Jaumé stopped him from sliding sideways into the water and heaved and wrestled Bennick's pack up. Bennick kept his sword, his throwing knife, his Stars. Even in his weakened state, he wouldn't surrender them. Or his bow, strapped over his back.

CHAPTER SIXTY-FIVE

THEY RODE NORTH, following first Hew, then Ebril, pushing through the humid, stinking jungle. In places the trees grew densely together, covered with leprous fungi, hung with vines, impenetrable. "May I take you down to the riverbed?" Ebril asked, the third time they'd come to a halt. His expression was harassed. "I swear there's no way through this, Cora."

The Szal was a good mile wide, braided with channels, some flowing, some dry, and long shingle bars. They stayed in the dry channels closest to the bank and made quicker time despite the river's meandering curves. Mid-afternoon, Petrus looked up and saw tongues of mist spilling over the riverbank from the jungle and rising in vaporous coils. He caught a whiff of sulfur. "Hot pools?" Katlen said, riding alongside him.

"Maybe." Petrus glanced back to where Justen rode, and then ahead to Cora and the prince. What had Innis told Cora last night? Cora had looked thoughtful, rather than angry. And why had Rand been summoned to join the discussion?

The smell of sulfur grew stronger. The horses didn't like it. They snorted, put their ears back. Streamers of mist curled around them and drifted into the sky. Ebril led them across a narrow creek that steamed and bubbled as it flowed into the Szal. The others exclaimed over it, but Petrus paid the simmering water scant attention. Anxiety was tight in his chest. What was he to do if Innis had lied to Cora? Protect her? Expose her?

His anxiety grew until it was close to anguish. It was almost a relief to notice that the curse shadows had grown darker.

"Cora!" Petrus called. "The curse shadows."

Everyone halted.

"Ah, yes..." Cora grimaced. "Well spotted, Petrus."

Rand glanced around, shivered. "Disconcerting. Was it like this in the desert?"

"The last few days before the anchor stone, yes. We need to be careful." Cora beckoned Ebril from the sky. "Select a defensible campsite tonight."

Prince Harkeld's gaze flicked from person to person, his eyebrows drawn together in a frown. "Can you see them?" Rand asked.

The prince's face tightened in frustration. He shook his head.

EBRIL TOOK THEM to where a river channel had changed course, isolating a portion of the riverbank. The small islet was grassy, flat-topped. The channels on three sides were dry, while the fourth held a trickle of water.

"There are lots of other islands," he said, gesturing at the broad river flats to their left. "But we'll get wet getting out to them, and if it rains upstream, we'll be in trouble. Here, we can get back to the bank if the water rises."

Cora surveyed the islet, chewing her lip.

"Looks defensible to me," Katlen said.

Still Cora hesitated. "We don't know what's out there. We lost eleven men, that first night in the canyon. I don't want a repeat..."

"We could pile driftwood around it, ready to set fire to," Petrus suggested. "And don't forget there's you and Katlen *and* Flin. We're actually better off than we were in the canyon, in terms of fire magic."

"And I didn't see anything that looked like graves today," Ebril put in. "Did you, Hew?"

Hew shook his head.

Cora blew out a breath. "Very well. We'll camp here."

CHAPTER SIXTY-SIX

THEY CLIMBED ROCKS like stepping stones. The river lay below, dull evening light on its surface. On the far shore, Jaumé saw dark humps amongst the foliage, like giant sleeping beasts.

Jaumé found a fissure leading into the rock. It was barely wide enough for Bennick, but once through the narrow opening it broadened, giving them room to sit but not lie down. He dragged in Bennick's pack and got food for them—dried meat and bread—and gave Bennick water. Bennick fell asleep with his head on his chest and his back against the wall.

Jaumé was afraid to sleep. The fissure ran up into the dark. Anything might live there. And breathstealers might come.

CHAPTER SIXTY-SEVEN

DARKNESS FELL WHILE they piled driftwood around the island. Petrus was sweating, panting, by the time it was done. He wiped his face, batted away the hovering gnats, and stood for a moment to catch his breath.

After they'd eaten, Cora brought out a map he'd never seen before. "Justen, I want you and Innis to fly to the anchor stone tomorrow. Check everything's all right. Look for Fithians."

Petrus leaned close to see the map.

"Looks a bit of a maze," Rand said.

"The delta mouth changes all the time, apparently, but back here, where the rivers join, it's stable." Cora tapped with one finger. "There's an island here, where the Szal meets the Yresk. The anchor stone is on it."

"It's a long way from the coast," Hew said. "I thought it'd be right at the mouth."

"No. And that's your second task tomorrow, Justen. Fly to the coast and see if you can see the ship that's meant to be meeting us."

Justen nodded.

Cora rolled up the map. "We don't know what will happen tonight. Hopefully nothing. If not... well, Flin can now help us fight anything off, so we shouldn't be overrun. In fact, we may not need the shapeshifters at all. Hew, if it does come to a battle with corpses, oliphants are best."

Hew nodded gravely.

"Petrus, you and Innis are splitting the watches tonight. Don't worry about overreacting. If you see or hear anything unusual—anything at all—wake us. Whatever comes may not be a corpse, it could be something else entirely, and I'd rather be short of sleep than dead."

Innis took the first watch. Petrus tossed and turned on his bedroll, worries churning in his mind. Beside him, Hew slept deeply, muttering and groaning occasionally. No noises came from outside the tent, but what if something had happened to Innis? What if corpses were silently creeping over the barrier of driftwood? What if everyone but he and Hew were already dead? And what exactly had Innis told Cora last night? Why had Rand been involved? And how could he ask her?

Finally Petrus gave up trying to sleep and crept out of the tent. Billowing mist covered the ground. Everything was peaceful. The driftwood barrier was intact, no skeletal figures lurched out of the darkness, the tent flaps were all closed.

A small, dark owl glided low. Innis. He beckoned her down.

Innis landed and changed into herself. "Is something wrong?"

"Can't sleep," Petrus said. "I'll take over from you."

"I've still got a couple of hours—"

"No point both of us being awake. Go to bed, Innis."

"Well..." She hesitated. "Wake me up early, then."

"Maybe. Seen or heard anything odd?"

She shook her head. "Nothing."

There was an awkward hesitation. *Innis, what did you tell Cora?* But he couldn't say the words aloud. What if they came out like an accusation?

"Be careful," Innis said. She went to her tent, her bare skin pale in the moonlight.

Emotions flooded through him. Jealousy at her infatuation with the prince. Anxiety that she might have lied to Cora. Fear that their friendship was over. And love.

He still loved her, whatever she had done.

"Innis..." He needed to know whether they were still friends. Needed to know what she'd told Cora.

She looked back at him. "What?"

A bird called harshly in the jungle. The sound jerked him back to awareness of where he was and what he was meant to be doing. "Sleep well." He changed into an owl and swept swiftly up into the sky.

CHAPTER SIXTY-EIGHT

ANOTHER MEAL, ANOTHER spoon, another nail dug out of the wood.

Britta went back to her pallet and ate the fish stew. It was cold.

She was chewing the last mouthful when the bolts on the door were drawn back. She swallowed hastily, put the bowl down.

The assassin who entered was one she'd seen before, his hair cut close to his skull. He put her rinsed chamberpot on the floor and held out his hand for the bowl, not speaking. His eyes—cold, hard—seemed to look right through her.

These men weren't like Duke Rikard. She wasn't a woman to them. They looked at her as if she was a piece of wood, a lump of rock.

Britta handed him the bowl and spoon.

"And the candle." His vowels were short, his consonants guttural.

She gave it to him.

The assassin bolted the door, left her in darkness.

CHAPTER SIXTY-NINE

HARKELD SLOUCHED IN the saddle, exhausted. He yawned for
what seemed like the hundredth time that day, while his horse
picked its way along the dry river channel. Mist curled out from
the jungle, dispersing in the bright afternoon sun. Beside him,
Ebril seemed almost asleep. His eyes were closed, his face almost
gray with fatigue beneath his red-tinted stubble. The mage had
reason to be tired—he'd flown all morning, finding the shortest
route through the twisting river channels—but Harkeld didn't.
He'd slept last night, his dreams a chaotic jumble that he
couldn't quite remember.

He glanced over his shoulder. Rand also slouched as he rode,
also yawned, and Katlen wasn't her usual erect self. She sagged
in her saddle, her face nearly as gray as Ebril's.

Rand looked up. "Innis is back."

Harkeld followed his gaze. Two hawks circled in the sky—
cream-feathered Petrus, whom they were following, and a
smaller, darker shape he recognized as Innis.

The dark hawk glided out of sight over the jungle. Half a
minute later, a third hawk flew into view. The bird was as large
as Petrus, but brown-winged. It landed and shifted into Justen.

Everyone halted. "Did you find it?" Cora asked.

"Yes."

"Any Fithians?"

"No."

"Any sign of the ship?"

Justen shook his head.

Harkeld closed his eyes while Cora and Justen talked, listening to the murmur of their voices. He must have dozed. When he woke with a jerk, Justen was dressed and mounted.

He glanced sideways. Ebril was definitely asleep, his chin sunk low on his chest, the reins fallen from his grasp.

"Ebril..." Harkeld gripped the mage's arm and shook him gently. "Wake up."

"Huh?" Ebril blinked and swayed in the saddle, and then straightened. "Thanks."

CHAPTER SEVENTY

BENNICK WOKE HIM at noon. "You did well finding us somewhere
safe to sleep," he told Jaumé, reaching out to ruffle his hair.
"Good lad. I'm proud of you."

They traveled north along the rocks. Rain started. Warm
rain, making puddles where they could fill their waterskins. It
seemed to keep Bennick fresher. He recovered enough to think
like a soldier again. He looked for a cave and found one large
enough to spread their sleeping mats in.

CHAPTER SEVENTY-ONE

THEY HALTED BEFORE dusk. Gray thunderheads piled in the sky. The site Petrus had chosen was much like last night's: a small island cut off from the jungle by a dry channel.

Rand sighed. "Do we have to fortify it?"

"Yes." Cora looked as exhausted as Harkeld felt, dark shadows beneath her eyes. "I'm sorry, Rand, but if you'd seen those corpses..."

Harkeld was gasping for breath by the time the barrier of driftwood was built. His legs trembled and his head ached. *Why am I so tired?*

He wiped sweat from his face and looked around. Justen was the only one of them who didn't seem tired. He'd hauled logs and now was pitching tents, wielding the mallet with a vigor that made Harkeld wince.

At least the horses were tended to and the stewpot was on the fire. Cora and Katlen had seen to that. *I should help with the tents.* But he couldn't make his legs move. He massaged his forehead, trying to ease the ache there.

Rand sat down at the campfire with a groan, his face almost bloodless beneath his whiskers. His closed eyelids looked bruised with exhaustion.

"Are we tired because the curse shadows are stronger?" Harkeld asked.

"Could be the mist." Ebril sat with his elbows on his knees, head hanging. "Or steam, or whatever it is. Maybe it's poisonous? It sure stinks enough."

Rand grunted and opened his eyes. "Doubt it. I spent a whole winter in Sondvaal once, hot pools all over the place, stank like this. None of us ever got poisoned."

"It's a thought, though," Cora said. Her plait was unraveling, but instead of tidying it, she brushed it back over her shoulder. "We could move further out into the river."

Silence greeted this suggestion, then Ebril groaned aloud and raised his head. "Tonight?"

"In case you haven't noticed, there's steam coming out of the river too," Katlen said. Fatigue robbed her voice of its usual curt edge. "This whole place is steaming. Must be hot springs all over. Going out into the river isn't going to help us—if it *is* the vapor."

"I doubt it is," Rand said, his eyes closed again. "The horses seem fine. They'd be like us if it's something in the air. Or water."

"Well, what is it then?" Hew asked. His face was so pale that his freckles stood out like flecks of mud. "Something to do with the curse?"

"The shadows *are* stronger," Ebril said.

"It's almost certainly the curse," Cora said. "Something Ivek did to protect the anchor stone, like the corpses. But what? And how do we stop it?"

No one answered. Harkeld looked around at the weary faces. Both Hew and Ebril seemed to be shaking with exhaustion. *This is not good.* "How many days to the anchor stone?"

"Three."

Alarm prickled up the back of his neck. "We need to figure this out."

Ebril grunted a laugh. "You think?"

Harkeld didn't smile. "If something attacks us tonight—"

Rand opened his eyes. "If something attacks tonight, we fight. However tired we are." He glanced at the simmering pot. "That stew ready, Katlen? We could all do with some food."

Innis ate a quick dinner as Justen, then shifted into an owl and patrolled while Petrus ate. To her surprise, it wasn't Hew who flew up to relieve her, but Petrus again. Cora took her aside once she'd landed. "Hew's in no state to shift. You and Petrus will have to patrol again tonight. I'm sorry, I know you've flown a long way today."

Innis shook her head. "I'm fine, but Petrus... I don't think he slept much last night."

"He's not as tired as Hew."

Innis glanced at Hew. He sat slouched, his face gaunt with exhaustion. "Shall I try healing him?"

"Anything's worth a try."

Innis dressed and went to Hew. She crouched alongside him. "Hew..."

He half-opened his eyes.

"I want to try something." She took one of his hands in both of hers and let her healing magic flow into him. What she felt shocked her. Hew's whole body was straining, from the hand trembling in her clasp to the labored beating of his heart and the effort it took to draw each breath. Cora was right; if he shifted shape, he'd not have the strength to change back into himself. His exhaustion was blood-deep, bone-deep.

Innis frowned, concentrating, pushing some of her own strength into Hew. When his hand no longer trembled, she stopped. "How do you feel?"

"Much better. Thanks, Innis."

She nodded and glanced at Cora. "Shall I do everyone?"

"As many as you can. Start with Flin."

Innis turned to the prince. His face was shadowed with stubble and tiredness, his expression impossible to decipher as he held out his hand to her.

She took it and let her magic flow into him. The familiar sense of who he was flooded through her. Honor, stubbornness, confidence, pride, determination, courage.

When she'd healed him in Lundegaard, fear and confusion and hatred had been his dominant emotions. Those were gone. Worry was at the forefront of his thoughts now. His sense of humor was buried deep tonight, he was too tired for laughter, but he wasn't as exhausted as Hew. His hand didn't tremble in her clasp, although he was wearier than she liked and he had a bad headache.

Innis let some of her strength flow into him, spent a few minutes banishing his headache, then released his hand and turned to Ebril.

Ebril was even weaker than Hew. Innis gripped his hand, pouring her magic into him, and looked across the fire at Cora. "Ebril mustn't shift shape."

"No?" Cora grimaced. "Very well."

She healed Ebril until his body stopped trembling and his heart beat more strongly, then released his hand reluctantly. He needed more of her magic, but there were still Rand and Katlen and Cora to go.

"Don't shift tonight," she told him as she stood. "I mean it, Ebril."

Ebril grinned faintly and sketched a salute at her.

Innis healed Katlen, her magic noting the rigid discipline that seemed to stiffen Katlen's bones, the grumbling undertone of righteousness and the edge of asperity that flowed in her blood. Rand was next. He was marked by a deep and innate kindness, a strong sense of humor, a tingling, lively curiosity. Cora was last. As kind as Rand, and more weighted by the responsibility of leadership than she let show; deeply worried.

Innis sat back on her heels, weary, and looked up at the pale blur of Petrus overhead. "Should I heal Petrus? He barely slept last night."

"That, I think, is the crux of this," Cora said. "The only people who're not affected are Petrus and you and Justen—and you're the ones who were awake last night. Whatever caused this, it happened while we slept. And it may happen again tonight. Keep your eyes open."

Innis nodded.

"We're too vulnerable. If anything should attack us..." Cora rubbed her forehead, as if it helped her to think. "I want you and Petrus—and Justen too—to sleep as wolves, here, by the fire, when you're not patrolling. I know it means breaking a Primary Law, but it will give us a few seconds' advantage if something should happen." She raised her voice slightly: "Ebril, Hew, no shifting tonight, whatever happens. Is that understood?"

Both mages nodded.

"Innis, you take first shift. When you finish, check in each tent, just to make sure."

"I shall." Innis stood.

"Night," Ebril said, and Rand gave her a half-smile and a flick of his fingers.

INNIS FLAPPED SWIFTLY upwards. There was no moon tonight, no stars. Clouds blanketed the sky. The campfire was bright to her owl's eyes. Below her, Hew took off his boots and crawled into his tent, and the prince and Ebril entered theirs. On a physical level the three of them had felt similar—young, male—but on a deeper level they'd been utterly different. Hew so serious, Ebril cheerful even in his exhaustion, levity running in his veins, and Prince Harkeld halfway between the two of them, not as light-hearted as Ebril, not as ponderously grave as Hew.

Petrus stripped and became a wolf. He trotted around the island, sniffing, checking the barrier of driftwood, the piled supplies, the horses, the tents, then curled up by the campfire, his pelt silver in the firelight.

Innis circled, watching. Steam crept from the jungle and poured over the riverbank like water. It covered the island, gathering around the tents, moving in slow eddies. Tiny bats swooped and darted, hunting moths. The jungle was alive with noise. Frogs croaked and boomed. Crickets sang. Birds shrieked.

CHAPTER SEVENTY-TWO

HARKELD STOOD AT the water lily pond, waiting for Innis. His memories of last night's dreams were vague, but he was certain she hadn't been in them. He always remembered the dreams she was in. He hoped she'd come tonight; he woke more rested when she visited.

The sky was a strange bruised color, yellow tinged with purple, and the garden was curiously still. No dragonflies hovered over the water lilies.

He heard footsteps behind him and turned. "Innis?"

But it was Broushka who came towards him, her sultry mouth curved in a smile. "Prince Harkeld."

Harkeld gaped at her. "What—" And then he realized he was naked. He covered his groin with his hands. "What are you doing here?"

Broushka uttered a throaty laugh. "Don't be shy." She brushed aside his hands and reached for his cock, began to stroke him.

Harkeld gave an involuntary grunt of arousal. He felt his cock stiffen—

And then he was flat on his back on the grass and it wasn't Broushka who rode him, but the serving maid from Gdelsk, her breasts jiggling deliciously as she moved, and his hands were at her waist, urging her on until he climaxed.

And then he was on top, but it wasn't the serving maid beneath him, but Lenora, laughing and coy, kissing him with that skilled, sinful mouth. Harkeld groaned and thrust into her, deeper, faster, more urgently, until he spilled his seed. He closed his eyes, savoring the moment, and opened them to find himself on his back again. Someone was sucking his cock. He raised himself on an elbow. It was Lenora, her blonde hair spilling across his belly. He lay back with a sigh of pleasure—

The dream took him back through every sexual experience he'd ever had. By the time he lost his virginity again, Harkeld was breathless and exhausted. He stretched out on the grass with a groan and closed his eyes.

Footsteps came towards him. He slitted his eyes open. Broushka stood there. Harkeld didn't have the strength to stand. "Enough," he said.

But his dream ignored him. Broushka knelt on the grass and massaged his cock, bringing him to aching arousal—and then the serving maid took Broushka's place, and he was burying himself in soft, warm, willing flesh.

When he'd climaxed, Harkeld staggered to his feet. "Enough," he said again, more loudly. But the serving maid was gone and Lenora now advanced across the grass towards him.

Harkeld turned and ran, lurching and stumbling.

Lenora pursued him along the crushed marble paths, laughing, relentless, cornering him eventually in a rose bower. "No," Harkeld said, panting, dizzy. "I don't want to have sex with you." He sank down on the silk cushions, too weak to stand, shielding his groin with his hands.

Lenora smiled and tilted her head to one side, voluptuous, beautiful, terrifying. "No?" She sat beside him and stroked his bare thigh with teasing, tickling fingers. "I think you'll find I can change your mind..."

INNIS LET PETRUS sleep for two thirds of the night before gliding down to wake him. He stretched and yawned, showing sharp white teeth, and shifted into his own shape.

"How do you feel?" The words came out of her mouth stilted and awkward.

"Fine."

The fire was little more than glowing embers. Mist swirled around them. Petrus's face was shadowed, his green eyes black. "Seen or heard anything worrying?"

"No."

For a moment she thought he was going to say something more, but he changed into an owl and flew up into the sky.

Innis twisted her fingers together, trying to follow him with her eyes. *Are you still my friend, Petrus?*

She shifted into a wolf and padded through the campsite, mist billowing around her, thrusting her head into each tent. People breathed, sighed, muttered, groaned. Prince Harkeld whimpered, thrashing weakly in his blanket as if trying to run. Was he dreaming that his brother was cutting off his hands? Across the tent from him was Ebril, still and silent. A sword lay naked and ready between the two men.

Innis's ears pricked forward. Was Ebril breathing?

Yes, very faintly.

She hurried to her own tent, changed into herself, threw on her clothes, crawled back outside. Without wolf eyes, she was practically blind. Innis groped her way to the fire, grabbed a smoldering stick, and ran back to Ebril's tent, mist billowing around her legs. "Ebril," she said, thrusting the flaps open. "Are you all right—"

Crouched on both men's chests, leaning over their faces, kissing them, were plump, naked babies. No, not babies. The creature sitting on Prince Harkeld's chest lifted its head and looked at her. It had a wizened man's face, with a damp mouth and black, malevolent eyes.

"Harkeld!" Innis cried. "Ebril! Wake up!"

The creature leered at her, unafraid. The one kissing Ebril didn't lift its head.

Innis threw down the smoldering stick and snatched the sword lying between the two men. "Harkeld! Ebril! Wake up!"

The prince stirred, groaned.

"Give me light!" Innis shouted, slashing at the creature on Ebril's chest. The tip of the blade caught it beneath its chin, slicing but not killing. The wide mouth opened in a high-pitched scream. The sound echoed painfully in her skull.

Innis swung again, severing its neck. The thin, high scream stopped. A stench of sulfur and decay flooded the tent.

Prince Harkeld groaned again, struggling to push up on one elbow, dislodging the creature on his ch·est.

"I need light!" she yelled at him.

Light flared weakly in the tent. The second creature was scrambling over the prince's torso. Innis grabbed one soft, plump leg and swung the sword. The prince jerked up his arms as if he thought she was attacking him.

The sword slid through the creature's neck as easily as if its bones were made of lard. The head tumbled to the ground, the damp mouth still leering, the black eyes still open.

The prince slowly lowered his arms. He stared at the remains of the creature dangling in her grip, and then at the severed head, and then at her, his eyes wide and his mouth open, apparently speechless with shock.

Innis threw aside the creature's body, dropped the sword, and scrambled over to Ebril. "Ebril! Wake up!" She shook him. "Ebril!"

Ebril's head lolled limply.

Innis cupped his face in her hands, sent her magic urgently into him. "Ebril, wake up."

But he couldn't wake up. His heart wasn't beating. Blood didn't flow in his veins. He was dead.

"Is he all right?" the prince asked, crouching at her shoulder, golden flames flickering on his right hand.

"He's dead." Her voice came out thick with tears.

"What? No!" He pushed her aside, bent over Ebril. "Can't you do something? Your magic—"

"His heart has stopped."

"But he's still warm!"

"I can't heal death. Healers who try that die."

She jerked around as someone thrust their head into the tent. Petrus, his face alarmed. "What's wrong? I heard shouting—"

He saw the small, naked, headless body of the creature that had been kissing Prince Harkeld and recoiled. "What's that? His voice rose in pitch. "Innis, what's going *on*?"

"I don't know. But there were two of them, and they've killed Ebril." She looked at the creature's remains. The baby-like body was no longer quite so plump and dimpled. It seemed to be slowly deflating, although no blood leaked from the severed neck.

The creature lay on its front. Prince Harkeld picked up the smoldering stick and turned the body over, holding his right hand up to illuminate it. They all flinched from the sight of the swollen, ruddy, male genitals.

"How did it kill Ebril?" Petrus asked, his voice hushed.

"It was crouched on his chest, kissing him." She glanced at the prince. "And you too."

The prince looked as if he wanted to vomit. He scrubbed a hand over his mouth.

"When I checked as a wolf, I didn't see anything. But Ebril was barely breathing, so I changed and came back to heal him, and then I saw them—" Tears choked in her throat. Innis pressed her hands to her mouth. *My fault.* If she hadn't let Petrus sleep so long, if she'd checked the tents sooner, Ebril would still be alive.

"I didn't see *that* until it was dead." The prince poked the body again with the stick, flipping it back over, hiding the engorged testicles and penis. "I thought you were attacking *me*. I just about burned you."

Innis shook her head. She turned back to Ebril and gently brushed the red hair back from his brow. *My fault.* Tears filled her eyes and spilled down her cheeks.

"Why aren't the others awake?" the prince said. "Innis shouted loud enough. Did you see anyone out there, Petrus?"

"No," Petrus said. And then, low-voiced, with a note of panic: "By the All-Mother!" He backed out of the entrance.

Prince Harkeld snatched the sword and followed. "Innis, come on!"

CHAPTER SEVENTY-THREE

HARKELD SCRAMBLED OUTSIDE, gripping the sword, holding his left hand out to give them light. Mist billowed around his legs. Petrus ran to the nearest tent, his naked skin pale in the firelight. The mage ripped open the fastenings, jerked the flaps open.

Harkeld thrust his hand into the tent.

Petrus looked inside. "Rand! Hew! Wake up!" His voice rose to a shout. "Innis, get over here!"

Harkeld moved aside, making room for her. Innis crawled into the tent. He peered in after her.

Rand and Hew lay face-up on their bedrolls, wrapped in blankets, open-mouthed and asleep.

"The sword!" Innis cried. "The sword!"

Harkeld thrust the hilt at her, staring into the tent, straining to see whatever it was she saw.

Innis grabbed for something and swung the sword. A creature materialized in her hand. A baby, his eyes told him, dangling by one ankle, decapitated. An instinctive cry of horror filled his throat.

Innis tossed the small body aside. It landed near the entrance, belly-up.

No baby had such massive balls and crimson cock. Harkeld barely managed to control his recoil. His gaze jerked from the body and found the creature's head. A large, moist, red-lipped mouth in an old man's face. Eyes as black and shiny as obsidian.

Revulsion rose in him. *One of those things was kissing me?*

Innis swung the sword again, tossed another small, naked body aside. She dropped the sword and bent over Rand.

Harkeld eyed the second body. The creature's cock was just as red and distended as its fellow's.

He glanced at Petrus. "I didn't see those until she killed them. Did you?"

"No."

"They're both alive," Innis said. "But Hew's in a bad way."

Petrus nodded, and jerked his head at Harkeld. "We need to check the other tent."

Harkeld scrambled outside and ran with Petrus to the last tent.

Petrus tore the flaps open and crawled inside. Harkeld dropped to his knees and thrust his flame-covered palm into the tent, peering in. "How are they?"

Cora and Katlen lay on their bedrolls. Petrus crouched between them, his expression frantic beneath his tousled white-blond hair. "Katlen's dead and I can't wake Cora. Innis!"

Harkeld moved hurriedly aside.

Innis scrambled into the tent, sword in hand. "Get back, Petrus."

Petrus pressed himself against the end of the tent.

Harkeld watched Innis, but his eyes made no sense of the skirmish. She grabbed something that wasn't there, hauled it into the air, chopped with the sword—and suddenly a creature dangled in her grip, limp and headless.

This time he did recoil as she flung it towards him. He didn't want the thing touching him.

Innis grabbed again, raised the sword again. Petrus crammed himself further back against the end of the tent. Harkeld winced. *If I was naked, I'd be afraid of that sword too.*

But the sword swipe came nowhere near Petrus, and another headless creature hung in Innis's grip.

There was a moment of silence, and then Harkeld swallowed and said, "Is that all of them?"

"All I can see." Innis tossed both sword and creature aside and bent over Cora.

Petrus peeled himself away from the back of the tent and knelt by Katlen. He touched her throat, grimaced, shook his head.

Harkeld reached for the sword. There was no blood on the blade. He prodded the nearest creature cautiously, then levered the blade under the body and lifted it. The creature was almost weightless. No blood spilled from that severed neck, but the body was slowly deflating, like a wine bladder that had lost its stopper. The engorged cock was becoming flaccid, the plump testicles shriveling. Whatever leaked from the body wasn't visible. Air? Mist? Vapor? It stank foully. Harkeld backed out of the tent, the body balanced on the blade, and flung the creature away.

"I need to heal them," he heard Innis say. "Hew first. He's the worst. Then Cora. Best bring Cora into their tent. They all need to be in one place, so I can see if any more of those things come."

Harkeld helped them drag Cora out of the tent on her bedroll. She didn't stir when Petrus lifted her in his arms. She looked lifeless, her face slack, her arms dangling limply.

Harkeld went ahead to Hew and Rand's tent and parted the tent flaps. Rand and Hew hadn't moved. They lay face-up, asleep. The air stank. The two creatures Innis had killed had deflated into shriveled pouches of skin. Harkeld picked them up with the sword, unwilling to touch them, and tossed them out into the mist. He chivvied the heads out with the sword. They were shrinking, dissolving. The black eyes seemed to have melted away.

He flinched as Innis uttered a wordless cry at his shoulder. She grabbed the sword from him and scrambled into the tent, reaching for something on Rand's chest.

Harkeld held his hand out, giving her light, deeply unsettled. There'd been a live creature in the tent? How had he not seen it?

He didn't see the death blow, but the stink of decay and sulfur came to his nose. He moved back, letting Innis toss the corpse out of the tent.

Petrus crouched and laid Cora down. "I'd best get back up there." He jerked his thumb at the sky. "I'll keep close to the camp. If you need help, yell."

Innis nodded.

Harkeld helped her lay Cora between Rand and Hew. Then he fetched candles and lit them.

"Thanks." Innis touched his wrist, checked him with her magic. "You need to sleep."

Harkeld shook his head. "I can't see those things until they're dead. This tent could be full of them and I wouldn't know."

"I'll see them." Innis knelt by Hew and cupped his face in her hands. "The more you sleep now, the less time it will take me to heal you."

Still he hesitated. One of those things had been feeding on him. He imagined it crouched on him, tumescent cock pressed against his chest.

"Go to sleep. I promise I won't let any of them get you."

Harkeld lay down in the cramped space between Rand and the side of the tent.

Innis turned her attention to Hew. Her eyes were narrowed, her expression inward-looking.

The nervous energy that had sustained him began to leak away. Harkeld grew aware of his fatigue. He was as exhausted as he'd been in his dream, limbs trembling, head aching. His eyes blurred. Innis was right. He needed to sleep.

Innis released Hew's face and grabbed the sword, raising it threateningly, hissing at something.

Harkeld sat up with a jerk, dizzy, blinking to clear his vision.

She hissed again, waved the sword, then muttered, "Stupid rutting thing," and scrambled across Hew, stabbing at something.

He blinked, missed the kill, but saw the corpse. Innis threw it outside and crawled back to Hew, sword in hand. She glanced at Harkeld. "Go to sleep."

Harkeld lay back down, his heart racing. Sleep? Impossible. He closed his eyes for a brief moment to ease their ache, and opened them to find himself lying beside the water lily pond. The sky was blue and sunny, the grass green and soft. He was alone. No Broushka, no serving maid, no Lenora.

He closed his eyes again and lay exhausted, soaking up the sunshine. Gradually his dizziness faded, the ache in his head eased, his limbs stopped trembling. Slow hours passed. He knew when the dream-Innis finally came, he felt her hand in his, felt contentment flowing from that clasp.

HARKELD WOKE, FEELING deeply rested. Someone stirred alongside him. He heard Rand's voice, and Cora's, and Innis answering.

Memory returned. His eyelids jerked open. He sat up abruptly.

Alongside him, Rand was peeling off his blanket and Cora sat upright. Hew's bedroll was empty. Innis sat on it, her face pale with exhaustion.

The tent flaps were open. It was daylight.

"You need to sleep," Cora said. "Take this blanket and lie down."

"But Ebril... his grave."

"We'll do that," Rand said. "Cora's right; you need to sleep. Now. Or you won't be any use to anyone."

"We'll wake you once the graves are dug," Cora said.

Harkeld crawled from the tent and stood. The day was heavily overcast, no sun visible, but it felt as if it was mid-morning. Hew was at the fire, stirring a steaming pot. A hawk soared overhead: Petrus.

Something lay on the ground at his feet. A smear of jelly? Mucus? He crouched. The substance looked like something from the seashore—a decaying jellyfish, gelatinous, translucent, dissolving even as he watched.

Harkeld glanced around, looking for the creatures' corpses. No limp, deflated bodies met his eyes; just a dozen or more of the mucous stains.

"Careful," he said to Rand, now crawling from the tent. "I think these are what's left of those creatures."

Rand stood, placing his feet cautiously. "You saw them?"

"Only once they were dead."

Cora emerged from the tent, her face grim. "Food," she said. "Then the graves. And then we must press on."

HARKELD HELPED DIG the graves. The stony soil made it difficult. Grief rose in him as he dug. He'd liked Ebril, had come to think of him as a friend. And now he was dead.

They piled cairns over both bodies and said the words to the All-Mother. Harkeld felt like crying. *Farewell, Ebril. I'll miss you.*

He and Rand loaded the packhorses. A light rain started falling. Harkeld fished out his cloak and looked around. Cora crouched by the last tent, talking with Innis. Hew circled overhead and Justen stood at Ebril's grave. *So few of us left.*

"I need to talk with Justen," Harkeld said, fastening the cloak. "Won't be long."

Rand nodded.

Harkeld walked across to Ebril's grave. "Justen?" he said quietly. He hadn't spoken to the mage since the morning he'd punched him.

Justen gave him a scant glance. His mouth was tight, his eyes damp.

"I'm sorry about Ebril. I know you trained with him, I know he was your friend."

Justen's mouth tightened further. He gave a brief nod.

"I liked him," Harkeld said. "He was a good companion."

Justen's mouth twisted. He looked away.

"I'm sorry I hit you," Harkeld said. "I apologize. It was wrong of me."

For a moment he thought Justen was going to ignore the apology, then Justen turned his head and looked at him. His expression was hard to interpret. Was it grief, or hostility, that made his jaw so stiff?

"If you wish, I'd like you to be my armsman again."

Justen blinked, and surveyed him for several seconds with an expression Harkeld had no difficulty interpreting: surprise. "I lied to you."

"I know." But he was no longer angry. Justen had been his friend, just as Ebril had. *That* hadn't been pretence. He held out his hand. "I apologize for hitting you."

Justen hesitated briefly, then gripped Harkeld's hand. "It's forgotten."

"Thank you." He released Justen's hand and glanced at the grave. "I'll let you say goodbye to Ebril alone."

Harkeld walked back past the tent where Cora and Innis were talking. He finished loading the packhorses, then turned his attention to saddling the riding mounts. Justen was gone. Innis knelt at Ebril's grave alone.

Cora was dismantling the final tent. Harkeld went to help her, then hefted the heavy roll on his shoulder and carried it to the packhorses.

"Here," Rand said, gesturing to a horse. Harkeld heaved the tent onto the packsaddle and glanced back at Ebril's grave.

Innis was no longer alone. Petrus stood there. As he watched, Petrus pulled her to her feet and hugged her.

An absurd shaft of jealousy stabbed Harkeld in the chest. *Don't be a fool,* he told himself. What did he care whether Petrus hugged her or not? The real Innis wasn't the dream-Innis. He had no feelings for her.

He strapped the tent into place and looked at the graves again. Petrus was still holding Innis. His head was bowed, his mouth pressed against her hair, his lips moving as he talked to her. He cradled her head in one hand, protective and tender. Harkeld had a sudden moment of insight. *He loves her.*

He looked away, feeling like a voyeur, and busied himself checking that the packsaddle was balanced.

"All done?" Rand asked.

"Yes."

He helped Rand clear away some of the piled driftwood and lead the packhorses off the island. Rain pattered down.

Cora joined them. Hew flew overhead. "Where are the others?"

"Asleep," Cora said. "A Primary Law broken, but it can't be helped. We'll need them awake tonight."

"Asleep?"

"As mice. Innis is in my pocket. Rand has Petrus and Justen."

Oh. His eyebrows rose.

"We need to talk about what's happened," Rand said. "Those creatures—"

"Yes. But later. Once Innis is awake. For now, let's move as fast as we can."

CHAPTER SEVENTY-FOUR

THE RAIN KEPT on, but the cave Bennick had found stayed dry. In moments when the rain thinned, Jaumé saw a low black headland on the other side of the river, half a mile long, and beyond that, more water.

"It's the island," Bennick said. He almost looked like his old self, cheerful. "It's where the prince is going. This will do."

CHAPTER SEVENTY-FIVE

THE DRY RIVER channels began to flow with water. Mid-afternoon, they were forced to leave the riverbed and retreat to the bank, where they picked their way through thick vegetation and tangled vines. "Only a couple more leagues of this," Hew said, gliding down to speak with Cora. "Then it opens up. Marshy, with lots of hot pools."

"Good," she said, batting gnats from her face. "Keep an eye out for tonight's campsite."

Harkeld found himself looking over his shoulder frequently, peering into the dense jungle. Sulfurous steam drifted between the trees. He felt exposed, vulnerable, with only two other riders. "You said more mages will join us soon?" he asked Cora.

"Shapeshifters, yes. The others only if the ship can get close enough—which depends on the shallows."

He had a sudden, vivid memory of Ebril. *The Drowned Man's Shallows are meant to be quite a sight. Some fleet or other got wrecked there ages ago, and you can see the old hulls rotting and masts sticking up out of the water.*

Harkeld's throat tightened. He cleared it. "If we sail, what will we do with the horses? Not leave them?" The beasts wouldn't survive once the sacks of grain the packhorses carried were empty.

"Hopefully we can get them aboard. But chances of us being able to sail are slim. I expect we'll need to go overland. And frankly, I'm worried the ship won't arrive. It should be here by now."

"It'll come," Rand said.

Cora blew out a breath. "You think?"

"Yes. Don't borrow trouble."

"No," she said dryly. "We have enough of that already, don't we?"

Harkeld glanced around, seeing the wide braided river, the dense jungle, the long string of horses with just two riders other than himself. *What if we die here? What if we fail to destroy the curse?*

Failure seemed a very real possibility.

CHAPTER SEVENTY-SIX

THE FINAL NAIL came out. Britta stood for a moment, her heart galloping in her chest. *Do it now, or wait?*

Wait. Until after her bowl had been collected.

She hurried back to the pallet and ate fast, but the food didn't want to stay in her stomach. She pressed one hand to her mouth. *Don't vomit. Don't vomit.*

An assassin came, left her rinsed chamberpot, took the bowl and spoon.

When he was gone, Britta sat on the pallet hugging her knees. Now. She should do it now.

She was afraid of dying.

Britta laid the arguments out in her head again, and the answer was as clear as it had always been, as obvious.

The longer she sat here, the more her nerve would fail her. And if she did it now, in daylight, there was a chance a passing ship would see her in the water.

Britta got to her feet. She crossed to the window, opened it, inhaled the fresh, cold sea air. Sunlight sparkled on water. Was that a sail on the horizon, heading towards them?

You can do it. I know you can, Karel's voice said in her ear.

GETTING OUT OF the window was harder than she'd thought it would be. Britta tipped the chamberpot upside down and used it as a step. She squeezed her arms through the narrow opening, and scrabbled her feet on the wall, trying to haul herself up and out.

Her shoulders scraped through, tearing cloth and skin. A shout came from high overhead. A sailor, in the rigging.

Panic seized her. She heaved, pushed, scrabbled.

The side of the ship was sheer. The sea rushed past a dozen yards below, fierce and foaming. Britta dug her fingernails into the wood, hauling herself out. Behind her, the bolts shot back on the door.

Her body slid through the window—waist, hips, thighs. She was falling—

Someone grabbed her ankles.

Britta kicked, connected with someone's nose, kicked again.

The Fithian didn't release her. More hands seized her, hauling her upward.

Britta kicked, screamed, clung to the side of the ship, tearing her fingernails. She kicked even harder when they dragged her back through the window, bit and scratched, flailed her fists.

The Fithians overpowered her silently. Her scream—rage, despair—was the only sound in the cabin.

A hand clamped over her mouth. Now all she heard were panted breaths.

She lay on the floor. An assassin knelt on her back, squeezing the air from her lungs. Another gripped her legs. A hand was fisted in her hair, screwing her head round, grinding her cheek into the floor.

Someone walked into her field of view and crouched: the leader of the assassins. He had a broad, flat face with wide cheekbones. A bruise reddened one cheek, and his nose dripped blood.

"Manacle her."

CHAPTER SEVENTY-SEVEN

"So," Rand said. "Tell us what happened last night."

They sat around the campfire, Rand, Cora, Hew, Innis, and himself. Justen and Petrus were patrolling.

Their camp was on the riverbank. Branches overhead kept off the worst of the rain.

Harkeld put down his bowl and listened intently to Innis.

"They stopped at dawn?" Rand asked, when she'd finished.

"Yes."

"And you couldn't see them when you were a wolf?"

"No. But as soon as I changed into me I could."

Rand glanced at Harkeld. "You and Petrus saw them too, but only once they were dead?"

"Yes."

"Could you hear them?"

Harkeld shook his head. He'd not heard the high-pitched screams Innis had described.

"They attacked everyone—but not Petrus. And not the horses." Cora looked at Hew. "Tonight you sleep as a wolf."

Hew nodded, his face grave.

She turned back to Innis. "They're made of vapor?"

"Vapor inside, skin outside. No bones that I could see."

"How did they get into the tent? Through the entrance, or the walls?"

"The entrance."

"Good. Rand, Flin, and I will sleep in one tent tonight. You'll guard the entrance."

Innis nodded. Despite sleeping all day in Cora's pocket, she looked pale and exhausted and miserable.

"Flin," Cora said. "You're from the Seven Kingdoms... have you heard of creatures like this?"

He shook his head.

"I have," Rand said. "In Sondvaal. They're meant to be a myth. Breathstealers."

Everyone looked at him.

"They spawn in hot underground vapors—or so the tales go—and rise up through vents in the ground and seek humans to feed on. Only virgins can see them." He glanced at Innis. "Human virgins, evidently, since you couldn't see them when you were an owl or a wolf. And virgins are the only people they won't feed on. Or *can't* feed on. According to legend they were wiped out in Sondvaal centuries ago."

"How do they kill?" Harkeld asked.

"They suck your life from you through your breath. They're meant to give the person they're feeding on quite vivid sexual dreams."

"They do," Harkeld said.

Rand's eyebrows rose. "You remember?"

"You don't?"

Rand shook his head. So did Cora and Hew.

"You were the only one who woke," Innis said. "Maybe that's why you remember."

"Yes," Rand said, frowning. "And that's another point. How were you able to wake up? Why did it affect you least of all?"

Harkeld shrugged. "I didn't like the dream. I was trying to stop it. Maybe it couldn't feed off me as much?"

"Maybe."

"They're here because the curse shadows got darker, aren't they?" Innis said. "Guarding the anchor stone. Like the corpses."

"They certainly weren't here before," Cora said. "Sentinels have been coming here for centuries, checking on the stone. Someone would have noticed."

Rand snorted.

"They can't possibly be natural," Hew said.

"They're not, or at least the ones in Sondvaal weren't. They were created by magic." Rand's voice became mellow and sing-song, like a story-teller's: "Once upon a time, long, long ago, when the moon was young in the sky and the oceans were newborn, there lived a maiden so lovely that skylarks sang of her beauty." His tone became brisk again. "Beautiful virgin betrothed to powerful mage. Mage goes off on a quest and doesn't *quite* trust his intended's fidelity. Lays a curse that will kill her if she's unfaithful—and, incidentally, almost every adult nearby." He grimaced. "And she *is* unfaithful. And the mage is so righteously enraged that he refuses to remove the curse, and it takes a couple of centuries before someone figures out how to destroy it. Or so the tale goes." He shrugged. "Who knows how true it is?"

"It's safe to say Ivek knew the tale," Harkeld said.

Rand tilted his head in agreement.

"And we can assume the breathstealers will stop once Flin destroys the anchor stone," Cora said. "Like the corpses. All we have to do is survive another couple of nights and we'll be all right. Thank the All-Mother you haven't finished your training, Innis, or we'd be dead. It was a great stroke of fortune to have you with us."

An emotion briefly crossed Innis's face. Grief? She shook her head.

"Training?" Harkeld said, not following that last comment.

"One of the last things a mage is trained in is sex," Rand said.

"Trained in *sex*? You're pulling my leg, aren't you?" He glanced at Cora for confirmation.

Cora shook her head. "Losing one's virginity can be dangerous for mages. In the past, deaths weren't uncommon. Nowadays... well, there was a terrible incident about fifteen years ago, but no deaths since then that I'm aware of. And very few for the past century."

Harkeld gaped at her. Ebril hadn't mentioned training in *sex*. "Dangerous how?" he asked, disbelief clear in his voice.

"It depends whether you're male or female, and what your magic is," Rand said. "A young male fire mage such as yourself could lose control of his magic while experiencing the, er, throes of passion for the first time and burn his bed partner. A shapeshifter such as Hew"—he nodded across the fire—"might inadvertently change shape and harm whoever he's lying with. Or just scare her half to death."

Harkeld realized that his mouth was still open. He shut it.

"It's much more dangerous if the mage is female," Cora said. "That's when the deaths usually occur. Losing one's virginity can hurt, you see. Quite badly, for some girls. And sometimes mages panic, even though they know what to expect. That's what happened with young Ana, fifteen years ago. She set fire to her instructor, burned him to death. Very distressing for everyone. Ana never got over it. Killed herself a while later."

"And a female shapeshifter can badly maul her bed partner if she panics," Rand said. "It's natural to fight back, after all, if someone hurts you. Hence the training."

Cora nodded. "To lose your virginity in controlled surroundings, after theoretical instruction, with someone who knows what he—or she—is doing, considerably reduces the risk."

Harkeld opened his mouth again, and then closed it, speechless with astonishment.

"For healers like me, the risk is somewhat different," Rand said. "Our magic doesn't harm, but it... how to put it...? it *nurtures*. If a healer has strong feelings for his bed partner, he'll impregnate her every time he lies with her, even if sponges or dung-root juice are used. A casual tup with a serving maid, probably not..." There was a sly gleam of amusement in Rand's eyes. "But with someone he loves, yes. And she'll probably give birth to triplets or even quadruplets."

Harkeld shook his head. His mouth had come open again. He shut it.

"Female healers such as our Innis have a similar problem. Extreme fertility. Especially if they're deeply attached to a lover.

With training, they can learn how *not* to become pregnant every time they have sex, and how to have only one or two babies at a time, not four or five."

Harkeld shook his head again. Not because he didn't believe Rand, but because it was almost too much to take in. "Ebril told me a bit about your training, but he never... " His thoughts wouldn't sit still long enough for him to catch them. He tried to grab one of them. "But I'm a fire mage and I've been having sex for years without any accidents!"

Rand's lips quirked. "Yes, Katlen was horrified when you went off with that maid. She wanted to stop you."

"If you'd been a female and a virgin, we *would* have stopped you," Cora said.

Harkeld tried to assimilate this. *They discussed stopping me?* He felt indignant and affronted, and then alarmed. "But... I could have burned her, couldn't I? The serving maid, I mean. I didn't know about my magic before then, so all the others were safe, but by Gdelsk..." He trailed off in response to Rand's headshake.

"It doesn't work like that. You've had the ability to do magic since you were about eleven or twelve. You could easily have burned a bed partner. In fact, it could have been the first expression of your fire magic. You obviously keep magic and sex quite separate up here." Rand tapped his temple.

Harkeld sat for a moment trying to think this through. Another thought spun past. He grabbed it. "But Ebril said that some mages only stay a year or two at the Academy. Do they get this... this kind of training before they leave? They'd still be children!"

"Of course not," Cora said. "They come back when they're older. And if their ability is slight, it's often not necessary. A fire mage with no more strength than it takes to light a candle wouldn't need the training."

Harkeld absorbed this information, his thoughts settling into place. "So... there are instructors at the Academy who just spend their lives giving lessons in sex?"

"There's an instructor who teaches the theory," Rand said. "But not the practice. She's in her fifties now, I believe."

"The practical instructors are strong mages, often Sentinel strength, whom the Council judge to have the right qualities," Cora said. "They make themselves available for a year or two, between their other duties."

Harkeld's eyebrows rose. "Sentinels?"

"Some Sentinels choose not to. It's certainly not required. Sex is a very intimate thing, after all, and losing one's virginity to someone who's little more than a stranger is... awkward, and can be embarrassing and even distressing if it's not handled correctly."

"Or deadly," Rand said, with a grimace. "I knew Keran, the instructor who was burned. It was extremely upsetting for everyone. Especially his wife and children."

Harkeld's eyebrows hitched even higher. "He was married?"

"Some instructors are, some aren't. Obviously one's spouse must support the choice. Not all do."

The mages must have a very odd society if it was acceptable for married men—and women?—to give sexual instruction to strangers. *But very sensible, too,* a tiny voice in his head pointed out. Especially if the risks were so high.

He glanced from Cora, to Rand, and then back to Cora again. *Have either of you been instructors?* But he couldn't bring himself to ask the question aloud.

"Late-twenties to mid-thirties is the age range for instructors," Rand said. "Old enough to be confident and experienced, but not *too* old. Someone who's as old as your mother or father is obviously... hmm." Rand left that thought unsaid. "Patience, tact, a sense of humor... What other things do they look for, Cora?"

"Probity. Integrity. I'm sure you appreciate that the system is open to abuse if the wrong instructors are chosen."

Harkeld nodded.

"An instructor receives tuition himself, before he or she begins," Rand continued. "Teaching someone how to control their magic during sex is quite different from bedding a lover, or a quick tup with a casual bed partner. It's demanding, and I don't just mean physically. Trying to give magical instruction at the same time as performing a, er... complex physical act— without giving the student a distaste for sex, or even worse, a fear of it—is... well, it's not easy."

Yes, Rand had done it.

Harkeld stared at him, fascinated. Rand was in his mid-forties, wiry and weather-beaten, but a decade or two ago, he'd instructed young female mages in sex. Young healers probably. Like Innis.

He glanced at Innis. Who would instruct her?

It was an unsettling thought. He barely knew Innis, but he didn't like the idea of a stranger bedding her. It gave him an uncomfortable feeling in his chest.

"If it's Sentinels who instruct, and Sentinels who're the students... wouldn't that mean that people can end up working with the person who instructed them? Wouldn't that be, um, awkward?"

Cora shook her head. "Dareus was my instructor."

Harkeld gaped at her. And then consciously shut his mouth.

He examined Cora's face. Dareus had been her instructor. Had Cora been an instructor in her turn? He thought she probably had. Cora was a good teacher. Patient and matter-of-fact.

"Are you married?" he asked abruptly. Did Cora have a husband waiting for her?

Cora nodded.

Harkeld glanced at Rand. "And you?"

Rand nodded too.

"Children?"

Both mages nodded.

Cora and Rand had children. The knowledge gave him a leaden, constricted feeling in his stomach. *I mustn't let them die for me.*

"What about Dareus?"

"A wife and three children," Cora said. "Two of his children are training to be Sentinels."

"And Katlen? Gerit?"

"Katlen's husband died several years ago. One of her sons has nearly finished his Sentinel training. Gerit was married too, but his children aren't old enough for the Academy yet."

Young children? The leaden feeling in his stomach swelled. It felt like a tumor sitting inside him, heavy and malignant. Harkeld recognized it for what it was: guilt.

"Their families don't know they're dead," he said. "Do they?"

"Dareus's may, by now. Katlen sent word back from Stanic."

Did she tell them it was my fault?

Harkeld rubbed his face. The skin felt stiff beneath the scratchy stubble. "What about Ebril? And Frane and Susa? Were they married?" *And why did I never ask Ebril that myself, while he was alive?*

"No."

But they'd have parents, brothers and sisters, people who loved them, who would grieve for them. Harkeld squeezed his eyes shut, feeling the guilt swell inside him.

"Sentinels' families are aware of the risks," Rand said. "We all know, every time we leave, that it could be the last time we see each other." Harkeld opened his eyes and looked at him. Rand's face was as calm as his voice. He'd accepted that he might never see his wife and children again.

If I can help it, you will see them.

"And most missions are achieved without loss of life," Cora said. "It's rare for Sentinels to die. Truly." She glanced at Innis as she said this, her expression difficult to interpret. Sympathy?

Harkeld looked down at his hands. *No more dead because of me,* he vowed.

But even as he made the vow, he knew it was impossible to keep. Until the last two anchor stones were destroyed, he needed the mages' protection, and while they protected him, they were at risk.

"Did you never consider..." He looked up, swallowed. "Did you never consider cutting off my hands and taking my blood?"

Cora recoiled slightly. "All-Mother forbid! Of course not!"

"It would be easier for you to travel. Safer. Quicker. Shapeshifters could take them and fly ahead. If you'd done it back in Lundegaard, then—"

"Flin," Cora said, uttering a laugh that was more horrified than amused. "Do you *want* us to do that?"

"No." He wanted to live. But so had Ebril. "But I don't want any more of you to die because of me."

Cora's horrified amusement faded. Her eyes narrowed slightly. Her gaze seemed to see inside him. "It's not your fault they're dead."

He set his jaw. *Yes, it is.*

Cora glanced at Rand. "What is it about young people?" she asked, her tone wry.

Rand shrugged and shook his head.

"Flin, you're not responsible for the corpses, or the breathstealers, *or* the bounty on your head. And as for Ebril and Katlen, Innis claims those deaths as her fault, for not changing shift with Petrus sooner."

"What?" Harkeld frowned. "They're not her fault, they're *mine*."

"Actually, Ivek is to blame," Rand said. "As he is to blame for all of this. So stop fighting for a share of the guilt, the two of you."

Innis shook her head. "If I'd woken Petrus when he asked me to—"

"You did what you thought best at the time," Cora told her. "And you were right; Petrus *did* need the sleep. And there was no sign of any threat to us. Now, enough of this nonsense, both of you. When I think one of you *is* to blame for someone's death, I promise I'll tell you."

Innis shook her head again and looked away—and stiffened. "There's a breathstealer."

Everyone jerked their heads around. Steam curled across the ground. Harkeld held his breath, staring as hard as he could.

"I can't see anything," Rand said.

"About a foot above the ground. Where the steam is thickest."

Rand shook his head. Harkeld did too.

"What exactly do you see, Innis?" Cora asked.

"Its eyes. Black eyes."

"Disturbing," Rand said. "To know it's there and not be able to see it."

Harkeld nodded. The back of his neck prickled uncomfortably.

Innis turned her head, scanning the darkness. "There are more of them." She climbed to her feet and unsheathed her sword.

"Rand, Flin, to the tent," Cora said calmly. "Innis, check it for us, will you? And Hew, perhaps it's best if you shift now."

Harkeld scrambled to his feet. "Will you be all right?" he asked Innis. It felt cowardly to leave her to face the breathstealers alone.

"I'll be fine." Her eyes weren't on him. She was watching something he couldn't see.

Cora brought a handful of candles and two brass soldiers' lanterns. One lantern, she placed inside the tent, the other she hung from a branch above the entrance.

"If you have any trouble, Innis, just yell," Rand said.

BREATHSTEALERS WATCHED FROM within the writhing steam, seeming to float a few inches off the ground. Innis gripped the sword hilt. Those black eyes were unnerving.

One creature, bolder than the rest, drifted towards the tent.

Innis cut it in half and flicked both pieces away. A pungent stink filled the air.

A second breathstealer came a few minutes later, closely followed by a third and a fourth, drifting in the tendrils of steam. How did they hunt? Did they smell human breath?

The rain became heavier, drumming down. The white billows of steam didn't dissolve; they grew thicker, piling up from the ground, breathstealers hidden in their folds. Every so often Innis peered into the tent, checking none of the creatures had found a way inside. Cora and Rand and Prince Harkeld slept crammed side-by-side in a tent made for two, their faces illuminated by candlelight.

Midnight came and went. Petrus glided down and shifted shape. His white-blond hair was plastered to his skull. "That's forty-six, by my count."

"What?" Innis pushed back her dripping hood.

"Forty-six of them. So far."

She spotted another breathstealer hovering at the tent entrance, trying to slip inside. "Forty-seven." She grabbed it, killed it, tossed the body away. "How many of the wretched things are there?"

"Could be thousands. There are so many vents round here, the jungle looks like it's smoking." He echoed Cora's words: "Thank the All-Mother you haven't finished your training, Innis."

Innis lowered the blade. "Ebril..."

"Don't." Petrus stepped closer and put his arms around her. "Don't say it, Innis. It wasn't your fault."

She squeezed her eyes shut. *But he was still breathing when I first checked. If I'd just been a few minutes earlier...*

"Ebril would be the last person to blame you for his death. You know that."

Innis leaned her forehead against his damp, bare chest, trying not to cry.

Petrus tensed. "Innis, the tent flaps are moving. I think there's—"

She pushed away from him, grabbing the breathstealer before it could slip inside.

"I'd best get back up there," Petrus said, once she'd killed it. "You don't need any distractions. I just wanted to check you're all right."

"Thanks." Innis tried to smile. "I'm fine."

She watched him shift and leap upwards, his wings catching the air. Petrus seemed to have forgiven her for willfully breaking a Law. Ebril's death had erased the awkwardness between them.

But what a terrible way to become friends again.

Innis checked inside the tent. No breathstealers crouched over the sleepers' faces, sucking their life from them. Rand stirred as she watched, muttered, rolled over, sank into sleep again.

More hours passed. The carpet of steam thickened, swirling around her hips. Innis lit fresh candles in the lanterns. Her count of kills crept above one hundred. The stink of the breathstealers' deflating bodies grew stronger, choking in the back of her throat with each breath she took. The smell didn't deter the creatures, though, nor did the occasional high-pitched screams when she failed to kill with her first stroke. The breathstealers were as relentless as the corpses had been, as unafraid of death. *No, not unafraid; uncomprehending.* There was no intelligence behind those gleaming black eyes, just a dumb, vegetable cunning, as if they sought human breath the way plants sought sunlight.

"One hundred and eight." Innis flicked the body aside, and jerked around at a sudden rush of movement. Petrus swooped low over the embers of the campfire. Three owls followed, shimmering slightly. Shapeshifters.

CHAPTER SEVENTY-EIGHT

THE SHAPESHIFTERS LANDED and changed into human form. One, a woman, flicked her fingers, relighting the fire. The other two were men; one she didn't know, but the second...

Innis put a finger to her lips as the younger male shapeshifter grinned at her and opened his mouth.

His eyebrows rose and he obediently closed his mouth. She ran across to him, hugged him. "Justen!" she whispered. "I can't believe you're here!"

He hugged her back. "Ach, how could I not come, knowing you were all here?"

"Where is everyone?" the other male shapeshifter asked in a low voice, looking at the single tent.

"And what are those things?" asked the woman, pointing at the tiny pink corpses visible beneath the swirling steam.

"Breathstealers," Innis whispered. "Wait here, I'll wake Cora and Rand. If Prince Harkeld wakes, you need to shift, Justen. He mustn't see you."

Justen's brow creased. "What?"

"Cora will explain."

She hurried back to the tent. A breathstealer was halfway through a gap between the fastenings. Innis jerked it out and killed it, then undid the ties and crawled inside. "Cora," she whispered, shaking her gently. "Wake up."

Cora's eyes jerked open.

Innis laid a finger over her lips, then pointed to Rand and jerked her thumb outside. Cora understood. She quickly, quietly woke Rand. "There's trouble?" Cora whispered, as she crawled from the tent.

"More shapeshifters have arrived."

Cora's worried frown lifted. "Thank the All-Mother." She hurried towards the fire, the mist curling around her as if she was a ship cutting through waves.

Hew had found the new shapeshifters blankets to wrap themselves in. They stood, the flames illuminating their faces. "You must be Justen," she heard Cora say.

"Yes." Justen's brow creased slightly in bewilderment. "And you are...?"

"Cora. And this is Rand. Sit down, all of you, we need to talk. Hew, set some water to boil. I'm sure our friends would like something hot to drink."

"First," Rand said, halting them with an upraised hand. "The rest of your party... they're not camped in the jungle, are they?"

"Aboard ship, a couple of miles off the coast," the male shapeshifter said.

"Ah, good. Then have a seat. We have a lot to discuss."

The two strangers sat, but Justen walked a few steps towards Innis. "I see Petrus and Hew," he said. "But where's Ebril? And Susa and Frane? Are they all right?"

Her expression must have told him. His face drained of color. He shook his head. "No."

"Susa and Frane died a while ago," Innis said. "And Ebril..." Her throat tightened. "He died yesterday."

Justen shook his head again.

"I'm sorry." Innis hugged him tightly, tears choking in her throat, then gave him a gentle push towards the fire. "Go sit. Cora will explain everything."

CORA AND RAND and the shapeshifters talked for more than an hour, their voices low murmurs. Hew bustled around the campfire, setting water to boil, steeping herbs. He brought Innis a steaming, fragrant mug. For the length of time it took to drink, the scent of peppermint pushed away the stink of the breathstealers. At one point, Rand stood and fetched a creature she'd just killed, carrying the limp corpse back to the fire for the newcomers to see.

Innis watched in quick glances, studying the strangers' faces, trying to guess what they were like. The woman was small, with olive skin and black hair and an expressive face. The man was barrel-chested and bearded. His voice rumbled below everyone else's.

The shadows of Ivek's curse had rested only lightly on the newcomers when they'd arrived, but as the three of them drank, the shadows darkened. Innis's skin prickled as she watched the curse take full hold of them.

The male shapeshifter noticed. He brushed his skin, as if trying to rub the curse shadow off. The rumble of his voice became louder for a moment: "...must say these are horrible..."

Her gaze kept straying to Justen. *We got the shape of his nose wrong. And the color of his eyes.* And even though it was marvelous to see him, she felt terror. What if he died too? Wouldn't it be better if he was a stranger? Someone she didn't like so much?

At last everyone stood. The shapeshifters put aside their blankets. Justen came to her with quick steps, churning the mist, and hugged her and whispered, "See you later." The newcomers changed shape and flew away.

Cora and Rand and Hew sat again. Cora and Rand talked, heads bent together, while Hew listened. His was the only face she could see. It was impossible to tell anything from his serious expression.

Dawn lightened the sky, but the heavy rain didn't ease. Visibility was less than a hundred yards. The river rushed and foamed.

With the dawn, the breathstealers stopped coming. Innis sheathed her sword and crossed to the fire. Cora looked up with a smile. "This makes things so much easier!"

Innis nodded and crouched, holding her hands to the flames.

"Have you met Serril and Linea before?"

Innis shook her head.

"Excellent Sentinels, both of them. And Hedín is with them, and Nellis and Bode, and they managed to recall Malle in time, which is what I'd been hoping for, so *she's* here too."

"And it looks like the ship will be able to land," Rand put in. "So we won't have to slog our way through the jungle to Krelinsk."

Innis nodded. "Who's Malle?"

"A water mage." Cora looked years younger than she had last night, as if she'd sloughed age along with worry. "An extremely strong one. We'll need her once we're in Sault."

"That we will," Rand said. "Innis, did you wake Flin?"

"No."

"I'll put some gruel on and roust him out." Rand stood and stretched and headed for the piled packsaddles. His step was jaunty.

"You'll still need to sleep during the day, unfortunately," Cora continued, flicking her plait back over her shoulder. "You're the only one who can see the breathstealers. But Justen can patrol for us, and Petrus and Hew won't need to stay shifted for so long any more. And did you notice that Linea looks remarkably like you, once she's shifted?"

Innis shook her head.

"We'll need to wait till we're on board for Justen to become *our* Justen, though. Did Petrus tell you, Flin wants Justen back as his armsman?"

Innis shook her head again. A flicker of relief kindled in her chest—*I can be his armsman again*—followed by quenching realization. No, she couldn't. The real Justen was here now. That would be his role.

"You and Petrus will need to tell him everything he needs to know about Flin, and his appearance will have to be tweaked slightly, but it will all be so much easier than it has been."

Rand set the gruel pot on the fire and crossed to the tent. He crouched and stuck his head inside.

The prince emerged a couple of minutes later. Innis watched as he stretched and combed his hair roughly with his fingers. He and Rand surveyed the dissolving corpses. Rand grimaced and waved his hand in front of his nose and said something her ears didn't catch.

No more lies, no more deception. Why, then, did she feel so miserable?

"How many new mages are there?" she asked.

"Five shapeshifters, four fire mages, a couple of healers, and Malle and her journeyman. Thirteen altogether." Cora stirred the gruel. "We're so much better off than we were this time yesterday that it feels like a dream!"

CHAPTER SEVENTY-NINE

BENNICK SHOWED JAUMÉ how to use the spyglass. The long, low
island leapt closer. He saw the higgledy-piggledy black rock,
saw the narrow neck of water that separated the island from the
steaming, marshy shore, saw the great brown river that flowed
on its other side, and the dense jungle beyond that.

"Where's the stone?" he asked. "The one the prince has to
break."

"Must be that gray thing at the end."

Jaumé shifted the spyglass—the island sliding past
jerkily, making him feel almost seasick—and found it at the
northernmost end. A gray lump. The stone that had cursed Da
and killed Mam and Rosa. Hatred for it burned in him. He
gripped the spyglass tightly, digging his fingers into the brass.

Bennick took the spyglass and put it away. Jaumé stared
through the rain at the stone. Soon it would be gone. The prince
would cut it in half with his axe.

CHAPTER EIGHTY

THEY MADE SLOW progress in the heavy rain, riding along the riverbank with the Szal rushing past on one side and dense jungle pressing against them on the other. Several times, where the bank had slipped into the river, they were forced to detour into the jungle, fighting their way yard by slow yard through a gloom that stank of decaying vegetation and sulfur. Steam coiled up from the ground. Vines wound around them. Clouds of gnats, sheltered from the rain by the thick foliage, crawled into ears and mouth and nose, despite Rand's oil. Harkeld sweated, swore, gritted his teeth. He clung to Hew's promise that the jungle ended shortly. He could do this for another mile, perhaps two. *And then I shall go mad.*

It was closer to a league before the trees grew spindlier and further apart. The horses picked up their pace, sensing open space ahead. The jungle thinned further, he could see stretches of land ahead—and then they emerged from the trees.

Marshland stretched before them. Here and there, outcrops of dark basalt thrust up and the occasional finger of jungle made an incursion, but for the most part it was water and steam.

Harkeld spat a gnat out of his mouth. *Thank you, All-Mother.*

They set out across the marshland, two hawks flying ahead: Hew, and one of the new shapeshifters. A dark-haired man, he thought, from the bird's size and color.

The sulfur stink was pungent. The horses didn't like it. They put their ears back, became skittish. Harkeld stared around as he rode. He saw a pool that bubbled with a sound like a pot boiling, and one where a bright yellow crust had formed around its rim, and another where the crust was orange-red, streaked with white. He saw steaming sapphire-blue pools, steaming lurid green pools, and a pool of what looked like steaming mud. The sound of bubbling came from all around, and once, steam gusted vigorously from a vent in the ground, making his horse rear.

Harkeld wrestled with the reins, eyeing the vent. Were breathstealers spawning inside it?

In the early afternoon, they halted briefly to share out strips of dried meat. Petrus, Innis, and Justen had slept the morning in Rand and Cora's pockets. Now Petrus flew overhead in wide circles and Justen came to ride beside him, his smile slightly cautious. "What a place!" Harkeld said. "Have you ever seen anything like it?"

Justen's smile became more relaxed. He shook his head.

It felt good to have Justen back at his side. They didn't talk much, but their silence was companionable. "Look, yellow water," Justen said once, and a couple of miles later: "The ground looks like it's covered with snow over there, doesn't it?"

Once a bird with a large yellow beak and bright green-and-red feathers flashed past with a squawk. It looked as improbable as the colored pools. Harkeld blinked. "That was one of the new shapeshifters, wasn't it?"

Justen shook his head. "No, it didn't have—" He shut his mouth, looking uncomfortable.

"Didn't have what?"

Justen shook his head. "Ach, it's not important."

"I'm not going to stop asking until you tell me," Harkeld said, exasperated by this evasion.

Justen screwed his face up in a grimace. "It's... kind of like the curse shadows. I don't think you'll be able to see it."

"Like the curse shadows?" His mind leapt to a new possibility. "You mean... mages can *see* when someone is shapeshifted?"

"It's complicated," Justen said, in a tone that indicated he didn't want to discuss it. "We can try teaching you once we're on the ship. Now's not the time."

Harkeld wanted to argue this point, but he didn't want to risk fracturing their new friendship. He rode, frowning, turning Justen's words over in his mind. Something mages could see... and he *was* a mage, so he should be able to see it.

He looked up at the birds gliding overhead—Petrus and the unknown shapeshifter—straining to see anything that would tell him they were mages, not ordinary birds. Did they shimmer slightly, as if sunlight struck their feathers even though it rained? He narrowed his eyes, but couldn't be sure.

"Look," Justen said, craning in his saddle. "It's bright orange. Over there, around that pool."

"There was one like that before," Harkeld said, squinting up at the hawks, frustrated by his inability to see whatever it was that Justen clearly saw. *I wish I could go to the mages' Academy and learn all this properly.*

The thought jolted him out of his frustration. He stopped staring at the birds. *What* had he just wished? To go to the mages' Academy?

No! a part of himself insisted loudly. *Of course I didn't wish that!* But another part of him knew that he had... and thought the idea interesting enough to consider.

In the late afternoon, they came close to the Szal again. The large dark hawk landed, shifting into a muscular man with a short, black beard. Cora and Rand halted. The man began to speak, gesturing at the river, unselfconsciously naked.

"...best place for the horses to cross," Harkeld heard him say in a rumbling voice as he and Justen rode up.

"Even though it's in flood?" Cora asked.

"It's the broadest point. Downstream it gets narrower and faster."

Rand shrugged. "We should make an attempt. Otherwise we have to abandon the horses. Serril, this is Prince Harkeld. Flin, we're calling him."

The shapeshifter gave a nod of greeting.

Harkeld returned the nod. "We're crossing here?" What little he could see of the river didn't look promising.

"The packhorses are," Cora said. "We'll camp here and ride to the anchor stone tomorrow. It's about nine miles north of here. We could make a push for it tonight, but it'll be dark by the time we get there and I prefer to be cautious."

"Any sign of Fithians, Serril?" Rand asked.

"No, but with the breathstealers, I'd hardly expect—"

"They survived the corpses," Cora said. "They could probably survive breathstealers, too."

"Only if there's a virgin among them," Serril pointed out. "And how likely's that?"

"Fithians are like cockroaches; they can survive cursed near anything. They were waiting for us at the last anchor stone. We need to proceed as if they're waiting for us at this one too."

"We're patrolling from here to the coast," Serril said. "The steam makes it more difficult than I'd like. We can't smell anything other than sulfur and we can barely see past our noses."

"Hmm." Cora glanced around at the flat, marshy ground and the steaming pools.

Harkeld followed her gaze. The nearest basalt outcrop was a good half mile away, barely visible. There were no stands of trees within view.

"Not much cover here. It'd be hard for someone to creep up on us. All right." Cora slid from the saddle. "We'll camp here. Serril, join us for a meal. Say, an hour?"

INNIS CHANGED INTO herself once the packhorses were unloaded and fed. She walked to the riverbank and looked out over the Szal, rain dripping steadily from her hood. Less than a furlong of the wide river was visible. The channels ran full spate, water rushing and hissing between the shingle bars. It seemed impossible that anyone could cross it. *The horses will all drown.*

Footsteps crunched towards her. She glanced back. Petrus. The real Justen now circled in the sky above the camp.

"Isn't it great that Justen is here?" Petrus said.

"In a way I wish he wasn't. Or you. I don't want either of you to die."

"Well, I don't want *you* here, either."

Innis looked at the river. "I told Cora she should send me home, but she said she needed me here."

There was a long moment of silence. "Innis... would you mind telling me what she said?"

"Oh..." Innis sighed. "She said she'd need to tell the Council, and that she'd recommend a comment is put on my record, but she wasn't as angry as I thought she'd be." In fact Cora hadn't seemed angry at all. Worried and concerned, but not angry. She glanced at Petrus. "She said it was a good thing I listened to you."

He shrugged.

"Thank you," Innis said seriously. "I owe you, Petrus."

He smiled. "No, you don't."

Yes, I do.

Petrus's smile faded. "Innis... what did Rand have to do with it? Why did she ask him to talk with you?"

"Oh..." Innis looked away from him and sighed again. "It was the dreams. Cora wanted to know more about them."

"What dreams?"

Innis frowned at the foaming brown water in the nearest channel. Where to start?

At the beginning. Back in Lundegaard, when she'd first shared fragments of dreams with Prince Harkeld.

"Let's sit over there." She walked across to a log on the riverbank and sat.

Petrus sat down beside her.

Innis tucked her hands into her cuffs and took a deep breath and told Petrus everything, not looking at his face, talking to the hissing, rushing water. She finished with Rand's comments. "He says we need to tell Flin. He says this kind of attachment is rare."

Petrus said nothing. Innis glanced at him. His expression wasn't thoughtful, as she'd expected, but almost grim. "You and I have never shared dreams."

"No," Innis said. "Our bond is different."

Petrus pushed to his feet in an abrupt movement.

Innis scrambled to stand. "Petrus... are you angry?"

Too late, she remembered that he didn't like the prince.

"Petrus, this isn't something either of us have any control over," she said hurriedly. "It just happened—"

Petrus turned away from her.

"Petrus..."

He didn't stop at the campfire. He kept going, his strides fierce, his cloak flaring, steam billowing behind him.

Innis stared after him, dismayed, with the river rushing and hissing behind her.

CHAPTER EIGHTY-ONE

THE MANACLE WENT around one ankle and was bolted into the floor. The chain was short. She could lie down on the pallet or stand, but not walk. The window—nailed shut again—was out of reach.

Britta sat on the pallet, gripped the chain in both hands, and tugged.

The bolt stayed firmly anchored in the floor.

She heard Karel's voice, fierce with conviction. *You can do it. I know you can.*

Britta tugged again. And again. And again. Another ten days until they reached land. She'd pull the bolt out by then.

CHAPTER EIGHTY-TWO

THE SMELL OF sulfur was so strong that Harkeld barely tasted the stew. He could have been eating boiled shoe leather for all the flavor the meat had.

After they'd eaten, Cora unrolled the map of the river junction and delta, sheltering it from the rain with her cloak. They crowded close, crouching.

"You're about thirty miles from the coast," Serril said. "We're anchored here." He tapped the map, leaving a wet fingerprint. "There's a sand bar formed here"—he traced a curve to the west of the delta—"and a deep channel on the lee of it where we can come in close and load the horses. If we can get them across the river, that is."

"Can the water mage stop the river flowing?" Harkeld asked.

"Not that volume, no." Rand grunted a laugh. "Nice thought, though."

"But *we* need to cross," Harkeld said, staring at the map. "You and me and Cora. How do we do that?"

"Serril has an idea. If it doesn't work..." Rand shrugged. "I hope you can swim."

"An oliphant could cross the Szal here," Innis said.

Serril glanced at her. A grin flashed in his beard. "You a mind-reader, girl?"

"We'll ride across on oliphants?" Harkeld asked, startled.

"It's an option," Serril said. "But we'll try something else first. Something quicker. I'd like to get you all aboard tomorrow, and if you three have to come back here to cross, and then ride ten leagues to the coast—*if* we manage to get the horses across... well, it'll mean another night out with the breathstealers, and I'd like to avoid that. Now, tomorrow..." His finger moved south on the map to where the two rivers merged. "The anchor stone is still high and dry, but the ridge of rocks between the island and the riverbank is underwater. You're going to get wet crossing to it."

Rand grunted another laugh. "We're already wet. In case you hadn't noticed, Serril, it's been raining the last couple of days."

"Well, you're going to get wetter. There's about three foot of water flowing over those rocks. If it gets any deeper, you'll need an oliphant to cross."

Harkeld examined the map—the converging rivers, the island where the anchor stone was, the spreading fan of the delta. By this time tomorrow, the stone would be dust, destroyed by his blood and his handprint. He wished he could ride there now. He wanted it over with.

Nine miles to the anchor stone, twenty more to the coast. *And then we'll be gone from here.* The curse would be two-thirds destroyed and the end of the nightmare would be in sight.

In sight? Yes. *But it gets harder after this.* Masse and Ankeny were the easy anchor stones. In Sault, the curse would be active. If they drank even one drop of water they'd go mad.

"Any questions?" Cora asked. "No?" She rolled up the map.

Innis glanced around and stiffened.

Harkeld followed the direction of her gaze, but saw only writhing steam. "Breathstealers?"

Innis stood, her hand on her sword. "Lots of them. Lots and *lots* of them."

Harkeld pushed to his feet.

"More than last night?" Rand said.

"There are hundreds. They're everywhere." Innis seemed to make a conscious effort to relax. She lifted her hand from her sword. "They're not advancing. They're just watching."

"Waiting for dinner," Harkeld said.

Rand snorted. The tension around the campfire eased.

"How far away are they?" Cora asked.

"About five or six yards."

Harkeld glanced around. He couldn't see anything but steam and darkness.

"I don't think they like the fire," Innis said. "They're not moving any closer. And last night they hung back until the fire had died down."

"Do they burn?" Rand asked, with a glance at Cora. "Care to try?"

Cora shrugged. "Why not?" She raised her hand. "Where, Innis?"

"Anywhere you like. They're all around us. About knee height."

Cora threw a bolt of fire to their right. Something flared alight with a sizzling burst of flames.

Innis flinched back, covering her ears with her hands.

Harkeld blinked to clear the afterimage of flames from his vision.

"Well?" Rand asked. "I take it that was a breathstealer burning?"

"Two of them." Innis lowered her hands. "Couldn't you hear them scream?"

Everyone shook their heads.

"Are they leaving?" Serril asked.

Innis shook her head. "They're not afraid at all. They don't seem to understand death." She massaged her temples, as if the breathstealers' screams had given her a headache.

"Hundreds of them?" Rand asked.

Innis nodded.

"I have two suggestions," Serril said. "One, the fire mages burn the breathstealers that are already here. More will come, if they spawn in the steam vents, but it will reduce their numbers for now." His eyes narrowed thoughtfully as he observed Innis. "But their screams hurt you, don't they? So perhaps that should be our second choice."

"And the first choice?" Rand asked.

"Fires. A ring of them around the tent. It'll keep them back, and if a few do make it through, Innis will be able to deal with them."

Innis nodded. "That could work."

"If I'm wrong and too many get through, Innis only needs to shout, doesn't she? Once you're awake, you're in no danger."

THEY BUILT BONFIRES around the tent, hauling driftwood from the riverbank and stacking it in huge piles. Steam billowed around them as they worked. Harkeld imagined breathstealers jostling one another, plucking at his trews and clutching at his cloak.

Cora lit the fires. "I don't want them too hot," she told him. "They need to burn slowly."

Harkeld nodded, looking at the flames. They were a mild orange-red, licking the wet wood lazily.

"Touch them. See if you can feel what I've done."

Don't burn me, he told the flames, and put his hand in the fire.

"I've gone for stamina and endurance, rather than intensity. Feel it?"

The flames licked his hand. The rain wouldn't put them out—he knew that without knowing how or why. The fires would consume the wood slowly, and only when no fuel remained would Cora's magic allow them to die.

"How did you do that?" he asked, removing his hand.

"I'll teach you. But not now." She stood and turned to the others. "Hew and Petrus, you'll sleep shifted tonight, and with so many breathstealers, I'll feel better if you're inside this ring. In fact, given the rain, it might be best if you sleep as mice, inside the tent."

Both shapeshifters nodded.

"Hew, take the first shift. Petrus, no patrolling for you. You get to sleep all night."

Petrus didn't return Cora's smile. Beneath his dripping hood, his face was expressionless.

"Now, bed, everyone. We need all the rest we can get. Tomorrow's going to be challenging."

CHAPTER EIGHTY-THREE

HARKELD'S EYELIDS JERKED open. His heart gave a kick in his chest. *This is it.* Today he destroyed the second anchor stone.

He heard conversation outside and rain pattering down. He pushed aside his blanket and scrambled out of the empty tent. "There you are," Rand said. "I was just about to drag you out. Breakfast is ready."

Harkeld was halfway through a bowl of steaming gruel when movement at the river caught his eye. Two massive shapes loomed out of the rain.

He almost choked before he realized what he saw: oliphants, lumbering across the Szal. A man was perched on one, swaying to the beast's movement, and on the other...

Harkeld blinked, stared, uttered a laugh. "A boat?"

Everyone turned their heads. "Ah," Cora said, sounding pleased. "They're earlier than I thought they'd be."

"What's the boat for?" Harkeld asked. The oliphants forded the final channel, water foaming and swirling around their bellies.

"You and me and Cora," Rand said. "After the anchor stone. If the river looks safe enough. Otherwise we'll come back here and cross."

A hawk swooped down and changed into Serril. The foremost oliphant gained the riverbank and went down on its knees, allowing its passenger to scramble down. "This is Arnod," Serril said. "One of our sailors. He'll be in charge of the boat." He made the introductions quickly.

The sailor grinned and nodded. His clothes were Grooten, like Justen's had been when Harkeld had first met him, with black and white geometric shapes embroidered along the hem of his cloak and the tops of his boots.

The second oliphant came up the riverbank and lowered itself onto all four knees, its movements slow and stately.

"Help me get this boat off," Serril said.

They untied the ropes, slid the boat off, and laid it to one side. It was a small, sturdy skiff, with oars and a mast and a rolled sail strapped inside. The oliphant stood and stretched and shifted into a man. He was as lean and weather-beaten as Rand, with light brown curly hair cut close to his skull and an impressive set of parallel scars running down one side of his ribcage, as if a lion had clawed him. "This is Hedín," Serril said. "And you haven't all met Linea, have you?"

Harkeld glanced over his shoulder to find that the first oliphant had become a woman, dark, petite, attractive—and naked.

He hastily averted his gaze.

"Did you make extra gruel, Cora?" Hedín asked. "You did? May the All-Mother bless you!"

WHILE THE NEWCOMERS ate breakfast, Harkeld helped Rand and Petrus and Justen load the packhorses. Petrus was silent, but Rand hummed cheerfully as he worked. The sound reminded Harkeld of Ebril.

"Linea and Hedín will try to get this lot across the river now," Rand said, tightening a girth as he talked. "Then fly up to join us."

"You think the horses will make it?"

"With oliphants to anchor them, hopefully they won't wash away." Rand patted the packhorse he'd just loaded. "Swim well, my friend."

The horse tossed its head with a snort.

"And the boat?" Harkeld asked. "How do we get that to the anchor stone? Will Arnod sail it down?"

"Too dangerous," Rand said, hefting another packsaddle into place. "There's a gorge with rapids ahead. Serril will carry it. And once we've sailed—*if* we sail—he'll bring our mounts back here and take them across the river. One or other of the shapeshifters will help him."

"And if it's too dangerous to use the boat... we cross here, like Arnod?"

Rand nodded, adjusting the packsaddle so that it was evenly balanced. "And sleep another night on land. Innis said the fires worked well last night, so the breathstealers shouldn't be a problem."

Harkeld made a final check of the packhorse he was loading. He gave the beast a pat and uttered the same blessing Rand had. "Swim well."

By the time everyone had eaten, the packhorses were roped into strings of five and the riding mounts saddled. Serril became an oliphant, and they lashed the boat to his back. Harkeld was aware of an itch of excitement in his blood. It was only nine miles to the anchor stone. They'd be there in a couple of hours. He checked his sword and swung up into his saddle.

Cora stood conferring with Rand, low-voiced. At the river's edge, an oliphant walked slowly into the rushing water, five nervous packhorses following.

Harkeld shifted restlessly in his saddle. *Come on, let's go.* He pushed back his dripping hood and went over the lessons Cora had taught him—burning arrows, burning throwing stars.

Justen mounted and nudged his horse up alongside Harkeld's. Petrus and Hew climbed into their saddles.

Cora strode towards them. "Petrus, Justen, Hew... stick close to Flin. If there are assassins, I want them to have a hard time guessing which one of you he is." She glanced up at Harkeld's unhooded head.

"Better field of view," he said.

Cora conceded this with a nod. "Hoods off, all of you. And make your hair as dark as Flin's. Stubble, too! The more similar you look, the more confusing it'll be for them."

Arnod jogged back from helping rope the horses to the second oliphant. He climbed clumsily into his saddle. Rand and Cora mounted.

"Ready?" Cora asked.

The itch of excitement grew stronger. Harkeld glanced at the river. The first oliphant had crossed two channels and was fording a third, all five horses still behind it. The second oliphant was starting out. The remaining packhorses stood tethered on the riverbank, awaiting their turn.

"Do you really think there'll be Fithians?" Hew asked.

Harkeld turned his head to hear the answer.

"It's unlikely, given the breathstealers, but let's take no chances, shall we?"

CHAPTER EIGHTY-FOUR

Misty rain hung in the air. Bennick peered out of the cave and drew back, stopping Jaumé from looking. "A hawk."

"Hawks can't hurt us."

"They can if they're shapeshifters. No, don't look, lad. A hawk can see a lizard on a rock half a mile away." Bennick took out the spyglass and aimed it at the island. He snorted. "Yes. Shapeshifter. It's landed. Look."

Jaumé took the spyglass and focused it. The island sprang at him. Black rocks, lapping water, the gray lump of stone at the northernmost end, and... "A dog?" Sniffing the rocks in ever-widening circles.

"Not a dog." Bennick took the spyglass back. "The prince is coming."

"They're looking for him!" Jaumé said, with a thrill of horror. "To kill him." He told Bennick the conversation he'd overheard in Droznic-Drobil.

Bennick laughed. "It's a good story."

CHAPTER EIGHTY-FIVE

THE FIRST FEW miles were much like the previous day—marshland, steaming pools, the occasional stand of trees or outcrop of basalt.

Gradually it changed. The outcrops of basalt became larger and more numerous, and the stretches of open ground between them dwindled in size. Harkeld began to look more frequently over his shoulder.

To their left, the Szal narrowed, pinched between basalt bluffs. The water flowed swiftly, turbulently. Harkeld understood why Serril carried the boat; the river would have swallowed the skiff, and spat it out as splinters.

They left the river's edge, skirting the basalt. Harkeld peered uneasily up at the looming black pillars. *If I was a Fithian, this is the sort of place I'd choose for an attack.* Two hawks flew with them, skimming over the thrusting rocks. They weren't birds he recognized. It was hard to trust the vigilance of mages he'd never met. He wished Innis was up there; she must be asleep in Cora's pocket again.

Half a mile to their right, an outcrop of basalt rose from the ground, gradually increasing in height. As they rode, the outcrop veered towards them and the open ground narrowed until it was barely a furlong wide. It was like being in the canyon again, except that the walls were black, not red, and the ground steamed.

The rain fell more heavily, streaming over his face, making it hard to see, hard to hear. Harkeld's nervousness grew. How far had they come? Six miles? Seven? *Not much more of this,* he told himself. They'd be at the anchor stone soon.

A hawk arrowed down and landed.

Harkeld reached for his sword, certain something was wrong—but the hawk was Hedín. "We got all the horses across," the mage said. "One broken hock, a couple of sprains, and some bad scrapes, but nothing a healer can't fix."

Harkeld slid his sword back into its scabbard.

"Excellent," Cora said. "Stay close, will you? And Linea, too. I don't like this territory."

"How much more of this is there?" Rand asked, gesturing at the basalt bluffs.

"Another mile or so. It gets narrower first, then widens right out." Hedín changed back into a hawk, spread his wings, and sprang upwards.

Hedín was right; the strip of open ground narrowed still further. They rode at a cautious trot, wary of steam vents and half-seen pools. "I don't like this," Justen muttered, riding so close that his knee almost touched Harkeld's.

"Neither do I." The looming basalt on either side was ideal for an ambush—

Something silvery flashed through the rain and buried itself in Hew's throat. A hawk's shriek echoed, simultaneously.

Harkeld snatched for his sword, his mouth opening in a shout as his brain caught up with what his eyes had seen: throwing star.

Another silvery blur came from his right. Petrus's horse reared, squealing.

Harkeld threw himself from his saddle at the same time Justen shoved him. He hit the ground hard, knocking the sword from his grip and the breath from his lungs. He scrambled to hands and knees, gasping, shaking rain from his eyes. *Where's the rutting sword?*

Justen landed alongside him, grabbed his shoulder, and thrust him back. "Stay down!" All around was a chaos of rain and panicking horses and billowing sulfur-scented steam. Something screamed; animal or human, he couldn't tell.

A throwing star sliced towards them. Harkeld stopped scrabbling for his sword and grabbed for his magic instead. *Burn.*

The throwing star ignited with a flash of white-hot flame. Somewhere a lion roared, deep-throated.

Justen shoved him further back. "Get behind me."

Harkeld crouched, struggling to fill his lungs. He dashed rain from his eyes. A throwing star arced towards them. *Burn.* And there was another one. *Burn.* Justen jerked back, his shoulder hitting Harkeld's, as the throwing star ignited less than a yard from his face.

"Did I burn you?" Harkeld asked, still wheezing for breath.

Justen gave a shaky laugh. "No."

An oliphant trumpeted. Serril. The ground shook as he charged past, the boat ludicrously perched on his back.

Harkeld cast a quick glance around. Hew lay with his arms outflung, clearly dead. He had a flash of memory: Innis, the night Ebril had died. *I can't heal death. Healers who try that die.*

Petrus was on the ground too, trying to roll to his feet, pain stark on his face.

A small, dark hawk swooped low. A throwing star came out of the mist, catching it in its breast, shearing through flesh and bone, flinging the bird backwards with a spray of blood and feathers.

Harkeld opened his mouth, but no sound came out. Horror emptied his lungs of air. "They killed Innis," he said numbly, then turned to Justen, almost shouting: "They killed Innis!"

"No, they didn't," Justen said, peering through the steam and rain in the direction the throwing stars had come from.

"I just saw it," Harkeld said. For some reason he didn't understand, he was shaking.

"That was Linea," Justen said flatly. "Get down. There's at least one Fithian still out there."

Harkeld crouched lower. "Are you sure it was Linea? It looked an awful lot like Innis."

"I'm sure—" Justen recoiled as a throwing star hurtled towards them.

Burn.

A lion bellowed somewhere to their right. Harkeld couldn't see any horses. Hew lay where he'd fallen. Petrus was gone. A dozen yards behind them, a figure crouched close to the ground. Arnod, his face white and frightened.

A lion padded through the mist, its jaws blood-stained. It shifted into Hedín. "We think we've got them all," he said grimly, wiping his mouth with the back of one hand. "But stay here. Don't move yet." He raised his voice: "You, too, Arnod. Stay put."

They crouched for another ten minutes, while warm rain pattered down and steam rolled across the ground. A few yards to their right, a pool bubbled like a simmering pot.

After a while, Justen said, "You saved my life. Thanks."

"You've saved mine often enough."

Finally Hedín came striding back. "We've caught the horses. Arnod, can you help settle them?" He jerked his thumb in the direction he'd come from. "Justen, Rand wants you up front as fast as you can. And Flin..." He turned to Hew's body and sighed. "Can you help me with Hew, please? We'll take him with us."

"Linea is dead, too," Justen said, standing, but not sheathing his sword.

"What?" Hedín jerked around. "Linea?"

"Flin saw it."

Hedín's gaze fastened on him. "Are you certain?"

Harkeld rose from his crouch. "I saw a throwing star cut a hawk in two. A small, black one."

The color leached from Hedín's face. "Where is she?"

"I'll show you."

"Are you sure it's safe for him?" Justen asked.

"I'll be with him," Hedín said. "And Oren." He pointed upwards, where a hawk hovered.

* * *

INNIS HURRIED THROUGH the steam. She saw the horses, milling nervously, and Petrus standing, clutching his right arm, his face alarmingly pale beneath the unfamiliar dark hair, and the looming shape of Serril, half-hidden by wreathing coils of steam. And Rand sitting on the ground, Cora crouched in front of him.

She cast a worried glance at Petrus and went over to Rand. "You wanted to see me—? Oh!" All the fingers on his left hand were missing. She hastily crouched, reaching for his hand.

"Not yet," Rand said through gritted teeth. "First do the horse and Petrus."

"But—"

"I've stopped the bleeding and Cora's found the fingers. One minute on the horse and five on Petrus, then come back to me."

"Wash the fingers," Innis told Cora hurriedly, pushing to her feet. "Use your waterskin. Make sure you rinse them completely clean. Completely clean, mind!"

The horse was Petrus's, and it was missing half an ear. Blood streamed from the wound. Arnod held the animal still while Innis hastily sealed the blood vessels. Then she turned to Petrus. "What—?"

"Dislocated shoulder." His face was pale, strained. "If you can put it back, I can do the rest."

Innis helped him out of his cloak and jerkin. "What happened?"

"My horse dumped me."

She eased off his shirt, wincing when she saw his shoulder. "This may hurt."

He uttered a hoarse grunt of laughter. "It already does."

Innis gripped his wrist in one hand and extended his elbow. She let her magic flow into him, coaxing the spasming muscles to relax. "Ready?"

Petrus held his breath, his eyes tightly squeezed shut. He groaned as the shoulder joint slid into place, and swayed, as if about to faint.

"Sit," Innis said.

He obeyed without protest, looking drained and exhausted. Innis crouched alongside him and laid her hands on his shoulder.

"You should do Rand," Petrus said. "His hand—"

"Let me check whether anything's damaged." She let her magic flow into him, exploring the tissues in his shoulder—muscles, tendons, ligaments, nerves—and frowned. It wasn't the injury that alarmed her, it was Petrus himself. The person she knew—even-tempered, patient, quick to laugh and slow to anger—was buried beneath a turmoil of bitterness and jealousy and anger.

What?

She let her magic flow more deeply into him, healing the swelling and bruising around the shoulder joint, but also searching for the source of those turbulent emotions. What had upset him so much?

But even as she asked the question, her magic told her the answer.

The depth of Petrus's love shocked her. It was far beyond the friendly affection she'd always sensed in him. *He wants to marry me?*

Mixed in with the churning, bitter emotions was shame. He was deeply ashamed of his jealousy, deeply ashamed of his behavior last night. And he was exhausted and in pain and terrified for her safety.

"Petrus..."

"What?" he said, his head bowed and his eyes closed.

I'm sorry I didn't know. Regret pierced her. She touched her knuckles lightly to his cheek. "You know I love you."

Petrus opened his eyes and frowned at her.

"You're my family."

His frown deepened. "We're not related."

"It's not about blood." She let her magic flow into him. *Calmness. Ease. Love.* "Do you remember the day I arrived at the Academy?" It was branded in her memory. She'd been newly orphaned, scared and bewildered and grieving, painfully shy, painfully alone.

He did remember. Her magic felt the surge of protectiveness the recollection invoked.

"You've been my brother since then."

"Justen," Cora called.

Innis leaned forward and kissed Petrus's cheek, even though she was Justen. "I will *always* love you," she said, and then she released his shoulder and pushed to her feet and hurried back to Rand.

Cora had washed all the fingers. Three of them lay on a scrap of cloak looking—grotesquely—like scrawny brown sausages. Rand held the forefinger in place on its stump.

Innis sat on the muddy ground and reached for the middle finger.

"Justen's not a healer, is he?" Cora asked.

"No." Innis hesitated, holding the finger. "Flin'll be here shortly. If he sees this..."

"You're helping me hold them in place," Rand said. "While I do the healing. Cora doesn't have the stomach for it."

Cora snorted and stood. "How's Petrus?"

Upset. "His sword arm's weak."

"How weak?"

"Fine to ride, but he won't last long in a fight. He'll need more healing before he's fully recovered."

Cora grimaced. "Can't be helped." She strode over to help Arnod with the horses.

Innis carefully fitted the finger into its place. "Throwing star?"

"Mmm."

She explored the damage, then bent her attention to repairing it—mending the blood vessels and coaxing blood to flow again, repairing the severed bone, encouraging the flesh to knit together. She was aware of Rand's healing magic working alongside her own.

"Leave the tendons and nerves, I'll do those later."

"Are you certain? Your dexterity—"

"We haven't the time." Rand reached for the last two fingers and gave her one. "Hew's dead?"

"Yes." She fitted the little finger into place. "And Linea."

Rand's mouth twisted. He said nothing.

Innis released her healing magic, exploring, assessing. "How many Fithians were there?"

"Two."

Innis rotated the little finger a fraction of an inch, until the sheared edges of bone matched perfectly. "How did they survive the breathstealers?"

"Only the All-Mother knows that. Though they must have been weakened by them. If they'd been at full strength, our losses would be greater."

Prince Harkeld and Hedín came out of the steam, carrying Hew's body. "Over here," Cora called, beckoning them, holding the reins of Hew's horse.

Innis mended Rand's little finger as swiftly as she could while Hedín and the prince slung Hew over the horse's saddle and lashed his body in place.

Cora came over and crouched. "How's it going?"

"They're not going to fall off again," Rand said. "But I can't use my hand yet." He raised his voice slightly as the prince came to join them. "Thanks for holding them in place for me, Justen."

"What happened?" the prince asked.

Rand displayed his left hand. "Fingers came off."

The prince grimaced. "Ouch." He bent, took Rand's elbow, and helped him to his feet.

Innis stood and glanced around. Steam rose curling from a pool on her left, and behind that—

She flinched back a step, reaching for her sword, before realizing the sprawled man was dead.

Prince Harkeld jerked round. He drew his own sword. "What?"

"Sorry," Innis said, while her heart beat thunderously with fright. "A dead Fithian. Over there."

The prince slid his sword back into its scabbard. "Must be from Issel. Look at the color of his skin."

"The other one's a big blond brute," Rand said. "Took two lions to bring him down. Let's go. Get this over with." He headed for the horses, Prince Harkeld at his heels.

Cora touched Innis's arm, halting her. "How are you? You were up all night, and now this healing..."

"I'm fine," Innis said. "Better than Rand and Petrus, anyway." She rubbed her forehead. She was tired, even if she didn't want to admit it. "Are you worried there'll be more of them?"

"Aren't you?"

Innis blinked, and looked at her uncertainly. "But, surely just one ambush...?"

"Fithians always turn up when you least want them to." Cora looked towards the horses, where Arnod and Prince Harkeld were helping Rand to mount. Her gaze followed the prince as he went to his horse and swung up into the saddle. "Stay close to him."

"I will."

Cora nodded, took a step towards the horses, and turned back. "Oh, and—"

A throwing star buried itself in the back of Cora's skull, knocking her sharply forward. Her head struck Innis's chest, directly over her heart.

CHAPTER EIGHTY-SIX

INNIS FELL BACKWARDS, clutching Cora. She hit the ground hard and thrust the body from her, rolling, shouting, reaching for her sword. A hawk shrieked overhead. She heard the muffled detonation of Prince Harkeld's fire magic. The ground shook; Serril was charging. A lion roared to her right. Fire magic flashed.

Innis scrambled to her feet and ran for the horses, sword in hand. "Flin!" she bellowed. "Petrus!"

Fire magic flashed again. The prince was alive.

She thrust her way through panicked, riderless horses. There was Rand, crouched low on the ground. And Arnod. And Petrus standing with his sword drawn, and behind him, Prince Harkeld, his hand raised to throw fire.

Petrus's gaze snapped to her. His face flooded with relief.

Innis ran to them. "You all right?"

"Get down," the prince said brusquely. "You, too, Petrus. Give me space to see."

Innis grabbed his left arm, hauling him to his knees. "You, too."

The prince shook her hand off, but didn't stand again.

They waited, crouching. Innis strained to hear past the patter of rain and the faraway bubbling of boiling water and the hard hammering of her heart. Beneath the alertness was knowledge: *Cora's dead.*

They all tensed as a figure strode out of the steam. Hedín, his face grim. "We got him."

"I thought you had them all last time," Rand said tersely. "How do we know there aren't more?"

"We don't. Now hurry. Help me with the horses. We've got to get out of here. This place is a cursed trap."

Innis stood. "Cora's body—"

"We'll take her with us. Arnod, Petrus, Flin—the horses. Justen, help me with Cora."

Innis followed Hedín to where Cora lay, face up, a bloody, razor-sharp point protruding from her forehead. Rain splashed in her open eyes. Her lips were slightly parted.

Innis stared down at her. *What were you going to tell me?*

Hedín crouched and touched Cora's cheek, a gesture of farewell.

Innis sheathed her sword; it took two tries, her hands were shaking so badly. Justen's cloak, jerkin, and shirt were torn above her heart. Blood trickled from a stinging scratch on her skin. "He was aiming for me? He thought I was the prince?" *He can't have seen me kiss Petrus, then.*

"He went for all three of you," Hedín said. "You first, then Petrus and Flin. Thank the All-Mother Flin can burn steel, or more'n Cora would be dead."

Innis crouched and looked at Cora's face. *You died instead of me.*

CHAPTER EIGHTY-SEVEN

BENNICK PUT THE spyglass to his eye. "Horses."

Jaumé squinted. He saw ant-like movements on the marshy shore opposite the southern end of the island.

"And bodies. Two of 'em. There's been a fight."

"Can you see Nolt and Gant and Ash?"

Bennick lowered the spyglass. "They're dead."

"How do you know?"

"The prince is there."

"With his army?"

"With mages. Those men are mages, Jaumé. What you call witches."

"They've caught him?"

"They've saved him."

"No." Jaumé shook his head. Witches didn't save people. They were evil.

Bennick handed him the spyglass. "Look."

Jaumé looked—and couldn't keep back a cry as something huge and gray filled the spyglass. It was as big as a house, with a long nose and vast flapping ears.

"It's an oliphant, Jaumé. A mage. A shapeshifter." Bennick took the spyglass back. He watched for several minutes. His mouth widened in a grin, almost of admiration. "Three of them. Clever bastards. Here..." He thrust the spyglass at Jaumé. "Tell me when they cross to the island."

Jaumé looked for the oliphant, but it was gone. He shifted the spyglass back and forth, looking at the people on the shore. They were all men. Two were naked. "Which one's the prince?"

Bennick grunted a laugh from the back of the cave. "You tell me, lad."

Jaumé studied the men again. None of them looked like he was being held prisoner. *The witches are helping him? They're good witches?*

But witches were always bad. Everyone knew that.

Three of the men stood together. They were younger than the others, all dark-haired. *He breaks the curse stone in half with a giant axe,* Jaumé thought. But none of the men had an axe.

Behind him, he heard Bennick stringing his bow.

CHAPTER EIGHTY-EIGHT

THE ISLAND WAS at the confluence of the Szal and the Yresk. Columns of basalt rose in irregular tiers to its highest point. "Is the anchor stone at the top?" Harkeld asked.

"At the northern end," Justen said. "Where it flattens out."

The skiff lay on the shore. Arnod was in discussion with Serril and Hedín, gesturing at the shallow, swirling water that separated the island from the shore. Cora and Hew lay in the boat's prow, along with the small bundle that was Linea, wrapped in the ripped-off hood of Hew's cloak.

Three more who've died because of me. What did that make his count now? Twenty-seven?

His gaze rested on Cora's huddled form. Grief clenched in his chest. Why her? *You were a good teacher,* he told her silently, regretting that he'd never told her while she was alive. *Thank you for everything you taught me.*

And Cora had a husband and children. Who didn't know she was dead.

Harkeld looked away. He cleared his throat, took a deep breath.

Rand crouched near the horses, holding his left hand in his right, his eyes closed, intense concentration on his face. Harkeld scanned the marshland behind the healer. The rain had eased to a drizzle, and the visibility was improving. Nothing moved except drifting steam. "Where's Innis?" He felt a prickle of alarm. Had she been sleeping in Cora's pocket? "Was she hurt when Cora—"

"She's fine," Justen said. "I think Rand has her."

"Look," Petrus said.

A swallow swooped across the twenty yards of water separating the island from the riverbank. Even though the sun wasn't out, sunlight seemed to glimmer on its wings.

The swallow landed on the rim of the skiff and looked at them with bright eyes.

Serril broke off his discussion with Arnod. "All clear?"

The swallow dipped its head.

"He's been on the island all morning," Serril said, turning to Harkeld. There were red marks on his skin where the ropes tying the boat had rubbed. "He's looked in every crack and crevice a dozen times. You can trust there are no Fithians there."

Harkeld nodded.

"Arnod reckons this is the safest point to enter the current, so we'll leave the boat here. Rand, you stay with him. Oren'll keep watch over you both." Serril jerked his thumb at the hawk circling overhead.

"You don't want me to come with you?"

"The rocks on the island are slippery and you've only one good hand."

Rand conceded this with a nod.

"Petrus and Justen, stick close to Flin. The three of us will be with you." Serril gestured to Hedín and the swallow. "Now let's move, before any more Fithians show up."

PETRUS SHUCKED HIS cloak before entering the water. It was only thigh-deep, but too murky to see the bottom. His feet told him it was a jumble of slippery blocks and ledges. The water flowed in swift eddies, surging around his thighs, nudging him this way and that.

He stumbled on a rock, sat heavily in the water. Prince Harkeld grabbed his jerkin and hauled him up.

"Thanks."

Petrus reached the island, scrambled up on black rocks and slipped again, landing hard on one knee. He bit back a curse. "Careful," he called back. "There's some kind of fungus on these rocks. They're rutting slippery."

He waited until both Justen and the prince were ashore before setting off round the island. It was like traversing a gigantic, crazy muddle of stepping stones. Their progress was slow, slipping and sliding, grabbing at rocks for balance, sometimes clambering on all fours. Prince Harkeld fell once, with a loud yelp of pain.

It took twenty minutes to reach the northern end of the island. His shoulder was aching by the time they got there. The anchor stone stood on a ledge of basalt, a barrel-shaped lump of pale gray rock with a contorted sausage of white marble running through it. It was more thickly covered with curse shadows than anything he'd seen yet in the Seven Kingdoms.

Prince Harkeld unsheathed his dagger.

Petrus glanced around. The drizzle had stopped. The Szal rushed brown and fast on their left; the Yresk, green-black and fast on their right. Ahead, where the two met, waves jostled one another.

He measured the distance to the riverbanks with his eyes. More than a hundred yards to the western bank, a good seventy to the eastern. Too far for a throwing star.

Petrus turned back to the anchor stone.

He watched Prince Harkeld cut his palm, wipe his dagger on his trews and sheath it, and place his left hand on the stone.

CHAPTER EIGHTY-NINE

"THAT'S HIM," BENNICK said. He thrust the spyglass at Jaumé and picked up his bow.

"Who?" Jaumé cried in alarm. Someone was going to kill the prince? *They can't! The curse won't be stopped.* He hastily focused the spyglass.

The three men on the island's tip sprang into view. One had his hand pressed to the curse stone. Two others stood, half-blocking him. A couple of hawks hovered overhead and a swallow dipped and swooped. Jaumé frantically scanned the rocks, the air, the water. Where was the threat Bennick had seen?

CHAPTER NINETY

THE PRINCE'S LIPS moved, as if he was counting. He glanced at Justen, "Long enough, I reckon," and tried to lift his hand from the anchor stone.

It didn't come off.

The prince frowned and tried again. Petrus saw the tendons flex on the back of his hand.

"I'm stuck to it."

Justen grabbed Prince Harkeld's wrist and tugged. The prince's hand didn't move. It appeared to have adhered to the anchor stone.

"Use your fire magic," Petrus suggested. "Try to burn—"

The prince wrenched hard. His hand came free. He staggered back, falling to one knee.

"You all right?" Justen said, hauling him to his feet.

The prince's face screwed up in a grimace. "It rutting *hurts*."

"Let's have a look." Justen took Prince Harkeld's hand and turned it over.

Petrus flinched. The prince's palm looked as if it had been flayed. The skin was completely gone. He saw pink flesh, beaded with blood.

He glanced instinctively at the anchor stone. Yes, the skin was there. A perfect handprint. He frowned and looked more closely. The skin was dissolving into the anchor stone.

"Petrus," Justen said. "You need to heal him. Stop the bleeding, at least."

"Yes," Petrus said, staring at the anchor stone. "It's eating your skin. Look."

The prince stepped closer. "What's going to happen at the third stone, d'you think? Maybe it'll take my whole hand off?" Flippant words, but with an undertone of unease.

We can hope so, Petrus thought, then quashed the thought as unworthy.

"Of course not," Justen said firmly. "Petrus, his hand."

CHAPTER NINETY-ONE

"MOVE," BENNICK MUTTERED. "Move." His voice was hoarse with the effort of holding the bowstring taut, his breathing strained.

CHAPTER NINETY-TWO

A CRACK APPEARED in the anchor stone, snaking across its surface. The thick curse shadows covering it frayed, dissolving like the prince's skin.

"Petrus," Justen said. "His *hand*."

"Yes, yes," Petrus said, watching another crack spring to life. A groaning noise came from within the anchor stone, as if it was about to disintegrate.

"Petrus!"

"All *right*." He turned and reached for the prince's hand.

The prince grinned. "Should be a nursemaid, shouldn't he?"

Petrus found himself grinning back. He broke their eye contact, looking down at the prince's hand. *Rut it, I don't want to like you.*

He gathered his healing magic and turned his attention to stopping the bleeding.

With a brief, whirring thud, an arrow buried itself in Prince Harkeld's chest. The prince fell backwards, his hand wrenching from Petrus's grip.

CHAPTER NINETY-THREE

"The prince!" Jaumé screamed. "You shot the prince!"

Bennick, fallen on one knee, panting, with the bow on the ground beside him, grinned. "Saved our honor, Jaumé. Made the kill."

CHAPTER NINETY-FOUR

PETRUS DUCKED AND scrambled after the prince.

Justen reached him first. "Harkeld!"

The prince's eyes were open, blinking, his mouth gasping. The arrow embedded in his chest quivered with each beat of his heart.

"We've got to get out of range! Take his legs." Justen seized Prince Harkeld under his arms.

The anchor stone disintegrated behind them with a gritty sigh. Gray dust billowed outward.

Petrus grabbed the prince's legs. They were as limp as if he was already dead.

They carried the prince fifty yards around to the far side of the island, panting, scrambling, crouching low. Petrus felt as if he had a target painted on his back. The shoulder he'd dislocated ached fiercely. He gritted his teeth and glanced back. The far bank of the Yresk had slid out of sight behind the island. "Here. This should do."

They laid the prince down. Justen tore open his jerkin and shirt. Petrus winced at sight of the arrow impaling Prince Harkeld's chest. There was no doubt it had gone through his heart. *It's a killing wound.*

But the prince was still alive, his eyes still blinking, his mouth still gasping, the arrow still quivering.

Serril dropped down beside them. "Hedín's fetching Rand. Can you keep him alive?"

"Yes," Justen said. His head was bowed, his hands pressed to Prince Harkeld's chest.

Petrus caught Serril's eye and shook his head. *He's dead.*

"One chamber of his heart, and an artery," Justen muttered. He raised his head. "Petrus, I need you to pull the arrow out a quarter of an inch when I say so. Just quarter of an inch, mind!"

"What?" His gaze jerked to Justen. "Are you sure?"

"Yes. The arrow's not barbed, it—"

"No. Are you sure you can heal him?"

"Yes. Now hurry!"

Petrus was alarmed by the desperation in Justen's voice, the wildness in his eyes. *Is Innis prepared to die with the prince? Does she love him that deeply?*

Justen's voice rose. "Help me, curse it!"

"Not unless you promise to stop if he dies."

"Petrus, there's no time—"

"Promise me, Innis. He dies, you stop. *Promise.* Or I'm not helping you."

"Petrus is right," Serril said. "It would be a waste of your life."

Justen glanced frantically from Serril to Petrus. "All right! I promise. Now help me!"

Petrus reached for the arrow.

"Quarter of an inch," Justen said, bending over the prince. "On my say-so."

Petrus gripped the arrow shaft. He wasn't sure he trusted Innis's promise. *I'm hauling you off the instant he dies,* he vowed grimly.

INNIS PATCHED THE artery with rough haste. "Half an inch," she said, her hands pressed to the prince's chest, her magic wrapped around his heart, keeping it beating despite the arrow buried in it.

The arrowhead jerked up, blood flooded outwards, Prince's Harkeld's heart stuttered. Innis concentrated fiercely, mending the sliced muscle, keeping the rhythm of his heart going as best she could. This patch couldn't be rough. It needed to be strong, robust. She poured her magic into him, encouraging the muscle fibers to knit together.

"Is the arrow still in his heart?" she heard Serril ask.

"Yes," Petrus said. "It went through one chamber and pierced the artery underneath." She felt his healing magic alongside hers, a faint presence, not distracting her, just monitoring. "She's fixed the artery and she's now onto the chamber, mending the lower hole... if that makes sense?"

Apparently it did, for Serril asked no more questions.

Innis glanced at Petrus. "All right, all the way out of his heart."

"But not his body?"

She shook her head and turned her attention back to the prince.

Petrus pulled the arrow upwards. Blood gushed, some of the tendons anchoring the valve tore.

Innis worked frantically, sealing the wound, mending the valve, keeping his heart pumping.

Petrus and Serril were silent.

At last the muscle was healed, the valve firmly attached to its thread-like tendons, the heart beating with a strong, regular rhythm.

Innis looked up, feeling drained, and smiled at Petrus. "You can pull it all the way out now."

"Are you sure you don't want to wait for Rand? He'll be here soon."

She shook her head.

"You're shaking, you know."

So she was, a trembling that went right inside her body. Even her bones felt like they were shaking.

"Best wait for Rand," Petrus said, gripping the arrow shaft. "You've almost reached your limit."

Innis sat back and wiped her face. Petrus was right. She felt suddenly dizzy. Tiny lights like fireflies swooped across her vision. She closed her eyes.

"Serril," Petrus said. "Hold the arrow, will you?"

An arm came around her, holding her, supporting her.

"Is she all right?" Serril asked worriedly.

"That was faster, stronger healing than we'll ever see again in our lives," Petrus said. She felt his healing magic touch her, felt a little strength trickle into her, faint and welcome. "That was amazing, Innis," he said in her ear. "I didn't think anyone could heal like that."

Innis opened her eyes and leaned her head against his shoulder. "Thanks."

The prince stirred, lifting his head, his expression dazed.

"Lie down," Serril told him, before he could see the arrow protruding from his chest.

Prince Harkeld obediently lowered his head. After a moment his hand fumbled across his chest. Serril caught it before he could find the arrow. "And don't move, either."

"It hurts," the prince said, his voice hoarse. "What happened? Have I been kicked by a horse?"

"Something like that," Serril said. "Rand'll be here any minute. Just lie still. You'll be fine."

"Where are we?" the prince said. "I thought..." He coughed, a raspy sound, his chest heaving.

"Don't cough!" Innis cried.

HARKELD SWAM SLOWLY back to consciousness. He blinked, looking up at the anxious faces clustered over him.

"Was it the arrow?" the black-bearded man said. "Did I push it in again?"

Harkeld groped for a name. Serril?

"It was the artery. The patch tore when he coughed," Justen said. Something was wrong with his appearance. Harkeld blinked slowly. His hair. Justen's hair was too dark.

His chest ached and his throat was tight, dry. His breath caught as he inhaled.

"Rut it!" Justen said. "Petrus, stop him coughing!"

The third anxious face disappeared from view. Harkeld's

brain tried slowly to identify the man while he coughed. Petrus? No. Petrus had white-blond hair, not dark brown.

Hands clasped his throat. Whoever the face belonged to had healing magic. A weak, soothing sensation spread from those hands. The spasming muscles in his throat relaxed. It became easier to breathe.

"Don't let him cough," Justen ordered. His hands were pressed to Harkeld's chest. Healing magic flowed from his touch.

Justen was a healer?

Harkeld blinked at this knowledge, and turned it over in his mind, examining it. He didn't feel angry or betrayed by this new secret of Justen's.

The two healing magics felt different. Whoever held his throat had a blunter, simpler magic. Justen's magic felt like Innis's, complex and precise.

"Don't forget to take my hands and my blood if I die," Harkeld whispered. "It'd be... ironic, don't you think? ...if you got to Sault and found... you'd forgotten them."

Someone snorted a laugh by his ear and then said dryly, "If he's making jokes, I don't think he's going to die." He recognized the voice: Petrus.

Justen gave them both a that's-not-funny look. "He's not going to die. I just need to patch this artery properly."

Harkeld wrestled with the question of why both Petrus and Justen had dark hair. Memory sluggishly returned, moving in hazy swirls like steam from the hot pools. They'd been riding to the anchor stone and...

Cora's dead. Memory hit him with a jolt that he felt physically. The breath choked in his throat again. He coughed—

THIS TIME, WHEN consciousness returned, no one was looking at him. Justen had his eyes closed, a fierce frown on his face. Serril was beckoning something down from the sky. A swallow swooped low, landed, shifted into... Justen?

"How far away's Rand?" Serril asked. "We need him *now*."

"About five minutes," the new Justen said.

He wasn't quite Justen, Harkeld decided. His nose was too short. His ears too big. His eyes the wrong color.

His Justen shimmered all over, as if sunshine lay on him. The new Justen didn't. How odd.

"Any sign of the archer?"

"No."

"Keep an eye out for him—but stay out of range."

The new Justen nodded and changed back into a swallow. Now he shimmered too.

Harkeld watched the swallow swoop upwards. "Are you twins?" he asked.

Justen's eyes opened.

"That's torn it," Petrus said dryly.

Serril grimaced, but Justen didn't answer. His face was strained, haggard.

More memory hazily returned. The anchor stone. It had been gray and white this time, and his hand had stuck to it. His palm began to burn, now that he'd remembered.

And something else had happened. Something that had given him this ache in his chest, as if a draft horse had kicked him.

Memory returned with shocking, vivid clarity. An arrow had struck him. Right through the heart.

Harkeld's heart gave a terrified leap. He inhaled sharply, coughed once.

"Rut it!" Justen said.

"Innis," Petrus said sharply. "That's enough. Stop."

Innis? Where was Innis?

"I only need one more minute," Justen muttered. "It didn't tear that time."

"Rand'll be here in five minutes—"

"And he could die before then!" Justen said fiercely.

"So could you!"

"I just need to patch this properly, so it doesn't rip open every time he coughs—"

"You *promised*."

Justen glanced at Serril. "May I shift, sir?"

"If it will save his life, yes."

Shift? Harkeld stared muzzily at Justen. What was he talking about?

Justen's body shrank within his clothes. His face became smaller, changed shape, no longer square, but oval, with gray eyes instead of brown. Pale skin. Long, curling black hair.

Innis?

Harkeld blinked, and blinked again. He opened his mouth, but no sound came out, not even a cough.

Innis closed her eyes and frowned deeply. The hands pressed to his chest hadn't moved. The sensation of healing magic flowing from them became stronger.

Harkeld stared at Innis, still blinking, still trying to understand what had just happened.

Innis opened her eyes and lifted her hands from his chest. "There. That'll hold, however much he coughs."

"Good," Petrus said. "Now get away from him and don't touch him again. I mean it, Innis."

Innis sat back. Justen's clothes hung on her, far too large, the shirt gaping open at her throat. Harkeld caught a glimpse of the Grooten amulet dangling there like a small round moon.

Justen's amulet. Justen's clothes. Worn by Innis.

She no longer shimmered. Her face was bloodlessly pale, exhausted.

"Where did Justen go?" Harkeld said, bewildered.

"Hmm. Still feel like coughing? No?" Petrus released his throat. "How's your hand?"

Harkeld recognized evasion when he heard it. "What happened to Justen?" he said more loudly.

Petrus moved into Harkeld's field of vision. He reached for Harkeld's left hand, turning it palm up. "Ouch. That's got to hurt."

Harkeld pulled his hand free. "Justen. Where is he?"

Petrus glanced at Serril.

"The truth, I think," the black-bearded mage said.

Petrus looked at Harkeld. "We made him up. All right? We took turns being him. The real Justen came with Serril on the ship. You saw him just now."

Harkeld shook his head. "No." But he could tell from their faces it was true—Petrus slightly belligerent, Serril uncomfortable.

Serril turned his head. "Here's Rand. Thank the All-Mother."

Justen didn't exist? Harkeld felt dizzy, even though he was lying on the ground. There was a hollow feeling inside him.

He glanced at Innis. She was watching him. Yes, the truth was on her face too.

She hadn't been sleeping in anyone's pocket this morning. She'd been at his side the whole time.

No wonder Justen had known the dead hawk was Linea, not Innis.

Rand scrambled into view, panting. "How is he? Hedín said an arrow in the chest."

"Through the heart," Petrus said. "Innis has healed all but the last bit. Neither of us has the strength for it. Do you?"

Rand crouched. Harkeld felt fingertips touch his chest, felt healing magic slide beneath his skin. "For this, yes."

Harkeld stared up at the gray sky. His armsman didn't exist. Had never existed.

It was a death of sorts, even though there was no body, no blood.

A hawk circled above them, its feathers shimmering. Shapeshifter. *The truth was there all along for me to see.*

The hollow feeling inside him began to fill with emotions. First was a sense of betrayal, as painful as the arrow in his chest. It was swiftly followed by humiliation and anger.

"Pull it out, Serril," Rand said.

Harkeld didn't flinch. He was far too angry.

CHAPTER NINETY-FIVE

THE WITCHES HAD carried the dead prince away. The curse was coming. It couldn't be stopped. The only person who could have stopped it was dead. Bennick had killed him.

"The curse doesn't matter," Bennick said. "It's not worth crying over. We all go to the All-Mother in the end. Doesn't matter how or when."

Didn't matter? Mam didn't matter? Or Rosa? Or Da?

Jaumé held them tightly in his mind—Mam and Da and Rosa—and wouldn't let Bennick's words touch them. They mattered.

As for everything else, he would help Bennick down from this cave and back through the jungle to Loomath's house. Bennick had taken care of him; he would take care of Bennick. That mattered. Bennick mattered.

Half a mile away, people crossed from island to shore. Two of the huge gray monsters helped them.

"Taking the body back," Bennick said. "I'd like to have his head and hands and blood. They should turn him towards his home and leave him. Ah, well. At least I got him." He held out the spyglass. "Here, lad. Watch and tell me when they're gone." He leaned his head wearily against the black rock.

Jaumé wiped his face and put the spyglass to his eye. A small boat with a square sail; he could see that much. No body. No prince.

People moved. Some wearing clothes. Some naked. The monsters were gone.

He didn't want to see the prince's body. But he looked, looked more closely, held his breath. The man getting into the boat, the dark-haired man with the bare chest and the red scar over his heart...

Jaumé's world turned quietly over. He felt sorry for Bennick.

"What?" Bennick said. "What is it?" He took the spyglass, looked, hissed between his teeth. "He's still alive."

HERE ENDS BOOK TWO OF
THE CURSED KINGDOMS TRILOGY

JULIET E. McKENNA'S
CHRONICLES OF THE LESCARI REVOLUTION

BOOK ONE
IRONS IN THE FIRE

ISBN: (UK) 978 1 906735 82 1 • £7.99
ISBN: (US) 978 1 84416 601 5 • US $8.99/CAN $10.99

The country of Lescar was born out of civil war. Carved out of the collapse of the Old Tormalin Empire, the land has long been laid waste by its rival dukes, while bordering nations look on with indifference or exploit its misery. But a mismatched band of exiles and rebels is agreed that the time has come for change, and they begin to put a scheme together for revolution. Full of rich characters and high adventure, this novel marks the beginning of a thrilling new series.

"Magically convincing and convincingly magical."
– Dan Abnett

BOOK TWO
BLOOD IN THE WATER

ISBN: (UK) 978 1 84416 840 8 • £12.99 (Large Format)
ISBN: (US) 978 1 84416 841 5 • US $7.99/CAN $9.99

Those exiles and rebels determined to bring peace to Lescar discover the true cost of war. Courage and friendships are tested to breaking point. Who will pay such heartbreaking penalties for their boldness? Who will pay the ultimate price?

The dukes of Lescar aren't about to give up their wealth and power without a fight. Nor will they pass up some chance to advance their own interests, if one of their rivals suffers in all this upheaval. The duchesses have their own part to play, more subtle but no less deadly.

"If you're not reading Juliet McKenna, you should be."
– Kate Elliott

BOOK THREE
BANNERS IN THE WIND

ISBN: (UK) 978 1 906735 74 6 • £12.99 (Large Format)
ISBN: (US) 978 1 906735 75 3 • US $7.99/CAN $9.99

A few stones falling in the right place can set a landslide in motion. That's what Lescari exiles told themselves in Vanam as they plotted to overthrow the warring dukes. But who can predict the chaos that follows such a cataclysm? Some will survive against all the odds; friends and foes alike. Hope and alliances will be shattered beyond repair. Unforeseen consequences bring undeserved grief as well as unexpected rewards. Necessity forces uneasy compromise as well as perilous defiance. Wreaking havoc is swift and easy. Building a lasting peace may yet prove an insuperable challenge!

"Shows McKenna at her best."
– Paul Cornell

 WWW.SOLARISBOOKS.COM

Follow us on Twitter! www.twitter.com/solarisbooks

ROWENA CORY DANIELLS

BESIEGED

BOOK ONE OF THE OUTCAST CHRONICLES

'Page-turning, plot-twisting, breakneck adventure.'

UK ISBN: 978 1 78108 010 8 • US ISBN: 978 1 78108 011 5 • £7.99/$7.99

Sorne, the estranged son of a King on the verge of madness, is being raised as a weapon to wield against the mystical Wyrds. Half a continent away, his father is planning to lay siege to the Celestial City, the home of the T'En, whose wyrd blood the mundane population have come to despise. Within the City, Imoshen, the only mystic to be raised by men, is desperately trying to hold her people together. A generations long feud between the men of the Brotherhoods and the women of the sacred Sisterhoods is about to come to a head.

With war without and war within, can an entire race survive the hatred of a nation?

Rowena Cory Daniells, the creator of the bestselling *Chronicles of King Rolen's Kin*, brings you a stunning new fantasy epic, steeped in magic and forged in war.

ROWENA CORY DANIELLS

EXILE

BOOK TWO OF THE OUTCAST CHRONICLES

'Page-turning, plot-twisting, breakneck adventure.'
SFX on *The King's Bastard*

UK ISBN: 978 1 78108 012 2 • US ISBN: 978 1 78108 013 9 • £7.99/$7.99

Slowly losing himself to madness, King Charald has passed his verdict on the mystic Wyrds: banishment, by the first day of winter. Their leader, Imoshen, believes she has found a new home for her people, but many are still stranded, amidst the violence and turmoil gripping Chalcedonia. A reward is offered for their safe return, and greedy men turn to abduction.

Tobazim arrives in port, to ready the way for his people, and finds their ships have been stolen. Sorne, the king's halfblood advisor, needs to find his sister and bring her to safety. Ronnyn and his family, living peacefully in the wilderness, are kidnapped by raiders eager for the reward.

Whether the ships are ready or not, the Wyrds must leave soon; those who remain behind will be hunted down and executed. Time is running out for all of them.

ROWENA CORY DANIELLS

SANCTUARY

BOOK THREE OF THE OUTCAST CHRONICLES

UK ISBN: 978 1 78108 014 6 • US ISBN: 978 1 78108 015 3 • £7.99/$7.99

For over three hundred years, the mystic Wyrds lived alongside the true-men, until King Charald laid siege to their island city and exiled them. Imoshen, most powerful of the female mystics, was elected to lead her people into exile. She faces threats from within, from male mystics who think they would make a better leader. and her people face threats from true-men, who have confi scated their ships. they must set sail by the fi rst day of winter. Those who are left behind will be executed.

Once they set sail, they face winter storms, hostile harbours and sea-raiders who know their ships are laden with treasure. Imoshen relies on the sea captain, ardonyx, for advice, and Sorne, the half-blood mystic, who has lived among the true-men kingdoms of the Secluded Sea.

But Imoshen knows the mystics can't run for ever. They need somewhere to call home. They need... Sanctuary.

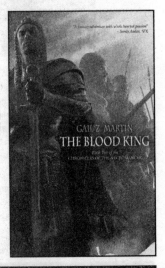

GAIL Z. MARTIN'S
THE CHRONICLES OF THE NECROMANCER

BOOK THREE

DARK HAVEN

ISBN: (UK) 978 1 84416 708 1 • £7.99
ISBN: (US) 978 1 84416 598 8 • $7.99

The kingdom of Margolan lies in ruin. Martris Drayke, the new king, must rebuild his country in the aftermath of battle, while a new war looms on the horizon. Meanwhile Jonmarc Vahanian is now the Lord of Dark Haven, and there is defiance from the vampires of the *Vayash Moru* at the prospect of a mortal leader.

But can he earn their trust, and at what cost?

"A fast-paced tale laced with plenty of action."

– SF Site

BOOK FOUR

DARK LADY'S CHOSEN

ISBN: (UK) 978 1 84416 830 9 • £7.99
ISBN: (US) 978 1 84416 831 6 • $7.99

Treachery and blood magic threaten King Martris Drayke's hold on the throne he risked everything to win. As the battle against a traitor lord comes to its final days, war, plague and betrayal bring Margolan to the brink of destruction. Civil war looms in Isencroft. And in Dark Haven, Lord Jonmarc Vahanian has bargained his soul for vengeance as he leads the *vayash moru* against a dangerous rogue who would usher in a future drenched in blood.

"Just when you think you know where things are heading, Martin pulls another ace from her sleeve."

– A. J. Hartley, author of The Mask of Atraeus

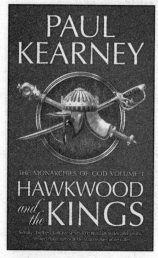
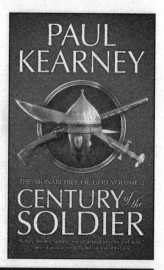

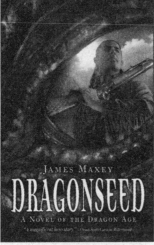

The warrior woman known as Infidel is legendary for her superhuman strength and skin tough as chain mail. She's made few friends during her career as a sword-for-hire, and many powerful enemies. Following the death of her closest companion, Infidel finds herself weary of life as a mercenary and sets her eyes on one final prize that will allow her to live out the rest of her days in luxury, the priceless treasure trove of Greatshadow.

Greatshadow is the primal dragon of fire. His malign intelligence spies upon mankind through every flickering candle, patiently waiting to devour victims careless with even the smallest flame. The Church of the Book has assembled a team of twelve battle-hardened adventurers to slay the dragon once and for all. But tensions run high between the leaders of the quest who view the mission as a holy duty and the super-powered mercenaries who add power to their ranks, who dream only of Greatshadow's vast wealth. If the warriors fail to slay the beast, will they doom mankind to death by fire?

"Maxey's newest novel plunges us into one of the most extravagantly fantastical worlds I've ever seen... this one is worth reading right now."
— Orson Scott Card

WWW.SOLARISBOOKS.COM

Follow us on Twitter! www.twitter.com/solarisbooks

ISBN: (UK) 978 1 78108 016 0 (US) 978 1 78108 017 7 • £7.99/$8.99

The invulnerable, super-strong warrior Infidel has a secret: she's lost her magical powers right at the moment when she needs them most. To keep a promise to a fallen friend, she must journey to the frozen wastelands of the north.

Her quest leads her through the abstract realms of the Sea of Wine, where she uncovers a conspiracy that threatens all life. Hush, the primal dragon of cold, has formed an alliance with the ghost of a vengeful witch to murder Glorious, the dragon of the sun, plunging the world into an unending winter night.

Without her magical strength, can Infidel possibly survive her battle with Hush? If she fails to save Glorious, will the world see another morning?

> '*Greatshadow's level 30+ adventure is charming, not po-faced, with a group of flawed, sarcastic, quick-witted and oddball adventurers that are equally comfortable with set-piece battle and rapid fire sarcasm.*'
> *– Pornokitsch on Greatshadow*

WWW.SOLARISBOOKS.COM

Follow us on Twitter! www.twitter.com/solarisbooks

A hell of a ride,
but heaven to read:
eerie, compelling
and very funny.'
MICHAEL MARSHALL SMITH

BLOOD AND FEATHERS

LOU MORGAN

UK ISBN: 978 1 78108 018 4 • US ISBN: 978 1 78108 019 1 • £7.99/$9.99

Alice isn't having the best of days – late for work, missed her bus, and now she's getting rained on – but it's about to get worse.

The war between the angels and the Fallen is escalating and innocent civilians are getting caught in the cross-fire. If the balance is to be restored, the angels must act – or risk the Fallen taking control. Forever. That's where Alice comes in. Hunted by the Fallen and guided by Mallory – a disgraced angel with a drinking problem he doesn't want to fix – Alice will learn the truth about her own history... and why the angels want to send her to hell.

What do the Fallen want from her? How does Mallory know so much about her past? What is it the angels are hiding – and can she trust either side?

 WWW.SOLARISBOOKS.COM

Follow us on Twitter! www.twitter.com/solarisbooks

ISBN: (UK) 978 1 78108 053 5 (US) 978 1 78108 054 2 • £7.99/$9.99

An ANTHOLOGY of the ESOTERIC and ARCANE

They gather in darkness, sharing ancient and arcane knowledge as they manipulate the very matter of reality itself. Spells and conjuration; legerdemain and prestidigitation – these are the mistresses and masters of the esoteric arts.

From the otherworldly visions of Conan Doyle's father in Audrey Niffenegger's 'The Wrong Fairy' to the diabolical political machinations of Dan Abnett's 'Party Tricks', here you will find a spell for every occasion.

Jonathan Oliver, critically acclaimed editor of *The End of The Line* and *House of Fear*, has brought together sixteen extraordinary writers for this collection of magical tales. Within you will find works by Audrey Niffenegger, Sarah Lotz, Will Hill, Steve Rasnic and Melanie Tem, Liz Williams, Dan Abnett, Thana Niveau, Alison Littlewood, Christopher Fowler, Storm Constantine, Lou Morgan, Sophia McDougall, Gail Z. Martin, Gemma Files and Robert Shearman.

 WWW.SOLARISBOOKS.COM

Follow us on Twitter! www.twitter.com/solarisbooks